Emile Gaboriau

The slaves of Paris

Emile Gaboriau

The slaves of Paris

ISBN/EAN: 9783744738798

Printed in Europe, USA, Canada, Australia, Japan

Cover: Foto ©Andreas Hilbeck / pixelio.de

More available books at **www.hansebooks.com**

VIZETELLY'S ONE-VOLUME NOVELS.

"The idea of publishing cheap one-volume novels is a good one, and we wish the series every success."—*Saturday Review.*

In Crown 8vo, good readable type, and attractive binding, price 6s. each.

PRINCE ZILAH.

By JULES CLARETIE,

AUTHOR OF "THE MILLION."

TRANSLATED FROM THE 57TH FRENCH EDITION.

"M. Jules Claretie has of late taken a conspicuous place as a novelist."—*Times.*

T   E.

"There is a good de:
"One of those books   dity."—*Society.*

The Book that n   rench Academy.

F   E.

TRANSLATED, W   RENCH EDITION.

"This excellent ver   the Channel."—*Londo*
Figaro.

By   A.,

"In many respects   are drawn with powe:
and without pity; th   able colours, and with
a skill that fascinates.

BETWEEN MIDNIGHT AND DAWN.

By INA L. CASSILIS,

AUTHOR OF "SOCIETY'S QUEEN," "STRANGELY WOOED: STRANGELY WON," &c.

"An ingenious plot, cleverly handled."—*Athenæum.*
"The interest begins with the first page, and is ably sustained to the conclusion."—*Edinburgh Courant.*

In small 8vo, price 3s. 6d. each. Sixth Edition, carefully Revised.

A MUMMER'S WIFE. A Realistic Novel.

By GEORGE MOORE, Author of "A Modern Lover."

"A striking book, different in tone from current English fiction. The woman's character is a very powerful study."—*Athenæum.*
"'A Mummer's Wife' holds at present a unique position among English novels. It is a conspicuous success of its kind."—*Graphic.*

3s. 6d. each.

FIFTH EDITION.

THE IRONMASTER; OR, LOVE AND PRIDE.

By GEORGES OHNET.

TRANSLATED WITHOUT ABRIDGMENT FROM THE 146TH FRENCH EDITION.

" This work, the greatest literary success in any language of recent times, has already yielded its author upwards of £12,000."

THIRD EDITION.

MR. BUTLER'S WARD.

By MABEL ROBINSON.

" A charming book, poetically conceived, and worked out with tenderness and insight."—*Athenæum.*

" The heroine is a very happy conception, a beautiful creation whose affecting history is treated with much delicacy, sympathy, and command of all that is touching."—*Illustrated News.*

" All the characters are new to fiction, and the author is to be congratulated on having made so full and original a haul out of the supposed to be exhausted waters of modern society. A writer who can at the outset write such admirable sense and transform the results of much minute observation into so pathetic and tender a whole, takes at once a high position."—*Graphic.*

SECOND EDITION.

THE CORSARS; OR, LOVE AND LUCRE.

By JOHN HILL.

AUTHOR OF "THE WATERS OF MARAH," "SALLY," &c.

" It is indubitable that Mr. Hill has produced a strong and lively novel, full of story, character, situations, murder, gold-mines, excursions, and alarms. The book is so rich in promise that we hope to receive some day from Mr. Hill a romance which will win every vote."—*Saturday Review.*

THIRD EDITION.

COUNTESS SARAH.

By GEORGES OHNET.

AUTHOR OF "THE IRONMASTER."

TRANSLATED, WITHOUT ABRIDGMENT, FROM THE 118TH FRENCH EDITION.

" The book contains some very powerful situations and first-rate character studies."—*Whitehall Review.*

" To an interesting plot is added a number of strongly-marked and cleverly drawn characters "—*Society.*

THIRD EDITION.

NUMA ROUMESTAN; OR, JOY ABROAD AND GRIEF AT HOME.

By ALPHONSE DAUDET.

TRANSLATED BY MRS. J. G. LAYARD.

" ' Numa Roumestan ' is a masterpiece; it is really a perfect work; it has no fault, no weakness. It is a compact and harmonious whole."—MR. HENRY JAMES.

" ' Numa Roumestan ' is a triumph for the art of literary seduction."—*Spectator.*

THE SLAVES OF PARIS.

THE GABORIAU & DU BOISGOBEY
SENSATIONAL NOVELS.

UNIFORM WITH THE PRESENT VOLUME.

THE STANDARD says :—"The romances of Gaboriau and Du Boisgobey picture the marvellous Lecoq and other wonders of shrewdness, who piece together the elaborate details of the most complicated crimes, as Professor Owen, with the smallest bone as a foundation, could re-construct the most extraordinary animals."

The following Volumes are already Published :

IN PERIL OF HIS LIFE.
THE LEROUGE CASE.
LECOQ, THE DETECTIVE.   2 Vols.
THE GILDED CLIQUE.
OTHER PEOPLE'S MONEY.
THE SLAVES OF PARIS.   2 Vols.
DOSSIER, NO. 113.
THE MYSTERY OF ORCIVAL.
THE COUNT'S MILLIONS.   2 Vols.
THE LITTLE OLD MAN OF BATIGNOLLES.
THE OLD AGE OF LECOQ, THE DETECTIVE.   2 Vols.
INTRIGUES OF A POISONER.
THE CATASTROPHE.   2 Vols.
IN THE SERPENTS' COILS.
THE DAY OF RECKONING.   2 Vols.
BERTHA'S SECRET.
WHO DIED LAST ?

To be followed by :

THE THUMB STROKE.
THE MATAPAN AFFAIR.
THE CRIME OF THE OPERA HOUSE.   2 Vols.

Other Volumes are in Preparation.

GABORIAU'S SENSATIONAL NOVELS.

IX.

THE

SLAVES OF PARIS.

By EMILE GABORIAU.

IN TWO VOLS.—VOL. II.

THIRTIETH THOUSAND.

LONDON:
VIZETELLY & CO., 42 CATHERINE STREET, STRAND,
1886.

Perth:

S. COWAN & CO., STRATHMORE PRINTING WORKS.

THE SLAVES OF PARIS.

XXVI.

Yes, he was in a hurry, this dear, good Tantaine, in such a hurry indeed, that although he was usually almost as perpetual a pedestrian as the Wandering Jew, he now hailed a cab, engaged it by the hour, and promised the driver five francs gratuity providing he drove fast. The first direction he gave was in the Rue de Douai, at the corner of the Rue Blanche, where he alighted, and bidding the cabby wait for him, walked towards the house where young Gaston de Gandelu had rented such a sumptuous apartment for Rose. Father Tantaine seemed to know the whereabouts of the place, for he asked no questions of the concierge, but went straight upstairs and rang at the door of the "Viscountess de Chantemille's" abode. It was some time before his ring elicited any reply, but at last the door was opened by a stout girl, with a red face, whose cap was all askew. This was Marie, Zora's cook, the girl who on a previous occasion had acquainted Mascarot with everything that transpired at Madame de Chantemille's house-warming. On recognizing the old clerk, she received him right cordially. "What, is it you, Father Tantaine?" she cried. "You're as welcome as flowers in May."

"Hush! hush!" said he with an anxious air.

"Eh? why hush?"

"Your mistress might hear you."

The girl burst out laughing. "No fear of that," she answered; 'madame's in a certain place it isn't so easy to escape from. The more precious the jewel, the more carefully you lock it up."

This remark, which implied that Rose had been arrested, seemed to astonish the old man prodigiously. "Impossible!" he cried.

"It is so, though. But come in and we'll tell you the whole story, while you drink a glass with us!"

In the dining-room, whither Tantaine was now conducted, six guests, seated round a table covered with bottles, were finishing a meal begun several hours previously. Four of them were women whom Tantaine recognised as clients of the agency, the two others being men of highly questionable appearance. "We are amusing ourselves as you see," said the cook, after pouring out a glass of wine for Tantaine. "Ah! what a funny affair it was yesterday! I had just started my dinner, when two military looking men called and asked to see madame. They were shown in, and at once said they had come to take her to prison. When she heard this she shrieked so loud that you might have heard her as far as the Rue Fontaine. She wouldn't budge an inch, but clung to the furniture. So they caught hold of her, one by the heels and the other by the head, carried her down-stairs, and bundled her into a vehicle waiting at the door! That's the fourth mistress of mine I've seen carried off like that—But, Father Tantaine, come, you're not drinking anything!"

Tantaine by this time, however, had discovered all he wished to know, and so he retired from the festivity, which seemed likely to terminate only with the last bottle in the cellar.

"All goes well here," he muttered to himself, as he entered the cab again. "Now for the next!"

They drove to the Champs Elysées, and Tantaine bade the driver stop not far from the house the elder Gandelu was building. Here he accosted an alert little fellow who was driving back the foot passengers with a lath, bidding them beware of the debris that was constantly falling from the scaffolding above. "Anything new, La Candèle?" asked the old clerk.

"No, Monsieur Tantaine, nothing; but please tell the master that I am keeping my eyes open."

The old clerk then hurried on his way, interviewing in quick succession one of De Breulh's footmen, and a woman in the employment of Madame de Bois d'Ardon. Then dismissing his cab, he started on foot for the establishment of Father Canon, in the Faubourg Saint-Honoré, where he found Florestan, who, humble enough in the presence of Mascarot, was haughty and supercilious to a degree with poor Tantaine. To air his superiority he insisted on entertaining the old clerk at dinner, but he could tell him nothing new, except that Mademoiselle Sabine was frightfully sad.

It was nearly eight o'clock when Tantaine got rid of Florestan, and jumping into a fresh cab, ordered the Jehu to drive to the "Grand Turc," that famous establishment, the object of Toto-Chupin's convivial aspirations. It is in the Rue des Poissonniers at Montmartre that the sign of the "Grand Turc" swings to the wind, inviting passers-by to walk inside and enjoy themselves. The pleasures provided are of an edible, potable, and saltatory nature. After a good *table d'hôte* at six p.m., one may indulge in coffee, beer, or other beverages, and then comes a dance by way of aiding digestion. There are two entrances, one conducting straight to the ball-room, and the other to the *table d'hôte*, which is extensively patronized by clerks, artists starting in life, and old bachelors living on their incomes. The repast is barely over before dishes and plates and glasses and tablecloths disappear, the restaurant becomes a café, beer flows freely on all sides, and in lieu of the clatter of knives and forks one may hear the rattle of dominos. Then all of a sudden a pair of large folding doors are thrown open and harmony pervades the entire establishment. The orchestra in the neighbouring ball-room has struck up the first waltz. One peculiarity of this ball-room is, that quadrilles are never danced there. The programme is a long succession of polkas, mazurkas, and waltzes—the latter being predominant. The rotunda forming the centre of the hall is edged round with benches dispersed in circular fashion. The dome above, on which a number of amorous doves are depicted disporting themselves in an azure sky, would be none the worse for a little cleaning, but the floor is kept marvellously shiny and smooth. Germany is always largely to the fore in the dancing hall of the "Grand Turc," and the gallant cavalier who wishes a partner for the mazy waltz, must at least be acquainted with the pleasing dialect of Strasbourg. Here, indeed, behold Alsatian maids and cooks, turning for hours round and round, stiffly erect, with lips just parted, and eyes half closed, displaying in fact, the same automatic grace as the little wooden figures one sometimes sees on barrel organs.

When worthy Father Tantaine entered the ball-room, having duly paid his fee, the master of the ceremonies had just called "take your places for the waltz," for the tenth time that evening. The scene was animated, and the atmosphere impregnated with strange emanations and perfumes. Many a new comer would have felt suffocated, but the old clerk, like Alcibiades, was always at his ease no matter where his profession called him. He had never before set foot inside the "Grand Turc," and yet you would have sworn he was an *habitué*, so thoroughly at home did he look as he roamed among the tables reserved for refreshments, both on the ground floor and on a circular gallery overhead. But in vain did he wipe his spectacles, dimmed by the vapour and dust of the ball-room—he could see nothing of either Toto-Chupin or Caroline Schinmel, the cook. "Have I come on a useless errand?" he grumbled, "or am I simply too early?" Finding a vacant table near the counter of the lady-cashier, he sat himself down, ordered some beer, and so as to while away the time, began to study a huge symbolical picture on the wall before him. This brightly coloured transplendent work of art, if such it may be called, represented a black bearded and exceedingly portly man, wearing a white turban and a blue robe, seated in a red chair near a green curtain, having a mauve border, with his feet on a yellow carpet.

With one hand he was apparently rubbing his stomach, but with the other he held out a glass so that it might be filled with tipple. Plainly enough, he was the "Grand Turc" in person, for on one side of him figured an enormous pipe, and on the other a crouching lion, whilst there was also a sultana who most graciously filled his glass with foaming beer. This sultana, a most bewitching fair-haired woman of massive build, had evidently been born in Alsace; the painter thus paying a delicate and merited compliment to the ladies who mainly frequented the establishment. Tantaine was looking at this work of art with considerable wonder, when all at once he heard a high-keyed voice behind him. "That's certainly Toto-Chupin," he said; "the young scamp! Where on earth can he have got to—for me not to have seen him?"

He turned round, and two tables off, in a dark corner, he perceived the object of his quest. It was not, after all, so surprising that he had passed Toto without recognising him, for the young rascal was transformed. He had planned out a new life for himself on the day he extorted a hundred francs from Tantaine, resolving to madden all his friends with envy. He had apparently succeeded, for he was now gorgeous to behold. He had laughed at young Gaston de Gandelu and called him a monkey, but he now imitated him even to exaggeration, so that of the two, Toto himself now looked the more genuine ape. His light coloured jacket was wonderfully short and tight, his waistcoat was of a most surprising pattern, and his trousers had such little width, that it was a wonder he had ever been able to get into them. Formerly he had despised shirts, but now his neck was imprisoned in a stiff stand-up collar, and as a finishing touch a hairdresser had curled his lank tow-like locks. Several empty jugs of beer stood on his table, and in front of him sat a couple of "pals," who with their "Newgate knockers," high caps and loosely knotted neck-cloths, looked as thorough a pair of reprobates as could be found. Toto-Chupin's haughty air and condescending smile told that he was standing treat—enjoying the superior position which belongs to those who pay over those who accept.

Tantaine was rising to go and pull the young monkey's ears, when a fresh thought crossed his mind, and he hesitated. Slowly and cautiously, mindful not to attract attention, he climbed over a couple of benches and hid himself behind one of the columns which supported the overhanging gallery. By this stratagem, the performance of which occupied at least five minutes, he found himself at last so near Toto's table, that he could hear every word the young reprobate and his associates exchanged. "You needn't call me a boaster," said Toto to his friends, "nor a dandy either; as you see me now you'll see me always, at least I hope so. A man must be properly dressed to work on a grand scale as I mean to do." His companions laughed until tears stood in their eyes. "I know what you mean," continued Toto. "You think I look queer in my new togs. That's because I ain't used to 'em. But just give me a little time, and, besides, I mean to take lessons in deportment."

"Well, well!" said one of his friends; "wonders will never cease. I say, Chupin, when you drive about in your carriage, will you give me a lift?"

"Why not? What's wanted to have a carriage? Coin of course. Well, and who are those that make coin? Why, the fellows that have a 'dodge.' Now, I know a 'dodge' that has filled the pockets of those who t ught it me, so why shouldn't it fill mine?"

Tantaine was quite terrified on noticing that Toto was tipsy. What did the young rascal really know, and what was he going to say? The old man made ready to fly at the boy's throat and choke down the first compromising word. Toto's guests also knew that he had drank too much. But as he seemed disposed to tell them a secret, they became very attentive, and exchanged a knowing look. They were ready to believe that this precocious scamp had, as he asserted, some special way of obtaining money; for his new clothes and his liberality were in their eyes highly suspicious. How had he got hold of so much coin? That was the question; and to induce him to talk, they freely filled his glass, each of them, moreover, offering remarks suited to hasten his revelations. The younger of the two shook his head laughingly. "I don't believe you've any dodge at all," said he.

"Yes, I have.

"And why not, after all," quoth the elder "loafer," soothingly.

"Let's hear what it is, then," interposed the other. "You can't expect us to believe it unless we know something about it."

It's as simple as 'how do you do,'" answered ⌐oto. "Suppose I saw Polyte there steal a couple of pair of boots from a shop front—"

At this Polyte protested with so much energy that Tantaine, who had not lost a word of the conversation, was convinced that the individual in question had some peccadillo of the kind on his conscience.

"You needn't make such a fuss about it," said Toto. "I'm only supposing a case. Let's say you did it, and that I found it out. Do you know what I should do? I should go and find Polyte, and say to him: "'Go halves, my dear fellow, or I shall peach.'"

"Perhaps you would, but I should knock you down."

Forgetting that he was desirous of seeming a regular swell, Toto made a mocking gesture familiar to Parisian *gamins*. "You wouldn't do anything of the kind," he cried, "for you are not a fool. You'd say to yourself ·

'If I hurt this boy, he'd make a row, and then I should be arrested, and with his evidence be sent to prison.' No, indeed, you wouldn't knock me down. On the contrary, you'd speak very gently, and end by doing just what I asked."

"And is that what you call your 'dodge?'"

"Yes, indeed, and a good one it is too? Fools run all the risks, and the wise men reap the profits."

"But there's nothing new in all this. It's simply blackmailing."

"I never said it wasn't. On the contrary, I'm proud to say that it's blackmailing reduced to a system." And, thereupon, Toto took up an empty jug, and calling a waiter, haughtily bade him replenish it.

In the meantime his two friends looked at each other with manifest disappointment. Toto's "dodge" was in no way new to them, nor did it strike them as especially practicable. Blackmailing is a speculation of primitive simplicity, which almost every one is acquainted with. The difficulty is to find a mine to work, and be sure it will pay for working. "Of course," said Polyte, "every now and then a good stroke of business may be done in that line ; but a man isn't woke up every morning by some one shouting down the chimney : 'Come and see how I steal boots.'"

"Of course, not," answered Toto, scornfully. "The calling's like all others, a man must be active if he wants to earn his living. Instead of customers coming to you, you must search for 'em, and you find 'em too—"

"And where, pray?"

"Ah! that's the point."

There came a long pause, of which Tantaine was tempted to avail himself, so as to prevent any further revelations on Master Toto's part ; but on the other hand, he deemed it wise to learn exactly what the young scamp could, and was inclined to do. So he cautiously crept still nearer to the party. Toto was reflecting. "Ah!" said he, at last, "and why not after all?" Then leaning forward, he whispered mysteriously : "I suppose I can trust you?"

"Of course you can."

"Well, then, it's in the Champs Elysées that I make my money, and I'm sure of a stroke of business not once, but twice a day."

"But there are no bootmakers' shops there?"

Chupin shrugged his shoulders disdainfully. "Do you think," he said, "that I address myself to thieves? Not at all. That would be a wretched business. No, I watch honest people—people who are supposed to be honest—people who consider themselves honest. They are the ones that can be made to pay, they're the most liberal."

Tantaine shuddered. He remembered that he had heard B. Mascarot use almost the same words. Toto must have listened at the door.

"But honest people have no need to 'pay up,'" cried Polyte.

Toto cracked his glass, so heavily did he bang it down on the table. "Let me speak, will you?" he cried impatiently. "When I'm in want of funds I go to the Champs Elysées, and sit down on a bench in one of the avenues, between the main one and the quays. Then I watch the cabs, and as soon as one stops, I take a squint to see who gets out of it. If it's a respectable woman I haven't lost my time."

"And you think you know a respectable woman, do you?"

"I should say I did. When a respectable woman gets out of a cab she oughtn't to be in, she looks in an awful state of mind. She squints out of the window right and left, pulls down her veil, and when she fancies no one's looking at her, out she scrambles and rushes off as if the devil was at her heels."

"And then?'

"Then? why, I take the number of the cab, and follow the lady home.' Tantaine saw that Toto's hearers were now deeply interested. "Then," continued the young scamp, "as I can guess she's come from seeing a lover, or doing something she oughtn't to do, I just allow her time to get up stairs into her rooms again. Then I rush into the house, go to the concierge and say, excuse me, but please give me the name of the lady who just came in. I always take care, mind, to have a pretty little purse in my pocket; and so, when the concierge looks at me suspiciously, and says, 'I don't know,' I pull the purse out of my pocket, and say, 'I'm very sorry for that, for she dropped this just outside the door, and I wanted to give it back to her.'"

Enchanted at the effect he produced, Toto paused to imbibe a huge glass of beer, and then proceeded: "The concierge at once becomes amiable and polite. She gives me the name, and the floor, and tells me to go upstairs. The first time I content myself with finding out if the lady's married or single. If she's single, I give it up; but if she married, it's all right, and up I go."

"Well, what do you do next?

"I go again the next morning and loiter about till I see the husband go out. As soon as he's gone, I go straight to his apartments and asks to see the lady. Ah! a fellow needs all his bounce just then, I can tell you. Well, I say something like this to her. 'Madame, I took a cab, yesterday, number so and so, and unfortunately left my purse in it with four or five hundred francs. I happened to see you get into the same cab, just afterwards, and so I've called to know if you found my purse.' Well, as you can guess, the woman flares up, denies it, defends herself and so on, but I politely rejoin, 'All right, madame, I see I must apply to your husband.' Then, of course, she's frightened—and pays!"

"And you leave her?"

"Yes, for the time being. But, when my funds run low, I call on her again, and say: 'It's I, madame, the poor young man you know who lost his money in a cab number so and so, on such and such a day last month.' And when a fellow has a dozen such clients, he can live on his income! So now, pr'aps, you understand why I want to be well dressed. When I used to wear my blouse folks would have given me five francs, but now I can go and ask for a bank note."

Toto-Chupin's guests had lost their gaiety, they were evidently reflecting, and it seemed to Tantaine that each of them was minded to try Toto's "dodge," albeit that their faces expressed intense contempt. Polyte was the first to speak. "There's nothing new in this!" said he.

"No, nothing at all," added the other.

And they were right. This abominable form of speculation is as ancient as marriage, treason, and jealousy; and it seems likely to last as long as there are jealous husbands tenacious of honour, and women forgetful of their duty. Alas! who would be able to count, in Paris alone, the unhappy women who, for a brief moment of passion, long and bitterly repented of, have been subjected to the intolerable and revolting tyranny of blackmail. One day, when happy and careless, they have hurried away to a rendezvous, some scoundrel has watched and followed them, and a few days later he arrives with a prayer on his lips, and threats in his eyes to, ask for the price of his silence. For the luckless victim life thenceforward be-comes one long agony. Good-bye to happiness, serenity, and peace of mind. At each ring at the door bell, the victim starts and turns pale. "Who is coming?" she asks herself with a shudder. Is it he, that execrable scoun-drel, about to make some fresh claim, some fresh demand, after the style suggested by Toto-Chupin. "Madame will not refuse a little help to the poor young man who was unfortunate enough to lose his purse in the cab, which madame took just after him."

It is only right to add, that when blackmailing in this or any other form comes under the eyes of justice, it is most severely dealt with. There are no halfway measures; but retributive vengeance falls right heavily on the guilty parties. But then how few there are who dare apply to the law for redress—who dare reveal their faults, their sins, their frailty? Despite their disdainful airs, Toto-Chupin's companions had been greatly interested by what he had told them. They had heard of blackmailing of course, their remarks proved it; but although they had plied many a shameful calling they had never thought of resorting to this one, which, as explained by Toto, struck them as being of fascinating simplicity. Hence they ad-visedly "ran it down," trusting that these tactics would fire Toto and make him more explicit. "All that's very fine," said Polyte. "Things like that are talked about, but they're never done."

"Yes they are," answered Toto stoutly.

"Come now, you're romancing. I bet you've never done as you've told us."

At any other moment the young rascal's conceit would probably have prompted him to answer, "Yes I have," but he was fuddled, and so may be excused for speaking the truth. "Well," said he, "if I've not done it myself, I've *seen* it done often enough—on a large scale, too—and a fellow can always imitate a big thing in a milder way with a better chance of success."

"You've seen it done, do you say?"

"Of course I have!"

"Did you lend a hand, then?"

"Yes, I did. Ah! bless my eyes, how many cabs I've followed, how many ladies and gents, real swells, all of the tip-top class! Only I wasn't working for myself! I was like the dog that catches the game and never eats it. It was hard lines, I can tell you. If I'd had a bone thrown me occasionally, even! But no, it was dry bread, and kicks and cuffs for dessert. I'm not going to stand it any longer. I've made up my mind now to go into business for myself."

"And who have you been working for like that?"

Chupin drew himself up in the most haughty fashion. Far from intend-ing to do Mascarot the smallest harm, he thought only of extolling his merits and extraordinary ability, as if, indeed, the "guv'nor's" glory shed some lustre on himself. "The folks I've worked for," said he, "haven't their equal in Paris. They don't stick at trifles, either, you may be certain of that—and they are so rich, it would frighten you to try and count their money! They can do anything and everything in the world they please; and if I told you—"

He stopped short, with his mouth open and his eyes dilated with terror, for in front of him stood the old clerk, that dear, good, genial Tantaine. Chupin's terror had no apparent ground, for never had the old man's face worn such a benign, good-natured look. "Ah! Toto, my boy, so here you are !" he exclaimed in a bland, paternal voice. "Why, I've been looking for you everywhere. Mercy on me ! how fine you are ! Any one would take you for a young prince ! "

Tantaine's kind looks and cheery voice seemed quite to disconcert poor Toto. The mere sight of the old clerk had dispelled the alcoholic fumes with which his brain had been burdened, and as he regained full conscious ness he remembered how indiscreetly he had been talking. He was con scious of his folly, and had a vague presentiment of some impending mis fortune, which was none the less fearful although as yet veiled in mystery. Artlessness was by no means a distinguishing characteristic of this child of Paris. His mental ability had been sharpened by stern necessity, and his intelligence was far beyond his years. Thus he at once doubted the sincerity of Tantaine's genial smile, and realised that perhaps his very life depended on the promptness of his decision at the present emergency. Had the old fellow heard anything of the conversation? Yes, or no. Everything de pended on that. "If the old rascal has been listening," thought Toto, "I'm lost !" And the lad watched Tantaine with the keenest attention, as if determined to decipher this living mystery. He was skilful enough to conceal his anxiety. Silence would have betrayed his suspense, and so with affectedly boisterous gaiety he answered, "I was waiting for you, sir ; and it was in honour of you that I put on my best clothes. I didn't wish you to blush for me."

"That was very good of you, I'm sure, and I'm really very much obliged."

"And now will you allow me to offer you something—a glass of beer, or a drop of brandy, perhaps? "

Toto must have been rapidly regaining his courage, for to patronise Tan taine in this way amounted almost to a piece of impertinence. But he would have done even more to exalt himself in the opinion of the two friends whom he wished to crush with his superiority. He half expected that his invita tion would be most peremptorily refused. However, the old clerk graciously replied that he was much obliged, but must decline the offer, having re freshed himself only a moment before. "You haven't my thirsty disposi tion, sir," rejoined Chupin. And pointing with an air of pride at the empty jugs and bottles on the table, he added, "We have drank all these, my friends and I, since dinner."

This was an introduction, or intended as such, and Tantaine slightly lifted his shabby hat, while Toto's friends bowed most profoundly. These gentlemen were not altogether pleased with the appearance of the new comer, and concluded that this would be a good time for them to make their escape, particularly as they were not without fears that Toto might repent of his generosity. At the "Grand Turc," as elsewhere, it is some times the invited guest who pays the score. A waltz had just struck up, and the master of the ceremonies was shouting his everlasting, "Take your places, ladies and gentlemen ! take your places ! " So Toto's friends shook hands with him, and bowing respectfully to Tantaine, disappeared in the crowd. "Good fellows ! " muttered Toto, looking after them. "Capital fellows ! " The young scamp never blushed for his compan ions.

Tantaine, however, whistled most contemptuously. "Ah ! my boy ! he said, "you keep very bad company, I fear. And you'll be sorry for it one of these days."

"I can look out for myself, sir, I fancy !"

"Go your own way, my lad. Of course it is no business of mine ; but you'll come to grief one of these days—be sure of it. I've told you so, as you may remember, more than once!"

This prediction, to which he had been so long accustomed, eased Toto of his last anxiety. "If the old rascal suspected anything," thought he, "I'm sure he wouldn't talk like that."

Unfortunate Toto! Little did he realise that at this very moment, when his spirits were going up like an india-rubber ball, his danger was most imminent. "This lad's altogether too clever!" Tantaine was at that instant saying to himself. "Too clever by far. Ah! if I were going on with our business and could make it worth his while, I should find him wonderfully useful. But just now, when we are thinking of winding up affairs, to leave such a smart lad who knows so much wandering about at his own sweet will, would be the height of imprudence on the part of people who know the importance of a stolen secret."

Meanwhile, Toto had summoned a waiter, and now threw a ten-franc piece on the table, haughtily exclaiming, "Pay yourself!"

But Tantaine pushed the money back, and handed the waiter another ten-franc piece from his own pocket. This generosity put the lad into the best possible humour. "So much the better for me!" he cried gaily. "And now, let's find Caroline Schimmel."

"But is she here? I couldn't discover her," said Tantaine.

"Because you didn't know where to look for her, then. She's playing cards in the café. Come on, sir!"

But Tantaine detained the lad for a moment. "One instant," he said. "Tell me, did you say precisely what I bade you to this woman?"

"Word for word, sir."

"Repeat to me what you said."

Chupin, who was standing, reseated himself. "For five days," he began, solemnly, "I've literally dogged your Caroline. We've played cards until all was blue, and I took care she should rise from table—a winner. I confided to her that I had a good uncle, fifty years old or thereabouts, still fresh and alert, perhaps a little bit foolish, but awfully amiable—in short, a widower without children, who was dreadfully anxious to marry again—with a woman she knew—in fact, herself; for having seen her he had fallen head over heels in love with her."

"Well done, Toto, well done! And what did she say in return?"

"Bless my soul! she grinned like a hyena. Only, she's a suspicious sort of a cat, and I saw very well she fancied one was after her money. I didn't look as if I guessed her thoughts; but I just mentioned that my uncle had a house of his own and made some four thousand francs a year."

"And did you mention me by name?"

"Yes, at the very last I did. I knew she must have often seen you at the agency, and said to myself, 'Father Tantaine's a worthy old gent, but—' dash it all, you'll excuse me, won't you?—'he isn't particularly handsome, nor over well dressed as a rule?' To say the truth, I thought she might cut up rusty, and so I kept the name back as long as I could. But as soon as I mentioned it she looked more pleased than ever. 'I know him!' she exclaimed, 'I know him well.' So you see, M. Tantaine, that you've nothing to do now but to fix the wedding-day. Now, come on; she expects to see you to-night."

Tantaine settled his glasses with a decided gesture. "I am ready!" he said.

Toto was not mistaken. The Duke de Champdoce's former servant was playing a game of cards, but as soon as she saw young Chupin's *soi-disant* uncle, in spite of the fact that she held a wonderfully good hand, she threw down her cards and received him with marked encouragement. Toto-Chupin looked on in delight. Never had he seen the old rascal—as he, in the recesses of his heart, irreverently termed him—so amiable, agreeable and talkative. It was easy to see that Caroline Schimmel was melting under his attractions, for never before in her life had such tender words been whispered in her ear by so musical a voice. Nor did Tantaine confine his attentions to tender words ; he ordered a bowl of kirsch punch, and loving talk and fiery liquor were allowed to alternate. The old boy's long-lost youth seemed to have come back to him—he drank, and he sang, and he danced. Yes, he really took her round the waist, and drew her into the ball-room ; and Toto, in open-mouthed astonishment, watched them as they whirled around. At all events Tantaine was rewarded for this super-human exertion, for at ten o'clock the marriage was arranged, and Caroline left the "Grand Turc" on the arm of her future husband. She had consented to allow him to offer her a betrothal supper at a restaurant hard by.

The next morning, when the street-sweepers came down from Montmartre, they found a woman lying face downwards on the pavement of the outer boulevard. They carried her to the nearest police station, but she was not dead as had been at first imagined ; she was only stunned. When she came to her senses the poor creature stated that her name was Caroline Schimmel, that she had been to supper in a private room at a restaurant with her future husband, but could remember nothing more. At her request she was put into a cab and sent to her home, in the Rue Marcadet.

XXVII.

"It is only a master's eye that sees," says La Fontaine, and once again the truth of this proverb was verified at the employment agency in the Rue Montorgueil. For more than a week B. Mascarot had ceased to preside in the Confessional Box, and the agency was already suffering from his absence. Continual complaints were made. Beaumarchef was all very well, but he was not Mascarot. The ex-sub-officer, frightened by his responsibility, had ventured on some timid remonstrances, but his master had so ill received him that he could only retreat with a sigh.

What indeed did Mascarot care for his agency now ? Thus on the morning after Tantaine's expedition to the "Grand Turc," while Beaumarchef answered each fresh applicant, with the same stereotyped phrase, "My master has gone out on business," his master was in reality shut up in his own private room. On the day in question, his face bore evident marks of fatigue. His eyes were greatly inflamed, and on his table stood a cup of *tisane* which he occasionally sipped, as if to moisten his parched throat and cool some internal fire. It was plain enough that this man, generally so cold and calm—so completely master of himself—was now a prey to terrible agitation. Great generals on the eve of a decisive battle may appear unmoved to those about them, but they are none the less the victims of that feverish excitement which always precedes action. Now with B. Mascarot, the hour had struck for the supreme conflict. He was about to take a step, after which there could be no possible turning back. He was, in fact, waiting for Catenac, Hortebize and Paul, to reveal to them his plan in its fullest details.

As usual, the first to appear was Hortebize. "I received your instructions, Baptistin," he said, as he entered, "and I have carried them out. I have just come from the Hôtel de Mussidan."

"How do they seem there?"

"Sad, but resigned. Mademoiselle Sabine was never particularly vivacious; she is graver and paler than before her illness; that's all the difference that I can detect."

"Were you alone with the countess?"

"Yes; and I told her that I was so harassed by the people who held her letters that she must be very guarded in her actions. She answered with a mournful smile, that she was in despair, but she was certain of her husband's consent, and could rely on her daughter's readiness to marry Croisenois."

Tantaine would have received this statement with enthusiasm, but Mascarot remained unmoved. However much he may have been pleased, it was coldly enough that he replied; "I saw Croisenois this morning, and if he obeys me, which I am sure he will, we shall get ahead of André, and M. de Breulh. The marquis will be Sabine's husband before they discover that the banns have been published. The marriage solemnized, we can afford to laugh at them; and, in regard to our grand idea, I have matured my plan of the company, and in a week the prospectus will be published. But to-day we have another subject for discussion, the Champdoce matter—"

At this point, he was interrupted by the arrival of Paul, who came in rather timidly, being a little uncertain of his reception after Tantaine's singular good-bye the day before. Contrary to his expectations, he was warmly welcomed. Either Tantaine had not repeated what had taken place, or Mascarot regarded it with different eyes. "Accept my congratulations," he said, "as regards your success with Monsieur Martin Rigal. You have'nt merely pleased the daughter, but you've fascinated the father as well."

"I'm glad to hear it. Last evening, however, he was away."

"Yes, I'm aware of that. He dined with one of our friends, who sounded him with regard to you. If Hortebize went to-morrow in your name to ask Mademoiselle Flavia's hand, M. Rigal wouldn't refuse it."

Paul closed his eyes, dazzled by the glare of Flavia's millions.

"Hark!" interrupted Hortebize; "I hear Catenac bustling along the passage."

The worthy doctor's ears had not deceived him; it was indeed the lawyer, who came late, as usual. He did not apologise for his lack of punctuality, but tried to win forgiveness by the smiles and honeyed words he lavished on everyone in the room.

However, Mascarot hastily rose and confronted him with such a threatening mien that Catenac started back. "What the deuce do you mean?" he asked.

"Can't you guess?" rejoined the agent, in a tone that was more appalling even than his manner. "I have measured the depth of your infamy. I was certain the other day that you meant to betray us. But you gave me your word to the contrary, and you—"

"I swear to you, Baptistin—"

"No oaths, they are needless. One word alone from Perpignan enlightened us.   Were you ignorant of the fact that the Duke de Champdoce had unfailing means of recognizing his child—that there are ineffaceable scars— "

"I had forgotten— " The words died away on his lips, for even his usually marvellous self-possession deserted him under Mascarot's contemptuous glance.

"Let me tell you what I think of you," continued the agent.   "You are a coward and a traitor !   Even convicts keep their word to each other.   I knew you to be vile, but not to this degree— "

" Then why do you employ me, against my wish ? "

The impudence of this reply exasperated B. Mascarot to such a degree, that he caught Catenac by the collar, and shook him as if he would have strangled him.   " I use you, viper," he cried, " because I so hold you that you cannot harm us.   And you will serve me well when I prove to you that your reputation, your money, your liberty, and even your life all depend on our success.   Fortunately, I know where that body is !   The proofs— the most absolute proofs of your crime—are in the hands of a person who knows precisely what to do.   When I give the signal he will move, and in another hour you are a lost man."   A terrible pause followed.   " And it would be as well," resumed Mascarot at last, " for you to pray that no accident may ever happen to Paul, Hortebize, and myself.   If one of us should happen to die suddenly, your fate is sealed.   You are warned ; so now look out ! "

Catenac stood with his head bowed, motionless and rooted to the ground as it were.   There was a gleam of fury in his eyes, but what did the others care ?   He was so bound and gagged that he could move neither hand nor foot against them.   No more tergiversation, no hope of vengeance was possible.   He owed his position to blackmail, and it was now blackmail that threatened him !

Mascarot turned away, swallowed some of his *tisane*, and tranquilly, as if nothing unusual had occurred, took his seat again by the fire and calmly adjusted his spectacles, which had been deranged by the violence of his movements.   " I ought to tell you, Catenac," said he, " that with the exception of this one detail, I know far more about the Champdoce matter than you do.   In fact, what do you know?   Nothing in the world except what the duke has seen fit to confide to you and Perpignan, and you imagine that you are in possession of the truth, do you ?   You were never more mistaken.   Fortunately I know the truth, and my knowledge won't surprise you when you learn that for years I have been investigating this matter."

" Yes, for many years." interrupted the doctor.

" And perhaps it would interest you to know how I first got on the track of this affair.   Do you remember that scrivener who had his room near the Palais de Justice, and who tried blackmailing on a large scale ?   Well, through an unfortunate speculation he came to grief, and was lodged in prison for two years."

" I think I remember him."

"He was intelligent and ingenious.   He bought old manuscripts and letters, invoices, and so on, papers written upon all sorts and kinds by weight, and he carefully sorted and read them all.   It is, of course, impossible to say what treasures he found in these papers, abandoned to the rag pickers and dust-carts, but I believe he came across several.   Do you think there was ever a man who hadn't reason to regret, at least once in his life, having had pen and ink within reach at some given time !   Was there ever a *cause célèbre* in which letters did not play an important part? These facts have struck me so often and so forcibly that I ask myself why prudent people do not invariably use those inks which, after a few days, fade away and leave the paper without a mark. To be brief, I decided to follow the scrivener's example. I bought old papers, and, among other curious things, I found this." So saying he took from his desk a bit of paper, fumbled, torn, and dirty, and handed it to Hortebize, adding, "Look at it well."

Some one had inscribed on this paper, with a trembling hand, the following enigmatical assemblage of letters: "*dlihcruoevahemtelemnoytipevahtnec onnimaiycrem,*" while beneath ran the one intelligible word, "Never!"

"It was clear to me," continued Mascarot, "that I had before me a cryptogram, that is to say, a letter composed according to particular rules and intended to place a compromising correspondence beyond all risk of exposure. Of course, it was equally clear that such a precaution was not employed in ordinary correspondence. I concluded, consequently, that this scrap of paper contained some tremendous secret."

Catenac listened to this explanation with a lofty and supercilious air. He belonged to that class of combatants who never know when their shoulders touch the ground, and who, even when exhausted and panting, persist in denying their defeat. "The conclusion seems to me evident," he said patronisingly.

"Thank you," answered Mascarot coldly. "At all events, it had to be found. I became deeply interested in deciphering this enigma—the more so, as I have the honour of presiding over an association, each individual member of which owes not only his daily bread, but even the esteem in which he is held by the world at large, to the manipulation of other people's secrets."

Hortebize smiled a wicked little smile, and with a glance at Catenac, murmured, "Take that to yourself!"

Mascarot thanked his friend with a gesture. "One morning," he continued, "I closed my door, and swore not to leave my room until I had deciphered the meaning of these letters."

In turn, Paul, the doctor, and Catenac now attentively examined the paper handed them by Mascarot. The letters seemed to them to be placed quite at random on the paper, and conveyed no sense or meaning to their minds. "No," said the doctor impatiently, "it's no use; I can make nothing out of it."

Mascarot smiled complacently. He had never been over modest, and he had, moreover, his reasons for prolonging his companions' astonishment as much as possible. "You can detect nothing?" he asked, as he took the letter from Paul's hands.

"Nothing whatever," answered Catenac sulkily.

"I assure you," resumed Mascarot, "that at the outset I was quite as much at sea as yourselves; and yet I carefully preserved this scrap of paper, soiled and old as it was—the age is evident from its hue and the faintness of the ink. A secret instinct bade me guard it closely, a presentiment seemed to tell me it meant fortune, wealth for myself and all of you. All human minds have a certain dose of curiosity, inquisitiveness, and seek to learn hidden things. Riddles, rebuses, and charades are successful simply for that reason. It might be that, on deciphering these letters, I should only arrive at some insignificant, childish phrase—or I might, of course, make some startling discovery. The chances were equal, and this, of course I fully realised. At the outset I had detected that there were two distinct handwritings. If it were a woman who had composed the rebus, a man had added the word 'Never!' Was that 'never' a reply to the previous letters? If this surmise were correct, then the woman asked some favour and the man refused it. But then, why had two different languages, so to say, been employed? Why those mysterious letters, followed by this ordinary word? On reflection this is what I thought: The woman's request was of a dangerous nature, and might reveal something it was her interest to conceal, while this laconic 'never' was in no degree compromising. But how happened it, you ask, that the request and the refusal were written on the same paper? This question, also, I soon solved to my own satisfaction. This letter was never intended for the post, and never went into a letter-box. It was exchanged between two neighbouring houses, perhaps between two floors in the same house, and perhaps, who could say, between two rooms in the same apartment. In a moment of intense excitement a woman penned these mysterious letters, and sent them by a servant to a man whose help or whose pity and mercy she implored. He, in a fit of rage, snatched up a pen, wrote that one word 'never,' and then handed the paper to the servant, saying, 'Take that to your mistress.' Having settled these points in my own mind, I next attacked the enigma. I was unaccustomed to this sort of work, and I found, as you may imagine, considerable difficulty in the task; in fact, I worked fourteen hours without success. It was the merest chance that gave me the clue I was vainly seeking. While I was studying the letters, I happened to hold the paper between myself and the light, the back of it turned towards me, and to my utter surprise I read it at once. It was the simplest, most childish cryptograph in the world. The letters, instead of going from left to right, went from right to left, and to obtain the sense, it was only necessary to replace them in their proper order. I took a pencil and copied each letter in turn, beginning at the last one. 'M. e. r. c. y. i. a.,' etc. I next divided the letters into words, and obtained this significant result: 'Mercy, I am innocent. Have pity on me. Let me have our child.'"

Dr. Hortebize snatched the paper from the desk.

"You are right," he said; "it is the infancy of art."

B. Mascarot smiled. "I had succeeded in reading it," said he; "but that was only the beginning. This scrap had been found among five or six hundred pounds of paper, bought at the sale of a château near Vendôme. How was it to be traced back to its possessors? I should have despaired if, in one corner—see there—I hadn't noticed the faint trace of a crest and motto, originally stamped on the paper. I knew literally nothing about heraldry, but one of my friends knew a great deal. He examined the crest with a magnifying glass, and at once pronounced it to be that of the noble house of Champdoce." At this point B. Mascarot rose, stationed himself erect, with his back to the fire, and then resumed: "That was how I started, gentlemen. Faint was the light that guided me, wavering and uncertain. Another man would probably have been discouraged; but I rarely give up an idea. I am patient, and I wake each morning with the same idea in my mind that was there when I went to sleep. Six months later, I knew that these appealing words had been addressed by the Duchess of Champdoce to her husband; and I knew under what circumstances they had been written. Since then I have fully investigated the secret first suggested to me by this scrap of paper. If I have not achieved my task earlier, it was because one single link was wanting. But I have it now; I obtained it yesterday.'

"Ah!" said the doctor; "so Caroline Schimmel has spoken?"

"Yes. The secret she kept for twenty-three years dropped last night from her tongue, which had been loosened by wine." As he spoke, B. Mascarot opened a drawer of his desk and drew out a voluminous manuscript, which he brandished with an air of triumph. "This is my masterpiece!" he cried, "and the explanation of my manœuvres for the last fortnight. After you have read this you will understand how it happens that I hold the Duke and Duchess of Champdoce and Diane de Sauvebourg, Countess de Mussidan, all in the same noose. Listen, doctor, you who have the blindest and most unquestioning confidence in me. Listen, Catenac, you who wished to betray me, and then tell me if I am in error when I affirm that I hold every element of success in my hand." He held the manuscript out to Paul. "And you, my dear child," he added, "read this aloud—I have written it more especially for you. Read it carefully, weigh every syllable, give it all the attention you are capable of; it is the history of a great and noble family. And remember that there is not one detail, however trivial it may seem, that is not fraught with importance as regards your future."

Paul opened the manuscript, and in a voice which trembled at first, but which gathered strength as he went on, he perused the heart-stirring narrative prepared by Mascarot under the title of "THE CHAMPDOCE SECRET."

END OF PART I.

PART II.

I.

In journeying from Poitiers to Loudon, it is best to engage a seat in the diligence, which plies between the capital of the department of the Vienne and Saumur, the gayest and most prepossessing of the many towns that stud the banks of the rapid Loire. The diligence office is but a few yards from the Hôtel de France, between the restaurant of the Coq-Hardi and the Café Castille. Travellers are received there by an exceedingly polite clerk, who in return for the advance of a five franc piece, promises a good seat in the *coupé* for the following morning. "But be careful," he invariably adds, "be careful to come here, punctually at six o'clock." So the next morning the traveller has himself awakened at daybreak, dresses as quickly as possibly, and hastens to the office as fast as his legs can take him. But he has hurried himself without reason. In the office there is only a stable-lad, just sufficiently awake to give a sullen reply to the questions asked of him. It is of no use remonstrating or flying into a rage, for he simply turns round on his bench, and dozes off again. Over the way, however, a shop where hot coffee can be obtained eventually opens, and furnishes a convenient refuge for those who are waiting. Half an hour afterwards, the clerk of the office turns up, yawning and rubbing his eyes. The old diligence is dragged out of the courtyard, the postilion and the ostler harness the three horses, while a couple of porters hoist the luggage and goods on to the roof of the vehicle. "Take your places, gentlemen," shouts the clerk, "take your places!" It is a false alarm. So far most of the passengers have not put in an appearance. It is necessary to wait for M. de Rocheposay, who lives in the Rue St. Porchaire, for M. Nadal, the notary, who resides near Blossac, for M. Richand, of Loudon, who arrived at Poitiers on business yesterday, as well as for several others. One by one, however, they eventually turn up, laden with parcels and carpet bags, which they stow away under their seats. At last the vehicle is full; half past seven is striking; the conductor swears a last oath, the postilion cracks his whip; and the heavy old coach rolls off, the bells of the horses gaily jingling. Down through the town go the nags at a sharp pace; the bridge across the Clain is crossed almost at a gallop; the vehicle bounds over the paving stones of the Faubourgs, the highroad is reached, and then—alas! for those who like to travel rapidly—the horses knowingly subside into the jog trot they will keep up till the end of the stage.

The driver now complacently fills his pipe, and the passengers, if they be so minded, may look out of the windows and admire the scenery. This is upper Poitou—a succession of fertile plains, far-stretching pasture lands and dense forests. Valleys follow valleys, and as far as the eye can reach, come fields, with ruddy-tinted soil, and chestnut-trees with branches bowing to the ground, planted here and there in their midst. See here are the moors and woods of Bivron where game is most abundant; for their owner, the Count de Mussïdan, has not once shot over them since he killed poor Montlouis three-and-twenty years ago. The château de Mussidan is farther off on the right hand side. Two years ago, come Christmas, old Madame de Chevauché died there, leaving all her property to her niece, Mademoiselle Sabine. On the other side of the road, half hidden by the trees of a lordly park, rises the proud castle of Sauvebourg, with its balconies and cornices, carved by one of the favourite sculptors of Francis the First. And here a few miles farther on, on the summit of an isolated hill, stands the ancient feudal manor of Champdoce, whence plains and villages and forests may be viewed for many a long mile around. How gloomy, how desolate it looks! Once the most stately pile in all Poitou, it is now falling to ruins; for, for five-and-twenty years, its owners have abandoned and seemingly forgotten it. The left wing has already half crumbled to pieces. The storms have carried away the weather-cocks and the roof. Rain and heat have rotted the shutters and window-frames, and the rusty iron balconies barely cling to the stone work.

Here, however, in 1840, there lived with his only son, the possessor of one of the most illustrious names in France—César-Guillaume de Dompair, Duke de Champdoce, three times a marquis, twice a count, and seven times a baron.

He was looked upon as a most eccentric nobleman. He might be met on the highways clad like the poorest peasant, wearing an old coat, darned and patched, a dingy leather cap and wooden shoes. In winter time he would throw an old sheepskin over his shoulders, and in all seasons he invariably carried a stout ash stick. He was then some sixty years of age, but still endowed with wonderful strength and nerve. His eyes bespoke his iron will, turning from grey to black whenever he became enraged. He had been an *émigré*, and had fought in Condé's army; and a sabre stroke had cut his upper lip in twain, leaving a scar which imparted almost a fiendish expression to his face. He was not, however, an evil-minded man, though for violence, obstinacy, and despotism, he was probably without an equal. Fortunately for those around him, his anger might be measured by his three favourite oaths. When he was merely dissatisfied he would exclaim, "*Jarnicoton!*" In a state of irritation he shouted, "*Jarnidieu!*" and when fairly enraged he burst forth into a terrible cry of, "*Jarnitonnerre!*" Then was the time to keep beyond reach of his bludgeon. He was greatly feared, and the folks of Bivron bared their heads with mingled terror and respect when, followed by his son, he passed by on Sundays on his way to high mass at the church, where he had a pew of his own, the first in front of the altar. As the service proceeded he read his huge prayer-book half aloud, or sang with the choir in a deep bass voice. At the collection he regularly deposited a five-franc piece in the plate, and this weekly offering, with his subscription to the *Gazette de France*, and the five crowns a year he paid the barber who came to shave him twice a week, made up his personal expenditure. It must not be thought, however, that he starved at home; plump fowls, savoury vegetables, and exquisite fruit abounded on his table. But the *menus* were invariably limited to things that had been caught, killed, or gathered on his estates, and so butcher's meat was never seen at Champdoce, for the simple reason that it would have had to be paid for. Although frequently invited to the entertainments of the neighbouring nobility, who looked upon him as their senior representative, the duke regularly declined the compliment, declaring that no nobleman, with any feelings of self respect, could accept hospitality without returning it; and in this instance, returning it implied a pecuniary outlay.

It was certainly not poverty that compelled the Duke de Champdoce to practise such rigid economy. His estates in Poitou, in the Angoumois and Saintonge, were worth more than twelve hundred thousand francs, and this without counting the forest of Champdoce, which, skilfully managed, yielded some ten thousand silver crowns a year in timber. It was said, moreover, that his personality in ready coin and invested money was yet more considerable; and the report was by no means a false one. People, of course, looked upon him as a miser; and yet he was not one, at least, as the term is usually understood. The fact is, this obstinate nobleman was simply following out a scheme, planned after long reflection, and executed with great perseverance and energy. His past life might in some degree explain his conduct. César-Guillaume de Champdoce had, as we have already stated, emigrated from France at the outset of the Revolution. For a time he had served in Condé's army, and then, when the Empire dawned upon Europe and Legitimists were reduced to wait and hope, he had journeyed to England, taken refuge in London, and earned a scanty livelihood by giving fencing lessons. At the restoration of the Bourbons he had returned to France, and by a very great piece of good luck he had obtained possession of a part of the old family estates. But what was that part to him? He thought of the princely opulence of his ancestors, and, contrasting it with his present belongings, pictured himself in a state of miserable poverty. As an additional pang he saw a new, young aristocracy spring out of the ranks of commerce and industry, active, proud of its wealth, and ambitious to win the influence and prestige of the listless, enervated old nobility. Then it was that M. de Champdoce, whose family pride was almost a form of monomania, conceived the plan to which he afterwards devoted his whole life. He considered he had discovered a means of restoring all the past power and splendour of his house; three or four generations must sacrifice themselves for the benefit of their descendants. "By living like a peasant," said he, "by denying myself every luxury, I can triple my capital in thirty years. My son must imitate me, and in a hundred years, thanks to a colossal fortune, the Dukes of Champdoce will have regained the rank to which their birth entitles them."

In 1820, following out this scheme, he espoused, as a matter of business, a young girl who was as ugly as she was noble, but who possessed a magnificent dowry. The marriage was far from being a happy one; and folks even accused the duke of brutality towards his poor young wife, who failed to understand how a man, whom she had enriched with a portion of half a million francs, could possibly refuse her a dress she needed. However, after a year's matrimony, she gave birth to a son, christened by the names of Louis-Norbert; and six months later, worn out, no doubt, with the hard life she was compelled to lead, she died, somewhat suddenly. In his heart, her egotistical husband rejoiced rather than otherwise. He had a sturdy young heir, and the mother's fortune now belonged to him. What else did he care for? Henceforth unhindered, he might carry his mania for economy to the farthest limits. Rising before daybreak, he accompanied his labourers to the fields and toiled beside them. He attended all the fairs and markets in person, selling his crops and live stock at the highest possible price, and haggling over a few francs like the closest-fisted peasant. As for his son, his only care was that the little fellow might grow up strong and healthy, so as to fittingly continue the task of retrieving the family fortunes.

Young Norbert was brought up like a petty farmer's son, neither better nor worse. At first he was allowed to ramble along the hedges, roll on the manure heaps, and wade about in the ponds at his own sweet will—going barefooted in summer time, and wearing wooden shoes, stuffed with straw, at winter tide. However, when he was nine years' old, his rural education commenced. To begin with, he kept the cows in the pasture lands, or at the outskirts of the woods, carrying a long perch to prevent the cattle from nibbling at the young shoots. He went off at dawn, with his daily pittance in a basket, slung over his back. Then, as he grew older, he learned to guide a plough, to mow, sow, and reap, to value a standing crop at a glance, to attend on cattle and sheep afflicted with rot and foot-and-mouth disease, and finally, to drive a bargain. The Duke de Champdoce long hesitated before allowing his son to be taught to read. What was the use of education, as the lad must lead a rough, country life? Still, on the other hand, the man who cannot read, write, and count, can scarcely manage a large estate to advantage. Finally, the priest of Bivron ventured on some timid remonstrances, and his grace consented that Norbert should be taught the first rudiments of knowledge.

Everything went as the duke desired it, till Norbert reached his sixteenth year, or rather till the day when his father took him to Poitiers for the first time. At sixteen, Louis Norbert de Champdoce looked fully three years older, and was certainly as handsome a youth as could anywhere be found. His features had that pensive expression common to tillers of the soil, who live alone, absorbed in their own thoughts, face to face with nature. The sun had bronzed his cheeks and brow; he had a magnificent crop of wavy black hair, and his big blue eyes with their melancholy gleam, strikingly recalled his mother's. Poor woman! Those eyes of hers had been her only beauty. The hard labour he had been subjected to had imparted uncommon strength to his muscles, but without tampering with his graceful build, and his hands, hard as they were, were albeit of perfect shape. From a moral point of view, he was altogether a young savage. Under his father's harsh rule he had never wandered a league from the château, and Bivron with its sixty houses, its little church and great inn, seemed to him a delicious locality full of stir and bustle. So far he had not spoken to three strangers, and the labourers and workpeople whom the Duke de Champdoce employed feared his grace too much to talk openly in the lad's presence. He had never heard a word likely to enlighten him as to his real position, or cause him to reflect. Brought up in this fashion, he could barely imagine any life different to his own. To wake when the cocks crowed, labour all day in the fields, and fall fast asleep after supper, such seemed to him the sum total of life. Happiness in his eyes consisted in good crops; and misfortune came in the form of a severe frost or a heavy hail storm. Still he had his amusements. High mass on Sunday mornings was almost a *fête* for him; and after the service he took infinite pleasure in surveying the groups of villagers rigged out in their best clothes. At times too he eagerly listened to the discourse of some helmeted charlatan vaunting the superiority of his "pencils" or "pain killer" from the top of a travelling van. For more than a year the young peasant girls had favoured him with sheepish glances, and blushed to their ears whenever he spoke to them, but he was far too simple to notice it. After mass, he accompanied his father on an inspection of the week's work, or else obtained permission to set snares for birds. He had no notion of real life, of the world, society, men's relations with each other, and the value of money. Somewhat alarmed by his natural intelligence, his father had purposely kept him in the dark on all these points. Such, indeed, was Norbert, when one evening the duke bade him hold himself in readiness to accompany him to Poitiers on the morrow.

The Duke de Champdoce had just received the rents of several of his tenants, as well as the price of a large stock of timber, and it was necessary he should invest this money, for he never let capital lie idle. If he took his son with him, it was because he began to feel that he must initiate him into the management of the large fortune he would one day inherit; so, soon after daybreak, they both set off in a light cart, with forty thousand francs in silver, in stout bags, under their feet. Norbert was radiant. For more than a year he had been longing to see Poitiers, which he had never visited, although it is only some five leagues distant from Champdoce. Poitiers, be it mentioned, is not precisely the gayest city in France, and many of the students there naturally sigh for Paris and the Quartier Latin. The streets are narrow tortuous and extremely ill paved. The tall black houses seem to date from half forgotten centuries. No matter, Norbert was fairly dazzled. As the horse was walked through the town, to prevent any mishap, he perceived the most beautiful, most astonishing things in the shop windows. It happened, moreover, to be market day, and such, to the lad's mind, was the stir and bustle, that he felt almost dizzy. He had perhaps never imagined that the earth contained so many inhabitants; and he was, indeed, so preoccupied that he did not notice that the horse had stopped of its own accord in front of a stylish house, having a notary's name inscribed on a bright brass plate.

"Come, come, Norbert," cried the Duke. "Here we are!"

The lad at once alighted, but his mind still wandered through the town. He helped, in purely mechanical fashion, to carry the bags of silver indoors. He did not notice the obsequious manner in which the notary received his father, he did not hear a word of the interminable conversation respecting investments that followed. His brain was busy with the marvels of Poitiers—to him an earthly paradise.

At last the duke left the notary's office, taking his son with him. They stabled the horse and cart at a large inn, on the market-place, and breakfasted off a bit of bacon, washed down with a glass of sour wine, on the corner of the common table where peasants and herdsmen were haggling and tippling. However, M. de Champdoce had not come to Poitiers merely on account of his investment. He intended, as it was market day, to avail himself of the opportunity to ferret out a miller, who had owed him a small sum for more than a year. Accordingly as soon as the frugal meal was over, he bade his son wait for him, and hurried off. Norbert was standing in front of the inn, somewhat perplexed at finding himself abandoned in the midst of so many strangers, when suddenly he felt some one touch him on the shoulder. He turned at once, and found himself face to face with a young fellow of his own age, who exclaimed with a laugh: "What! have you forgotten your old friends?"

It was a moment before Norbert recognized this young fellow; but suddenly remembering him, he responded: "Why, Montlouis, is it you?"

This Montlouis. the son of one of the Duke de Champdoce's farmers, had formerly been Norbert's comrade. In earlier days they had ofttimes driven their cows to the same pasture lands, had spent long afternoons playing together, fishing and bird-nesting; but for five years they had not met each other. Norbert's hesitation on recognizing his old playmate, was in some measure due to the latter's costume—a tall hat and a long black coat with metal buttons. This was the uniform of the college where Mont-louis was completing his studies; for whilst his grace the duke was making a peasant of his son, the humble farmer strove to turn his lad into a gentle-man. Norbert was in fact so struck by the difference of Montlouis' attire to his own, that beyond a few words of recognition he could find nothing to say. "What are you doing here?" asked Montlouis, at last.

"Waiting for my father."

"Just as I am for mine. However, we've still time to take a cup of coffee together." And without waiting for his old mate's acceptance of the offer, Montlouis drew him into a little café at a few yards from the inn. The young collegian's superiority was evident, and he seemed dis-posed to make it yet all the more apparent. "If the billiard table were free," said he, "I should have proposed a game. To be sure it costs money, and I don't suppose your father allows you much." Norbert had never held in his hand a fi'penny bit he could call his own, and he felt cruelly mortified on hearing his friend talk like this. "My father," resumed Montlouis, "never refuses me anything. But to say the truth, I work hard, and I'm certain of two prizes this term. When I've taken my degree, M. de Mussi-dan will engage me as secretary—he has promised it—and I shall go to Paris, and amuse myself. And you—what do you mean to do?"

"I? I don't know."

"Don't know? Then I know for you. Why, you'll dig and toil in the fields like your father. Does it amuse you? To think you're the son of a great noble, of the richest man in Poitou, and yet you're not so happy as I, a mere farmer's son. Well, well, I suppose there's no help for it."

They parted; and when the Duke de Champdoce returned to the inn, he found his son on the spot where he had left him, and noticed nothing unusual in his manner. "Come," said the duke, "let's harness." The drive home was a silent one. Montlouis' remarks had fallen into Norbert's mind like subtle poison into pure water. Twenty careless words from an incon-siderate boy were about to destroy the result of sixteen years' patience and obstinacy. From that day, indeed, Norbert was transformed, though no one suspected it.

It is in secluded rural districts that diplomatists should go and study dissimulation. This young fellow, ignorant as he was, at least knew how to control his temper. His smiling face never revealed the storm raging in his heart; and it was with all his usual alacrity that he started each morning to perform his daily task, once pleasant enough, but now held by him in horror. To gain some inkling of his thoughts, it would have been necessary to follow and watch him. Often when he thought himself alone, he would remain motionless for hours, leaning on his spade, with contracted brows, and absorbed in dismal reflections—he, who formerly had known no more of care than the bird warbling in the bushes. His intellect, aroused by Montlouis, was now on the *qui vive*, and many circumstances which he had never before heeded, at present seemed to him so many revelations. For instance, noting his father's relations with the surrounding peasantry, he realised, that despite apparent familiarity, they were separated by a perfect chasm. He divined that he must seek for his equals among the great landowners of the district, who lived on their estates in the summer time, and repaired on Sundays to the Church at Bivron. The old Count de Mussidan, so imposing with his snow white locks, the proud Marquis de Sauvebourg, to whom the peasants bowed so humbly, were always eager to shake hands with the Duke de Champdoce and his son. And, moreover, the most beautiful and most disdainful of the ladies of the nobility, who bore themselves like queens when they crossed the market-place, sweeping the dust with the trains of their gorgeous dresses, ay, the most imposing amongst them, seemed flattered and delighted when his grace, who, despite his coarse garments, retained the manners of the old *regime*, gallantly kissed their hands.

All this was calculated to enlighten Norbert. He felt that he was the equal of these haughty folks ; and yet, what a difference there was between them and him ! Whilst he and his father walked to mass in their heavy hob-nailed shoes, the others drove up in superb carriages, drawn by valuable horses, and were surrounded by footmen obedient to their bidding. What could be the cause of this difference? It certainly did not consist in the poverty of the Champdoces, for Norbert was sufficiently well acquainted with the value of lands and crops to realise that his father was as wealthy, if not even wealthier than these people. Thus everything he had heard whispered since his transformation must be true. The Champdoce labourers declared that the duke was an old miser, and that rather than spend his gold or give it to the poor, he buried it in the vaults of his castle, rising from bed in the dead of night to go and worship his treasures. " Our young master, Norbert's badly off," they said to each other. " He might have every pleasure in life, but he's treated even more severely than our own youngsters." Thereupon others would rejoin in a threatening tone, " Ah, I wouldn't stand it, if I were in his place."

The labourers were not the only ones who pitied him. He remembered very well that on one occasion, whilst his father was talking to the Marquis de Sauvebourg, an old lady who accompanied the latter, probably the marchioness in person, had looked at him most compassionately, and, carried away by her feelings, perhaps, had murmured, " Poor lad ! what a pity he lost his mother so early."

What did all this mean ? Did it not signify that folks pitied him, because he had to submit to his father's despotic will ? To crown everything, these gay, grand nobles had sons of their own, young fellows of Norbert's age or thereabouts. He wept with jealousy when he compared himself with them. Sometimes as he trudged along, bringing a pair of oxen home after ploughing a field, he met some of these young aristocrats riding dainty thoroughbreds. If they knew him they just exclaimed, "Good day, Norbert," and galloped on. The greeting seemed almost an insult to him ; these young fellows were as insolent as happiness itself and he hated them. What life did they lead in Paris, whither they invariably returned as soon as the cold weather set in ? *He* had to sow his crops, but how did they find occupation for their hours of idleness? This was a point he could not solve, and his absolute ignorance led him to make the most absurd conjectures. He in no degree envied such "pleasures," as he had hitherto heard of. The peasantry shut themselves up in a tap-room, emptied countless flagons of wine, shouted, disputed, and finally fought together. That was what they called "amusement ;" but, to Norbert it seemed just the contrary. However, the young scions of the nobility, whom he knew by sight, must have more refined enjoyments, a different gaiety to that of the tippler stumbling home. But then came the question as to what these superior pleasures really were. Across the desert with which the paternal will had encompassed him, he divined there must be another marvellous, unknown world. Who could describe it to him? Whom could he talk to, ask for information, make his friend? He felt indignant at having been kept so frightfully ignorant, whilst Montlouis, the farmer's son, went to college. Hitherto he had yawned at the sight of a printed page, but now, although obliged to spell almost every third word, he devoted all his spare time to reading. However, this could not possibly please his father; and one evening the duke imperatively declared there was nothing he disliked so much as a bookworm. Still Norbert did not relinquish his new pursuit. Opposition only strengthened his resolution. He read in secret. He had heard that one of the upper rooms of the château was full of books, and so, picking the door lock, he entered and found a library of fully three thousand volumes, including some five hundred novels which his mother had perused in the weary, lonely hours of her married life. Norbert fell on these books like a starving man on bread. He read everything indiscriminately, without discernment or reason, jumbling the past with the present, and history with romance. Still two ideas rapidly evolved from the confusion which filled his mind. He considered himself the most wretched being on earth, and he began to hate his father. Yes, he hated him with a cold bitter hatred, with all the violence of the covetous longing that consumed him ; and if he had dared—But he did not dare. The duke inspired him with invincible terror.

Such had been the situation for eighteen months, when M. de Champdoce considered it was time he should acquaint his son with his schemes, so that the lad might, in his turn, fittingly labour for the restoration of the family fortunes. It was one Sunday, after supper in the common hall, and when all the servants had retired. Never had Norbert seen his father look so solemn. Usually somewhat bowed, like all who have toiled long years in the fields, the duke had now drawn himself up to his full height. All the pride of birth, generally so skilfully concealed, glittered in his eyes. He related to his son the history of the house of Champdoce, the origin of which is lost in the legends of medieval times. He related the lives of all the heroes who had made the name illustrious. He recapitulated the honours conferred upon them, the sovereign alliances they had formed, and told what was the wealth and power of the family in the days when the Dompairs of Champdoce raised taxes like princes, possessing their strongholds and their army, and tiring out the strongest horse ere they had crossed their domains. "That is what we were," he cried in a ringing voice; "but what is left to us of all that splendour? A house in Paris, in the Rue de Varennes ; this castle ; a few patches of ground ; a few stocks and shares ; at the utmost, an income of three hundred thousand francs—barely eight millions of capital !"

Norbert knew that his father was wealthy, but not to this degree. He was stupified on hearing these figures—eight millions ! and then a thousand conflicting thoughts flashed like lightning through his mind. Eight millions ! And he had to toil like a labourer who earned thirty sous a day ! An income of three hundred thousand francs ! And this room where he now sat listening to his father looked like some pauper's dwelling ! His ancestors had had an army of retainers, and yet all the clodhoppers of the district treated him with patronising familiarity ! How could he accept such humiliation and such poverty, being so wealthy and so nobly born ? A first impulse of rage almost overcame his usual timidity, and he half rose to reproach his father for his avarice and cruelty ; but his strength was not in keeping with his audacity. Overwhelmed with emotion, he sank on to his stool again, unable to speak a word, choked by the sobs that rose from his heart.

The duke had not noticed this explosion of feeling. Prostration seemed to have followed the excitement with which he had recorded the glories of his house, and now he was walking heavily up and down the room, his head bowed upon his breast. "Barely eight millions," he repeated ; "'tis little, very little."

Little indeed ! And yet Norbert knew that not one of the so-called wealthy families of the neighbourhood possessed a third of this large capital. The Mussidans certainly did not enjoy an income of more than eighty thousand francs. The Sauvebourgs, at the very most, had half as much again. There was certainly a so-called M. de Puymandour, who was said to be over and over again a millionaire ; but he was by no means of authentic nobility, and, according to popular report, the origin of his wealth would not bear anything like close inspection. Thinking of all this, Norbert looked hatefully at his father, as the latter paced to and fro muttering unintelligible words ; and the lad needed all his reason, all the energy of his honest conscience, to repell the frightful ideas that assailed his mind.

At last the Duke de Champdoce paused in front of his son. "My fortune is nothing," he said bitterly ; "no, nothing, in these days when vain and insolent upstarts of the middle classes carry all before them. Because they have bought our estates and affixed the names of their château to their own ridiculous cognomens, they fancy they belong to the nobility, and copy, not our qualities, but our vices. The real aristocracy has not understood the times ; it leads a wretched, beggarly life, and will soon die of hunger. Money is everything now-a-days ; and for a Champdoce to fight against all these parvenus, all these financial princes whose escutcheon is stolen coin, he must, at the very least, have an income of a million francs. Do you hear me, my son, a million." Norbert looked at his father in astonishment ; despite all his attention, he could not understand the drift of these explanations. "Neither you nor I, my son," proceeded the duke, "will ever have the capital of such an income in our coffers ; but, please God, our descendants will find it in theirs. Our ancestors established the power of our house by valour and the sword ; we must show ourselves worthy of them, and consolidate what they have bequeathed to us by dint of labour and privations." The old nobleman paused, and for some moments his emotion prevented him from proceeding. "Well, I have done my duty," he resumed at length, growing somewhat calmer. "It is for you to do your's. When I set about the task, I hadn't fifteen hundred thousand francs I could call my own. I have just told you what I now possess. You must imitate me. You shall marry some wealthy young girl who will bear you a son. He must be brought up like I have brought you up. By living in the same style as myself, and even if you are unlucky in crops, you will at the very least be able to bequeath your son some fifteen millions. Let him imitate us, and then, in his turn, he will leave his descendants a regal fortune ! This is what must and shall be, for so have I decided."

Now, indeed, Norbert fully understood. Still he remained silent, utterly overcome with wonder and surprise.

"It is no doubt a painful task," resumed his father, "but it is by no means unknown to illustrious families. In seeking to establish a great house a man must live entirely in the future, and forget himself to think of his posterity. There are certainly moments when a man's frivolous or evil instincts try to gain the upper hand, but they may be crushed and stifled if you always keep your great and noble object in view. Follow my example. I only live for my descendants, and picture to myself the splendid existence they will owe to our exertions." As Norbert listened, he half fancied he was dreaming. "You have seen me," continued M. de Champdoce, "haggle for hours over a paltry twenty-franc piece. I did so, saying to myself that some day one of our descendants would nobly throw it to a beggar from his carriage window. Everything I amass is intended for them. Next year I will take you to Paris and you shall see the house we possess there. You will find it full of tapestry, such as other people cannot obtain for love or money, full of furniture of marvellous workmanship, and masterpieces of painting and sculpture. I preserve, and embellish this house as a lover embellishes the home he means for his bride ; for I intend, Norbert, that it shall belong to our children, to the Dompairs de Champdoce of the future." The duke spoke in a tone of triumph, he seemingly divined the future and pictured his descendants in the proud position he had described. "If I have spoken to you in this fashion," he resumed, imperatively, "it is because you are old enough to know the truth. What I have told you must be your rule through life. You are now a man, and of your own free will you must do what you have done, hitherto, merely out of obedience. That is everything. To-morrow, you will have to load twenty-five sacks of wheat, and take them to the bakery at Bivron. You may now retire."

Norbert staggered from the room. Like all despots, unused to contradiction, the terrible old nobleman did not admit the possibility of his son hesitating. He foresaw no obstacles to his pet scheme, and yet at this very moment Norbert was swearing to himself that he would never obey his father. His rage, which fear had restrained whilst he was in the duke's presence, now burst freely forth. He had gained the broad walk, lined with old walnut trees, behind the château ; and rushing along, he thundered out his despair. He pictured himself condemned, condemned beyond appeal. As long as he had imagined that his father was simply a miser, he had indulged in hope—all passions have their fluctuations ; but now, despite his inexperience, he understood that such a mania as the duke's could never be shaken off. "My father's mad," he repeated, "my father's mad." Everything he had heard seemed to him monstrous and absurd, and he longed to free himself from such atrocious tyranny. But then how could he hope to gain freedom? What could he possibly do?

Alas ! Evil counsellers are only too easily found, and on the very morrow, Norbert was fated to meet one at Bivron, in the person of a man named Dauman, who bore the Duke de Champdoce no good will.

II.

This man Dauman did not belong to the district, and, indeed, folks were quite ignorant of his antecedents. He asserted that he had formerly been a huissier at Barbezieux ; and after all this was quite possible, nobody having made inquiries. One thing is certain, he had long lived in Paris, for he spoke of the capital like a man well acquainted with its ins-and-outs and the ups and downs of life there. He was a scraggy little fellow, some fifty years of age, with the face or rather the snout of a weasel. With his long pointed nose, his cunning restless eyes, and his thin lips, he hardly looked the sort of a man to be trusted. He had arrived at Bivron some fifteen years previously, looking inexpressibly seedy and with little or no worldly possessions. However, he showed himself remarkably eager to make money, and was ready for anything. He had, indeed, prospered during his sojourn in Poitou, and owned fields and vineyards and even a house at the Croix-du-Pâtre, where the highway and the cross road to Bivron meet. In addition, he was rumoured to have a nice round sum in cash put by. He had no real profession, but he dabbled in everything and had a finger in every pie. He had something to do with everything that was estimated or sold. He bought standing crops of the farmers who were "hard up," and gave himself out as a clever surveyor. Those who needed money or grain for seed purposes applied to him, and providing they produced suitable guarantees, he willingly accommodated them at the rate of fifty per cent. In one word, he was the confidential adviser of all the folks with tarnished reputations, and the evil genius of all the madcaps for five leagues round. He was said to be exceedingly skilful, able to rescue anyone from a false situation. Was he really such a master of the law as he pretended? At all events, he could not speak for a minute without quoting some clause of the code. He pretended that his one great desire in the world was to improve the lot of the peasantry, and thus, whilst squeezing heavy interest out of them, he tried to stir them up against the nobility, the merchant classes and the priests. Owing to his facile verbiage, his legal knowledge, and his long frock coat, the farmers had nicknamed him the "lawyer" or the "judge." His enmity towards M. de Champdoce, dated from an occasion when he had almost come to grief. He had found himself on the threshold of the assize court, and would have been severely sentenced had he not managed to bring forward four or five false witnesses to swear in his favour. However, the duke having openly declared against him, and endeavoured to persuade the peasantry not to let him dabble in their affairs, Dauman had sworn he would have his revenge, and for the last five years he had been watching for a favourable opportunity. Such, physically and morally, was the man whom Norbert met at the mills of Bivron on the morrow of the foregoing interview with his father.

In accordance with the instructions he had received, the young fellow brought his five-and-twenty sacks of wheat from Champdoce, and unassisted he had removed them from the waggon and carried them on his shoulders up to the mill loft. He had just put on his jacket again, and was preparing to return home, when Dauman approached him, and bowing to the ground begged him to give him a lift as far as his house. "I hope," said he, "that Monsieur le Marquis will excuse the liberty I take in asking for this favour, but the rascally rheumatism that troubles me prevents me from walking. I'm growing old and weak, Monsieur le Marquis."

Dauman knew how to give folks their fitting titles; he had read that a duke's son was known as a marquis, and so he lavished the apellation on Norbert. It was the very first time that the latter had ever been so addressed. A few days earlier, his common sense would have induced him to look on the flattery for what it was worth, but now his famishing vanity was delighted. "Yes, I've a seat for you, 'judge,'" said he, "I'm only waiting for a sack that was forgotten at the last delivery."

Dauman made a low bow, and smiled obsequiously. But whilst expressing his thanks he watched Norbert, askance, and noting that the lad's features had a most unusual expression, he said to himself: "Something out of the common must have happened at the château de Champdoce." Perhaps the opportunity to revenge himself, which he so longed for, was about to be offered; indeed, he had a presentiment to that effect, and reflected that he might surely and terribly strike the father through the son. However, one of the mill hands had just brought the sack Norbert was waiting for. Dauman climbed into the waggon and settled himself on some straw, whilst the young marquis sprung on to one of the shafts and started his horses. At first the "judge" remained silent; he was thinking with what trivial remark he might best open the conversation he desired to have with his noble young driver. "You must have risen betimes, Monsieur le Marquis," he began at last, "to have finished your work so early." Norbert offered no rejoinder. "His grace the duke," resumed Dauman, "is lucky indeed, to have such a son as yourself. I know more than one father in Bivron, who says to his lads: 'Look at the example our young marquis sets. He doesn't shirk work for fear of hardening his hands, and yet he's a noble, and wealthy too, and might cross his arms if he chose and let others work for him.'" Here a sudden lurch interrupted Dauman's verbiage, but he soon began again. "I was watching you as you lifted those sacks of wheat; they seemed like feathers in your hands! What muscles! What shoulders!"

At any other time Norbert would have been delighted to hear this praise, but it now displeased and irritated him, as the way he whipped up his horses plainly showed. "There are impudent busy-bodies" resumed Dauman, growing bolder and bolder, "who dare to deride you, Monsieur le Marquis, because you are as well conducted as a young girl; but I always reply that you are a sensible fellow. A regular life is far better for a man's health and purse than wasting time and money on billiards and women, like a number of young fellows I know of, do."

"But I should do just the same, if I could," answered Norbert with sullen frankness.

"What did you say?" asked his companion, who looked amazed, although he had heard perfectly well.

"I said that if I were my own master I should live like other young men."

He stopped short, but Dauman's eyes flashed with joy. "Ah, ha!" he said to himself, "the game's in my hands. I'll teach the duke not to meddle with my private affairs." And then speaking aloud, he added: "Some parents are certainly too severe!" A gesture of Norbert's showed him he was on the right track. "Yes, it's always the same," he continued. "Men grow old, their hair falls off, their blood runs slow, and they forget the days when things were different. They forget that young men must sow their wild oats. Your father was very different when he was young."

"My father!" exclaimed Norbert in surprise.

"Yes, ask his friends, if you doubt what I say!"

The waggon had now reached the cross roads. "Here we are," said Dauman. "How shall I thank you, Monsieur le Marquis? If you would allow me to offer you a glass of real cognac, I should esteem it a great honour."

Norbert hesitated. Instinct warned him that he was doing wrong, that he had better refuse, but he would not listen to his forebodings. He tethered his horses, and followed the "judge" indoors. The house had a comfortable aspect. Dauman was served by an old woman, a stranger to the province like himself, and of somewhat questionable reputation, albeit exceedingly devout. She was certainly on terms of surprising familiarity with her master. The latter's "study" as he called it was almost as ambiguous as himself. A stock of pigeon holes ran along one wall; there was a desk covered with ledgers; sacks of wheat and rye stood in sundry corners; a book case replete with legal tomes faced the fireplace, while from the ceiling hung numerous bunches of dried herbs. It was with great respect that the "judge" ushered the son and heir of the Duke de Champdoce into this apartment. He brought forward his own leather chair, and, as soon as his guest was seated, went in person to the cellar whence he speedily returned with a venerable looking bottle. "Taste this, Monsieur le Marquis," he said, when he had filled two glasses. "A grower at Archiac gave me this brandy in return for a great service I did him; for, let me tell you without boasting, I have done many people a good turn in my time." So saying, he raised his own glass and smacked his lips. "Good, is it not? One can't buy anything with a bouquet like that!"

All this obsequiousness was not thrown away, for in less than half an hour Norbert had opened his heart. His conduct was in some measure excusable. He was in one of those situations when it is positive relief to be able to confide a secret to any one, and besides he knew little or nothing of the "judge's" true character. So he poured forth his most secret thoughts. The story was a long one, and Dauman chuckled secretly as he listened; though all the time, he retained the grave face of a physician, called in for a serious consultation. "This is frightful!" he said, at last. "Poor fellow! were it not for the respect I owe to Monsieur le Duke, I should say he was not in full possession of his intellectual faculties."

How could such a lad as Norbert distrust such marks of commiseration? "Well, as I've just said," he continued with tears of rage starting from his eyes, "That's the way I'm situated! My destiny is settled, it seems, and I'm helpless. Unless, indeed, I kill myself." And he added with clinched teeth, "After all, it would be better to rot under ground than lead such a life as mine." At these words Dauman smiled so singularly that Norbert asked, "Do you think that a mere child's threat?"

"By no means, marquis; you have suffered too much not to have thought of suicide; but excuse me if I say that you are foolish to talk in this way of your future."

"Future!" cried Norbert angrily. "Why do you talk to me of a future, when you know that my present life may endure twenty years more? My father is young still."

"What of that? In three years you will be of age, and then you will have a right to claim your mother's fortune." Norbert's astonishment convinced the "judge" that the youth was even more simple than he had supposed. "When a man reaches his majority," continued Dauman, in an explanatory tone, "he may claim whatever he is legally entitled to. Such is the law. Your mother's fortune would render you independent of your father."

"But how could I ever dare to claim it?"

"It would not be necessary for you to claim it in person. A notary would transact the business. Of course, you have to wait three years before making the demand?"

"But that's impossible," answered Norbert. "I can never wait. I must put a stop to this tyranny at once."

"Fortunately there are ways—"

"Do you think so, 'judge'?"

"I will point them out. If you were of age, I would suggest applying to the courts to have your father placed under interdict, as, being inflicted with monomania, he is unfit to manage his fortune properly. That is done every day in great families. But then, unfortunately, you are *not* of age. Let us think of something else." Worthy M. Dauman swallowed another glass of brandy, and then resumed, "You are eighteen, and wish to escape from your father's tyranny. Well, to begin with, you might enlist as a soldier."

"Ay," exclaimed Norbert, "that's always a resource."

"A bad one, marquis, believe me. However, you might forward a complaint to the Public Prosecutor."

"A complaint?"

"Yes. Do you suppose our laws do not provide for the case of a father abusing his authority? Tell me, has your father ever struck you?"

"Never."

"Never mind, you might say it all the same; and besides you could urge that you are not brought up in accordance with your rank, that you are denied the advantages of education, that you are treated as a servant, whilst your father is several times a millionaire. All those points would hit hard; and, besides, all the countryside would bear testimony that you are pitied by everyone, and commonly known as the little Champdoce savage."

Norbert started to his feet. "Who ever dared to speak of me in that way?" he cried, in a threatening voice. "Name him."

This explosion in no way amazed the "judge," who had indeed artfully provoked it. "Be calm, be calm, Monsieur le Marquis," he answered, adding as Norbert resumed his seat, "The term is used by all your enemies, or rather by your father's foes, and I can tell you they are no few in number, thanks to his despotic habits. You yourself might count many friends. For instance, several ladies of your own rank take great interest in you. Only the other day, Monsieur le Marquis, when you were being spoken of, Mademoiselle Diane de Sauvebourg turned scarlet at the mere mention of your name. Do you know Mademoiselle Diane?"

The young man flushed. "*Sufficit,*" resumed Dauman. "Well when you are free you will do as you please. And now, in reference to your complaint—"

But Norbert, who had just caught sight of the clock, started up once more. "Twelve o'clock," said he, "dinner-time. What on earth will my father say?"

"Are you afraid of him as much as that?" asked the "judge" with a touch of sarcasm.

But Norbert did not hear the taunt; he was already in the road, and, springing into his waggon, drove off at full speed. Standing on the threshold of the house, Dauman gazed after him. "Make haste, my lad," said he. "You didn't say good-bye; you'll come again. I've a third little plan in my mind to rid you of your father, and that's the one you shall adopt. Ah! ah! my Lord Duke of Champdoce, you wanted to send me to the galleys, did you? Well, you shall see where I'll send your son."

III.

DAUMAN had not exaggerated when he said that Norbert was generally called, "that little Champdoce savage," only no one attached an insulting meaning to the nickname. At that time gold was god in Poitou, and it would have been blasphemy to outrage the son of a man who had an income of three hundred thousand francs. It should be mentioned that among the nobility, opinions had singularly changed in reference to the Duke de Champdoce during the course of twenty years. He had been laughed at the first time he was seen wearing a rough jacket and wooden shoes; but he did not care a straw for this merriment, relying on the power and re- spect his great wealth must ultimately conduce to; and he was right. When the nobleman's neighbours saw him add vineyards and pasture-lands and fields of wheat and rye to his ancestral forest, they began to reflect. Though they had not the courage to imitate him, they admired his energy and perseverance. He was no longer a madman in their eyes, but the masterly manager of a superb estate. And after all, was the son really to be pitied? Would he not ultimately possess the largest fortune in the province? Mothers were especially interested in Norbert, and thought what a triumph it would be, if they could only marry a daughter of theirs to the Champdoce savage. But then his father watched him most jeal- ously; the lad was seemingly not to be got at.

However, the task which mothers considered too difficult to grapple was to be attempted by a young girl, audacious Mademoiselle Diane de Sauve- bourg. She was rightly considered to be one of the beauties of the province. She was tall and very fair, with abundant sunny hair, a milk like complexion, and a charming smile. In her eyes, however, there gleamed at times the fire of concentrated energy and ambition. She had been educated at a convent, and her parents had wished her to take the veil; but at her own repeated request, and at the earnest solicitation of the Lady Superior, who was kept in a constant state of anxiety by her threats to scale the walls, they had recently called her home. Her father was wealthy, but she had a brother ten years older than herself, and the Marquis de Sauvebourg had openly declared that he meant to arrange matters, so that the entire pro- perty should go to the heir of the name. All he could do for his daughter, said he, was to give her a trousseau, and a dowry of 40,000 francs. She must renounce all other expectations. "So I suppose, my girl," he added, speaking to Diane, "that you have come home, armed and equipped to con- quer a husband. Study your cards, mind; for if you don't succeed, I've virtually nothing to offer you."

Diane had quite accustomed herself to the idea of being disinherited in her brother's favour, so she quietly replied, "Well, I'll have a try; and, at all events, it will be time enough to shut me up in a convent again in ten years from now."

M. de Sauvebourg had roundly blamed M. de Champdoce for sacrificing his son, but to sacrifice his daughter seemed natural. "I shall succeed," thought the girl; "I know it." And indeed, one day when a friend of her father's spoke of Norbert, and the great fortune he would one day inherit, in her presence, she asked herself, "Why shouldn't I marry him?" In fact, she at once decided to try and fascinate the

"Champdoce savage." It would be bliss indeed, to become a duchess with an income of three hundred thousand livres. Of course there would be the old duke and his avarice to contend against, and besides, she must first of all see Norbert and try and study his character. He was pointed out to her at church, and she was struck by his handsome looks and noble bearing, which even his shabby garments could not hide. Moreover, with feminine intuition, she divined that Norbert suffered, and a feeling of pity crept into her heart. Pity leads to love, remember; and when Diane left the church she had taken a solemn oath to be Norbert's wife. However, she did not breathe a word of this to her parents, preferring to carry on her designs without counsel. She was at once determined and practical, prudent and calculating. She had learned many things at the convent where she had been brought up, and frank and open as was her expression, she possessed considerable insight into character, and never lost sight of the main chance. To carry out her plan, however, she must meet Norbert and talk to him under favourable circumstances. To her parents' surprise, she suddenly seemed inspired with interest in the poor and made it her occupation to relieve them. She was constantly to be met in the lanes carrying soup or meat to some of her *protégés*, and her father exclaimed, "Diane has missed her vocation; she was evidently meant to be a Sister of Charity." He did not notice, however, that the poor folks she took an interest in all lived near Champdoce. Meanwhile, several days elapsed, and her wanderings proved vain. The "Champdoce savage" seemed invisible, and, to make matters worse, she did not even have the consolation of meeting him at mass.

The fact is, Norbert had changed his life. One evening, a week or so after the conversation in which the duke had confided his hopes to his son, he again detained him after supper. It was harvest-time, there were still several sheaves to be got in, and Norbert was on the point of starting afield again with the labourers when the duke bade him remain. "The way I confided in you the other night," said the old nobleman, "should have warned you that a great change was about to take place in your position. In future you will not toil as you have hitherto done. I mean to allot you less tiresome but more difficult duties. You shall act as overseer of the estate." Norbert looked up quickly, and his father resumed, "You are no longer a child, and I wish you to become accustomed to independent action, so that at my death you may not be intoxicated by your liberty." With these words the duke rose and produced a very beautiful gun. "I am pleased with you," he continued, "and this is the token of my satisfaction. My forester has this morning brought me a fine dog, which is also to be yours. A young man must have some relaxation, and in your spare time you may shoot over the domain. In going about you may have to incur some trifling expenditure, and so here is some money which I beg you to husband; for remember that the least prodigality will certainly delay the restoration of the family fortunes." The old nobleman talked on for some time in this strain; but Norbert literally heard nothing. He was even too stupified to take the six five-franc pieces which the duke held out. His strange manner was certainly not to the liking of M. de Champdoce, who at last impatiently exclaimed, "Eh! *Jarnicoton!* I thought this new arrangement would please you."

With a great effort, Norbert managed to stammer, "Yes, certainly it does. You will find that I'm not ungrateful."

The duke looked at him in surprise, turned his back, and hurriedly strode away. "What does the boy mean?" he muttered. "Could the curé have been right?"

The fact is, this new arrangement, as his grace called it, had been pressingly advised by the only man M. de Champdoce ever condescended to listen to—the village priest of Bivron. However, the relaxation came too late. Norbert's hatred against "his tyrant," as he called his father, was too deeply rooted to be so easily dispelled. And besides, what was this great concession after all? A gun, and a matter of thirty francs in all! It would have been different had his father decided to complete his education; but no, he was still to remain the "Champdoce savage." Nevertheless, availing himself of his father's authorisation, he spent long days in the cover, less engaged in shooting than in thinking over his position. In his rambles he was invariably accompanied by the dog the forester had brought for him, and the animal was so intelligent and faithful that he felt he had found a friend. He still thought of Dauman; and although he had asked questions, and ascertained that the "judge" was a most dangerous man, who would stop at nothing, he none the less determined to return to him for further advice. It was in vain that conscience warned him; he spurned its counsels, longing more ardently than ever for the life of freedom and enjoyment he had dreamed of.

IV.

DAUMAN was expecting to see him, as certain of his coming as the birdcatcher of a capture, after carefully arranging his perfidious mirror. Had he not ensnared Norbert with a mirage of enjoyable liberty? Dauman, like all who speculate in cupidity and misery, had his spies everywhere, and knew precisely what was going on at the château. He even knew the very words the duke had used during this last conversation, and was aware of the privileges granted to Norbert. Still, he was convinced that by this relaxation M. de Champdoce only hastened his son's revolt. Of an evening after dinner he often roamed along the high road, with his pipe in his mouth, and whenever he sighted the château de Champdoce, he was wont to shake his fist at it threateningly, and mutter, "He'll come back! Yes, he'll come!"

And indeed, a week later, one day when Norbert was supposed to be shooting as usual, he knocked at the door of his father's enemy. From his window Dauman had seen him approach, and it was with quite as much respect as before that he received "Monsieur le Marquis," as he took good care to call the lad. Still, he seemed embarrassed, and in lieu of saying anything to the point continued repeating, "Your very humble servant, Marquis; your very humble servant."

Norbert, who had expected a very different greeting, was disconcerted by this coldness, and thought of withdrawing. However, his vanity withheld him, and he said to himself that if he retired without attempting anything, the "judge" would certainly consider him a fool. So, mustering up his courage, he began, "I wish to consult you, M. Dauman. As I have no experience of my own, I desire to avail myself of yours."

"I am sure, sir—I am sure—" replied the "judge" with an absent air.

"Come," exclaimed Norbert, "you really ought to help me after what you said the other day. When I left so hurriedly you were explaining the different plans I might resort to with the view of altering my position."

"Do you really remember those idle words I uttered?" asked Dauman with an admirably affected air of embarrassment.

"Most certainly I do."

The rascal was inwardly delighted; still he rejoined with a forced smile, "Oh, you know, sir, a great many things are said which mean nothing. There is a wide distance between intention and act. I am so outspoken that my tongue is apt to get me into trouble."

Norbert was no fool, and besides, the hot blood of the Champdoce race coursed in his veins. "You took me for a fool, then, it seems?" he asked indignantly, striking the floor with the butt end of his gun.

"Oh! Monsieur le Marquis!"

"And you fancy that you can trifle with me. You induced me to open my heart to you; but your amusement may cost you dear."

"Monsieur le Marquis! is it possible you suppose me guilty of such infamy?"

"Then what on earth do you expect me to think of your conduct?"

Dauman hesitated at first; but suddenly seeming to regain courage he exclaimed, "You will be angry, but I must tell you the truth."

"I shan't be angry. Speak without fear."

"Well, Monsieur le Marquis, this is the case. I'm only a poor man, and can't afford to run any risk. What could I gain by encouraging you to brave your father? Why, it's madness to think of opposing the powerful Duke de Champdoce! He would take such steps that I should be popped into prison in the twinkling of an eye."

"And why, pray?" asked Norbert.

"Have you never studied law at all, marquis? Good heavens! how negligent parents are! You are not nineteen yet, and I know a certain clause in the code which could be twisted in such a way that your humble servant would simply be shut up in durance vile for five years. The law severely punishes any one who tampers with a minor, the son of a millionaire to boot. If your father ever discovered—"

"How could he ever learn it?"

Dauman did not answer, and his silence so clearly signified disbelief in Norbert's discretion that the youth indignantly repeated his question.

"Well," said the "judge," "to speak frankly, you are a dutiful son, and besides, you fear your father so much—"

"You think I should tell him everything if he asked me?"

"Well, you yourself told me that when he looked at you in a certain way you couldn't resist him."

"I may be a savage," rejoined Norbert, "but I'm not a traitor. When I promise to keep a secret, neither threats nor torture could extract it from me. Certainly I fear my father; but I am a Champdoce, remember, and prize honour above aught else. Do you understand me, sir?"

"But—"

"No human being," interrupted Norbert, "shall ever know from me that you have spoken to me. I swear you that."

As the "judge" listened, his features gradually assumed that expression of sympathetic interest which had originally inspired Norbert with confidence in him. "People might think," said he, "by my hesitation, that my object was an evil one. However, it is not my habit to give bad advice; I know the law besides. Behold my breviary, my rule of conduct." And so saying he proudly brandished a volume of the code.

"Well," exclaimed Norbert hastily, "now that I have given you a solemn promise of secrecy, will you tell me what I am to do?"

Dauman winked as he answered, "Nothing, marquis—bide your time, you have only three years to wait. Be patient. Your father is an old man. Let him nurse his hobby for three years more, and—"

But he was suddenly cut short by Norbert, who, bringing his fist down with a bang on the table, exclaimed, "If that's all you have to say, I am sorry I came." At the same time he turned as if to leave the room.

"You are too hasty, marquis," rejoined the "judge."

The young man hesitated. "Well, go on then," he said abruptly.

"Please notice, marquis," resumed Dauman, "that while advising you to be prudent, I don't suggest that you should endure all the hardships you have hitherto had to bear. In fact, I should simply like to see you both happy. I am like a justice of the peace seeking to reconcile two adversaries. Now, while seeming to be submissive, can't you arrange a plan of life for yourself?" Norbert returned to the centre of the room. He wondered what the "judge" was driving at. "You have more liberty already, I think," continued Dauman. "Does your father know how you employ it?"

"What can I do but shoot

"Well, I know very well what I should do if I had your age.

"What would you do?"

"To begin with, I should stop at home just enough to avoid all suspicion, but the rest of the time I should spend at Poitiers, which is a very pleasant town. I should rent there a nice apartment, where I could be my own master. At Champdoce I should perforce wear my old coat and wooden shoes, but at Poitiers I should wear clothes made by a good tailor. I would find some jolly companions among the students; have male and female friends; dance, sing, and generally amuse myself." He hesitated for a moment, and then abruptly asked, "There ought to be some fast horses among those your father breeds? Very well, then; why not take one for your own use. In the night, when you are supposed to be sound asleep, you could quietly slip out of doors, with your gun and spaniel, mind, harness the horse, and reach Poitiers in a wink. Then dress yourself like the handsome young lord you are, and join your friends. If you don't choose to go home the next day, well, seeing neither gun nor dog, folks would think you were out shooting."

Norbert was naturally straightforward, and the idea of this duplicity was intensely repugnant to him. Still it was the natural result of circumstances. On the other hand, the coarse picture of pleasure, sketched by Dauman, appealed to his imagination with such force that his eyes sparkled with covetous longing. "What is there to prevent your doing this?' asked Dauman, insidiously.

"The lack of money," sighed Norbert. "A large sum would be needed, and I have none. If I asked my father he would refuse, and besides—"

"Have you no friends who would consent to oblige you for three years?"

"None whatever." And Norbert, overwhelmed by a sense of his powerlessness, dropped heavily on to a chair.

For a moment Dauman remained reflecting. It seemed as if a struggle were going on in his mind. "Well, no, no, Monsieur le Marquis," he exclaimed at last, "I can't see you unhappy without doing my best to save you. It's a foolish thing to slip one's fingers between the bark and the tree, but no matter; I'll risk it. Some one shall lend you what you want."

"You, 'judge?'"

"Unfortunately, no. I'm only a poor devil; but I have the confidence of several of the farmers hereabouts, who bring me their savings to invest for them. Why shouldn't I secure them for you?"

Norbert caught his breath. "Can it really be managed?" he asked, anxiously.

"Yes, marquis. Only you must understand it will cost you dear. The interest will be far above the legal rate, on account of the risk incurred. The law does not recognise such transactions, and I myself don't approve them. In your place, I shouldn't borrow this money, but wait until some friend can accommodate you."

"I have no friends," was Norbert's reply.

Dauman shrugged his shoulders, as if to say, "Decide as you please, I wash my hands of the consequences," and then he exclaimed aloud, "After all, marquis, this would be but an insignificant matter, given the great wealth you will come into one of these days." Thereupon he explained in full detail on what conditions he could consent to part with the funds intrusted to him by his clients, the farmers, pausing at each particular point to ask, "Do you understand me, marquis?"

Norbert understood so well that in exchange for two thousand francs in banknotes he joyfully signed two I O U's of forty thousand francs each in favour of a couple of petty farmers of bad repute, who were entirely under Dauman's thumb. The young fellow, moreover, gave his word never to disclose to any one that the "judge" had had anything to do with the transaction.

"Prudence, marquis! That must be the rule of your life. Come here only after dark." Such was Dauman's parting advice to his client; and as he stood alone in his office, he carefully re-perused the acknowledgments, which Norbert had given in exchange for the money. Yes, he had forgotten nothing. His knowledge of the law had served him well. These I O U's would certainly be paid when the marquis came into his property, if merely to avoid a scandal. The wily trickster intended to let Norbert have all his savings, some forty thousand francs, on similar terms, so as to be able to claim a perfect fortune on the day the lad succeeded to his father's title. It is true that all this fine plan hung on Norbert's discretion, for at the first suspicion the duke would turn round and spoil everything. However, all things considered, Dauman felt pretty sure that the young marquis would keep his promises of secrecy.

As Norbert walked home, he was compelled to keep his hand in his pocket and feel the crisp, silky bank-notes to satisfy himself; that it was not all a dream. That night seemed a year long; and at day-break, with his gun and dog, he strode along the road to Poitiers. "I will hire a small apartment," he said to himself, "and make the acquaintance of some of the students to begin with."

In fact, he meant to do precisely what Dauman had advised. However, he reached Poitiers, which he had only visited on one occasion, and at sight of the houses and people felt terribly confused and embarrassed. He sauntered along the streets not knowing how to begin, not daring to enter a shop or make a single inquiry. He was like a newly fledged bird, at a loss how to use its wings. At last, feeling cruelly mortified, he went to the inn on the market-place, where he had been with his father, and, after an unsatisfactory breakfast, returned, sadly downcast, to Champdoce. Late that evening he saw Dauman, and related his misadventure, which greatly amused the worthy "judge." But the latter was a man of resources, and so he kindly put the young marquis in communication with a friend of his, who, for a good commission, piloted him about, hired furnished apartments for him, and took him to a tailor, of whom he ordered such clothes as he needed. Norbert was now elated again, and fancied himself on the high-road to the gratification of his desires; but the result was far below his hopes. He was too timid and ignorant to enjoy himself. He needed a friend and knew not where to find one. One evening he entered the Café Castille, and although it was then the long vacation he met several students there. But their noisy merriment scared him, and he hastily withdrew. Thus he lived alone at Poitiers as at Champdoce, spending most of his time in the rooms he had rented, in the company of his dog Bruno, who would certainly have preferred the open fields. Altogether, he only had five enjoyable evenings which he spent at the theatre; and to attain this paltry result, he had to lead a life of perpetual dissimulation. M. de Champdoce had noticed his son's frequent absence from home; but his surmises were far from the truth. One morning, however, he rallied Norbert on his lack of success in the cover, for the lad seldom brought as much as a hare or a rabbit home. "Come, Norbert," said he, "do your best to-day. Let's have a full bag this time, for we shall have a friend to dinner to-morrow."

"To dinner! Here?"

"Yes," said M. de Champdoce, repressing a smile, "yes, here! M. de Puymandour is coming. The grand dining-room upstairs must be opened and put in order."

Norbert took up his gun and whistled Bruno. He was sorely perplexed as to what this visit meant. At all events, he could not spend the day at Poitiers, and it was essential he should shoot something. However, he was by no means an able marksman, and throughout the morning he rambled far and wide, burning a good deal of powder without result. About two o'clock, however, he was approaching the moors of Bivron, he fancied he could distinguish an imprudent rabbit, nibbling near a hedge. Now was his opportunity. He raised his gun, fired—heard a shriek of pain or fright—and Bruno at once dashed into the hedge, barking furiously.

V.

DIANE DE SAUVEBOURG was the veriest woman that ever breathed. This seemingly artless girl, apparently occupied with a thousand frivolous whims, really possessed an iron will, and would have died before renounc-ing her project of becoming the Duchess de Champdoce. So far, all her rambles had been fruitless. The weather had become uncertain, and she would soon have to give up her long strolls round about Bivron and Champ-doce. Still she clung tenaciously to her idea. "The day must come," said she, "when the invisible prince will appear!"

The day came. It was mid November, and the weather was ex-tremely mild for the season. There was a blue sky overhead, the last leaves on the trees fluttered in the breeze, and the blackbirds sang in the hedges. Diane de Sauvebourg was walking along the path leading to Mussidan from the Bivron woods, when suddenly she heard a crackling of branches in the copse on her left hand. She turned at once, feeling some-what startled, and all her blood seemed suddenly to rush to her heart, for through an opening in the hedge she caught sight of the very man she had been watching and waiting for during two long months. Norbert was cautiously advancing, his forefinger on the trigger of his gun, as if about to take aim at something he was watching. Emotion kept Diane spell-bound. She faintly realised the difference between intentions and facts, and all the phantasmagoria of her imagination vanished. Here was the very occasion she had so long and patiently watched for, and yet she could draw no advantage from it. What would happen! Norbert would simply bow to her in passing, she would return his salutation, and then she might wait another two months for a second meeting. How could she engage any conversation with him? Was there any possibility of her doing so? She was just deciding to make some heroic effort, when she saw Norbert level his gun in her direction, he was taking aim. She wished to warn him, but ere she had time she felt a sudden, sharp pain in one leg just above the ankle. With a shriek she raised both arms and fell at full length on the path-way. Still she did not faint, for she heard the report of the gun, a cry of alarm in reply to her own, and a crash through the underwood. Presently she felt a hot breath on her face, and then the touch of some-thing cold and damp. She opened her eyes and saw Bruno licking her hands. At the same moment the hedge was torn apart and Norbert ap-peared before her. She at once realised the advantages of her position and closed her eyes again.

Norbert, as he stood over this fair creature, stretched white and motion-less before him, felt as if he were going mad. He had killed Mademoiselle de Sauvebourg, and at the thought, his first impulse was to take to his heels, his second, to aid his victim. He knelt beside her, and soon perceiving she could not be dead, carefully raised her head, exclaiming, "Mademoiselle, I beseech you, speak to me!" But she did not speak at once. She was absorbed in returning thanks to Heaven for her granted prayer. Presently she stirred, however, slowly raising her eyelids, and looked at Norbert with the surprise of a person just roused from sleep. "It is I," stammered the poor fellow—"Norbert de Champdoce. Will you pardon me? Are you suffer-ing?"

He seemed so distressed, that Diane really pitied him; so repelling his arm, she gently said, "It is for me to beg your pardon, sir, for fainting in this foolish way; for I am really more frightened than hurt."

Norbert breathed again. "However, I will go for help," said he.

"By no means. It is a mere scratch;" and she drew her skirt a little aside and showed an ankle that would have turned a steadier head than Norbert's. "Look!" said she, "it is there;" and she showed a spot of blood staining her white stocking.

Seeing this, Norbert's fright returned, and he started up. "I will run to the château," he said, "and in less than an hour—"

"No, do nothing of the kind," interrupted Diane. "It is really nothing. Look! I can move my foot perfectly well."

"But I beg of you—"

"Hush! we will soon see what it is;" and ripping her stocking with a pen knife she began to examine her wound. It was as she had said—nothing. Two shots had struck her—one had grazed the skin only, and the other had lodged in the flesh; however it was on the surface.

"You must have a surgeon," urged Norbert.

"For that? No it's not worth the trouble!" And with the point of her knife she loosened the tiny shot, which dropped on to the ground.

Norbert was gazing in ecstacy at this beautiful young woman. He had never heard a voice like hers before. He had never seen anyone so lovely, and he seemed perfectly entranced.

In the meantime Diane had torn her handkerchief into four strips, which she tied around her wound. "Now I am all right," she said gaily, at the same time extending her pretty slender hands to Norbert, that he might help her to rise. Once on her feet, she took several steps with a slight limp.

"But you are suffering!" cried Norbert, in despair.

"No, I am not, indeed; why, I shall have forgot it this evening," rejoined Diane, and she laughed like a merry school-girl, as with a little teasing air she added, "this is a droll meeting, marquis."

Norbert was struck by the way in which Diane uttered the word marquis, for no one save Dauman had ever before given him this title. "She does not despise me!" he thought.

"This melodramatic adventure will be a lesson to me. Mamma always insists on my keeping on the highway, but I prefer this path on account of its lovely view." So saying, she extended her hand, and it seemed to Norbert that a curtain rose, as in a theatre, and that he saw the familiar scenery for the first time. "Although it is very wrong to disobey mamma," continued Diane, "I come this way nearly every day when I go to see poor old mother Besson! Poor woman, she's dying of consumption; still I try to save her with nourishing food—good meat and soup. It is the only chance." She spoke on as unctuously as a Sister of Charity, and in Norbert's opinion, only lacked wings to be an angel. "The poor woman," she continued, "has three children, and their father does nothing for them, for he drinks all he earns."

Norbert had indited one of his I O U's for 4,000 francs in the name of this very Besson. He was, according to Dauman, one of those "clients" who wished to invest their savings. However, Norbert paid no attention to the matter; he was too preoccupied in looking at Mademoiselle Diane, who had already placed her basket on her arm. "Before leaving you," she said, with considerable hesitation, "I should so much like—if I dared—to ask a favour—"

"A favour of me, mademoiselle?"

"You will oblige me," she resumed, "by saying nothing of this accident to any one. Should it reach the ears of my parents, they would be very anxious, and, undoubtedly, deprive me of the little liberty they now accord me."

"I will never mention this terrible misfortune, mademoiselle," he answered.

"Thanks, marquis," exclaimed Diane, with a coquettish courtesy. "And another time, let me advise you, before you shoot, to ascertain that there's no one in the path!"

As she turned and departed, she limped no longer. Right lightly did her happy feet tread the earth. She had read Norbert's eyes like an open book; the game was in her hands. Women have a sixth sense which reveals to them things hidden from masculine perception. She had told Norbert in five careless sentences exactly what she wished him to know—that she was allowed some little liberty by her parents, and passed along that path almost every day. She was certain that the young marquis had not lost one word; and looking back, she saw him standing just as she had left him, as motionless as the trees around.

The poor boy felt, when Diane hurried off, as if she took with her all his vitality. He had felt a strange, unaccountable pang as she tripped away. What did it mean? Had he been dreaming? And as if to satisfy himself that the adventure was a real one, he knelt down and searched for the shot that Mademoiselle de Sauvebourg had picked with her penknife from her leg. Having found it he rose, and, lost in reverie, slowly sauntered home. To his great surprise, when he entered the court-yard, he found the grand entrance open, and on the steps there stood his father, who impatiently exclaimed, "Make haste, lad, I want to present you to our guest!"

VI.

SINCE the death of Norbert's mother, the state rooms of the château had remained closed, but they were kept in such order, that they could be utilised at any moment. The dining-room was really magnificent, with its huge sideboards of carved oak incrusted with steel and garnished with plate bearing the Champdoce arms. Everything was on a grand scale. The walls were hung with tapestry, the seats were covered with old stamped leather, the table was so huge and heavy, that four men could barely raise it from the ground. When Norbert entered, he found himself face to face with a fat little, red-faced man, looking altogether common and vulgar, although his clothes were cut in the very best style. This was the Count de Puymandour, to whom M. de Champdoce at once introduced his son, by his title of marquis. Norbert was surprised, and wondered what this ceremonious presentation meant. However, his reflections were suddenly interrupted by the sonorous peals of the great bell, which had not been rung for fifteen years. At the same moment a valet entered the dining-room carrying a large silver soup tureen. The dinner of three, seated at so huge a table, and in so vast a room, would have been a little dreary, but for M. de Puymandour's fund of anecdote and adventure. He was continually to the fore with a fresh story, which he told in a jolly but vulgar tone, interspersed with hearty laughs. Whilst talking, however, he ate, and went into ecstacies over the wine, which the duke had brought up from the cellar, where he preserved a large supply intended for his descendants. M. de Champdoce, generally so silent and morose, smiled benignantly whilst the Count de Puymandour rattled on, and seemed indeed to greatly enjoy his guest's jokes. Norbert who knew his father, and had long studied him, was quite at a loss to understand his urbanity. Was it merely such as a host should show, was it sincere, or did it conceal an afterthought? He could not tell.

M. de Puymandour resided with his only daughter in a charming château of modern date, less than a league from Champdoce. He was most hospitably minded, and his receptions were truly magnificent; but whilst the neighbouring nobility condescended to dine at his table, they none the less called him a "robber" and a "rascal." He could not have been spoken of with greater contempt had he made his fortune by highway robbery. The fact is, he was wealthy; folks who pretended to be well informed, asserting that he possessed no less than five millions of francs. He had acquired them honestly and legitimately enough, by trading in wool on the Spanish frontier. His great, his only crime was, that his real name was Palouzat. On becoming wealthy, he had purchased the title of count from the Pope, had ordered a coat of arms from a herald's office in Paris, and had endeavoured to convince the world that he was a born nobleman. With this object, indeed, he had left his native town, Orthez, to settle in Poitou, where the nobility tolerated him on account of his wealth, but without ever recognising his aristocratic pretensions. Still on this particular evening, he was greatly elated. It was no small honour to dine with the terrible Duke de Champdoce, and, indeed, M. de Puymandour considered it equivalent to a patent of social equality.

At ten o'clock, when the meal was over, and he talked of retiring, the duke insisted on escorting him as far as the high road ; and Norbert, who walked a little in the rear, managed to catch a few words of the private conversation the pair were having together. "Yes," said De Puymandour, "I will give a round million. That's a sum, mind."

"Oh, I must have half as much again," rejoined M. de Champdoce.

"Half as much again!" was the retort, "no, that can never be managed. And, besides, remember the million I speak of will be in hard cash."

"Not enough, I say," rejoined the duke. "You'll come to my figure; I'm sure of it. It's your interest to do so."

Norbert was too absorbed in thoughts of Diane to pay much attention to this talk ; but when M. de Puymandour had gone on his way the lad was roused from his reverie by his father exclaiming, "Did you note the bearing of that man, Norbert? He's a representative of our new aristocracy, and one of the best among them, too. Buffoon as he may be, he's still intelligent and honest. In another century the descendants of these folks will form a new nobility as greedy of prerogatives and influence as ours." During the walk home, M. de Champdoce enlarged on this subject ; but Norbert, despite his seemingly attentive bearing, had again relapsed into the land of dreams. He fancied he could hear Diane's harmonious voice and merry laugh ; he recalled all the circumstances of his melodramatic adventure that afternoon, and asked himself what impression he could have created on this young girl. Had he not made a fool of himself? Had he not behaved like a simpleton? Surely she would never take any notice of him.

However, he did not forget what she had said respecting her daily rambles in the same direction, and at the thought he might perhaps soon meet her again his blood tingled in his veins. He worshipped her already. Ah ! if such a woman as she was only smiled upon him, his life would be changed indeed ! He longed to see her, to tell her that he loved her ; but realising that at the decisive moment his tongue would no doubt fail him, he thought it preferable to write. However, what could he say? He began fifty fresh letters that night and tore them up in succession. He feared that the plain, simple words, "I love you," would prove too startling and abrupt, and tried to express his feelings in milder terms. At last he considered he had composed a masterpiece, and threw himself on his bed, not to sleep, however, but to think and wait for morning. At early daybreak he had left the house, carrying his gun and followed by his faithful spaniel, and hurried to the spot where he had met Mademoiselle Diane the day before. Alas ! he waited in vain. Hour after hour elapsed, and he strode up and down in feverish impatience, but she came not. He would have been much surprised had he been told that the young lady considered it not politic to show herself. And yet twice that day she ventured stealthily through the brushwood, watched him for several minutes, and then cautiously retired. On the morrow, after perceiving that Norbert was still there waiting for her, she would perhaps again have gone on her way without giving sign of life, but for a fortuitous circumstance. Bruno, Norbert's dog, scented her, and darted to the corner of the highroad where she stood watching. There was then, of course, nothing for her to do but to come boldly on. Norbert had started up as soon as he heard his dog bark, and then, perceiving Diane, he had hastened forward to meet her. She coloured deeply, wondering if he had seen her hiding and watching him; and he, although her suspicions were incorrect, seemed equally, if not more embarrassed. For a moment they stood speechless, and with downcast eyes.

"If I dare to appear before you, mademoiselle," at last said Norbert in a husky voice, "it is because I have been devoured by anxiety to know how you were. How did you regain Sauvebourg, wounded as you were?" He paused, waiting for some word of encouragement, but none came. "I almost wished to go to the château to ask about you," he proceeded; "but you had forbidden me to speak of that unfortunate accident, and I could not disobey you."

"Many thanks," stammered Diane.

"Yesterday," continued Norbert, "I spent the whole day here. Will you forgive this folly? I thought that, perhaps, having noticed my anxiety, you would take pity on me, and condescend—" He stopped short, aghast at his own presumption; but Diane did not appear to be in the slightest degree appalled.

"Yesterday," she answered with an innocent air, "I was kept at home by my mother."

"For two days," resumed Norbert, "I have constantly thought I could see you lying senseless on the ground. I have felt as if I had committed a horrible crime. I cannot forget how white you were, and how I lifted your head and held it on my arm. It lay there but a moment, and yet I still seem to inhale the perfume of your hair."

"Oh, Monsieur le Marquis!" murmured Diane so softly that Norbert barely heard her.

"When you were here the other day," said he, "I was so entranced I could not express what I felt; but as soon as you had gone, it seemed as if everything grew dark." He quivered at the remembrance of the sensation he had experienced. "Then," said he, "I searched for the shot which might have killed you, and at last I discovered it, and took it home with me. All the treasures of earth are nothing to me, compared with that holy relic!" Diane turned away her head to conceal the delight sparkling in her eyes. "Pardon me, mademoiselle," proceeded Norbert, "pardon me if I have offended you. You would pity me if you could form any idea of the life I have hitherto led. When I beheld you I hoped I had found a woman who might take some interest in my fate—a woman whose compassion could scarcely be repaid by life-long devotion." Norbert's eyes were aflame with passion as he spoke, and Diane involuntarily drew back. "Ah!" exclaimed the young marquis, wrongly interpreting her movement, "I see that I was mad—simply mad! And now I despair!"

"Ah, marquis! despair is not a word for us to use at our age," murmured Diane, who, cold and calculating as she usually was, was now profoundly touched by the young fellow's ardent manner.

The look which accompanied her words was significant enough to revive Norbert's hopes. "Do not trifle with me, mademoiselle," he said, "do not trifle with me; it would be too cruel."

As she hung her head without replying, he fell on his knees, and, snatching hold of her hands, covered them with kisses. Pale, and with compressed lips, Diane felt herself carried away by this whirlwind of passion. She panted for breath and fairly trembled. She found herself caught in the snare she had herself spread for Norbert, and it was only with a great effort that she succeeded in regaining some degree of self-possession. This situation must not be allowed to last. "I am forgetting my poor people!" she exclaimed.

"If I could only go with you, mademoiselle!"

"You may; but you will have to walk fast."

It often happens that a man's whole life is influenced by some apparently trivial circumstance. If on this particular day Diane had gone to see mother Besson, Norbert, who was with her, would have been put on his guard against Dauman. But it so chanced that she was bound on a visit to another of her *protégés*. Norbert watched her fulfil her charitable mission; and as he still had some of the money borrowed from Dauman about him, he laid a couple of gold pieces on the table before taking leave. He still walked beside Diane until they sighted the houses of Bivron, when she raised a finger to her lips, and, with the one word, "To-morrow!" turned into the path which led her home.

It was only then that Norbert regained in some measure his self-possession. Yes, he thought, this beautiful girl loved him; and, on his side, he was ready to shed his heart's blood for her. He tore up the letter he had written with so much trouble; for, in spite of his inexperience, he felt that Diane's promise to come the next day amounted to a confession of love.

Now, indeed, life seemed sweet and the future radiant; and Norbert was so unlike himself, so elated, that at supper the same evening the duke remarked, "*Jarnicoton*, lad! I'll wager a crown that you've had a good day's sport."

"You are right, father," answered Norbert audaciously. Fortunately enough, the duke did not ask to see his game-bag. But, on another occasion, he might be called upon to exhibit his spoils; and so, on the morrow, before going to meet Diane, he bought a couple of brace of partridges and a hare from a poacher he was acquainted with.

He had been waiting half an hour or so at the meeting-place, when Bruno's joyous barks warned him of Diane's approach. She was very pale, and the dark circles round her eyes testified to the anxiety which had kept her awake all night. As soon as she had left Norbert the day before, she had realised the risk she was running, and the extent of her imprudence. She was, so to say, trifling with her reputation, her future, in fact, with everything a young girl should hold most dear. For a moment she thought of confiding in her parents; but, on second thoughts, she rejected this salutary inspiration. "No," said she, "they would never understand me. My father would declare that the avaricious Duke de Champdoce would never give his consent. I should not be allowed to leave the château, and, perhaps, I might be sent back to the convent." This last prospect was not at all to Diane's liking, and, besides, she fancied she had considerable chances of success. Hence she resolved to persevere with her scheme. She remained for some time talking with Norbert in the pathway, but suddenly remembering her poor, as on the previous day, she declared it was time to be off. She must not neglect her patients, or otherwise her parents might think of curtailing her liberty. Norbert again accompanied her on her visits, and even made so bold as to offer her his arm whenever the path proved slippery or steep.

This kind of thing went on for several days, the young lovers meeting every afternoon at the same spot and rambling along the lanes together. They were more than once met by peasants and farmers, and there are, of course, as scandalous tongues in Poitou as elsewhere. Diane realised all the imprudence of her conduct ; but it was part of her plan to allow herself to be slightly compromised, though, at the same time, it must be understood that her behaviour, whilst in Norbert's company, was decorum itself. Unfortunately for their meetings, it was now the end of November, and cold weather was near at hand. One morning, when Norbert woke, he could see the rain falling in torrents, and hear a blusterous wind careering through the trees. He said to himself that Diane would never be allowed to go out in such weather as that, and so he despondently installed himself in front of the fire at home, and tried, or pretended, to read.

Contrary to his surmises, however, Diane *had* gone out, but in one of her father's carriages, having to visit a poor old woman called widow Rouleau, who lived near Bivron, and who had broken her leg the previous week. On reaching the miserable shanty where the widow resided with her only daughter, Diane found them both in tears. "What fresh misfortune has befallen you ?" she asked ; whereupon the widow, with many sobs and groans, related that she owed a matter of a hundred and thirty crowns and could not possibly repay them, so that her creditor threatened to seize her two cows—her only belongings of any value—and have them sold. It was Dauman the "judge," she added, who had caused her all this trouble. She had begged him to grant her a little time, but he had refused her application, adding, however, that if her daughter went in person to appeal to him he might perhaps change his mind. The inference was plain enough, for Françoise Rouleau was a comely, buxom young woman. Diane was intensely shocked on hearing this. "How shameful," she cried ; "I will go and see this man myself, and return here by-and-by." Thereupon, she hastily got into her carriage again, bade the coachman drive fast, and in ten minutes reached the "judge's" house.

Dauman was writing at his desk, when the woman he dignified with the name of house-keeper showed Diane into his office. He started up, offered her a chair, and with his velvet cap in his hand, bowed to the very ground. Diane, although she knew little of Dauman's reputation, was not as artless as Norbert, and was not imposed upon by this display of servile deference. She waved away the chair with a disdainful gesture, and with haughty mien and in a curt, cold voice, exclaimed, "M. Dauman, I have just left the widow Rouleau."

"Ah ! you know that poor woman ?" observed the "judge," who had been wondering what on earth could have caused this proud young lady to call upon him.

"Yes, and am much interested in her."

"Oh ! mademoiselle's compassion is well known," said the "judge" with a servile smile.

"Well, the poor woman is in great distress. She is confined to her bed with a broken limb, and is almost destitute."

"Yes ; I heard of her accident."

"And yet folks have threatened to seize her two cows, which are all she owns in the world."

Dauman assumed a benevolent expression. "Poor creature !" said he. "I have often heard that misfortunes never come alone."

Diane was aghast at this cool impudence. "It seems to me," she answered, "that this last misfortune can only be attributed to you. At least so I am told."

"Can it be possible?"

"Well, who persecutes this poor widow, but you?"

"I?" cried the "judge," striking his breast with his clenched hand. "I? Ah! mademoiselle, why do you listen to these vipers' tongues? They only speak to slander me! The fact is, this woman bought two sacks of wheat and one of potatoes, from a man at Mussidan, on credit. A month later she bought three sheep from the same man, on credit as before. Then something else, I don't quite recollect what. However, all these things represent a certain sum."

"One hundred and thirty crowns, I believe."

"I daresay. At all events, she over and over again promised to pay without doing so, and finally the man became impatient. I believe he needed the money. Well, he came to me, and I talked to him of patience, but I might as well have talked to the wind. He declared that if I did not do as he desired, he would go elsewhere. What could I say? Besides he had the law on his side." Dauman paused, and then *sotto voce*, as if talking to himself, resumed, "If I could only find a way of getting the poor creature out of this trouble; but it would be impossible without money, and money, ay, there's the rub." So saying, he opened a drawer and displayed some fifty francs in silver which it contained. "This is all I have in the house," he said, mournfully, "and 'tisn't near enough." He then paused again, and then as if suddenly inspired, resumed, "Dear me, how stupid I am. With a noble young lady as her protector, widow Rouleau need have no fear of losing her cows." Unfortunately, Diane had no money; she had so enlarged her circle of benevolence that she had already anticipated on her allowance. "I will speak to my father," she said, in a tone that told very clearly that she had small hopes of success.

The "judge's" countenance fell. "To the Marquis de Sauvebourg?" he said. "Oh! in that case we haven't done with the matter. He will make all kinds of inquiries, and valuable time will be lost. If I dared advise you, I should say it would be better to apply to some family friend— to M. Norbert de Champdoce, for instance. I know," he continued, "that the duke doesn't keep his son's purse full of gold, but the young man need have no difficulty in obtaining anything he needs, for he will soon be of age, and besides a marriage may even more speedily place large sums at his disposal."

Diane fell into the trap so cunningly set for her. "A marriage?" said she, with mingled surprise and apprehension.

"Oh! I don't know. I say marriage as I might say legacy. With his father's consent he might of course marry to-morrow, but if he has a whim of his own he'll have to wait at least six years."

"Six years! Why he will be of age in fifteen months."

"What of that? To marry against his parents' will, a young man must be twenty-five, not merely twenty-one."

This blow was so unexpected that Diane lost her head. "Impossible!" she cried. "Are you not mistaken?"

The "judge" smiled triumphantly. "I am never mistaken!" he replied, as he calmly opened his code and laid it before the young lady. While she read the passage he pointed out, he watched her as a cat watches a bird. "You see," said he, "at twenty-one M. Norbert will be an elector and his own master in every respect, barring this one point of matrimony. The law is precise."

Diane was convinced, and now drew herself erect with a pale face and anxious eyes. "After all," she said, "what does it matter to me? I will speak to my father about widow Rouleau. Good-morning." Then making a great effort, she tottered out of the house.

When she was alone in the carriage again, she abandoned herself to a paroxysm of tears and despair. This fatal hampering provision of the law seemed to thwart all her plans. She had hitherto said to herself: "The Duke de Champdoce will never accept me as his daughter-in-law, with my poor little dowry; but as soon as Norbert is of age he can marry me, notwithstanding his father, and we shall not have much more than a year to wait." But now she saw six years of dreary suspense and struggling before her, and possibly a final defeat; for could Norbert's passion, fervid as it now was, live on hope alone for six long twelvemonths? The old Duke de Champdoce was as sturdy as an oak. He might last much longer. And yet despite this crushing blow, Diane determined to fight on. Resistance whetted her energy, and she swore she would do everything in her power to carry the day. To begin with, it was of the highest importance she should see Norbert as soon as possible. Alighting at the widow's door, she entered the house and hurriedly exclaimed, "I've seen the 'judge.' Don't distress yourself, everything will be arranged." And then cutting the poor old crone's thanks short, she added, "Can you give me a slip of white paper?'

Françoise, the daughter, produced a soiled scrap, and Diane wrote thereon, in pencil, as follows :—" She would, perhaps, have gone there in spite of the storm if she had not been occupied with the troubles of a poor woman. The same troubles will compel her, to-morrow, no matter what the weather may be, to go and see a man named Dauman, at his house at two o'clock." Diane folded up her note, and then exclaimed, "I want this to be delivered to M. Norbert de Champdoce; to himself, mind, and no one else."

It so happened that Françoise had made a blouse for one of the Champdoce farm servants, and thus, having an excuse for going to the château, she willingly undertook the errand, albeit, Diane's conduct seemed to her passing strange.

It rained hard again the next day, but at two p.m. Norbert, punctually, arrived at Dauman's house. He had an excuse all ready for his visit, for he had exhausted the funds of his first loan and needed more money. He had no idea why Diane had selected the "judge's" abode for their meeting place, but he was inexpressibly downcast. He had thought of marrying Mademoiselle de Sauvebourg. As ignorant as herself of the law, he had fancied he might do so on attaining his twenty-first year; but, alas! he dared not confide his projects to his father, for the latter, in revealing his scheme for the restoration of the family fortunes, had added : "You must marry a woman of wealth." However, Norbert felt he could never carry self-sacrifice so far, never abandon Diane, and he was on the point of unburdening himself to Dauman, asking his advice and help, when a vehicle stopped outside, and a moment later Mademoiselle de Sauvebourg entered the room. At one glance Dauman realised the position, and cut short all pretended astonishment on the part of the young people by hastily explaining to Diane what he had done in regard to the Rouleau matter. "The *huissier*," he said, "consents to delay proceedings—I can even show you his letter to that effect." He turned and looked for this letter among his papers, with as much perseverance as if it had really existed. "I can't find it," he eventually exclaimed; "I must have left it in my bed-room. I have so much to do," he added, testily, "that sometimes I lose my head. I must find it, however. Excuse me, I will be back directly."

In point of fact the worthy "judge" was by no means anxious about this huissier's letter; only he had divined a rendezvous and considered he might best ascertain its purport by leaving the room. He went, however, no farther than the other side of the door, and then in turn applying eye and ear to the keyhole, he heard and saw all that he desired. The "judge's" absence seemed to Norbert a celestial boon. He had been painfully struck by Diane's pale face as soon as he saw her, and now he took her hands and looked into her very eyes. "Tell me," he said in a low, tender voice, "what has happened to you?" A sigh came from Diane, and then two pearly tears rolled down her cheeks. "In heaven's name," cried Norbert, "what has caused your grief? Diane, I implore you to tell me! Am I not your truest and most devoted friend?"

For a long time she refrained from giving any precise answer, and it was only after Norbert in utter despair had again and again renewed his prayers, that she finally declared that on the previous evening her father had spoken to her of a young man who had asked for her hand—a young man with every advantage of birth, character and fortune. Norbert listened, quivering from head to foot with jealousy. "And you did not refuse?" he asked.

She gave an evasive reply, asking; "What could a poor young girl do against her family, when she had only two alternatives offered to her—either a marriage she loathed, or a convent she dreaded."

With his ear close to the door, Dauman shook with laughter. "Not bad!" he muttered—"not at all bad for a little convent-bred girl. She has a clear head and a clever tongue, and under my tuition she would go the whole hog or none. If this simpleton doesn't declare himself now, I wonder what'll be her next move?"

"And you could hesitate?" resumed Norbert, reproachfully. "There would always be a chance of escape from a convent, but a marriage—"

Diane, looking more lovely than ever in her tears, wrung her hands piteously. "What reasons," she asked, "could she give her father for her refusal? Did not every one know she was virtually dowerless—sacrificed to her brother. Who but this man would ever ask for her hand?"

"Do you forget me?" cried Norbert. "You do not love me, then—"

"Alas! my friend, you are not free either."

"I am only a weak child, it seems?" he asked, with compressed lips.

"Your father is all-powerful," she replied, resignedly. "His will is inflexible, and you are in his power."

"What do I care for my father?" he exclaimed. "Am I not a Champdoce as well as he? Woe to the man, father or not, who comes between me and the woman I adore. For I adore you, Diane, and no human being shall take you from me." With these words, he clasped her to his breast, and pressed a burning kiss on her brow.

Dauman, at the key-hole, held his breath for a moment. "This sight," he muttered at last, "is worth at least fifty thousand francs to me."

Panting like a bird in its captor's hands Diane seemed for a moment terrified, but with a sudden effort she repelled Norbert, and escaped from his arms. She was a woman, be it remembered, young and passionate, despite all her diplomatic artfulness, and she felt afraid—afraid of him, afraid of herself.

"Do you refuse me, then?" he asked. "Do you really repel me when I implore you to be my wife—to become the Duchess de Champdoce?"

Mademoiselle de Sauvebourg answered with one look, which said as clearly as eyes can speak: "I am your's, I belong to you."

"Then, why frighten ourselves with these vain chimeras?" resumed Norbert. "Do you doubt my love? May be my father will oppose these plans which assure the happiness of my life. But before long I shall have shaken off his tyranny. In a few months' time I shall be of age."

"Alas! my friend," she answered, "your's are vain delusions. You must be twenty-five before you can give your name, unhindered, to the woman you love."

This was precisely the disclosure Dauman had been waiting for. "Bravo! he muttered, "bravo! young lady. So that's why she came. Well, there's some pleasure in giving her a lesson, for she doesn't forget a word of it."

"You are mistaken," Norbert had answered in reply to Diane's statement.

"Unfortunately, I tell you the precise truth, my friend. The law clearly defines the age I speak of—twenty-five. You will enjoy Paris, Norbert, from twenty-one to twenty-five, and will you remember that a sad-hearted girl—"

"Why do you talk to me of law? I shall have plenty of money when I'm twenty-one; and do you think I shall submit to my father's coercion? Not so, indeed I will wring his consent from him!"

The "judge" now thought it time to intervene. "I shall suddenly open the door," he said to himself, "accidentally hear a few words, make some remark upon them, and master the situation."

Norbert and Diane had so utterly forgotten Dauman's existence, that they started with alarm as he re-entered the room. But he was in no way disconcerted by the effect he produced. In the easiest possible tone, he exclaimed: "I can't find the letter; but I assure you that the widow's affair shall be speedily and satisfactorily arranged. I wish I could say as much of your own concerns."

Norbert and Diane exchanged a look, which testified to the anxiety they felt on finding themselves at this man's discretion. Their evident fear seemed to mortify Dauman most cruelly. "You have a perfect right," he exclaimed, "to tell me to mind my own business, but the truth is, injustice revolts me to such a degree that I invariably side with the weakest. The few words I overheard just now, as I came in, were a ray of light to me, and I said to myself, "Here are two young people made for each other—"

"Sir!" interrupted Diane, haughtily, "you forget yourself."

"I beg your pardon," stammered the "judge," "I am only a poor peasant; I speak too plainly. I meant no harm, and I trust you will forgive me." Then as Diane made no further objection, he resumed: "Well, I said to myself, here are two young people who love each other, and have a right to love each other, and yet they are kept apart by unreasonable, hard-hearted parents. Young and ignorant, knowing nothing of the law, they would certainly get into trouble if left to their own devices. But suppose I helped them, and no doubt I might do so advantageously, for I know the law thoroughly—I know its weak points and its strong ones—" He talked on sounding his own praises for fully ten minutes, and affected not to see that the young couple were whispering to each other near the window.

"Why not trust him?" said Norbert; "he has had experience."

"He will betray us; he is capable of anything for money."

"So much the better for us, then. He will hold his tongue if he is promised a magnificent reward."

"Do as you think best, my friend."

Thus encouraged, Norbert turned to Dauman. "I have perfect confidence in you," he said, "and so has this young lady. You know the situation. What is your advice?"

"Simply this," answered the "judge." "Learn to wait. The least step taken before your majority is fatal; but the day after you are twenty-one, I promise to show you more ways than one of bringing the duke down on his marrow-bones."

He could not be induced to speak more plainly, but he looked so confident and cheerful, that when Diane left the office she felt hopeful once more.

This was almost their last interview that year. The weather turned from bad to worse, so that it was impossible for them to meet out of doors, and the fear of being watched prevented them from availing themselves of Dauman's hospitality. Each day, however, the widow Rouleau's daughter carried a letter to Sauvebourg and brought back a reply to Champdoce. The cold weather had scattered the inhabitants of the various châteaux of the district. Only the Marquis de Sauvebourg, who was a great sportsman, lingered behind; but after some heavy snow storms even he decided to retire until the ensuing spring to the handsome mansion he owned at Poitiers. Norbert and Diane had foreseen this contingency, and acted accordingly. Two or three times each week Norbert mounted his horse and rode to town, changed his clothes and hurried to a certain garden wall where he walked up and down before a small door. At a certain hour, previously agreed upon, this door softly opened. Norbert slipped in, and there in the garden found Diane, lovelier than ever. This great passion, the beacon of his life, and the certainty of being loved, had dispelled much of his timidity. He had met Montlouis again, and often played a game of dominos with him at the Café Castile. Montlouis was to join the young Viscount de Mussidan in Paris, and become his secretary as soon as the winter was over; but this prospect, which had once so delighted him, was now scarcely to his taste, for, as he confessed to Norbert, he feared separation from a young girl in the vicinity whom he was desperately in love with. Confidence for confidence; and more than once Montlouis went with Norbert to the door that opened into the Marquis de Sauvebourg's garden.

April at last came round again. The châteaux refilled, and the lovers were able to meet in the lanes once more. They had now only a few months to wait until Norbert reached his majority, when Dauman had promised to help them. One day, however, when they had spent the afternoon in the woods together, preaching patience to each other, and just as Norbert, light-hearted and full of spirits, had reached home, his father sent for him.

"Marquis," said the duke, without the least preamble, "I have found you a wife, and you will marry her in two months from now."

VII.

A THUNDER clap would have terrified Norbert less than these words. But the duke did not see, or did not choose to see, his son's agitation, and simply added, in a composed, careless tone: "There is no need, I imagine, to tell you the young lady's name. She is, of course, Mademoiselle de Puymandour.

She cannot fail to please you. As you know yourself, for you have seen her, she is very pretty, tall and dark, with a very pleasing figure. Her teeth, eyes, and hair are admirable. Don't you think so?"

"Yes," stammered Norbert. "I think—in fact I've scarcely even noticed her."

"Pshaw!" rejoined the old nobleman, "I thought you were learning to use your eyes. Never mind, you will have ample time to look at your wife when you are married. And, marquis, there must be some alteration in your dress. To-morrow you will go with me to Poitiers and give orders to a tailor, who will see you are dressed as befits your rank. We mustn't frighten this young lady with our fustian jackets."

"But—"

"Wait a moment, if you please. I shall set aside some of the rooms in the château, and you will spend your honeymoon here. You will take care it doesn't last too long, and, after a while, we can introduce this young woman to our ways, make a frugal, economical housewife of her."

"But, father," said Norbert, hastily, "suppose I don't fancy this young lady?"

"Well?"

"Suppose I entreated you to spare me a marriage which would make me miserable?"

M. de Champdoce shrugged his shoulders. "This is childish," he said. "This alliance is in every way suitable, and I wish it—"

"But, father—" Norbert began again.

"Do you hesitate?" asked the duke angrily.

"No; I don't hesitate," said his son boldly.

"Very well, then. Let a mere nobody consult the dictates of his heart, if he sees fit, when he marries, but with a man of position, matrimony should be looked upon as a matter of business. I have managed things admirably. The marriage portion will be a million and a half of francs in hard cash, and ultimately, when Puymandour dies, and he's apoplectic mind, you'll come into the remainder of his fortune. Do you know what he's worth? Five millions. Think of that! And this is all the more reason for pinching and economising. Think of the restoration of our house, of the princely fortune of our descendants, and realise the beauty of self-abnegation." The duke walked for some minutes up and down the room, speaking incoherently, and at last stopped in front of his son. "You understand everything now," he said. "To-morrow you will go to Poitiers, and on Sunday we dine with the Puymandours."

Norbert hardly knew what to say or do in this extremity. "Father," he began once more, "I don't see the use of going to Poitiers to-morrow."

"What do you say? What on earth do you mean?"

"I mean," answered the young man with sudden energy, "that I shall never love Mademoiselle de Puymandour, and that she will never be my wife."

The duke had not once foreseen this contingency, and his mind refused to believe the possibility of such monstrous iniquity. "You are mad!" he exclaimed, "and you don't know what you say or what you want!"

"I know very well."

"Reflect, my son."

"I have reflected."

M. de Champdoce was evidently struggling to keep calm. "And you think," he said, with a disdainful smile, "that I shall be satisfied with such an answer as this?"

"I hope you will yield to my entreaties."

"Do you, indeed? You think that I, the head of this family, after conceiving a magnificent plan for the restoration of its fortunes, am to be turned from my scheme by the mere caprice of a boy like yourself! Surely you ought to know me better!"

"No, father," rejoined Norbert, "it is no mere whim that impels me to refuse and claim independence. Have I not always been a good son? Have I ever disobeyed you? You have said, 'Go there,' and I have gone, 'Come here,' and I have obeyed you. I am the son of the wealthiest man in the province, and I have lived like the son of your poorest farm-hand. Have I complained or murmured? Bid me do whatever you choose except—"

"I bid you marry Mademoiselle de Puymandour!" said the duke, striking the floor with the stout ash stick he carried, according to his wont.

"Oh! all but that. I don't love her, I cannot love her. Do you wish me to be utterly miserable for the rest of my life? Do not exact that of me!"

"I have spoken, and you will have to obey."

"No," said Norbert quietly. "I will not obey!"

On hearing this the duke at first turned purple, and then every drop of blood seemed to leave his face, which became absolutely livid. "*Jarnidieu!*" he cried in a voice that once would have made Norbert tremble. "How do you dare to brave me in this way? What on earth has given you this audacity?"

"The consciousness of being in the right."

"How long has it been right for children to disobey their parents?"

"Ever since fathers ventured to give unjust orders."

This was more than the Duke de Champdoce could endure. "*Jarnitonnerre!*" he cried; and he rushed towards his son with his bludgeon raised, but suddenly stopping short when only midway, he threw the stick across the room, and in a hoarse voice exclaimed—"No! I will not strike a Champdoce!"

Maybe it was Norbert's fearless attitude that restrained his father's passionate fury. This once timid youth had not moved, not even sought to avoid the onslaught, but stood quite still and erect, with folded arms and head thrown back. And even now that the duke had flung his improvised weapon aside, Norbert retained the same attitude of defiance, thus speedily rekindling his father's anger. "I will not submit to such audacity," cried M. de Champdoce, and seizing his son by the collar, he dragged him to one of the rooms on the second floor, and roughly pushed him inside. Then before retiring and locking the door he exclaimed, "You shall have twenty-four hours to decide whether you will accept the wife I have selected for you."

"My decision is made," answered Norbert, calmly. He had not resisted his father, when the latter dragged him upstairs. Semi-prostration had followed his sudden courage, and yet it was urgent he should act, urgent he should warn Diane of what had happened and put her on her guard against all contingencies. But how could he escape? The door was of solid oak, more than an inch thick, and the lock was as enormous in strength as in size. Only the window remained; and this was forty feet from the ground. But Norbert reflected that some one would probably be sent to make up a bed for him, and then he would have two sheets at his disposal. These he could knot together, and thus obtain the means of descent. If he started off at night-time, with the intention of returning before dawn, he could not of course see Diane, but he might send her a warning through Dauman, whom it was also urgent he should see, with the view of obtaining proper advice. This plan decided upon, he threw himself into one of the arm-chairs in the room with a lighter heart than he had known for months, for the ice was now broken between his father and himself, and this seemed a very great point to Norbert. The first step was taken, and it is always the first one that is the most difficult. The rest would be easier work, and at all events he must conquer at any price.

In the meanwhile, downstairs, the duke was wild with rage. When he took his seat at the supper table, he looked so terrible that the farm-hands barely dared open their mouths to eat and drink. They all knew that a violent quarrel had taken place between M. de Champdoce and his son, and wondered what could have occasioned it. The meal was soon over, and the duke then summoned an old confidential servant, who had been in his employment for thirty years. "Jean," he said, "your young master is shut up in the yellow room on the second floor. There's the key; take him something to eat."

"Yes, sir,"

"Wait a moment. You will pass the night in his room. Whether he sleeps or not, you will watch him just the same. It may be he will think of running away. If it be necessary to employ force, employ it; that's all. If you are not strong enough, just call to me; I shall hear and come to your assistance."

This unexpected precaution destroyed all Norbert's hopes. He tried to induce his jailer to let him out for a couple of hours, swearing he would faithfully return, but his prayers were as vain as the threats to which he next resorted. Had he looked from the window, he would have seen his father pacing up and down the court-yard, absorbed in the dreary thought that perhaps, after all these long years, he was doomed to disappointment. "There is a woman concerned in it," the duke reflected. "Only a woman could change a young man's character from white to black in so short a time, and besides he would never have declined this proposal with such obstinacy if he had not been in love with some one else!" But who could this woman be? What steps could be taken to discover her? It would, of course, be useless to question Norbert himself, and at the same time the duke was very unwilling to institute any formal inquiry. He passed the greater part of the night in painful indecision as to the best course to pursue, when all at once he had an inspiration, which he regarded as direct from Heaven. "I have Bruno!" he cried. "And through this dog I can learn all my son's habits, discover what houses he goes to when he's out alone, and even ascertain the very woman under whose influence he acts!" Somewhat comforted by this hope, M. de Champdoce was more like himself when he appeared in the morning. At noon he took his seat at the table as usual, and ordered the prisoner's dinner to be carried upstairs, with no relaxation of watchfulness.

At last the moment he deemed favourable arrived. He whistled to Bruno, who seldom followed him, but in Norbert's absence the animal yielded to entreaties and condescended to accompany the duke as far as the end of the avenue. Three diverging roads started from this point, but Bruno did not hesitate, he turned to the left one, with the air of a dog who knows perfectly well where he is going. On he went for more than half an hour, the duke following him all afire with hope and expectation, and at last the pair reached the woodland path where Diane and Norbert had so often met. Sagacious Bruno halted at the precise spot where the young marquis had wounded Mademoiselle de Sauvebourg, ran round in a circle, sniffed in all the neighbouring bushes, and finding nothing, quietly lay down. His intelligent eyes seemed to say, "Let us wait!"

"This," thought the duke, "is evidently the spot where the lovers have been in the habit of meeting." Anxious to watch and escape observation, he next retreated into the neighbouring grove and sat down on a mossy stone at the foot of an oak. He was so pleased with his penetration respecting Bruno's abilities, that he was almost in a good humour. Moreover, on reflection, the danger seemed to him far less than he had feared. To whom could Norbert have lost his heart? What ambitious little country girl, thinking the youth simple enough to be duped, had made up her mind to marry him? The duke was thus reflecting when he heard the dog bark joyously. "Here she comes then!" he said, and he rose to his feet at once. At the same moment Diane appeared, and perceiving M. de Champdoce was unable to restrain a little shriek of terror. She hesitated, should she turn and run? But strength failed her to do so, and only just in time to avert a swoon did she grasp the nearest birch for support. The old nobleman was quite as much dismayed as she. He had expected a country girl, and he saw the daughter of the Marquis de Sauvebourg before him.

But his anger quite equalled his surprise. If he had nothing to dread from a peasant's daughter, he had everything to fear from this young lady of noble birth, who was legitimately entitled to try and win Norbert for her husband. Could he even have recourse to her family? Perhaps she was acting at her parents' instigation. He was sorely perplexed, and yet an explanation was necessary. "Aha!" he began, with a grimace intended for a smile, "you don't look overpleased to see me, my child!"

"Sir!"

"I understand. When one comes to meet the son and finds the father, the change is not altogether satisfactory. But you mustn't blame Norbert; for, poor boy, I assure you that it isn't his fault!"

Mademoiselle de Sauvebourg was no ordinary girl. Startled at first, she had by this time regained her self-possession. Some women would have taken refuge in denial; but this idea never occurred to her. A disavowal of her position would have been an act of absolute baseness in her eyes. "You are right, Monsieur le Duc," she answered; "it was to meet your son, the marquis, that I came. You will therefore excuse me if I retire."

She made a sweeping courtesy with charming grace, and was about to pass on, when the duke laid his hand on her arm. "My child, allow me to say a few words to you;" and he tried to speak in a paternal fashion. "Do you know why Norbert is not here?"

"I presume he has some excellent reason."

"My son is a prisoner in his room, guarded by my servants, who are ordered to restrain him by force if he makes any attempt to escape."

"Indeed! Poor fellow! How I pity him!"

The duke was amazed at this effrontery, as he called it in his heart. "I wish to tell you," he retorted, in an angry voice, "why I treat my only son, the heir of my name and fortune, in this manner."

His eyes flashed fire, but Diane quietly answered. "Pray proceed, Monsieur le Duc."

"Well then, I beg leave to inform you that I've found a wife for Norbert. She is about your own age, beautiful, clever, witty, and wealthy."

"And of high birth, of course?"

This sarcasm stung the old nobleman. "Fifteen hundred thousand francs as a dowry," he sternly replied, "are worth more than a tower argent on an azure field." This was the Sauvebourg blazon, and the duke paused as if to underline his uncourteous retort. "I will tell you," he at length resumed, "that the young lady in question has several millions coming to her, and yet my son is mad enough to refuse her hand. But I will not tolerate such disobedience."

"You are right, sir, I am sure, if you really think this marriage would ensure your son's happiness."

"His happiness! What does that matter if the supremacy of our house is insured by it? I have determined that Norbert shall marry this woman —and marry her he shall. I have sworn it, and I swear it again!"

Diane's agony of mind was well-nigh intolerable, but her pride sustained her; and, moreover, feeling sure of Norbert, she ventured to ask, "And what does Monsieur le Marquis say?"

"Norbert," angrily replied the duke, "will return to his duty as soon as it pleases me to free him from the pernicious influence he has been subjected to."

"Ah! indeed!"

"He will obey me when I show him that, though he may be in ignorance of the prestige of his fortune and his name, there are others who fully understand it. I can understand a woman longing to be Duchess de Champdoce! However, my son may be a mere child; but I have had some small experience of the world, and when I enlighten him as to the ambition which he, poor fool, mistook for love and unselfish devotion, he will return to his allegiance to me. I will tell him how to look on those haughty, high-born damsels, who, both penniless and proud, have merely their youth and beauty to win husbands with—scheming girls who, in pursuit of phantom dreams, are willing to run risks and perils which eventually leave them with tarnished reputations."

"Continue, Monsieur le Duc!" cried Diane, turning pale with anger and emotion. "Continue, pray; insult a defenceless girl—laugh at her poverty —it is a generous, noble thing to do, right worthy of a gentleman!"

"I thought," said M. de Champdoce, "that I was addressing the person whose influence had induced my son to rebel against my authority. Am I mistaken? You can prove me to be in the wrong by inducing Norbert to submit." Diane did not speak, but dropped her head. "You see," resumed the duke, more angrily than before, "I am right. Reflect well on what I say, and remember that persistency on your part will justify any reprisals on mine. You are warned—continue your intrigue if you dare!"

This word, "intrigue," spoken with an insulting sneer, was too much for Diane. She would have sacrificed at that moment her honour, ambition, and very life for the sake of revenge. Forgetting all prudence, she cast aside the mask, and haughtily throwing back her head, with her eyes flashing fire, and her cheeks blazing: "Listen to me!" she cried. "I, too, have sworn—and I have sworn that Norbert shall be my husband! Imprison him, have him guarded and ill-treated by your servants if you like, but you will never draw from him a shadow of assent. He will resist because I bid him resist—even unto death, if need must be. His energy, like mine, will never abate; and, believe me, before attacking the honour of a young girl, remember that she will one day become a member of your own family. Farewell !"

Diane was far down the path before the duke recovered his senses, and then he burst forth into a torrent of imprecations, threats, and insults. He believed himself alone, but never was he more mistaken. This strange scene had an invisible witness—none other than "judge" Dauman in person.

Informed by one of the servants at the château of the young marquis's imprisonment, Dauman had been eager to warn Diane ; but how was he to do so ? He could not go to Sauvebourg, and no power on earth would have induced him to write a line ; for handwriting is treacherous, and may turn up as evidence against one, even when least expected. The "judge" was thus greatly embarrassed, when it occurred to him he might repair to the lovers' usual meeting-place, whither Diane would come that afternoon no doubt. He was barely a few yards off, when he heard her cry of alarm on perceiving M. de Champdoce. This cry put him on his guard ; he crept and crawled to a hiding-place, where he could both see and listen. Bruno soon scented him out ; but he was known by the dog, who complacently allowed the "judge" to pat his head and fondle him. How eagerly Dauman listened to the talk between M. de Champdoce and Diane can easily be imagined. But he realised that Mademoiselle de Sauvebourg, despite her haughty bearing, was really sorely perplexed, and anticipated that, before returning home, she would hasten to his house to ask his advice. "If I am to carry out my plans," he said to himself, "I ought to strike the iron while it's hot ; and how can I do that, if I am not at home to receive her ?"

Accordingly, without any especial caution, he rose from his hiding-place and hastened through the woods, hoping, by means of a short cut, to reach his house before Diane arrived there. The noise occasioned by his passage through the underbrush attracted the duke's attention. "Who's there ?" he cried, going towards the spot whence the sound had proceeded. No reply. Still he had certainly heard someone or something stir. Summoning Bruno, he tried to put him on the scent ; but the dog merely sniffed about a little, and then lingered near the bush behind which Dauman had remained concealed. The duke eagerly scanned the ground, and at last distinctly detected the imprint of two knees on the velvety moss. "Some one has been listening," he said to himself, disagreeably impressed by this circumstance. "But who can it have been ? Has Norbert escaped from his room ?" This idea so alarmed him that he strode home in hot haste. "Where is my son ?" he asked of the first servant he perceived.

"Up-stairs, sir," was the reply.

M. de Champdoce breathed again. Norbert had not escaped, and therefore it was not he who had been listening.

"Our young master's in a terrible state, sir," added the servant whom the duke had questioned.

"What do you mean ?"

"Well, sir, he declared he wouldn't stay in that room a minute longer, and so Jean called for assistance. He's frightfully strong, sir, for it took six of us to hold him. He swore that if we would let him out, he would be back in two hours, and said it was a matter in which his honour and life were involved."

The old nobleman heard this account with a sarcastic smile. What did he care for the young fellow's struggles ! His grace's heart had grown hard under the pressure of fixed ideas during so many years. It was with the solemn air of a man who believes he is fulfilling a sacred duty, that he climbed the stairs and knocked at the door of the room where his son was confined. Jean, the confidential servant, at once opened it, and for a minute the duke stood on the threshold. All the furniture had been over-turned, and a great deal of it broken, the fragments strewing the floor. A stalwart farm-hand was seated by the window, and Norbert lay on the bed with his face turned to the wall.

"Leave us," at last said the duke to the servants, who instantly withdrew; whereupon M. de Champdoce added, "Get up, Norbert; I wish to speak to you."

The young fellow obeyed. Anyone but M. de Champdoce would have been startled by the wild, haggard expression of his face. "What does this mean?" asked his father, in his most arbitrary voice. "Are not my orders sufficient to insure obedience? It seems it was necessary to employ brute force during my absence. Tell me, my son, what you have gained by these hours of solitude? What plans have you formed, and what hopes?"

"I wish, and I intend to be free."

M. de Champdoce preferred not to heed this clear, decisive answer. "It was easy for me to divine," he continued, "from your obstinate resistance, that some woman had taken advantage of your inexperience, and employed her pernicious influence in inducing you to disobey your best friend." He hesitated. No answer came. "Well, I went in search of this woman who was flattering your pride and ministering to your worst passions, and, as you may imagine, I found her. I went to the Bois de Bivron, and there, I need scarcely tell you, I met Mademoiselle de Sauvebourg."

"And—did you speak to her?"

"Did I speak to her? I am inclined to believe I did. I told her what I thought of those adventuresses who fascinate the dupes they mean to take advantage of."

"Father!"

"Can it be possible, poor, simple boy, that you have been taken in by that young lady's pretended love. It is not you, marquis, she wants, but our fortune, title, and name. However, there are places where women who lead young men astray can be shut up, and I told her so."

Norbert turned perfectly white. "And you said that to her?" he asked, in a low, hoarse tone. "You dared to insult the woman I love, while you knew I could not protect her? Take care—I shall forget you are my father."

"*Jarnitonnerre!* He threatens me!" roared the duke. "My son threatens me!" And mad with rage, blinded by the blood that rushed to his brain, he raised his heavy stick and struck at Norbert.

Fortunately, the young fellow instinctively recoiled, so that only the extreme end of the staff hit him just above the temple, and then slipped, severely grazing his cheek. Norbert, in his turn infuriated, was about to rush upon his father, when he suddenly saw that the door was open. This meant liberty and salvation. With one bound he reached the stairs, and before the duke could throw up the window and call for help, the young fellow was running like a madman across the meadows.

VIII.

DAUMAN had hoped to take a short cut home, but his road proved longer than the one followed by Mademoiselle de Sauvebourg. However, he scrambled through the trees and hastened down the paths with wonderful agility and speed, as if he had never been troubled with rheumatism, and at last reaching his house, he darted without even drawing breath up to the garret, and from an artfully concealed hole in one of the rafters, drew forth a tiny black phial which he slipped into his pocket. Then going downstairs into his office he examined the phial with a sinister smile, and after ascertaining that there had been no tampering with its contents, he laid it on his table behind a pile of papers. Next, he wiped his brow, and donned his velvet smoking cap and shabby dressing-gown. Mademoiselle Diane might come now as soon as she pleased : he was quite ready for her. And why on earth did she not come? Had any other adventure befallen her? Dauman began to be anxious. He went to the window, and looked down the road ; he consulted his watch and swore impatiently, when, all at once, he heard a light tap at the door. "Come in," he cried.

Diane entered, indeed, tottered into the room, and sank on to a chair heedless of the "judge's" courteous welcome. He now understood why she had been so long in coming ; her strength had failed her—prostration and nervous emotion had followed anger and energy. But after a minute's repose, she made a vigorous effort, and regaining in some measure her self-possession, exclaimed, "'Judge,' I need advice. Listen to me. About an hour ago—"

With a gesture Dauman interrupted her. "Alas !" he sighed, "I know everything !"

"You know—"

"That Monsieur Norbert is a prisoner? Yes, mademoiselle, I know that. And I also know that you have just met M. de Champdoce in the Bois de Bivron. I know, moreover, all you said to the duke. I have heard every word from a person who has just left me."

Diane was unable to repress a start of terror and dismay. "Who told you this?" she gasped.

"A wood-cutter. Ah ! mademoiselle, woods are not safe places to tell secrets in. Behind every tree a pair of ears may be listening. Four wood-cutters heard every syllable you both said. As soon as you left the duke, they started off eager to tell their tale. I did my best to make the one I saw promise not to repeat it. He promised, of course, but then he's married, and will, naturally, tell everything to his wife. And then there are the three others, besides."

"Then I am lost !" murmured Diane, despondently, regretting for the moment, perhaps, that she had so trifled with her reputation. Dauman hung his head by way of answer. But this daughter of the once martial house of Sauvebourg was not the woman to abandon the fight so long as life was left her. "All is not over yet," she cried, grasping the "judge's" arm. "What are we to do? You must have some idea. I am ready for anything, now that I have nothing to lose. No, it shall never be said that the Duke de Champdoce insulted me, the coward ? without my having my revenge. Will you help me ?"

"For Heaven's sake!" said Dauman, "speak lower! Be calm, I implore you. You do not know this man, I assure you."

"You are afraid of him then, are you?"

"Yes, mademoiselle, I am afraid, and very much afraid. What a man he is! He almost always gains his ends at any cost. Do you know that he tried to injure me, to punish me, for having summoned him before a magistrate in the name of one of my clients? And so, when anyone comes to me with anything against the duke, I am apt to keep out of the business—"

"Indeed!" exclaimed Diane, contemptuously. "Then after inducing us to compromise ourselves, you now abandon us in this emergency."

"Oh, mademoiselle, can you believe—"

"Do as you please, 'judge.' Norbert is still left to me."

Dauman shook his head, sadly. "How can we be sure that at this very moment the marquis has not said Amen! to all his father's propositions?"

"No!" cried Diane, "I don't believe that of Norbert. He would kill himself first! He is timid, I know, but not a coward; and when he thinks of me he will have strength to resist."

"Oh we can reason coldly," retorted Dauman, "for we stand here free and in safety. M. Norbert, on the contrary, is exposed to all sorts of threats and dangers, moral and physical tortures. He is in the power of one of the most obstinately wicked men that ever lived. And, remember, there are moments in men's lives when even the firmest natures waver."

"Well, I admit it. I admit that Norbert may have abandoned me, that he will marry another woman, and that I am lost and dishonoured, destined to become the talk of the whole province. Nevertheless, I have still life left to me, and that life I would gladly give in exchange for revenge."

There was a ring of such terrible vehemence in her voice, that Dauman started; and this time his start was a real, not an affected one. "Ah me!" he said, "I also swore to have my revenge on the duke; but then he's so powerful, so dangerous an adversary, that I thought better of it. And there are many others who have done the same, men who threatened vengeance with frightful oaths, calling heaven and hell to witness them. 'A good shot in the twilight from behind a hedge would finish him,' they thought. Well, they loaded their guns and went forth to wait and watch; but, dear me, at the last moment their hearts failed them, and the duke lives on, as hale and hearty as ever. And yet, it seems to me, that judges don't look deeply enough into things. What looks to them like a crime is often a deliverance. Who can tell how many other crimes the Duke de Champdoce's death would avert, or how many people it would render happy?" Diane turned pale as she listened to these words. "Meanwhile," continued Dauman, "as I said before, the duke lives on. He is rich and powerful, and to a certain degree respected. He will die in his bed, there will be a great crowd at his funeral, and the curé will, of course, pray for him, as in duty bound." Whilst speaking, the "judge" had drawn the tiny black glass phial from behind his papers, and turned it round and round in his hands. "Yes," he repeated, "M. de Champdoce, the sturdy old veteran, will bury us all, unless—" He stopped short, uncorked the phial, and dropped a few particles of the fine white sparkling dust it contained into the palm of his hand. "And yet," he said, in a low, stern voice, "a little of this powder and no one would ever need fear the terrible duke again. A man who lies six feet under ground, with a heavy stone and a fine epitaph over him, doesn't inspire anybody with dread."

He ceased speaking, and watched the girl before him. They stood face to face, motionless and breathless, for two good minutes. The silence was so profound that the very beating of their hearts might have been heard. They each wished to ascertain, before breaking this intense silence, whether they both shared the same criminal thought. Yes, they understood each other, for Dauman at last spoke, in a hoarse whisper, as if he feared the very sound of his own voice. "There is no pain with this—. Imagine a man struck by a heavy blow on the temple. Ten seconds, and all is over. Not a cry, nor a gasp, nor a struggle—nothing—"

"Nothing?"

"And no traces either. One pinch dropped in wine or coffee would suffice. Nothing betrays its presence, no change of colour in the liquid, no smell, no taste."

"But if a very careful post mortem examination took place, might not some traces be detected?"

"Perhaps so, in Paris, or some large town—but not here in the depths of the provinces. And besides, never unless suspicion had been previously aroused. There are perhaps not four doctors in France who would remark ought else but the symptoms of apoplexy ; moreover, it is not enough to say it's there, it must be found. Then comes the question, how it got there."

"Yes, perhaps—"

"There is no perhaps. Investigations once begun would be carried to the end. However, this substance is not sold by chemists. It is rare, costly and difficult to prepare and obtain. At the most, four or five laboratories in France preserve a few pure grains for the needs of scientific investigation. It is impossible to imagine that any man in this part of the country possesses an atom of it, or even knows of its existence. For where, and how could he have procured it?"

"And yet you—"

"That's another thing entirely. Years ago, when I was many leagues from here, I rendered a very great service to an eminent chemist, and he made me a present of this—this product of his art. But it would be impossible to trace this bottle back to its origin, for it came into my hands more than ten years ago, and, moreover, the chemist is dead."

"Ten years ago !"

"Twelve, I think. And yet this substance has lost none of its precious qualities."

"How can you be certain of that?"

"Why, I experimented with it only a month ago. I threw a pinch of this powder into a bowl of milk and gave it to a bull-dog. He lapped the milk for ten seconds and then rolled over dead."

Overwhelmed with horror, Mademoiselle de Sauvebourg started back. "Horrible !" she stammered, "horrible !"

A smile played over the "judge's" thin lips. "Why horrible?" he asked. "The dog had been bitten. He might have gone mad and bitten me, and I should have expired in frightful agony. Wasn't it a case of legitimate self-defence? Ah ! men are at times even more dangerous than dogs. A man morally murders me—I suppress him. Am I guilty? the law says yes, and condemns me. In my opinion, however, it is better to kill the devil than—"

He said no more, for Diane abruptly placing her hand before his mouth, thus ended the exposure of his monstrous theories. "Listen !" she muttered.

A heavy step could be heard on the stairs.

"Norbert!" gasped Diane.

"Impossible! can his father—"

"It is Norbert," repeated Mademoiselle de Sauvebourg, and snatching the black phial from Dauman's hands, she thrust it into her bosom.

For one moment she had really been gifted with second sight. The new comer was indeed Norbert and none other. He opened the door and at sight of him both Dauman and Diane uttered a cry of terrified surprise. Everything in his appearance indicated some terrible catastrophe, his automatic motion, his haggard eyes, and the blood on his face. Dauman scented a crime. "You are wounded, marquis," he said.

"Yes; my father struck me."

"Can it be possible that he—"

"Yes, it was he!"

Diane had feared something worse than this; she quivered like a leaf as she went towards Norbert. "Let me examine your wound," she said softly, and standing on tiptoe the better to see, she took his head in her hands. "Good heavens! one inch lower down and—" She shuddered. "'Judge,' give me some water and some old linen—"

But Norbert gently disengaged himself. "We will attend to this trifle later," said he, "I avoided the blow, which would have felled me to the ground, had it come in full force; in fact, but for my alacrity, I should have been murdered by my father."

"By the duke? And why—what has happened?"

"He had insulted you, Diane: and he dared to tell me of it—to boast of it to me! Didn't he know that the blood of the Champdoces' runs in my veins as well as in his?"

Mademoiselle de Sauvebourg burst into tears. "And it is I," she sobbed—"I who brought all this upon you."

"You! You saved his life, probably. When he struck me with his stick, the thought of you withheld my hand. I turned and fled, and never again will I cross that threshold. We hear a great deal of a father's curse—a son's should have equal weight. The Duke de Champdoce is my father no longer—I know him no more. I wish I could forget his very existence, but no—I prefer to remember him, so that I may yet avenge myself."

Never in his life had Dauman felt such intense joy. Ah! his own vengeance also was near at hand. "At last, marquis," said he, "you will believe with me that there is some good in almost all misfortunes. Your father's imprudence will cost him dear. It now rests with us to shake off the paternal yoke just as soon as we choose. We now possess all the requisite elements for a formal complaint. We have sequestration, threats, violence connived at by third parties, wounds and blows which have imperilled life—in fact, we have everything we want. A physician will come, examine your head, and draw up a formal, written report. We can produce plenty of witnesses of the accessory facts—and, as to the wound, the scar will tell the story. To begin with, we shall pray in our petition, not to be ordered back to the paternal home, and sue for legal emancipation—"

"But tell me," interrupted Norbert, "if I am emancipated, as they say, from parental control shall I be able to marry whom I please without M. de Champdoce's consent?"

Dauman hesitated. In his opinion, under all the circumstances, Norbert might eventually obtain from the courts the authorisation to contract an honourable alliance, but this would mean litigation, and patience, so he thought it advisable not to say so.

"Then why petition? The Champdoce family have always washed their dirty linen at home, and I prefer to do the same."

This determination seemed to astonish the "judge." "If I dared," he began, "if I dared to advise you, sir—"

"No. No advice is necessary; my mind is made up. But I need some assistance, in fact, within twenty-four hours I must have a large sum—twenty thousand francs."

"You can have them, sir; but I warn you that it will be at a heavy cost."

"I care nothing for that!"

Mademoiselle de Sauvebourg tried to speak, but Norbert prevented her. "Don't you understand me, Diane?" he said. "We must fly! Let us go at once, and search for some retreat where we may live happy and obscure."

"But this is folly! you would be pursued," said Dauman.

Mademoiselle de Sauvebourg hung her head.

"Is it true, Diane," continued Norbert pleadingly, "that you hesitate to intrust yourself to me? I swear to consecrate my entire existence to you—all my thoughts, all my will. I ask you on my knees to go with me!"

"I cannot!" she murmured, "I cannot!"

"You do not love me!" he cried, in a tone of despair. "Fool that I am, I believed that your heart was mine, but I see now that you never loved me!"

"Thou hearest him! Oh, my God! Thou knowest that I love him!"

"Then why reject our only means of safety?"

"Norbert, my dear Norbert—"

"I understand only too well. The thought of the world's talk frightens you—there are prejudices, opinions—"

He stopped, checked by the reproachful expression of Diane's eyes. "Must it be?" she asked—"must I justify myself? You talk to me of prejudices—have I not defied them already, and has not the world sat in judgment upon me? And yet what have I done? I could repeat every word we either of us have breathed, to my mother without a blush; but would any one believe me? No, no one. The opinion of the world is already made up, no doubt. My reputation is unquestionably gone, and yet I am as guiltless as a child."

Norbert was furious. "Who has dared to mention your name except with the most profound respect?" he asked.

"Alas! my friend, everybody. And to-morrow it will be worse still. Some hours ago, while your father was talking to me with such appalling violence and contempt, four woodcutters, binding faggots in the wood, overheard him."

"That is impossible!"

"No, it's true," affirmed Dauman. "I heard it all from one of these four men—"

If ever a man received a quiet intimation to leave a room it was conveyed in a glance which Diane now gave the "judge." He took the hint at once, and hastily rose from his seat. "Excuse me," he said; "but I just heard some one calling, and I must prevent any one from coming in here!" With these words he left the room, banging the door behind him.

It needed this noise for Norbert to notice that he and Diane were now alone together. "And so," exclaimed the young fellow, "the Duke de Champdoce did not even take the precaution of ascertaining whether there was anyone to overhear his insults. And he was so blind that he did not realise that in dishonouring you he was dishonouring himself."

"Alas!—"

"Does he think he can force me to marry this heiress of his—this Marie de Puymandour?"

At last Diane knew the name of the woman whom the duke had chosen to become his son's wife. "Ah!" she murmured, "it is Mademoiselle Marie, then, whose hand is offered to you?"

"Yes, it's she, or rather her millions; but my hand shall shrivel before it takes hers. You hear me, Diane?"

She smiled sadly as she murmured, "Poor Norbert," speaking moreover in such a melancholy tone, that the young man's heart sank.

"You are cruel," he exclaimed; "what have I ever done to deserve your distrust? What oath shall I take that I will never have any other wife but you? Is it because you doubt me that you will not go with me?"

"No, it is not any distrust of you that deters me."

"But what is it, then? Is it not liberty and happiness that I propose? What keeps you from accepting?"

She rose, threw her head back with haughty pride, and answered, "My conscience! Yes, my conscience—the same that has hitherto enabled me to walk with head erect, despite all the slander I knew was being circulated. But now it bids me stop, and I dare not disobey its voice. Duty may be hard to perform, my heart may break; but I must not, I cannot go with you. If I were alone in the world, I should, perhaps, not hesitate; but I have ties, I have a family whose honour is a sacred trust."

"A family that sacrifices you to an elder brother!"

"That may be—so the more my merit if I do my duty. Where did you ever hear that virtue was easy to practise?" Norbert was too much oppressed with the thought of losing her to notice the contradiction of her conduct. She had preached insubordination to him, but pretended to practise duty herself. "Both my reason and my conscience," she resumed, "dictate the same course. The result is fatal when a young girl sets social rules and conventionalities at defiance. You would soon cease to esteem her whom others despised."

"Good heavens! what an opinion you have of me!"

"I believe you to be a man, my friend. Suppose I followed you to-day, and suppose to-morrow you heard that my father had fought a duel on my account, and had been killed—what then? Believe me, I give you the best possible advice in bidding you depart alone. You will forget me; indeed, you must!"

"Forget you!" cried Norbert fiercely. "I forget you! Can you forget me?"

He was so close to her that she felt his burning breath. "I," she stammered, "I—"

Norbert drew back that he might better look into her eyes. "And if I went alone," he asked, "what would become of you?"

At this question Mademoiselle de Sauvebourg turned extremely pale. A sob rose from her heart, and her strength seemed suddenly to fail her. "I," she answered, in as sweet and resigned a voice as if she had been a Christian martyr about to enter the arena, "I know my fate. We see each other now for the last time. I shall return to Sauvebourg, where everything is known—or will be known in a few hours. I shall find my father irritated, enraged, he will order me to a carriage, and to-morrow the walls of a convent will again close round me."

"Never! never! That life would be long agony to you; you have told me so over and over again."

"Yes," she answered, "it would be agony; but it is duty also. And when the burden grows too heavy—when I can no longer bear it—" As she spoke, she had drawn Dauman's black phial from her bosom, and Norbert, on perceiving it, at once understood what she meant. As he tried to snatch it from her, she resisted; but the contest soon exhausted her little remaining strength. As Norbert at last clutched the phial in his hands, her beautiful eyes closed, her head fell back, and she sank into her lover's arms, while he, with horror, asked himself if she were dying. Dying she might have been, and yet she murmured a few words in a low but distinct whisper. She implored Norbert to restore to her that precious phial, her only friend and liberator; and then, with truly wonderful lucidity, she contrived to repeat to him all the directions Dauman had given her. "Oh! my friend," she said, "return it to me. I shall not suffer—in ten seconds all will be over. A mere pinch of it in wine or coffee will suffice, and no one will ever suspect the truth; for it leaves no trace behind it."

At the thought that this woman loved him so tenderly and passionately that she would rather die than live apart from him, Norbert felt his senses reel. "Diane!" he repeated, as he leaned over her. "Diane!"

But she continued, as if in delirium, "To die after such fair hopes! Ah! M. de Champdoce, you are pitiless, indeed. You have robbed me of my happiness; you have insulted me, lowered me in the estimation of the world, blackened my reputation, and now you want my life."

Norbert uttered a cry of mingled rage and hatred—so terrible a cry that even Dauman, listening as usual at the key-hole, felt frightened. An execrable idea had just dawned on the young man's mind; and as he deposited Diane in the "judge's" arm-chair, he exclaimed in a hoarse voice, "No, you shall not kill yourself, nor shall I depart!" He looked at her once again; she smiled faintly, murmuring his name, with parted lips eager to be kissed. Norbert's last ray of reason fled. "You shall be mine!" he murmured. "The poison you intended for yourself shall serve my vengeance." A moment later and he had gone.

Dauman was livid, and his teeth were fairly chattering when he returned to his office. He had lost nothing of this scene, and, hardened as he was, it had greatly impressed him. He could barely fancy himself awake when he saw Diane—whom he had expected to find in a fainting condition—standing near the window, and carefully scrutinising Norbert as the latter hastened away. She was pale, no doubt, and her eyelids were red and swollen, but her eyes themselves flashed with all the pride of victory. "To-morrow, 'judge,'" she said; "to-morrow I shall be the Duchess de Champdoce!"

Dauman, the ready speaker, the man of many words, was so confounded that he made no rejoinder.

"I mean," resumed Diane, "providing the truth is not discovered to-night."

At these words Dauman felt a cold shiver along the spine; but summoning all his self-possession he replied, "I do not understand you; what could be discovered to-night? Pray, explain—"

She gave him such a contemptuous, ironical look, that his sentence ended in an inarticulate murmur. He recognized his error. He had fancied he might play with her like a cat with a mouse, but he was mistaken; it was she who had played with him. He had been her dupe. "There is no doubt of success, of course," she resumed coldly, "only—Norbert is awkward sometimes." Then, as she arranged her attire, she added, "I must return home—my father will be anxious. Ah! what a night of suspense is in store for me! When will to-morrow come? Good-evening, 'judge.' Everything will be decided when we meet again."

Dauman had shuddered on hearing these words: "Norbert is awkward sometimes." Could he really be sure of impunity; might not Norbert or Diane, rather, betray him? The "judge" sank into his arm-chair and tried to think. Perhaps, at this very moment, it was all over.

Meanwhile Norbert had hastened towards Champdoce. He had really lost his head, and yet, like a true madman, he fancied he could reason clearly. All his ideas, however, converged to the criminal purpose he had in view. All the work-folks at Champdoce, and Norbert with them, drank the common but healthy wine of the district; the duke alone reserving for his especial use a higher class vintage, grown on an estate of his in the Médoc. "The master's wine," as the servants said, was drawn direct from the cask, and served in a bottle which, after each meal, remained on a shelf in the common hall, within sight and touch of everybody. But no one ever dared to finger it. Now Norbert had thought of this bottle, and had formed his plan accordingly. Crossing the court-yard, without paying the least attention to the labourers who were loading straw there, he reached the common hall, and to his satisfaction found it empty. Then with singular prudence—remarkable on the part of a person in his state of mind—he opened each door in succession, and glanced out of every window to make sure he was not being watched. Next, with extreme rapidity and prodigious precision, he took his father's wine bottle from the shelf, swiftly uncorked it, and dropped therein, not one pinch, but three pinches of the powder contained in Dauman's phial. To dissolve it the sooner, he gently shook the bottle, taking care not to render the wine either turbid or frothy. He was certainly unconscious of his acts, and yet his carefulness and exactitude were remarkable. As some specks of the powder clung to the rim of the bottle's neck, he carefully wiped them off, not with a napkin, but with his own pocket-handkerchief; and then he replaced the bottle on the shelf, took his customary seat in the corner, and waited.

At this moment M. de Champdoce was striding up and down the avenue. For the first time in his whole life, probably, the headstrong, obstinate old nobleman had begun to regret his conduct. He had been thinking of the very same matters that Dauman had explained to Norbert, and was obliged to admit to himself that he had been exceedingly rash. Norbert had deserved punishment, no doubt; but the law does not trifle with cases of sequestration and ill-usage, and the duke feared lest a complaint might be lodged against him. In that case the courts would probably remove Norbert from his control, the young fellow would find evil advisers, and then good-bye to all his cherished plans. Such a catastrophe must, if possible, be averted, and so the duke resolved to act with all possible caution. He did not relinquish his views in regard to his son's marriage with Mademoiselle de Puymandour. No—he would sooner have renounced life itself; but he resigned himself to the conviction that he must substitute cunning for violence. The point of greatest importance now was to bring Norbert

back. But would the young fellow ever consent to enter the château again?
M. de Champdoce was ruminating, with a heavy frown, on this particular
question, when a servant came in haste to tell him that Norbert had returned. "I have him!" muttered the duke, and at once he hurried to the
château.

When he entered the common hall, Norbert, forgetting his customary
deference, did not rise, and this non-observance of the usual rules struck
the duke most forcibly. "*Jarnicoton!*" thought he, "does the young
scamp imagine he no longer owes me any deference?" However, he did
not audibly express his displeasure; in fact, the blood on his son's face
worried him exceedingly. "Norbert," he asked, "are you in pain? Why
haven't you had your wound dressed?" The reply he paused for did not
come. "Tell me," he resumed, "why haven't you had that blood washed
away? Is it left as a reproach for me? I didn't need it, I assure you, to
regret my anger—and violence." Norbert still offered no remark, and his
silence seemed to embarrass the duke frightfully. The old nobleman hardly
knew how to continue—he was so unfitted for the new part he had now decided upon playing; and thus, at last, more to gain time than to quench his
thirst, he took his bottle of wine from off the shelf and poured out half a
glassful. Norbert, who had watched him, quivered from head to foot.
"Come now, my lad," said the duke, "come now, try and make friends
with your old father. A man of honour is never ashamed to acknowledge
his mistakes." As he spoke, he took hold of his glass and raised it to the
light.

Norbert held his breath—it seemed to him as if the floor was giving way
beneath his feet; his brain whirled, his blood boiled, and yet he did not
move.

"It is cruel," continued the duke, "it is sad for a man to humiliate
himself thus before his son, and to do so uselessly."

In vain did Norbert turn away his head. He could still see M. de
Champdoce bring the glass nearer and nearer to his lips; he was on the
point of drinking—but no, Norbert could not suffer that. With one bound
he reached his father's side, and, snatching the glass from his hand, he
threw it out of the window, shouting in a terrible voice, "Do not drink it!"

The young fellow's expression, voice, and motion required no explanation. A terrible light flashed upon his father. The duke's features
quivered, his face became suffused, blood rushed to his eyes—he opened his
lips to speak, but only a hoarse rattle was heard; he extended his arms
convulsively, and then fell back, striking the back of his head against the
corner of a heavy oak dresser. Norbert had rushed out of the room.
"Come quick!" he cried. "Help! I have killed my father!"

IX.

The Duke de Champdoce had not underrated M. de Puymandour's mad
longing to be considered a genuine nobleman. He had been happier in his
earlier years when the name of Palouzat, his honest father's, had sufficed
for his ambition. Then, undoubtedly, he was a man of mark, respected
for the ability he had shown in honestly amassing an enormous fortune.
Matters changed, however, on the day when he took it into his head to buy
a title from the Pope, and sport address cards bearing the inscription,
"Count de Puymandour." From this moment his tribulations began.

With the nobility, who laughed and refused to recognize him as one of themselves, on the one side, and the middle classes, who sneered at his pretensions, on the other, he was like a shuttlecock between two battledoors, battered and banged about, and sent spinning to and fro. Still he clung more ardently than ever to his aristocratic pretensions, and eagerly desired that his daughter might marry the son and heir of the high and mighty Duke de Champdocc. He had agreed to sacrifice the third of his fortune for the honour of this alliance, and would, indeed, have given the whole of it to have dandled on his knees an infant-duke, with the blood of the Palouzats and that of the heroes of the Crusades mingled in his veins. This marriage was, in his estimation, calculated to silence all raillery. As the flag covers the merchandise, so would his son-in-law's authentic rank and ancestry prove his passport into aristocratic society, assuring him fitting deference and courtesy on the part of those who now so openly derided him.

As soon as arrangements were finally concluded with the duke, M. de Puymandour resolved to acquaint his daughter with his intentions. He never dreamed of any obstacle, and, indeed, he candidly believed that she would be as pleased as himself. Having come to this determination—it was one morning whilst he sat alone in his library—he rang the bell, and, as soon as his valet appeared, exclaimed, "Go and ask mademoiselle's maid if my daughter can grant me an interview."

Although given with an air of great solemnity, this order in no wise seemed to astonish the valet. In fact, M. de Puymandour was habitually ceremonious, and his deriders declared that the etiquette of the court of Austria was nothing in comparison with that which prevailed in his household. However, less than two minutes after the servant left the room, there came a tap at the door. "Come in," exclaimed M. de Puymandour, and at once his daughter Marie appeared, and flinging both arms round his neck, kissed him heartily on either cheek. The count frowned, as if this display of affection displeased him, and then inquired, "Why did you come here, Marie? I asked if you would receive me."

"To be sure you did, dear father; but I thought it more natural for me to come here; besides, it was much more quickly done. Pray don't be vexed."

"Always the same story. When will you acquire the dignity of manner which ought to distinguish a young person of your rank and position?"

Marie de Puymandour smiled, but oh! so faintly; for although she was conscious of her father's absurdities, she was not disposed to sit in judgment upon them, for she loved him very tenderly. She was a very charming girl, and the Duke de Champdoce had not flattered the portrait he had drawn of her to Norbert. Although her style of beauty was very different to that of Diane's, she was none the less of bewitching loveliness—tall, and of shapely form, and with all that languid grace of attitude and motion which distinguishes the women of the south. Her cheeks were two blush roses, her big black eyes were as soft as velvet, and she had a wondrous wealth of bluish-black hair. Unlike Diane in person, she was yet even more unlike her in mind. She had a tender heart, capable of intense devotion, and the angelic sweetness of her disposition at times even degenerated into weakness.

"Now, dear papa," she said, in answer to her father's words of blame, "come, don't scold me. You know that the Marchioness d'Arlange gave me lessons of dignity last winter, and I'm practising in secret. Why, you yourself will be intimidated when I've learned them perfectly."

"Ah! women, women!" muttered her father. "What frivolous creatures they are! The most serious matters only furnish them with food for jest and scoffing." So saying he rose, and assuming an oratorical attitude, resumed, "I ask myself with anxiety, Marie, whether you will be equal to the exalted position I have in view for you. You were eighteen last month, and it is time to consider your future. I have an important piece of news for you. In fact, I have had an application for your hand."

Marie dropped her eyes and endeavoured to conceal her confusion.

"Before coming to a decision on so grave a subject," continued M. de Puymandour, "it was, of course, necessary for me to give it serious reflection. I have made full inquiries, and I am certain that the proposed alliance offers every guarantee of human happiness. The young man is only a few years older than yourself. He is good-looking, his fortune is considerable, he is of noble birth, and bears the title of Marquis—"

"He has spoken to you, then?" interrupted Marie in an agitated tone.

"He? Who do you mean by 'he?'" As the girl did not answer, her father repeated his question.

"Why, M. George de Croisenois," replied Marie faintly.

"What have you to do with Croisenois?" retorted M. de Puymandour. "And who is this Marquis de Croisenois? Is he that fop with little moustaches whom I saw hanging round your skirts this winter?"

"Yes," she stammered, quite out of countenance; "that is he."

"Why should you suppose he has asked for your hand? Did you know he intended doing so?"

"My dear father—"

"There's no 'dear father' in this case. What! my daughter—a Puymandour—listens to a declaration and conceals it from me! Zounds! He has written to you, I suppose? What have you done with his letters?"

"Dear father—"

"Silence! You have preserved these letters, no doubt? Very well, I must see them."

"Dear father—"

"The letters!" interrupted M. de Puymandour in a formidable voice; "where are they? I must have them, even if I turn the whole house topsy-turvy."

Marie was incapable of dissimulation, and such was her father's anger that she dared not resist him; so she surrendered these precious missives, four in number, tied together with a blue ribbon. He at once opened the topmost one and read it aloud, interspersing his perusal with invectives and exclamations. "Mademoiselle, although I fear nothing in the world so much as your displeasure, I venture, notwithstanding your commands, to write to you once more. Forgive me, but I learn that you are on the point of leaving Paris for several months. I am twenty-four years of age. I am an orphan, and my own master. I belong to an old and honourable family, my fortune is considerable, and I love you with the most sincere and respectful love. May I entreat you, therefore, to authorise me to ask M. de Puymandour for your hand? My great uncle, the Duke de Sairmeuse, who knows your father, will act as my intermediary on his return from Italy, that is in three or four weeks' time at the utmost. Once more, imploring your forgiveness, I am, Mademoiselle, &c., &c."

"Very nice indeed—very nice," said the count as he finished reading. "The scamp doesn't beat about the bush. That's quite enough for me—I need read no more. And what did you write in return?"

"That he might apply to you, dear father."

"Indeed! you do me too much honour, upon my word. And you thought I should listen patiently to propositions from such a source? You love him, then?"

She averted her face, and tears streamed down her cheeks. This mute avowal, for avowal it was, exasperated M. de Puymandour. "You love him!" he exclaimed, "and you have the audacity to own it. Ah! what times we live in! Any girl is at the mercy of an adventurer!"

Marie looked up quickly. "The Marquis de Croisenois," said she, "comes of a good family."

"Pshaw! you know nothing about it. The first Croisenois was an errand boy of Richelieu's. Louis XIII. conferred this title upon him for some dirty piece of work he executed for him. Has your petty marquis any real means of subsistence?"

"Most certainly. Some fifty thousand francs a year."

"Stuff and nonsense."

"But am I not rich enough for both of us?"

"Ah! that's the point. That's what the scamp was after—your money! Do you think I've slaved for twenty years for the sake of a Croisenois! No, no. I won't hear of him. His conduct has been most disgraceful. When a man of honour is in love, he goes to his notary, and lays before him his intentions and position. This notary goes to the notary of the young lady's family, and when the two notaries have studied and found everything satisfactory, then the heart is allowed to speak. And, besides, we need not bandy words; you must forget this Croisenois as quickly as possible. I have chosen a husband for you, and have given my word of honour—you will have to keep it. On Sunday, the young man will be introduced to you; on Monday, a visit to the bishop, to ask him to bless your union; on Tuesday, a round of visits to announce the engagement; on Wednesday, the reading of the contract; on Thursday, a great betrothal dinner; on Friday, the examination of the *trousseau*; on Sunday, the banns, and at the end of the week after, the wedding will take place."

Mademoiselle Marie listened aghast. "For heaven's sake, dear papa, be serious!" she pleaded.

The count merely shrugged his shoulders. "Finally," added he, "the husband I have selected for you is the Duke de Champdoce's son, young Marquis Norbert."

Marie turned deadly pale. "But I don't even know him!" she stammered. "How can I love him?"

"I know him, then, and that is quite enough. I have decided you shall be a duchess, and I mean it."

Marie loved M. de Croisenois more than she had told her father—more even than she dared avow to herself. So she at first resisted with a heroism most unexpected on the part of a girl endowed with so mild a nature, and so weak a character. M. de Puymandour, however, was not the man to readily abandon the dream of his life. He did not leave his daughter for a minute in peace—he argued, insisted and domineered—until at last, on the third evening, Marie surrendered, and murmured the fatal "yes" amid sobs and tears.

The word had scarcely passed her lips when her father, not lingering even to thank her for the sacrifice, exclaimed, "I must go at once to Champdoce. I have had no news from there for the last three days, and there were still several points to be settled between the duke and myself."

Thereupon he hastened off, just adding as he closed the door, "I shall soon be back, my little duchess."

He had every reason to wish to see the duke, for when they parted, three days before, the old nobleman had said to him, "To-morrow you will hear from me," but not a word had come. The delay had suited M. de Puymandour, inasmuch as it had enabled him to conquer his daughter's resistance; but now that she was reduced to submission, he began to feel very anxious. Could anything have gone wrong? He walked on at a rapid pace, and had just reached the rising ground near Bivron, when he perceived "judge" Dauman talking earnestly with the widow Rouleau's daughter. Despite his haste, M. de Puymandour bowed affably and stopped, for he was now courting popularity, preparatory to coming forward as a candidate at the next election. Now Dauman, despite his villainous reputation, was undoubtedly an influential personage, and an able electioneering agent as well, whenever occasion required. "Good-day, 'judge,'" said the count, "what's the news?"

Dauman bowed to the ground. "Sad news, Monsieur le Comte," he answered; "I hear that the Duke de Champdoce is very ill."

"The duke! Impossible!"

"Well, this girl has just told me so. Tell us all about it, Françoise."

The girl curtsied and replied "I've just heard at the château that it is quite impossible for him to recover."

"But what's the matter with him?"

"I didn't hear."

M. de Puymandour stood aghast.

"That is always the way in this world," observed Dauman, philosophically. "In the midst of life we are in death—"

"Good-bye, 'judge'," interrupted the count, "as this is the case, I must try and obtain some further particulars." So saying, he hurried on, breathless and anxious. All the people belonging to the château—servants and farm-hands—were gathered together in the court-yard, talking earnestly, but as soon as M. de Puymandour appeared, Jean, the duke's confidential valet, advanced to meet him. "Well," cried the count, "tell me what is the matter?"

"Oh! Monsieur le Comte, a most awful misfortune! My poor master—"

"Is he dead?"

"Alas! he is hardly any better!"

"But how is it he has so suddenly fallen ill?"

"It came like a flash of lightning," responded Jean, after a moment's hesitation. "On the day before yesterday, at about this same hour, Monsieur le Duc was alone with Monsieur Norbert in the common hall, when we heard Monsieur Norbert suddenly shriek for help. We hastened in and found Monsieur le Duc lying on his back on the floor, unconscious, with his face all black and swollen."

"He had had a fit of apoplexy, then?"

"No, not exactly—the doctor called it a suffusion of blood to the brain, and said he would have died at once if, in falling, he had not struck his head against the oak dresser, cutting himself so that he bled profusely. We carried him to bed, he was stiff and—"

"And now?"

"Well, now, no one can say anything for certain. My poor master neither sees nor hears; and if he recovers, which I scarcely believe possible, the doctor says, that at all events his mind is gone for ever."

"Frightful! frightful! Such a noble, worthy, remarkable man! I don't ask you to let me go upstairs, for I could do him no good, and the sight would be a most painful one; but if I could see Monsieur Norbert—"

"Don't think of it, Monsieur le Comte, I beg of you!" said Jean, with a sudden start.

"I was his father's friend, his intimate friend; and if sympathy could soften the marquis's grief—"

"Impossible, Monsieur le Comte," rejoined Jean in a curt, gloomy voice. "My young master is with his father, he has not left him for a moment, and he has given orders not to be called on any pretence. But I must go to him now. We are expecting two physicians who are coming from Poitiers."

"I will retire, then, and to-night I will send for news."

M. de Puymandour walked slowly away, in a most anxious, despondent state of mind. The old servant's manner, voice and look had struck him as very singular. Had he told him the whole truth? The count recalled the fact that Norbert was alone with M. de Champdoce at the time of the accident; and bearing his own daughter's resistance in mind, he jumped to the conclusion that the duke had met with similar opposition from his son, that a violent quarrel had followed, and that, mad with anger, the old nobleman had been struck with this fatal fit. Interest, indeed, so sharpened M. de Puymandour's natural penetration, that he came singularly near the truth. "If this should really be the case," he thought, "it will be just the same whether the duke dies or loses his mind, for Norbert will certainly break off the negotiations." In that case, what could M. de Puymandour do, so as to escape ridicule? Only one plan occurred to him, that of immediately marrying his daughter to the Marquis de Croisenois, who, despite all he had said to the contrary, was in reality a most desirable husband.

The count was thus cogitating as he walked home, when suddenly he was startled by hearing some one ask him: "Was the girl right, Monsieur le Comte." Chance had again thrown Dauman across his path. "How is the duke?" resumed the "judge"—"and Monsieur Norbert? You saw him, of course?"

"No; the poor fellow is overwhelmed with grief. Fancy, his father has a suffusion of blood to the brain, and will remain an idiot even if he doesn't die."

"How awful!" answered the "judge." "For it really is a terrible thing indeed!" And then with a low bow, he turned towards his own house.

In point of fact, M. de Puymandour felt little or no pity for Norbert. He was mainly occupied in wondering whether his surmises as to the cause of the duke's attack were right; and supposing such to be the case, what was Norbert thinking of, what were his intentions.

At that moment the young marquis was kneeling at his father's bedside, and with his heart full of anguish and remorse, watching for some indication of returning life or reason. Three days of horror and self-abasement had made him a different man. It was only at the very last moment, when the poison all but touched his father's lips, that he had realised the horror and enormity of his crime. His whole nature had revolted, and a formidable voice seemed to cry to him: "Assassin! Parricide!" When his father fell back he had had strength enough to shout for assistance; but immediately afterward, he was seized with a wild fear, and ran into the fields, at hap-hazard, as if hoping to escape from himself. Jean, the duke's old confidential servant, had alone witnessed this precipitate flight, and a terrible presentiment had seized hold of him. He knew the cause of the estrangement existing between father and son; he was acquainted with the violence of their tempers, and with the fact that a woman was urging Norbert to resistance. After the frightful blow the duke had struck his son, he was amazed to see Norbert return home. What could be his intention in thus so speedily coming back to the château? Finally, Jean had been in the court-yard at the very moment when Norbert had flung the glass containing the poisoned wine out of the window. All these circumstances combined, made the old servant apprehensive of the truth, and so as soon as the duke had been put to bed, he went downstairs again into the common hall, convinced he should find something to confirm his fears. The bottle containing the duke's wine stood there on the table, three-quarters empty. What did this mean? With infinite care Jean poured several drops of the wine into the hollow of his hand; he tasted them cautiously, spitting them out again as soon as they had touched his palate. The wine retained its usual aroma and flavour. No matter. Obeying the inspiration of his devotion to the House of Champdoce, Jean carried the bottle to his own room, unperceived, and hid it there. He then bade another servant to remain with the duke until the doctor arrived, and went himself in search of Norbert.

He had searched in vain for fully a couple of hours, and utterly discouraged, was returning through the woods to the château, when on the turf, under a tree, he saw a human form extended. He advanced cautiously—yes, the man lying there was Norbert. The faithful old servant knelt down, and finding him all but unconscious, shook him roughly. With one bound the young fellow sprang to his feet. It seemed to him as if justice, human or divine, had just set its clutch upon him, and his eyes dilated with sudden terror. "It is I, Monsieur Norbert," said Jean.

"Ah! yes; what do you want?"

"I came to find you, sir, to beg you to return with me to Champdoce."

"Return to the château?" answered Norbert, in a hoarse voice. "No; not now."

"But you must, sir. Your absence would seem perfectly inconceivable. It would set people talking, and strange things might be said. Your place is at your father's bedside."

"Never! No, never!"

He said this; but he made no resistance when Jean slipped his arm through his, and drew him along. Thus led, Norbert retraced his steps, in automatic fashion, to the château, crossed the court, and ascended the stairs; but on reaching the door of his father's room he drew back, again in a state of abject terror, and tried to escape Jean's grasp. "I will not!" he gasped; "I cannot!"

"You can, and you shall," said the faithful old servant. "For, no matter what else happens, the family honour must not be tarnished in the eyes of the world."

These few words, the thought of the honour of Champdoce, gave Norbert just sufficient strength to stagger across the room and sink on the floor at the bedside. Once on his knees, with his forehead on his father's cold hand, he burst into tears. He sobbed aloud, and at the sound the farm-hands clustering in the room breathed sighs of relief. They were only simple peasants, but on seeing Norbert, as white as if every drop of blood had been drawn from his body, with his lips quivering, and his eyes blazing with fever, they had asked themselves if he were not mad? Indeed, he was not far from it. But with these tears relief came to his brain; and with thought, suffering returned. Still he had again become sufficiently master of himself, when the doctor arrived, to appear before him simply as an anxious son.

"There is no hope for your father, marquis," said the rough spoken country practitioner, by no means trying to soften the blow he dealt. "Even if we succeed in saving his life, we can't hope to save his reason. The truth ought always to be told to a patient's relations, and there you have it! I shall return to-morrow."

Norbert did not escort the doctor down-stairs. He had fallen on to a chair, with his hands clasped round his head, which throbbed as if about to burst. He sat in this way for half an hour or more, when suddenly he started to his feet with a stifled cry. He remembered the bottle he had dropped the poison into, and which had been left in the common hall. What had been done with it? Suppose one of the servants had profited of the duke's illness, to imbibe its contents. Everything might then be discovered. The intensity of Norbert's fears gave him sufficient strength to go down-stairs. The bottle was neither on the table, nor in its ordinary place on the shelf. He was searching for it in every corner, when suddenly the door opened and Jean appeared. At sight of his young master, the old servant was so impressed that he almost dropped the light he carried. "Why are you here, sir?" he asked, in a trembling voice.

"I wanted—" stammered Norbert; "I was looking for—"

The servant's suspicions were instantly transformed into convictions. He approached, and whispered in his ear, "You are looking for that bottle, are you not? Well, it's safe. I have it in my room. To-morrow we two will throw its contents away, and there will be no proof left."

Jean spoke so low, hardly articulating the syllables, that Norbert divined these words rather from the movements of his lips than from any sound. And yet it seemed to the young marquis that the valet's voice, recalling his awful crime, resounded like thunder, filling the whole château from roof to cellar. "Hush!" he said, looking around him with wild, affrighted eyes. "Hush!"

What more explicit confession than this was required? "Oh! we are alone, sir," murmured Jean. "Fear nothing. There are words, I know, which should never be spoken. If I have dared speak to you of a matter which I accidentally discovered, it was because it was my duty to reassure you, and warn you against any imprudence."

Norbert at once realised that the servant thought him more guilty than he really was. "Jean," he exclaimed, "what do you believe? My father never tasted that wine! I snatched the glass from him before his lips had touched it. I threw it out into the court-yard, and if you look you will find its fragments there."

"I am not your judge, sir, and you need give me no explanations. Whatever you bid me believe, I will believe."

"Ah! he doubts me," rejoined Norbert. "He will not believe me. I swear, in the name of all I hold sacred, I swear to you that I am innocent!"

The old valet shook his head sadly. "You must be so, sir, of course; for we two must save the honour of the house. But listen to me. Should it so happen that any suspicions are aroused, throw them all on me, I will defend myself, but in such a way that they will have all the more reason to believe me guilty; and now I think of it, I won't throw that bottle away, but keep it in my room, where it may be found. That would be all the proof required. What does it matter how a poor man like me is sent to another world? but you, a Champdoce—"

Norbert wrung his hands in despair. Jean's sublime devotion only proved to him that the man was convinced of his guilt. Once more he was endeavouring to explain, when suddenly a door was heard being banged to on the floor above. "Hush!" said Jean; "some one is coming down. We must not be seen whispering together like two conspirators; suspicion would then certainly be awakened. I can't get rid of the idea that the secret may be read on my face, or in your eyes. Quick, sir! go up-stairs and do your best to be calm. I entreat you not to risk the honour of your family, it is that which is now at stake!"

Norbert obeyed, and regained his father's room. The servant who had been watching there rose as he entered, and exclaimed, "The medicine the doctor ordered has just come, sir. I have given the duke a spoonful, and it seems to have had some effect already." Norbert looked—he was bound to do so, for hesitation would have been suspicious—and concurred with what the man had said. Then, as he wished to be alone, he told the man he might retire, for he would watch his father with Jean, and see that the medicine was regularly given. The servant thereupon withdrew, and Norbert wheeled a large arm-chair in front of the bed, and sat down. In the state of mind in which he found himself, he could only with difficulty recall the series of swiftly succeeding events which had culminated in his abominable crime. But as he appealed, again and again, to memory, it seemed as if a bandage fell from his eyes—perception returned, and judgment also. He could still hear his father roughly exclaiming: "That girl is an *intrigante*, she does not love you, she loves your name and your fortune." He had then been indignant, and had thought these words blasphemous. Alas! the duke had been right. He saw it now. How happened it he had not realised that this girl was throwing herself at his head; that her reserve and her frankness alike were artificial; that she it was who had impelled him into this fatal path leading to such an awful precipice? The monstrous meaning of the comedy enacted by Dauman flashed upon him. She whom he had believed to be a pure and noble young girl had been the "judge's" accomplice. Between them they had excited him to madness, and finally, placed in his hands the poison intended for his father. He quivered with anguish as he realised all this, and his love for Diane de Sauvebourg turned to loathing.

Day broke at last, and worn out, he fell asleep. It was noon when he awoke. The sun was streaming into the room, and the doctor stood at the patient's bedside. He turned as Norbert stirred, and coming towards him exclaimed, "We shall save his body."

The prediction came true; that very night the Duke de Champdoce was able to turn over in his bed. The next day he uttered a few unintelligible words, and later again, he made those about him understand that he was hungry. His life was saved; but would not death have been a mercy? The powerful will that had guided his athletic form had vanished; his eyes had lost their glitter; his expression had become painfully idiotic. And there was no hope of cure, no hope of restoring the mind. The duke would be always thus—always! After realising the enormity of his crime, Norbert was now to measure the immensity of his chastisement.

It was now that Jean ventured to speak of M. de Puymandour's visit, and such was the change in Norbert that he regarded this circumstance as a direct warning from Heaven. "So be it," he said. "At least my father's wishes in this respect shall be carried out." And without loss of time, he wrote to M. de Puymandour that he expected him, adding that he hoped the sad catastrophe which had just occurred would in no way modify the arrangements his father had made. Thus did Norbert de Champdoce seal his fate.

X.

LIKE the miner who has lighted his train, and draws aside and waits for the explosion, Diane de Sauvebourg had retreated home after leaving Dauman. Great as were her energy and strength of mind she could barely hide her anxiety, and at supper-time found it almost impossible to eat. However, neither her father nor mother took any notice of her strange excitement. During the day, they had received news that their son—the young fellow for whose sake Diane was to be sacrificed—had been taken dangerously ill in Paris, where he habitually resided. This intelligence made them very anxious, and they talked of starting for the capital almost immediately. Thus they made no objection, and expressed no surprise, when, on leaving table, Diane complained of a bad headache, and asked permission to retire. Alone in her room, she experienced inexpressible relief. The thought of going to bed never occurred to her. She wrapped herself in a dressing-gown, and opening a window, leaned out over the balcony. She gazed long and earnestly in the direction of Champdoce, for despite the lateness of the hour, it seemed to her impossible that Norbert should not attempt to see her, or at least try to find some means of informing her, whether he had succeeded or failed. The dawn almost surprised her, still watching with the same feverish anxiety ; and as soon as practicable she went downstairs, and stationed herself in the garden at a point whence she could view the high road, hoping at each moment to see Norbert or some messenger arrive. No one appeared, however ; the breakfast bell rang, and she had to take her place once more between her parents, and again pretend to eat.

Finally, at about three o'clock in the afternoon, she could bear it no longer ; and so making her escape, she hurried towards Bivron, intending to see Dauman, who must, she thought, know something. Indeed, if he were as ignorant as herself, it would, at least, be a relief to talk with him, and ask him when, in his opinion, this terrible suspense would come to an end. No doubt he would speedily allay her apprehensions. In this she was mistaken. The "judge" had passed as wretched a night as herself, and had nearly died of terror. He had remained in his office all the morning, starting at the least noise and not daring to go out, desirous as he was of information, but the only news he had obtained, derived from a miller, who had called upon him, was that the Bivron doctor had been summoned to Champdoce the night before to attend on the duke, who was supposed to be dying. Dauman had just learnt this, and was feeling more nervous than ever when Diane arrived. At sight of her his pale face flushed, and, regardless of respect or civility, he uttered a terrible oath. "It's you, is it?" he said, "Why, what do you want? You are out of your senses to come here to-day. Do you want all Bivron to know that you and I are Norbert's accomplices?"

"Good heavens! what do you mean?"

"I mean that the duke isn't dead, and if he recovers we're lost. When I say 'we,' I mean myself of course ; for you will get clear of it all, being a nobleman's daughter. We all know that the nobility take care of themselves, so I shall have to pay the piper."

"You said that the effect was instantaneous."

"I said that? It's false. Ah! if I'd only known! But I mean to deny everything. You deceived me and robbed me! Oh, I mean to defend myself, you'll see. I'll drag all you nobles down into the gutter. I'm an honest man, I am. You ought to have done the job yourself. You've some blood in your veins, but that fool, your lover's the veriest capon out."

At these insulting words from such a scoundrel, she started up, and tried to protest, but he interrupted her : "I've no time to choose my words, for I feel as though I had a rope round my throat already. Now, do me a favour ; take yourself off, and never show your face here again."

"As you please. I will send to Champdoce."

"No, you won't!" exclaimed Dauman with a threatening gesture. "Why, while you're about it, why don't you go and ask old Champdoce how he liked his poison?"

But Diane was not deterred by this sarcasm. Anything seemed preferable to further suspense, and indeed, after a long discussion, she at last prevailed on Dauman to try and find out what had really occurred at the château. Thanks, however, to Jean's precautions, none of the other servants were in a position to tell the truth, as Dauman ascertained after various discreet inquiries addressed to such of them as came to Bivron. There was but one resource left, that of dispatching the widow Rouleau's daughter to the château on the morrow, on the pretence of claiming some sixty crowns which were owed him by one of the duke's keepers named Méchinet. Françoise Rouleau, alas! had paid her mother's debts to Dauman by the sacrifice of her own virtue, and was now obedient to his behests. He instructed her so skilfully that she had no suspicion of her real mission, and he accompanied her halfway on her journey, to a spot where, it was arranged, he should meet Diane later in the day.

He did not wait long for his messenger's return. In less than twenty minutes he saw her coming back, and he rose in all haste to meet her. "Well!" he asked breathlessly, "has that scamp of a Méchinet got me my money?"

"Alas! no, sir. I couldn't even speak to him."

"He wasn't there, then?"

"I don't even know that. Ever since the duke has been laid up, the gates of the château have been bolted, and not a human being is admitted. It seems he's very low."

"Did you hear what the matter was?"

"No, sir ; and all I tell you I learned from a stable boy, who spoke through the gate to me. But he hadn't said ten words before Jean arrived."

"Do you mean the duke's valet?"

"Precisely," answered Françoise ; "and Jean was furious. He raved at the boy, and told him to go back to the stable and stay there ; and then he unbolted the gate and asked me, 'Well, my girl, what do you want?' I told him I had come to see Méchinet ; but before I could say for what, he interrupted me and said, 'Well, he isn't here ; you can call again next month.'"

"And was that all you did, simpleton?"

"Not exactly; I said I must find Méchinet. And then old Jean looked at me and asked, 'Who sent you here, you little spy?'"

The "judge" started. "Ah! and what did you answer?"

"Why, I said *you* sent me, of course."

"Ah! yes, that was right; and then?"

"Then Jean rubbed his chin and looked at me again, and said, very slowly, 'So—you come from the "judge," eh? I might have known it. Yes, I see, and he'll see too! You may tell him he'll have news from me.'"

Dauman, at these words, felt his legs quake, but he could not continue his questions, for at that moment he saw M. de Puymandour approaching on his way to the château. What transpired between the "judge" and the count has already been recorded. Dauman learnt what was the nature of the duke's illness, and in his ignorance of the real events, ascribed the fit to the effects of the poison. He decided in his own mind that Norbert had not hesitated, that if he, Dauman, were prosecuted the marquis must be prosecuted as well, and as this last was a highly improbable contingency he considered himself virtually saved. "The fact is," he said to Diane when the latter reached the meeting place, "M. Norbert can't have given a sufficient dose. The duke, you know, is as strong as an ox. However, it will be all right. If he lives, he'll be an idiot, and our object is achieved the same as if he had died."

Still Diane was uneasy. "But why doesn't Norbert write?" she murmured. "Why?"

"Why? Because he had a vestige of common sense. Don't you know that there may be a dozen spies at his heels! We must wait."

They waited—waited for a week, but still no sign from Norbert. Diane suffered intolerable agony, and each successive day seemed more and more interminable. At last Sunday arrived. The Marchioness de Sauvebourg had risen betimes and gone to early mass, arranging that her daughter should go to high mass at ten o'clock, accompanied by her maid. This arrangement suited Diane to perfection, for she hoped she should see Norbert. Alas! no. The service had begun when she entered the church, but the Champdoce seats were vacant. It would have been mockery for her to pray, still she pretended to follow the service, though all the while she was absorbed in anxious thought. However, at one moment, while rather less preoccupied, she noticed that the priest was just mounting the pulpit stairs. The congregation was all attention, and no wonder, for before preaching it was usual for the curé to publish the banns of marriage, a matter of immense interest for all the assembled villagers. Like a man who enjoys keeping his audience in suspense, the old priest looked blandly round the church, coughed, wiped his spectacles and his nose, and then leisurely drew a sheet of paper from between the leaves of his missal. "I publish the banns of marriage—" he began, and then paused artfully enough, so as to stimulate his hearers' curiosity—"Between Monsieur Louis-Norbert de Dompair, Marquis de Champdoce, minor and legitimate son of Guillaume-César de Dompair, and of his late wife, Isabelle de Barneville, of this parish—and Demoiselle Désirée-Anne-Marie Palouzat, minor and legitimate daughter of René-Auguste Palouzat, Comte de Puymandour, and of the defunct Zoé Staplet, his wife, also of this parish."

Such was the thunder crash, which came from the pulpit, and seemed to deafen Diane. Her heart ceased to beat. She thought she was going to die. However, the priest continued, "This will be the first and last public cation of banns in view of the dispensation the contracting parties have obtained from our lord the archbishop. Any one who may know of any impediment to this marriage is charged, under penalty of excommunication, to acquaint us with it; while at this same time it is forbidden under the same penalty to create any impediment either in malice or without cause."

"Impediment!" What frightful irony. Mademoiselle de Sauvebourg knew of more than one. A wild longing came to her to start up and shriek aloud before them all, then and there, that this marriage could not take place; that Norbert was her husband before God; that he was bound to her by a tie stronger than all other ties—by that of crime. However, her pride saved her from this folly. She made a prodigious effort and remained still, white as snow, but with a smile on her lips; and seeing one of her friends—a young girl of her own age—she made her a little sign, as if to say, "Who would have thought of that?" Now she devoted all her energy to retaining a bold, dispassionate countenance, and such was her wonderful strength of mind that she succeeded. Still, as soon as the service was over, she did not linger to converse with friends, but hurried homewards, followed by her maid. She longed to be alone, longed to allow her grief full course, unseen.

But a fresh calamity awaited her at Sauvebourg. As she entered the château, a servant, who seemed greatly agitated, rushed to meet her. "Ah, mademoiselle!" gasped the man, "such a terrible misfortune! Your father and mother are waiting for you. It is terrible."

She went slowly upstairs. No doubt she was going to learn that her intrigue with Norbert had been discovered, perhaps even something worse. When she entered the drawing-room, she perceived her father and mother sitting near each other and weeping. She went towards them, and the marquis, drawing her to him, pressed her tenderly to his heart. "Poor child!" he murmured; "poor, dear child; we have only you now."

Their son was dead. An express had brought the sad news while she was at church. She was an only child now, heiress to one of the largest fortunes in the province. If this catastrophe had occurred only one week before, it would have assured her marriage with Norbert, and she would never have committed that frightful crime. This was something more than the grim sarcasm of destiny—it was a chastisement. She burst into tears, not tears for her brother, but tears of rage and passion.

She could only think of Norbert, and still seemed to hear the old priest reading the banns of marriage. Why had her lover decided on marrying Marie de Puymandour, whom he did not even know, whom he had spoken of with loathing only a few days previously? Diane scented a mystery and determined to solve it. What had taken place at Champdoce? Had the duke, contrary to Dauman's predictions, recovered? Had he discovered his son's attempt, and pardoned it only on conditions he now yielded to his will? The day passed away in these futile conjectures, and in efforts to think of some means of preventing Norbert from marrying Marie de Puymandour; for Diane, cast down as she was, had not relinquished the struggle. She had a presentiment that she might triumph yet, providing she could only see Norbert for one minute alone. Had she not already, with one single look, influenced his career? Yes, she must see him, and instantly. The danger was urgent; so she determined she would go to Champdoce that very night.

A little after midnight, when she knew that everyone in the château was asleep, she threw a mantle over her shoulders, crept down the stairs on tip-toe, and passed out through a side door.

Norbert had often described to her the arrangements of the château de Champdoce, and she knew that his room was on the ground floor, with two windows looking on to the court-yard. This was all she needed. Still, on reaching her destination, she hesitated. Supposing she mistook the window! However, she had now gone too far to retreat; and so, after deciding that if any one else but Norbert opened the window, she would turn and fly, she rapped against one of the shutters, softly at first, and then more roughly. Her memory had not deceived her. It was Norbert who appeared at the casement and inquired, "Who's there?"

"It is I, Norbert; it is I—Diane," she replied, and as the window was but a few feet from the ground, she boldly sprung into the room before he could recover from his surprise.

"What do you want?" asked Norbert wildly. "What brings you here?"

She looked at him; his face seemed almost that of a stranger, so greatly had he changed. She felt frightened, but had strength to murmur, "Do you really intend to marry Mademoiselle de Puymandour?"

"Yes."

"And yet you pretended you loved me?"

All Norbert's feelings of resentment, born on that sleepless night he had passed at his father's bedside, were revived. "Yes," he answered, "I loved you devotedly—madly, with a love that drove me to crime. But you—you cared only for a princely fortune and the title of duchess."

Diane raised her arms with a despairing gesture. "Should I be here at this hour if that were true? My brother is dead—I am as rich as you, Norbert, and yet I am here. You accuse me of mercenary calculations; and why? I suppose, because I refused to fly with you from my father's roof. Oh! my friend, it was our future happiness that I defended; it was—" She paused, breathless, and her eyes dilated with horror. The door had opened, and the Duke de Champdoce appeared, babbling incoherently, and laughing in that meaningless style peculiar to idiots.

"Do you understand now," asked Norbert, "why the remembrance of our love has become intolerable to me? Can you talk to me of happiness, when my father's phantom will ever more rise between us?" So saying he pointed to the window, and a moment later she had sprung out into the court-yard once more.

But rage and jealousy were gnawing at her heart. She could not forgive Norbert this crime she herself had committed—this crime which had blighted all her hopes, and her parting words were threats. "I shall avenge myself, Norbert," she cried. "We will meet again!"

XI.

ONLY three days—busy days, it is true—had been needed to complete the preliminaries of Norbert's marriage with Mademoiselle de Puymandour. One Saturday evening the two young people were presented to each other. They were mutually displeased; and at the first glance each felt that instinctive repugnance for the other which often cannot be conquered after long years of companionship. Whilst her father was goading her into submission, Marie had thought of confiding the secret of her heart to Norbert, hoping that he might be generous enough to abandon his suit, when he learned that she loved another. But, alas ! she was weak and fearful, and at the decisive moment did not dare to speak ; thus losing the only chance of escaping a life of torture. At the first word on her part, Norbert would certainly have withdrawn, happy to avail himself of this pretext not to ratify the arrangements his father had made ; but then Marie remained silent, and thus events followed their natural course.

He was now allowed to pay his court, and presented himself each day at the Puymandour château carrying the traditional bouquet. He was regularly shown to the salon, where he presented the flowers to Marie with a compliment, while she accepted both bouquet and flattery with a burning blush. Then the two seated themselves, and, whilst an aged female relative played propriety, remained together for several hours ; Marie leaning over her embroidery-frame, and Norbert sadly out of countenance—both at a loss to keep up even a commonplace conversation. It was positive relief for both of them when M. de Puymandour proposed an excursion in the environs ; for with a man of his talkative disposition there was no irksome silence to fear. But then this seldom happened, the count declaring that he had not a moment to himself.

Never, indeed, had he seemed so gay and lively as since his daughter's marriage had been decided on. Despite the distressing condition of the Duke de Champdoce and Norbert's appeals, he had determined that the wedding should be a most magnificent affair, and incessantly busied himself with the preparations. The château was furnished anew for the festivities to be given therein. The carriages were all done up and repainted, with the Champdoce arms added to the Puymandour's. These arms were everywhere—over all the doors, carved on all the furniture, engraved on all the plate. Had it been at all advisable, M. de Puymandour would have even consented to their being burnt into his breast.

Amid this incessant stir and bustle, Marie and Norbert both grew sadder and more hopeless day by day. But M. de Puymandour pretended not to notice it. One afternoon, while they sat as usual in the salon, looking as woe-begone as two sinners performing penance, the count hurried in, all importance and excitement. "Well, well, children !" he exclaimed ; " your example is so good a one that all the world seems inclined to follow it, and the mayor and the curé will be kept pretty busy this year." Mademoiselle Marie tried to look interested. "Yes," continued her father, "I have just heard of a wedding which will almost immediately follow yours, and make some little commotion too."

"And whose is that ?" asked Norbert.

"I suppose you know the Count de Mussidan's son, Viscount Octave, who usually lives in Paris ? Well, he has been staying here lately with his father, and in one short week he has lost his heart. Can you guess to whom ? No, no doubt ; but I'll tell you. He is about to marry Mademoiselle Diane de Sauvebourg."

"I hardly think that possible," urged Marie. "Why, she lost her brother only a fortnight ago ! "

Whilst his *fiancée* spoke, Norbert had flushed scarlet and then turned absolutely livid. So great was his confusion that he nearly dropped the album he held.

However, M. de Puymandour proceeded . "I decidedly approve of Viscount Octave's choice. Mademoiselle Diane has not merely her beauty to boast of ; she seems to me a most accomplished young person. She has a most distinguished air ; and as to her mind, I have reason to think her wonderfully clever." Thereupon he turned towards his daughter and added, "Now there's a model, Marie, which I should like you to copy—which it would be well for you to imitate—as you are so soon to become a duchess."

Whenever he started on this topic, M. de Puymandour was not easily stopped, so his daughter calmly waited till he drew a long breath, and then left the room with a murmured apology of an order to give. However, the count was not much disturbed by her defection, for Norbert was left to him. "To return to Mademoiselle Diane," said he, "black is wonderfully becoming to her. Indeed, fair-haired beauties ought really to consider a relative's death as a piece of rare good luck. But I beg your pardon for singing her praises to you, who know her so much better than any one else."

"I, sir?"

"Yes, sir, you. I don't suppose you intend to deny the soft impeachment, do you?"

"I don't understand—"

"Well, I do, then. I understand that—that you have been making love to her, and that quite lately, my lad! Bless my soul! how you blush! What's in the wind now?"

"I assure you, sir—"

De Puymandour laughed aloud. "I have heard a good deal of your little walks and talks, and all that sort of thing," said he.

In vain did Norbert protest and deny. His words did not make the least impression on the count. Seeing this, and feeling excessively annoyed, the young fellow would not remain to dinner, as M. de Puymandour urged him to do, but declared he must return home to attend on his father. He was walking hastily back to Champdoce, lost in a reverie as usual, when suddenly he heard some one call to him by name. He turned, and to his surprise recognised Montlouis, the farmer's son, who had been his friend and confidant at Poitiers. "I'm glad to see you," said Norbert, with some little embarrassment, for Montlouis reminded him of much that he longed to forget. "How long have you been here?"

"A week or so," replied Montlouis; "I came here with my patron—for I have a patron now. The Viscount de Mussidan has engaged me as his private secretary. M. Octave is not the pleasantest man in the world to live with, for at times he flies into terrible passions; but after all, he is at heart the best of men, and so I'm very well content with my position."

"I am very glad to hear it, my friend, very glad."

"And you, marquis, I'm told, are to marry Mademoiselle de Puymandour. When I heard it I could hardly believe my ears."

"And why, pray?"

"Why? because I remembered the time when we used to wait outside a certain garden till we saw a certain gate open mysteriously."

"But you must forget all that, Montlouis."

"Oh, sir! my lips are sealed except to you; no one else could ever extort a word from me. But, nevertheless, there are some strange things in life. Just fancy, your castaway—"

"Stop!" cried Norbert with a threatening gesture; "do you dare imagine—"

"Imagine what, sir?"

"I wish you to understand that Mademoiselle de Sauvebourg is as pure to-day as she was when I saw her first. She was foolish, unquestionably, but guilty—no! I swear it before God!"

"And I believe you, sir; I believe you."

The fact is that he did not believe one word that Norbert said, and it was easy to read that it was so in his eyes. Still, he boldly resumed, "And all the more, too, as the young lady is to marry my patron."

"Then, it's really true," thought Norbert, and he added, aloud, "But when and where has Viscount Octave had means of seeing Mademoiselle Diane?"

"At Paris M. Octave was very intimate with her brother, and visited him constantly during his illness; so, as soon as the parents heard of his being in the neighbourhood, they sent for him to come and see them. He went at once, saw Mademoiselle Diane, and has ever since been most enthusiastic about her." Norbert's irritation was so evident that Montlouis checked himself, convinced that the marquis was still in love with Diane, and jealous into the bargain. "After all," he added, by way of consolation, "nothing is finally settled, as yet."

But Norbert was too much disturbed to endure Montlouis' chatter any longer. He pressed his hand and left him abruptly, walking off at a rapid pace. Did he really love Diane still? he asked himself. Could he never forget her? Was he such a coward as that, after all she had made him suffer? And then, love or passion apart, did not the future seem most threatening? Mademoiselle de Sauvebourg would marry the Viscount Octave de Mussidan, no doubt, and thus she must, constantly, come into contact with Montlouis, her husband's secretary. What would be her feelings in such a situation? Montlouis was acquainted with her meetings with himself (Norbert); he had often been intrusted with letters and messages for her. Besides, how would he behave on his side? Would he have the *sang froid* and tact required in so delicate a position? Norbert decided in his own mind that Diane would not be able to long endure Montlouis' presence near her person. Such being the case, she would seek some pretext for his dismissal, and if that happened, Montlouis, enraged at losing a comfortable livelihood, might retaliate by exposing her. Then, no doubt, M. de Mussidan would part from his wife. Diane would be cast on the world, beyond the pale of society, with all the social influence she had, undoubtedly, dreamt of, lost to her for ever. What would she do then? Would she not seek for revenge? And on whom? Why on himself, Norbert.

He had just asked himself if in these circumstances death would not really be a mercy, when suddenly, to his intense surprise, he saw the widow Rouleau's daughter, Françoise, standing before him. She had been waiting for him for two hours, hidden behind a hedge. "I have something here for you, sir," she said.

He took the letter she offered him, and opening it, he read as follows:—

"You said that I did not love you, you wish me to prove my love, possibly. Very well, let us elope to-night. I shall be sacrificed—but to you, by you, and for you! Reflect, Norbert. There is time still; to-morrow it will be too late." Yes, that is what Diane had dared to write. He stood with his eyes long fixed on this letter, which to him was thrillingly eloquent. Then did it not tell him something of the thoughts of her who penned it? Diane's usually firm, neat writing was here trembling and confused. The three last words were nearly illegible. In many places the writing was blurred and the paper blistered, was it with tears? But then writing may be

intentionally irregular, and drops of water sometimes do duty for tears.
"Does she love me?" he murmured.

He hesitated—yes, he hesitated, touched by the idea that she would
sacrifice for him her honour, family and fortune; that she was his if he
raised his finger; that in two hours, seated by her side, he might be driving
at full speed towards some foreign land. His heart beat madly, and he
gasped for breath, when suddenly, fifty paces down the road, he caught a
glimpse of a man's figure. It was his father. This was the second time
that by his simple presence the duke had triumphed over Diane and all her
power of fascination.

"Never!" cried Norbert, with such energy that Françoise retreated,
terrified. "Never! never!" And crushing the letter with unconscious
violence, he flung it on the ground (where Françoise picked it up a moment
later), and rushed forward to meet his father.

The duke, then, had recovered from his attack? Recovered, yes, in one
sense. In the sense that his life was saved—that he rose from bed, walked
about, ate and slept as of yore. He went to look at the labourers in the
fields, and thence strolled to the stables; but he had no recollection of
what he saw nor even consciousness of it. The state of his health had,
indeed, created many difficulties, which would have seriously embarrassed
Norbert but for M. de Puymandour's shrewd assistance.

The wedding was necessarily delayed. Still it came at last. Norbert
and his bride were driven to the mayor's, and thence to the church, every
formality was fulfilled, and the Marquis de Champdoce and Marie de Puymandour were yoked together for life.

Five days later, after a round of hypocritical festivities which the bride's
father obstinately refused to curtail, they were installed at Champdoce.
With a wife whom he could not love, and whose sadness was a perpetual
reproach to him, and with a father who had lost his mind, no wonder that
Norbert at times felt tempted to suicide. A prey to regrets and remorse,
seeing no object in life, no finish to his tortures, this fatal idea of self
destruction was daily gaining more hold on his mind, when one morning he
was told that the duke refused to get up. The doctor was sent for, and at
once declared that M. de Champdoce was in danger. A kind of reaction
was setting in, and all day long the invalid seemed to be in a state of great
excitement. His powers of speech, which had been much impaired, seemed
suddenly restored to him. Finally, he became delirious, whereupon
Norbert and Jean sent everyone else away from him, lest, in some incoherent phrase, those dread words, parricide or poison, should be pronounced.

At about eleven o'clock he became calmer, and seemed drowsy, but all at
once he started up in bed. "Come here!" he cried, whereupon Norbert
and Jean hastened to the bedside, and were much startled to find that he
had regained his old expression of face; his eyes flashing and his lips
trembling as in moments of great excitement. "Pardon me, father!" cried
Norbert, falling on his knees. "Pardon me!"

M. de Champdoce gently extended his hand. "My pride was unreasonable and God punished me," said he. "My son, I forgive you."

The young man sobbed aloud. "I renounce my projects, my son. I do
not wish you to marry Mademoiselle de Puymandour if you do not love
her."

"I have obeyed you, my father," Norbert answered. "She is my wife
already."

On hearing this, M. de Champdoce's features expressed the most frightful anguish ; he raised his arms as if to drive away a phantom, and, in a
hoarse voice, he cried : " Too late ! Too late ! " Then he fell back on his
pillows in convulsions. He was dead !

If it be true, as is asserted, that for the dying the veil of the future is
sometimes torn away, then the Duke de Champdoce must have had a
frightful vision of mental torture and misery, infamy, and bloodshed.

XII.

REPELLED by Norbert at that interview in his room at night time, Diane,
with death in her heart, turned towards the château de Sauvebourg, following the same road she had so lately traversed palpitating with hope.
The apparition of the Duke de Champdoce had terrified her ; but, with
her, impressions were fleeting, and at home once more, in the seclusion of
her own room, she even smiled at her alarm. She had threatened Norbert,
but she now realised that it was not he whom she hated, but rather that
rival who had robbed her of him—Marie de Puymandour. As this
marriage could not be broken off by bringing influence to bear on Norbert,
she must change her tactics, and see if on Mademoiselle de Puymandour's
side there was not some reason that would suffice to prevent the wedding.
With this object Diane commenced an inquiry into her rival's antecedents.

She was busy with her investigations when the Viscount Octave de Mussidan was introduced to her. He was a tall, handsome young man, highly
educated and possessed of a considerable fortune. When he was presented
to Diane de Sauvebourg, it was, on his side, a case of love—ardent, passionate love at first sight. But with Diane matters were different. Octave
was too much unlike Norbert to please her. There was no possible point
of comparison between this well-bred, accomplished young nobleman of
supremely aristocratic tastes, and that veriest child of nature, "the Champdoce savage." It seemed to Diane that nothing could ever efface Norbert's
image from her memory. How well she recollected their first interview—
his rustic garments, his shyness, his consternation at having wounded her !
She was the first woman he had ever dared look upon—ah ! how pleadingly eloquent had been the gaze of his bright blue eyes. At all events,
whatever may have been Diane's thoughts, Octave de Mussidan was fairly
smitten, and returned home more and more entranced from each visit he
paid to Sauvebourg. At last he could control himself no longer, and decided to ask Diane if he might dare to apply to her parents for her hand.
Having succeeded in finding himself alone with her, he presented his request in a trembling, respectful voice. Diane was exceedingly surprised, for
she had been so absorbed in her own affairs that she had not even suspected
his feelings. What should she answer? The viscount's prayer snatched
her as it were from dreamland, and brought her face to face with the reality
of life. However, she could not give a decided answer on the spot. She
must have time for reflection. Hence she replied, with well affected
timidity, that on the morrow she would tell him whether he might hope or
not. She hesitated all night long. Must she really relinquish Norbert?
Must she really abandon all hope of reaping the fruits of the crime she had
instigated ? The result of her meditations was the letter she intrusted to
the widow Rouleau's daughter—the letter in which she had offered to
elope with Norbert, and which he had so furiously flung aside at sight of

his father. Diane had been anxiously waiting at the end of the park for her messenger's return, and at sight of her hastened forward, asking, "Have you an answer? what did he say?"

"Nothing—that is, he made a furious gesture and cried out, 'Never! no, never!'"

As it was necessary this girl's suspicions should not be aroused, Diane had sufficient strength to laugh aloud, as she rejoined, "That is just what I thought!"

Françoise seemed inclined to say something more, but Diane hastily dismissed her with the present of a louis. There was to be no more uncertainty, doubt and anguish now, no more struggling, no other hope than that of vengeance. She was thankful now for Octave's love, and said to herself that, once married, she should be free, and able to follow Norbert and his wife to Paris.

When she returned to the château, Octave was there. He questioned her with his eyes, and with a slight grave bow she gave her assent. This consent, she thought, would free her from the past. But, alas! she was mistaken. She forgot her many follies and acts of imprudence, and most especially she was oblivious of that scoundrel Dauman. The latter had only felt fully reassured as to the consequences of the crime when he ascertained the duke had absolutely lost his reason, and that the doctor, regarding the case as hopeless, had ceased visiting Champdoce. Then as he heard, in succession, of Norbert's marriage and the duke's death, the horizon seemed fair indeed. All danger was over, and he recalled the important fact that he possessed twenty thousand francs' worth of notes signed by Norbert, which were worth their full amount now that the young man reigned at Champdoce.

Still after all, thought he, twenty thousand francs was but a small sum, quite inadequate to recoup him for all the risk he had incurred, all the suspense and anxiety he had endured; hence why should he not make a bold bid for a larger amount, which would enable him to spend his last years in comfortable retirement. Influenced by this idea, Dauman began roaming about Sauvebourg, hoping that he might meet Diane alone, and have a little private conversation with her. For several days he was unsuccessful, but at last one afternoon he perceived Mademoiselle de Sauvebourg walking towards Bivron. He followed her cautiously, and without accosting her as long as she kept to the high road; but as soon as she took a bye-path leading through a small wood he hastened forward and overtook her. "What do you want?" she asked hastily, as soon as she perceived him.

He did not answer at once, but after apologizing for his audacity, he began to congratulate Diane on her marriage, which everyone was now talking about, and which, he said, delighted him, especially as he knew M. de Mussidan to be far superior to—

"Is that all you have to say?" she asked; but as she turned away he had the impudence to restrain her by the corner of her shawl.

"I have something more to add," he replied, "if you will listen; something about—you know what."

"About what, indeed?" she asked, with no effort to conceal her utter contempt.

He smiled, looked round to see that no one was near, and then leaning towards Diane, whispered, "It is about the poison."

She started back as if fearing a serpent's sting. "What do you mean? What do you dare to say?" she asked.

But he had resumed his obsequious air, and relapsed into complaints and recriminations ! What an abominable trick she had played him ! She had stolen his black glass phial. If the truth had been discovered, he would have paid, with his head, for a crime he was innocent of. He had really been made ill by this suspense and mental torture ; he could not sleep at night, and he was haunted by remorse. .

"That's enough !" exclaimed Diane, stamping her foot; "that's enough !"

"Ah, well, mademoiselle, I cannot stay here at Bivron any longer ; I'm too uneasy. I wish to leave for some foreign land."

"Tell me what all this preamble means."

He answered in an obsequious, roundabout, desultory fashion, and Diane had great difficulty in bringing him to the point. At last, however, he confessed he wished for something to console him in his exile—a souvenir—a little help. In fact, he needed a sum which would bring him in a modest yearly income of some three thousand francs.

"I understand," she interrupted, "you wish to make me pay for what you call your devotion."

"Mademoiselle—"

"And you estimate it at sixty thousand francs. That's rather dear, I think."

"Alas ! that is not half what this miserable affair has cost me."

"Nonsense ! I know what to think of your demand."

"Demand," he retorted. "I come to you humbly, hat in hand, asking alms. If I demanded this money, I should approach you in a very different way. I should say : 'I want such and such a sum, or I shall speak.' What have I to lose after all, if everything were told? Almost nothing. I am a poor man, and I am old. Monsieur Norbert and you, mademoiselle, are the ones who are in danger. You are young, and rich, and noble, and the future is full of happiness for you."

Diane reflected for a moment. "You are talking," she said, "in a very foolish way. When certain charges are made against certain people there must be proofs."

"That's true, mademoiselle; but how do you know that I haven't proofs? But if you prefer to purchase them of course you have the best right as well as the first choice, so don't complain." As he spoke, he drew from his pocket a greasy portfolio, and took from it a paper which bore signs of having been crumpled up and then smoothed out again.

Diane gave it a glance, and then stifled an exclamation of mingled rage and fear. She recognized the last note she had sent by the widow Rouleau's daughter to Norbert. "Ah !" she cried, "Françoise has betrayed me—probably because I saved her mother from starvation." Then as the "judge" held out the letter, she tried to snatch it from him fancying he did not distrust her.

But wily Dauman was on his guard. With an ironical gesture he swiftly drew back his hand, and secured the note in his pocket again. "Oh no ! if you please," said he, "this letter isn't that little black phial. Still I will give it to you, with another I have, when you give me what I want. But nothing for nothing ! Mind, if I'm arrested, I prefer to be in good company when I stand in the dock."

Mademoiselle de Sauvebourg was in despair. "But I have no money," she cried. "A young girl has no money !"

"But Monsieur Norbert has."

"Go to him, then."

Dauman shook his head. "No," he replied, "I'm not quite such a simpleton. I know Monsieur Norbert; he's his father over again. But you, mademoiselle, can manage him. Besides, you are even more interested in the question than he is."

"Judge !"

"Oh, you'll find that there is something more than the 'judge' concerned. I came to you humbly enough, and you treated me like the dirt under your feet. However, I won't submit to such treatment, as you will find. I never poisoned any one ! But enough recrimination. This is Tuesday. If on Friday, before six o'clock, I don't receive what I want, your father and M. de Mussidan will hear from me. And perhaps you won't be married after all !"

Mademoiselle de Sauvebourg was absolutely aghast at such impudence, and Dauman had disappeared before she could think of a retort calculated to wither him. She understood perfectly well that he was the man to execute his threats, even if he seriously compromised himself, and gained no advantage whatever in doing so. Strong natures do not procrastinate, but try to cope with difficulties as speedily as possible. Thus it was with Diane; but then she had little or no choice in her decision. Indeed her only resource was to apply to Norbert. She of course knew that he would do all in his power to avert danger which threatened himself as much as her ; but the idea of applying to him for money—for this is what it amounted to— was odious to her pride. Her pride, indeed ! She, a Sauvebourg born, was at the mercy of that vile Dauman, and must do his bidding ! Ay, there was no help for it.

Thus instead of continuing her road, she repaired at once to the widow Rouleau's, and addressing Françoise as if she were not acquainted with her perfidy—indeed dissimulation was highly requisite—she bade her go to Champdoce, speak to Norbert alone, and tell him that a pressing emergency required that he should come that night to the little park gate at Sauve-bourg where she would be waiting for him.

Then she went home. For the rest of the day she endured intolerable agony of mind, and as the hour of rendezvous drew near, her heart beat as if about to burst, and the most terrible doubts assailed her. Would Norbert come ? Had Françoise seen him ? Suppose he had been away from home ! At last it grew dark, and the servants entered the salon with the lamps. Octave de Mussidan was there paying his court as usual : still Diane contrived to slip away, and reached the park gate in breathless haste. Norbert was already waiting for her, and as soon as she appeared, he sprung forward—but then, as if overtaken by a sudden remembrance, he drew back and in a grating, guttural voice exclaimed, "You sent for me, mademoiselle ? "

"Yes, Monsieur le Duc."

At this title, dropping without thought from her lips, they both started. This title Norbert owed to his father's death, and that death was due to Diane's wish to become a duchess.

She recovered her self-possession first ; and at once feeling the need of haste and decision, she began with extreme volubility to explain Dauman's insulting demand, exaggerating all his threats, albeit there was little need of doing so. She fancied that the "judge's" rascality would enrage Norbert, but he had suffered so intensely that he had now become insensible to misfortune. Hence, to Diane's surprise, he merely answered listlessly,

"Don't he troubled, I will see Danman." So saying, he turned as if anxious to withdraw.

"And you can leave me thus," she asked sadly, "without a word?"

"What can I say, mademoiselle? My dying father forgave me—I forgive you. Adieu."

"Adieu, then, Norbert, we shall see no more of each other. I am about to be married as you have probably heard. Can I resist my parents' will? Besides, what does it matter? Farewell! Remember that there is no one in the world who hopes so earnestly for your happiness as I do."

"Happiness!" cried Norbert. "I happy? Impossible! Can *you* be happy again? If you can, teach me your secret—tell me how to forget, and how to annihilate thought. Perhaps you don't know the dream I had indulged in—a dream of happiness, the memory of which will be the despair of my life. Were I to live a thousand years I could never forget it."

A gleam of triumph, of ferocious joy in fact, came into Diane's eyes as she heard these words. She had dreaded this interview, but to her surprise it had occasioned her little or no painful emotion. "He loves me still," she murmured, "and I no longer love him. My vengeance will be an easy task."

Two days afterwards, Jean, the old Champdoce servant, approached Diane as she was returning home from walking, and handed her a package. She opened it in the seclusion of her room, and found that it contained not merely the two letters Dauman had spoken of, but her entire correspondence with Norbert—more than a hundred missives, all of them lengthy and compromising. At first she thought of destroying them, but on reflection she carefully hid the package, together with the letters she had received from Norbert. "Who knows?" she murmured, "they may be of use some day."

The sixty thousand francs given by Norbert to Danman as hush money, and the twenty thousand due on the notes of hand, apparently represented the height of the "judge's" ambition, for, a week afterwards, he mysteriously disappeared from the neighbourhood in the company of Françoise, mother Rouleau's daughter. Mother Rouleau went about repeating that Diane had favoured this abominable intrigue; and the old woman who had served as Dauman's housekeeper, declared to the amazement of the villagers that the "judge" had never been a *huissier* at all, but had acquired all his legal knowledge in a convict prison, where he had been detained ten years. Diane was delighted to hear of the elopement of the "judge" and Françoise. She was now at least rid of two of her accomplices. Moreover, Norbert had started for Paris with his wife, and M. de Puymandour repeated on all sides that there was little chance of his daughter, the Duchess de Champdoce, returning to Poitou for a long time to come.

At last, Diane and Octave de Mussidan were married. She had literally enslaved him, so fervent was his passion, and she considered she would be able to mould their life in accordance with her pleasure. All the dark clouds had passed away, and the future seemed to be her own. She planned out a gay existence in Paris, an existence of fêtes and social successes, at the same time bearing in mind the vengeance she intended to wreak on Norbert and Marie de Puymandour.

On her wedding day she seemed radiant, though in point of fact, her apparent delight was only so much bravado. She knew that every eye was fixed upon her as she came out of the church, and she espied many an evil minded look on the faces of the villagers. The happy pair drove at once to the château de Mussidan, and there a terrible, unexpected misfortune awaited Diane. There indeed, in the drawing-room, stood her husband's secretary, Montlouis, and despite all her courage and audacity, she coloured to the roots of her hair when he was presented to her. He, fortunately, had foreseen this emergency, and having had time to prepare for it, retained an apparently impassive attitude. Still, respectful as was his obeisance, Diane—now Madame de Mussidan—detected, or thought she detected, in his eyes the same threatening expression of ironical contempt as she had so often seen in Dauman's. "That man cannot stay here," she thought. Still, however simple, it was withal a dangerous thing to ask her husband to send Montlouis away at once. The wisest course was to defer the secretary's dismissal until some good pretext offered itself. Nor was this occasion long in coming; for Montlouis, zealous enough in Paris, had wonderfully relaxed in punctuality since his arrival at Mussidan. He had, in fact, renewed his connection with the young girl he had courted before going to Paris. M. de Mussidan was by no means pleased with the change in his secretary's conduct, and indeed this sort of thing could not, of course, go on. However, the first blow struck at Diane's newborn happiness did not come from this direction.

She had been married a fortnight or so, and was strolling one afternoon with her husband through the woods, when all at once a dog was heard barking in the underbrush. A moment later and the animal appeared. It was Bruno. The sagacious spaniel immediately recognised Diane, bounded towards her, raised himself on his hind-legs, and, with his fore-paws resting on her breast, tried to lick her face. Diane was inexpressibly agitated. "Help me, Octave!" she gasped.

Her husband at once complied, driving Bruno on one side. "Has the dog frightened you, dear?" he asked.

"Yes," she answered faintly; "I am sick with terror." She was very pale and shuddered at this recognition—shuddered at the thought that it might excite her husband's suspicions.

M. de Mussidan was watching Bruno, who, quite surprised by this unfavourable reception, looked questioningly at Diane with his bright, intelligent eyes. "I'm sure the dog can have meant no harm," exclaimed the viscount.

"No matter. Pray drive him away." And as she spoke, Diane raised her parasol; but the dog, never supposing it to be a threat, fancied that his old friend wished to play with him as formerly, and at once began leaping round her, barking joyfully at every bound.

"Why, this dog knows you, Diane," remarked the viscount.

"Knows me!" As she spoke Bruno licked her hand. "Well, perhaps I may have met him before, but I hardly know where; his memory is better than mine. At all events I don't feel quite at ease. Come, Octave, let us go."

They turned their steps homewards, and Octave de Mussidan would have forgotten the occurrence if Bruno, delighted at having met an old acquaintance, had not obstinately followed Diane. "It's singular," repeated the viscount; "very singular. Look here, my man!" he cried, seeing a peasant at work in a field, "do you know this dog?"

"Oh yes, sir."

"To whom does he belong, pray?"

"Why, to our master, sir; to Monsieur Norbert de Champdoce."

On hearing her old lover's name, Diane could not repress a shudder.

"Ah! to be sure," she exclaimed, speaking with mingled haste and embarrassment. "I remember the dog now. I used to see him at widow Rouleau's; he was always following her daughter about. Oh yes, I know him now. Let's see, his name's Bruno, I think. Here, Bruno! here!" The dog hastened to her, and she stooped, less to fondle him, however, than to hide her burning face.

Octave and his wife walked home almost without speaking. The young husband was oppressed by a vague doubt, and Diane herself felt much disturbed. She cursed herself for having been so foolish—so cowardly. Why hadn't she recognised the dog at once? Her conduct had been preposterous. If she had immediately exclaimed, "It's Bruno, the Duke de Champdoce's dog," her husband would have attached no importance to the matter; but her own folly had transformed this simple incident into a great event. Octave indeed seemed greatly preoccupied, and she even detected a look of suspicion in his eyes. How could she make him forget this unfortunate occurrence? She took it into her head to feign the greatest fear of dogs, as if that might explain the incident; having her husband's chained up, and shrieking whenever she perceived one. But the device hardly answered her purpose as she realised; the very ground of Mussidan seemed to burn her feet; she longed to fly—to go away, no matter where. It had originally been arranged that the young pair should spend their honeymoon abroad; but events had decided otherwise, and from various causes they were compelled to linger at Mussidan from week to week. Diane did not dare to openly advocate a prompt departure; but she exerted all her feminine diplomacy with that end in view, for a presentiment warned her that delay could only bring about a catastrophe. Alas! her attempts were fruitless, and the catastrophe came.

It was one Thursday, the 26th of October, about four o'clock in the afternoon. Diane had just finished dressing, and was looking out of her bedroom window, when suddenly an excited crowd poured into the court-yard of the château. In the rear came a party of peasants carrying a litter covered with a blood-stained sheet, beneath which the outline of a human form could be distinguished. This appalling sight held Diane spell-bound; she could not tear herself from the window. That morning her husband and one of his intimate friends, the Baron de Clinchan, had started out on a shooting expedition, accompanied by Montlouis and a keeper named Ludovic. Had some fatality overtaken the party? Which of the four lay under that sheet? Was it her husband? No; for Octave now appeared, looking pale and haggard, and leaning on the arms of Ludovic and M. de Clinchan. So the dead man, then, was Montlouis, the secretary.

Ah! it would no longer be necessary for her to intrigue for his dismissal. He would never speak more, this side the grave. Diane felt as if her path had been cleared of a terrible danger; and anxious to ascertain how the catastrophe had occurred, she darted from her room down the stairs. But, midway, she encountered M. de Clinchan, who was coming up, and who, on perceiving her, caught her by the arm and exclaimed in a strange, harsh voice, "Go back, madame, go back!"

"But in heaven's name what has happened?" asked Diane, seized with a vague alarm.

"A frightful misfort e. Return to your room, I entreat you; your husband will be her presently." Then, as she still hesitated, he fairly pushed her upstairs again into her own apartment.

A moment later Octave appeared, and on perceiving his wife held out his arms, drew her to his breast, and burst into sobs.

"He weeps!" exclaimed M. de Clinchan. "He is saved! I thought he would go mad." Then, after many questions and incoherent replies, Madame de Mussidan learnt that her husband had accidentally killed Montlouis whilst aiming at some game.

She fully believed in this fatality. And yet the truth was not told her. Montlouis had really been killed by her, just as the Duke de Champdoce had been. He had died because he knew her secret, and had partially revealed it. In point of fact, the whole party had lunched together in the woods of Bivron, and M. de Mussidan, somewhat exhilarated by a bottle of Sauternes, had begun jesting with his secretary on account of his unpunctuality and frequent absence from the château. Some woman was at the bottom of it, no doubt, added the viscount; and his raillery became so displeasing to Montlouis, that the latter at last made an angry retort. M. de Mussidan immediately fired up, declared he would not allow such escapades to continue, and added that he was surprised his secretary should risk a comfortable position for the sake of some worthless creature. "Not another word, sir," cried Montlouis, who had become ghastly pale. "I forbid you—"

He spoke in such a threatening tone that the viscount fancied he was about to spring upon him, and accordingly he raised his hand to strike his disrespectful secretary. Montlouis avoided the blow; but fairly enraged, and altogether losing his head, he exclaimed, "What right have you to talk in that way; you, who have married another man's mistress? Why do you talk of worthless women, when your wife is but a—"

The word was barely spoken, when the unfortunate young fellow fell to the ground dead. M. de Mussidan in his exasperation had shot him in the heart.

It may be asked why Octave concealed the truth from Diane, why he did not try to discover what truth there was in Montlouis' accusations?

Alas! he loved his wife madly, passionately, and his love made him a coward. He felt he should never have the courage to separate from her; that whatever her faults and frailty might be, his passion would still insist on condonation. In that case, what was the use of enlightenment? Better uncertainty and possibly illusion.

Acquitted by the assize court, thanks to Ludovic's evidence, Octave, however, was not absolved by his conscience. The young girl Montlouis had loved had just given birth to a son, and, turned out of doors by her parents, she was on the verge of dying of destitution, when Octave came to her assistance and, without assigning any reasons for his conduct, undertook to assist her in bringing up her child, who had been christened Paul, after his father. A few days later, M. and Madame de Mussidan left Poitou for Paris, where Diane was more than ever anxious to reside. She had recently engaged a new maid, formerly employed by Marie de Puymandour, and had learnt from this girl that, prior to her marriage, the young Duchess de Champdoce had been in love with George de Croisenois. With this information, Diane considered that her vengeance would prove an easy task.

XIII.

NORBERT'S honeymoon was a dreary business indeed, and it could hardly have been otherwise. He did not love his wife, and she, on her side, had not the least sympathy for her husband. On the morrow of his father's death, the young duke had announced his intention of settling in Paris, a plan which his father-in-law, M. de Puymandour, highly approved of, considering that if he remained alone in the country he would be able to play the grand seigneur and manage the Champdoce estates. In fact, with Norbert's approval, he established himself at the château de Champdoce, and fairly slipped into the old duke's shoes.

It was not until the young duchess reached Paris that she fully realised that she was, in sad truth, the most miserable woman in the world. Champdoce had been almost the same as home to her; her eyes had rested on a familiar landscape, friends had come to see her, and whenever she went out she had met people she knew. But here, in the capital, everything seemed strange and hateful. The late Duke de Champdoce, although stingy and hard-fisted in all that concerned himself and Norbert, had always acted like a grand seigneur as regards his descendants; and thus the family mansion in Paris intended for their benefit was upholstered and decorated with marvellous luxury. Everything, moreover, was so completely in order, that when Norbert and his wife arrived, they might easily have fancied they were returning to their usual home after a brief absence. Old Jean had become the young duke's adviser, and was able to turn his knowledge of the old traditions to good account. In a fortnight he had filled kitchen, larder, and ante-rooms with suitable servants; valuable horses were stalled in the stables, and a number of handsome carriages garnished the coach-house.

However, despite this princely retinue of lackeys and the general stir and bustle of the household, the young duchess felt inexpressibly sad and lonely. Anguish filled her heart, and she thought with a pang of what her life might have been and what it had become. Alas! she had not even a friend to confide in. Norbert had forbidden her frequenting her old Parisian acquaintances, declaring that they were not sufficiently well born and well bred. "Moreover," added he, "we are in deep mourning, and cannot begin visiting till next year."

Under these circumstances, alone, deserted as Marie found herself, she could not help thinking of George de Croisenois. Ah! if her father had only been less obdurate, she would have been *his* wife now, and they would have been far away, hiding their happiness in some distant clime—in the sweet south, perhaps, at Florence, Naples, or Sorrento. Yes, George had loved her; but Norbert, alas! was he even her friend?

The young duke was leading one of those senseless lives that so often end in ruin or suicide. Presented at the most fashionable club in Paris by his uncle, the Chevalier de Septvair, he was received with enthusiasm. He bore one of the historical names of France—his fortune, large as it was, was supposed to be three times larger—he was sought after, surrounded, *fêted*, and flattered, a legion of sycophants and parasites being anxious to win his favour. His inferior education debarred him from certain successes, hence he sought for easy triumphs, those that are gained by dint of money, eccentricity, and cynicism. He started a racing stable, fought two or three duels that resulted to his advantage, and showed himself everywhere in the companionship of women without reputation. His days were spent in the saddle and in the fencing gallery, his nights in supping and gambling. His wife seldom even saw him. As a rule, it was daybreak when he returned home, more or less intoxicated, and having generally lost large sums at play. Old Jean, the faithful retainer of the House of Champdoce, sighed, not because his master scattered so lavishly the treasure his father had amassed, but because he was always surrounded by folks of questionable repute. "Think of the name, sir," he said at times, "the name!"

"Oh! what does it matter," answered Norbert, "providing I live fast and die soon?"

The truth is, that the young duke seemed a prey to vertigo. He was like a bark caught in the Maelstrom, whirling round and round, beyond hope of salvation. He rushed on without thinking, or rather, the only thoughts that came to him were thoughts of Diane. Ah! the recollection of others might fade away, but the memory of her still clung to him. Even amid the fumes of wine her image rose before him, luminous and attractive, like a lamp suddenly ignited in the dead of night.

For six months or more, Norbert had been leading this senseless life, when, one fine February afternoon, as he was riding down the Champs Elysées, he noticed a woman nod to him in friendly style. She was seated in a large open barouche, and swathed in furs. He fancied she must be one of the many actresses he knew, and nonchalantly rode towards the carriage; but when only midway, he discovered to his intense surprise that its occupant was Diane—Madame de Mussidan. Still he rode on, and as the carriage had just stopped, he drew his horse up beside it.

Diane seemed as much agitated as himself, and for a few moments neither of them spoke. Their eyes were fixed on each other, and they were as oppressed as if they had felt a presentiment of what Fate had in store for them.

At last, however, Norbert realised he must speak—speak, at any cost, no matter what he said, for the servants were eyeing him inquisitively. "You, madame! here in Paris?" he stammered.

"Yes, Monsieur le Duc."

"Since how long?"

"Oh! we have been installed here, my husband and myself, for a couple of months at least." Artfully enough, she accentuated these words, "my husband."

"Two months!" repeated Norbert, as if lost in a dream.

"Quite so, though I myself can scarcely believe it, for the time has passed so quick." She smiled strangely as she spoke, and a peculiar gleam came into her eyes as she added, "But give me some news of the Duchess de Champdoce. Does she amuse herself in Paris?"

Norbert made a furious gesture. "Oh! the duchess, the duchess!" he grumbled.

Diane interposed. Whilst the duke was speaking, she had disengaged her hand from among her furs, and now, as she held it out to him, she said in a half tender, half jesting tone, "I hope we shall always be friends—good friends. *Au revoir!*"

The coachman, as if the words "*Au revoir*" had been a signal, at once touched up his horses, and the barouche rolled rapidly away.

Norbert had not taken Diane's hand; he had been too bewildered. But he speedily recovered himself, and spurring his norse, rode swiftly towards the Arc de Triomphe.

"Ah !" he exclaimed, with despair gnawing at his heart, "I love her still. I can never love any one but her !"

He made several fruitless efforts to find her barouche again, but all in vain ; no doubt she had gone home. "But I will see her again !" he said to himself. "She has not forgotten me—her eyes and voice both said she hadn't." At this moment a gleam of sense darted through his mind. "After all," he murmured, "a woman like her could never forgive certain offences. Her cordiality must have been a snare. Did she not swear to revenge herself ?"

Unfortunately he did not long retain this common-sense view of the matter. In fact, the same evening, he asked a friend at his club if he could tell him the Mussidans' address. His friend smiled. "What! Champdoce," said he, "are you in love with the charming viscountess as well ? Hasn't she made enough victims already ?"

"Victims !" ejaculated Norbert in surprise.

"Ay, I know at least of four. To begin with, Octave de Mussidan, her husband ; then the youngest of the Sairmeuses ; next, Clairin, and then George de Croisenois."

The young duke turned aside in disgust, not daring to carry his inquiries any farther. However, the next day, in the Champs Elysées, he again encountered Madame de Mussidan's carriage ; and indeed, day after day, they met in similar fashion, merely exchanging a few words. However, at the beginning of the following week, after a great deal of hesitation, Diane promised Norbert that the next afternoon, at three o'clock, she would alight from her carriage in the Bois, as if desirous of walking, turn into a side avenue they agreed upon, and grant him a short interview there.

She had said at three o'clock ; but before two, Norbert was already at the rendezvous, boiling over with impatience and tortured by uncertainty. He asked himself, "Is this really I, waiting for Diane, as I did at Bivron?" How many events had taken place, and how many changes since then ! It was not Diane de Sauvebourg who was coming, but the Viscountess de Mussidan, another man's wife. And he himself was married. It was no longer the mere caprice of a father that separated them, but duty, law, and society. Still, in his mad excitement, he asked himself why Diane and he should not set absurd prejudices on one side. Couldn't she leave her husband ? couldn't he leave his wife ? In the meanwhile, time was passing, and Norbert half feared she might not keep the appointment. He had hardly expressed his anxiety to himself, when he noticed a cab stop some short distance off and a woman hastily alight. It was she. She rapidly approached—crossing an open space, careless of the brambles, so as to reach him the sooner. He bowed low as she drew near ; but without a word she took his arm and drew him deeper into the wood. It had rained for several days, and the paths were very muddy, but Madame de Mussidan did not seem to notice it. "Let us go on," she said. "I do not wish any one to see us from the road. I have taken every precaution, my carriage and servants are waiting for me outside the church of St. Philippe du Roule. I am supposed to be at confession ; but I came out by a side door and jumped into the first cab. However, I may have been watched and followed. Let us walk farther still."

"You were not so timid once upon a time."

"I was my own mistress then ; my reputation was all my fortune, but it was mine—I had a right to risk it, for if I lost it I only injured myself; but when I married I accepted a sacred deposit—the honour of the man who gave me his name. I must keep it—keep it intact!"

"Say that you love me no longer."

She gave Norbert one of those frigid looks she excelled in, and slowly answered, "Your memory is failing you, I think. However, I remember a certain letter."

With an entreating gesture Norbert interrupted her. "Mercy!" he stammered. "Have pity on me! You would have some compassion if you realised the horrors of my punishment. I was blind, mad, foolish then! But never have I so loved you as now."

A smile curved Diane's exquisite lips. Norbert told her nothing new; still, she took pleasure in listening to his confession.

"Alas!" she murmured, "what can I say? Nothing but the fatal words, 'too late!'"

"Diane!"

He tried to take her hand, but she hastily drew it away. "Oh! do not speak like that!" she cried with a wild look; "do not use that name, you have no right to do so. Is it not enough to have trifled with the young girl? Do not dishonour the wife! You must forget me—do you hear? It is to say that, I came here. The other day when I saw you I was not altogether mistress of myself—my heart, which you possessed, went forth to meet you, and I allowed you to see it. But draw no conclusions from my weakness. I said to you, 'We are friends;' 'twas folly. We cannot even be friends; we must become strangers."

Whilst listening, Norbert remembered what his friend had said to him at the club. "You are cruel," he exclaimed bitterly. "You have been kinder to M. de Sairmeuse, to M. George de Croisenois—"

"What do you mean?" she asked haughtily. "These gentlemen are my husband's friends; whilst you—" She paused, and then, taking both his hands and fixing her eyes on his, resumed: "You forget that the folks of Bivron said I was your mistress. Do you think this slander has never reached my husband's ears? One day when your name was mentioned in his presence, I read suspicion and hatred in his eyes. Good God! If he suspected on my return that your hand had just touched mine, he would drive me from his roof like a degraded wretch. Is not the door of our home closed to you for ever?"

"Ah! I am very miserable!"

"And I, what am I? But what is the use of complaining? Be a man; and if in your heart there still lingers one ray of affection for me, prove it by never trying to see me again."

Thereupon, despite all Norbert's entreaties and efforts to retain her, she hurried back to the cab, leaving in his heart even a more subtle poison than that she had once intended for his father. She knew what chords vibrated in him, and how to deal with them. She felt certain that before a month was over he would be at her feet, that she would be able to govern him more absolutely than ever, and that even against himself he would assist her in carrying out the infamous scheme of vengeance she had conceived.

Her calculations were correct. After following her about like a shadow for a fortnight, Norbert at last made bold enough to approach her again, one afternoon in the Champs Elysées. She showed her displeasure, but not in so marked a degree as to prevent him from renewing his offence. He accosted her again, she shed tears, and yet he persevered. Her defence seemed very heroic to Norbert, but by degrees it grew weaker, and at last she granted him one interview, then two more. But what were they? They took place in a church, in a museum, or in the Bois, and they hardly even had time to shake hands.

Still he did not dare complain, for she depicted the danger she incurred as something terrible. At last, after a great deal of hesitation, tears and expostulation, she finished by saying that she had found a means of making their interviews less hazardous. It was—but she dared not say it. However Norbert urged her to speak, and finally she allowed herself to be persuaded. It was that they might meet in comparative safety, if she could only become the friend of the Duchess de Champdoce! This time Norbert felt certain she was altogether an angel, and it was decided that on the very next day he would introduce her to his wife.

XIV.

IT was a Wednesday, early in March. Instead of breakfasting in his own room, or at his club with his friends, the Duke de Champdoce had seen fit to join his wife. He was in the best possible humour, gay and smiling, indeed his wife had never seen him so affable since their unfortunate marriage. Madame de Champdoce could not understand the change; it frightened her, for with an innate presentiment, she seemed to divine that it presaged some approaching misfortune. However, as soon as the servants had retired and Norbert found himself alone with his wife, he took hold of her hand and kissed it gallantly. "I have long wished, my dear Marie," said he, "to open my heart to you. Indeed a frank and friendly explanation has become positively necessary."

"An explanation!"

"Good heavens! yes—but don't let the word startle you. I have appeared, I fear, the saddest and most dismal of husbands."

"Indeed!"

"Permit me to explain. Since we came here, we have hardly seen each other. I go out early, and come home very late, and sometimes three days elapse without our exchanging a word."

The young duchess listened with the air of a woman who distrusts her senses. Could this be Norbert accusing himself in this way! "I have no complaint to make," she stammered.

"I know that, Marie. You are a noble and dignified woman. However, you are a woman, and a young one too; so it is impossible that you should not have judged me."

"Indeed, sir, I have not."

"So much the better then. In that case I shall not be obliged to defend or excuse myself. But I wish you to know, Marie, that you are my first thought, even when I am not with you."

He was evidently trying to appear good, kind, and affectionate, but his efforts were useless; for while his words were almost tender, his voice was not even friendly.

"I know my duty, sir," said the duchess.

"Pray, Marie," exclaimed her husband, "let there never be a question of duty between us. You know the causes of your isolation as well as I do. The people who were the friends of Mademoiselle de Puymandour could not be those of the Duchess de Champdoce. You know that."

" And have I ever questioned that decision ? '

" No, indeed. Besides our mourning prevents our visiting for four or five months yet."

" Have I asked to go out ? "

" Never ; which is all the more reason why I should try to make your home more pleasant. I should like to see some one by your side—some one whose society would be congenial to you. Not one of those foolish creatures who are always running after pleasure, and always occupied with dress, but a sensible woman of your own age, and your own rank—a woman you could, in short, make a friend of. But where is such a one to be found ? Such connections between young women are at times full of peril, and the happiness or misery of a home depends upon them."

He tripped over his phrases, and caught himself up, like a man who, having to express a difficult idea, turns it round and round in every possible way. "However," he at last resumed, more glibly, "after thinking about this for a long time, and giving it all my attention, I really do fancy I have discovered the person I dreamt of for you. I met her recently at the house of Madame d'Arlange, who sang her praises to me, and I hope to present her to you to-day."

" Here ? "

" Of course. What is there curious about it ? Besides this lady is not altogether a stranger to us. She comes from Poitou, from our own part, and in fact, you know her by sight." He coloured as he spoke, and knowing it, he bent over the fire as he added : " Do you remember Mademoiselle de Sauvebourg ? "

" Mademoiselle Diane, do you mean ? "

" Precisely." And Norbert, as may be imagined, waited right anxiously for his wife's answer.

" Oh ! I saw very little of her. Her father and mine were not over pleased with each other. The Marquis de Sauvebourg regarded us as too insignificant to—"

" Ah, well ! " rejoined Norbert, well pleased, for his wife's answer showed she had no knowledge of the past, no suspicion even of his intrigue with Diane, " ah, well ! I hope that the daughter will repair her father's faults. She married just after we did, and her husband is the Viscount Octave de Mussidan. In short, she is coming to call on you to-day, and I have told your servants you would receive."

Madame de Champdoce made no rejoinder. She lacked experience no doubt, but she was not deficient of that penetration which seems to belong naturally to women. She had noticed Norbert's embarrassment, and reflected, asking herself what it meant. The pause that ensued, was already growing embarrassing, when carriage wheels were heard grating on the sand in the court-yard. The next moment a servant entered and announced that Madame de Mussidan was in the salon.

Norbert eagerly rose, and taking his wife's arm, exclaimed, " Come Marie, come !—it is she ! "

It was only after considerable hesitation that Diane had decided on this strange and audacious step, in this visit paid in defiance of all ideas of social propriety. She exposed herself, as she well knew, to the most painful humiliations. For a minute or so, which seemed to her a century, so great was her anxiety as to the reception in store for her on the part of Norbert's wife, did Diane remain alone in the drawing-room, and then the door opened and the duke and duchess appeared. Diane's heart was beating pit-a-pat, and yet with a winning smile, and charming grace, she bowed to the young duchess, gaily excusing herself for her importunity. "She had not been able," she said, "to resist the desire of seeing her old neighbour, now that she was so near ; and so in disregard of all *convenances*, for which she trusted the duchess would forgive her, she had ventured to call so that they might talk together about Bivron, Champdoce, and all that beautiful country where she was born, and which she loved so dearly."

The duchess listened in silence to this flow of words. She had bowed with great coldness, and her face expressed more clearly, perhaps, than is customary in good society, the surprise this visit caused her.

Even a more perfectly self-possessed person than Diane might have been disconcerted. But present annoyance was so small in comparison to the advantages she hoped to reap, so that she appealed to all the resources of her wit and skill.

Norbert meanwhile wandered up and down the room feeling none too comfortable in the contemptible *rôle* he had accepted. However, as soon as he fancied that the ice was broken, and that the two women were conversing amicably, he left them, uncertain whether he ought to feel glad or sorry at the success of this unworthy comedy.

The task was more difficult than he supposed. After what Norbert had told her of his wife, Madame de Mussidan had fancied she would be received by the duchess as if she were an angel come down from heaven to visit and console a prisoner. She expected to find a simple, artless sort of woman, who, on her first visit, would throw her arms round her neck, and afterwards entirely abandon herself to her influence. But she speedily realised that she must be most cautious and skilful, if she wished to win the duchess's confidence. Still this unexpected difficulty rather exhilarated Diane than discouraged her, and such, when she chose, were her powers of fascination, that when she left, the first step was achieved.

That same evening, Madame de Champdoce said to her husband: "I think that the countess is an excellent woman !"

"Excellent is just the right word," answered Norbert. "All Bivron wept when she left ; she was the providence of the poor."

He was flattered by Diane's success. For had she not displayed all this address for his sake—were not her efforts a fresh proof of the sincerity of her passion ! However, his satisfaction diminished considerably the next day, when he saw Madame de Mussidan in the Champs Elysées. She looked sad and preoccupied. "What has gone wrong ?" he asked.

"I—I repent bitterly having yielded to my own heart and your entreaties. Alas ! we have been terribly imprudent."

"We imprudent ? And how ? "

"Norbert, your wife suspects something."

"She—impossible ! She sang your praises after your departure."

"If that is the case, she is cleverer than I supposed, for she is able to conceal her suspicions, and has determined to verify them."

Diane's tone was so serious, that Norbert was positively startled. "What is to be done, then ? " he asked. "What can we do ? "

"It would be best to give up seeing each other."

"Never ! never ! "

"Let me think, then ; and in the meantime, be prudent. Yes, in the name of heaven be prudent."

The result of Diane's reflections and artful advice was that Norbert entirely changed his mode of life. No more club bouts, or suppers, or nights spent in gambling and drinking. He went about with his wife in the daytime, and often spent his evenings at home. His friends charged him with having become a model husband. This great change did not take place without many an inward revolt on his part. He was humiliated by the constant hypocrisy he was condemned to, but then Diane's small white hand, apparently so slender and so frail, was yet as firm as steel.

" You *must* live like this," she said, in reply to his complaints—" first, because it must be so, and next, because I wish it. On your present con- duct all our future security depends. I wish Madame de Champdoce to feel that happiness entered her doors with my introduction to her."

What could be said in reply to this? Norbert was more in love than ever, and a terrible fear froze every objection upon his lips. " If I displeased her," he thought, "she wouldn't hesitate to throw me over !" and so he obeyed her, hard as it was to do so.

After remaining for a long time on the defensive, the duchess yielded at length to the charms of the friendship which seemed so frankly offered her, and finished by abandoning herself absolutely to her mortal enemy. Finally, she had not a secret from her ; and one day, after many long and confidential conversations with Diane, she confessed, amid tears and blushes, her one girlish love—the memory of which remained in her heart like some precious perfume. She even spoke of George de Croisenois by name. That day Diane was thrilled with joy. " I have her at last," she thought; "my vengeance is at hand !"

The two young women were now constantly together. In fact, they seemed like two fond sisters. Norbert, however, was scarcely pleased thereat ; for Diane's intimacy with his wife had by no means conduced to that liberty of intercourse he had desired and anticipated. In fact, now that Madame de Mussidan went daily to the Hôtel de Champdoce, Norbert saw her even less than before. Sometimes weeks elapsed without their see- ing each other alone for a single moment, and she devised everything so artfully that his wife always rose up, as it were, between him and her— just as in the pantomimes, when the clown, wishing to kiss Columbine, al- ways finds Harlequin there to prevent him. At times Norbert waxed wrathful ; but Diane always had reasons, either good or bad ones, to close his lips with. At times she ridiculed him mercilessly, and then at others she assumed her grand air and said, " In heaven's name, what did you ex pect ? What infamy did you suppose me capable of ? "

Norbert was, in fact, managed by Diane precisely as if he had been a child or a fool. He knew it and realised it fully. If he could only have followed her about as before ! But she was always guarded in the Bois or at the races, in fact, wherever she went, by some *cavaliere servente* riding beside her carriage—now by M. de Sairmeuse, now by M. de Clairin, and most frequently by George de Croisenois. These men were one and all dis- agreeable to Norbert, and De Croisenois especially so ; for he looked upon him as impertinent and absurd, in which opinion he was altogether wrong.

At twenty-five, the Marquis de Croisenois was one of the cleverest and most witty men in Parisian society, and his high reputation, contrary to what often happens, was well deserved. Many persons were envious of him, but he had no enemies. He was greatly esteemed, for his honour and probity were beyond question. Moreover, his character was not destitute of certain chivalric, adventurous *traits*. However, Norbert could not brook him, and in his mad jealousy often asked, " I should like to know what you see in this impertinent fop to have him about you so much ? "

To which she invariably replied, with an equivocal smile, " You are too curious—you will know some day."

Ah ! if Norbert had been less carried away by his passion, if he had studied Diane's tone of voice when she spoke to him, if he had investigated her conduct ! But no, love had blinded him ; he saw, he divined nothing.

In the meanwhile, not a day passed without some conversation between Diane and the duchess about Croisenois ; and the viscountess had artfully accustomed Marie to look certain probabilities, or rather, possibilities, in the face, from the mere idea of which, a few months before, she would have shrunk with horror. This point gained, Madame de Mussidan now considered it advisable to bring the old lovers once more together ; an unexpected meeting, thought she, would have more effect than all her insinuations. Accordingly, one day when Madame de Champdoce called for her friend, she was asked to wait in the salon for a few minutes. She entered, and found herself face to face with the Marquis de Croisenois.

An exclamation of surprise escaped them both as they recognised each other, and they turned very pale. But the emotion of the duchess was such, that she sank half fainting on to a chair near the door. M. de Croisenois was scarcely less moved ; for he had loved Marie de Puymandour deeply and truly, and was not yet consoled. "I had faith in you," he murmured, hardly knowing what he said ; "but you forgot me."

"You do not believe what you say," answered the duchess proudly. But a moment afterwards, unconscious of the gravity of her words, she added, "What could I do ? I obeyed my father. I was weak, no doubt ; but I have forgotten nothing."

Behind the door Madame de Mussidan was crouching and listening, and as she heard these words, her eyes glittered with infernal triumph. She said to herself that an interview that commenced like this was not likely to be the last one. She was not mistaken ; for she soon discovered that George and the duchess understood each other enough to meet regularly at her house. However, she did not appear to notice it. She waited calmly ; things were proceeding as she wished, and sooner or later the mine she had prepared must surely explode with terrible force and effect.

XV.

SEPTEMBER had come round, and although the weather was atrocious, the young Duke de Champdoce, accompanied by his faithful Jean, was sojourning at Maisons, where his racing stable was installed. The truth is, that having had a tiff with Diane, he wished to try the effect of absence in reducing her to submission, having, indeed, heard say that absence is like the wind that fans a fire and extinguishes a candle.

Norbert had been at Maisons a couple of days, and was already growing very anxious at not having heard from Madame de Mussidan, when one evening, as he came in from a last look at his horses, he was told that a man wished to see him. He found this man to be a poor old fellow, well known in the place, who lived partially on the alms he received and the errands he was intrusted with.

"Did you wish to see me ? " asked the duke.

The old fellow half drew a letter from his pocket, and with a knowing wink replied, "This is for you."

'Very well—give it to me."

"But I was told, sir, to wait until you were alone, for—"

"Never mind. Make haste!"

"If you say so, I suppose I must."

Norbert took it for granted that this letter came from Diane, so tossing the man a louis, he hurried with the letter to the nearest stable lamp. But the direction was not in the aristocratic, delicate handwriting of the Countess de Mussidan. Indeed, Champdoce was written with two s's instead of with a c. "Who the deuce could have sent me this?" thought Norbert. However, he broke the seal.

The paper was soiled and greasy, and as coarse as the envelope. The writing was atrocious, and the mistakes in spelling innumerable. The missive ran as follows: "Sir, it gives me pain to tell you the truth; but I can't help it, for I must relieve my conscience. I cannot endure to see a woman, without heart or honour, persistently deceiving a man like yourself. I write therefore to tell you that your wife betrays you, and daily laughs at you. You may believe me, for I am an honest woman; and it is easy, too, for you to satisfy yourself that I don't lie. Conceal yourself this very evening, from half-past ten to eleven, in any place where you can see the small door in your garden wall, and you will certainly see the lover arrive. He has had a key for a long time. The hour for the rendezvous is well chosen, for there won't be a servant in the house. But I implore you, sir, don't be severe; for I would not do your wife any harm on any consideration.

"FROM ONE WHO KNOWS."

Norbert read this infamous letter at one glance. The blood rushed to his brain, and he gave vent to a roar of rage. All the servants rushed towards him. "That man!" he cried, "where's that man?"

"What man?"

"The fellow who brought me this—this letter. Run after him. Bring him here instantly."

In a minute or two the man appeared, dragged along by two stalwart grooms. "I didn't steal it," he cried; "it was given me. I'm ready to restore it!" He spoke of the louis tossed to him by Norbert; for the largeness of the sum had awakened his doubts as to its having been intended for him.

"Keep the money," said the duke. "I gave it to you. But answer my question. Who gave you this letter?"

"A man I don't know, sir," replied the old fellow trembling.

"Is that really true?" asked Norbert.

"Oh! may my next pipe poison me if I am lying. It was about four o'clock when he jumped out of a cab near the bridge. I was passing by, and he stopped me and said, 'Do you see this letter? At half-past seven just take it to the Duke de Champdoce, in the house at the stables on the forest road.' 'Yes, I know the place,' says I; and then he put the letter and a five-franc piece into my hand, jumped into the cab again, and drove off."

"What was he like?" asked Norbert.

"Like? Well, sir, I don't know. He had a gold watch-chain across his waistcoat; but I didn't notice anything else. He wasn't old, nor young, nor short, nor tall—"

"Enough! You may go."

At this moment Norbert's anger was solely directed against the writer of this anonymous letter. He did not place the smallest belief in the charges against his wife; for if he did not love her, he respected her.

"My wife," he said, "is an honest woman, and this must come from some servant she has discharged, and who takes this mode of revenge."

However, he re-perused the note, and on reflection it seemed to him that the bad spelling was somewhat forced. Moreover, the mention that there wouldn't be a servant in the house struck him as especially singular. Anxious for information on the point, he summoned Jean. "Is it true," he asked, "that there won't be any of the servants at the house in Paris to-night?"

"Doesn't Monsieur le Duc remember? It's the head coachman's wedding to-day, and madame was kind enough to say she would not deprive any one of the ball, and that if the concierge and his wife remained at home as usual that would do."

"Ah, yes, I remember now," said Norbert with affected calmness.

But in point of fact, doubt had now crept into his mind, and as we know suspicion cannot be reasoned away. "After all," thought Norbert, "why shouldn't my wife betray me? I believe her to be virtuous, and attached to her duties; but all husbands who are deceived undoubtedly believe the same. Why shouldn't I profit by this advice? Why shouldn't I see for myself?—No," he continued, "I will not descend to such baseness. I should be as vile as the person who wrote this letter, if I played the spy, as she suggests."

He looked up and saw that all the stablemen were watching him with intense curiosity. "Go to your work!" he cried, angrily; "put out your lanterns and shut the windows."

He thought the men looked sneeringly at him, and intensely aggravated, he at once made up his mind. He took out his watch. It was eight o'clock; he had just time to get to Paris, he thought. Accordingly he summoned Jean once more. With this devoted servant there was no need of dissimulation. "I must go to Paris at once, Jean," said Norbert.

The old man shook his head sadly. "On account of that letter?" he asked, respectfully.

"Yes, on account of this letter."

"Some one has made charges against my mistress."

"How do you know that?" asked Norbert.

"It was easy enough to guess, sir."

"Well, quick, a change of clothes for me. Have horses put to the carriage, drive to the club, I will go on foot."

"It can't be done like that, sir," said Jean gravely; "the other servants may have the same idea as myself. You ought to go without anyone knowing it. Let the servants here suppose you have never left Maisons. I will take a horse from the small stable, secretly saddle him, lead him across the bridge, and you can come and join me there."

"Very well; but there is no time to lose."

Jean hurried away, and Norbert heard him say to an under valet, "Put some cold meat on the table, the duke says he's famished."

Entering his bedroom M. de Champdoce donned an overcoat and riding boots, and slipped a loaded revolver into his pocket. The night was very dark, a fine, icy rain was falling, and the roads were almost impassible. However, at the appointed spot he found the old valet with the horse. Norbert at once leaped into the saddle, exclaiming, "No one saw me leave."

"Nor me either," answered the faithful servant. "I shall go back and attend to things just as if you were at supper. But in three hours from now I shall be in that wine shop on the left. When you return just touch the window lightly with the handle of your whip."

The horse champed the bit impatiently, Norbert was off like the wind. Jean had made a wise choice, for the animal stretched himself out and took the muddy road at an even, regular pace. Still Norbert, by this time in a state of great excitement, applied the spurs.

As he reached the Faubourg St. Germain, he had a new idea. Suppose some of his club friends had sent him this letter as a practical joke? In that case, they would of course be watching for him, and would keep him on the *qui vive* near that gate for two hours, and then suddenly appear and overwhelm him with ridicule. This fear made him prudent. What was he to do with his horse? The wine shops were still open; he might perhaps go into one, and find some man who would take charge of the animal. Whilst he was hesitating, he perceived a soldier tramping along on his way, probably to his barracks. "Eh, my good fellow," asked Norbert, "are you inclined to earn twenty francs?"

"Of course I am, if it's honestly and in no way contrary to the regulations of the service."

"It's only to hold my horse and walk him up and down, while I pay a visit near here."

"Oh, all right, I can stay out a couple of hours more."

Norbert thereupon alighted, told the soldier where to wait for him, and went rapidly on his way. To make sure of everything, for he still dreaded a practical joke, he took a circuitous route to the Rue Barbet de Jouy where the side gate of the Champdoce grounds was situated. Almost in front of it on the other side of the way was the *porte-cochère* of an aristocratic mansion, and Norbert slipped into a dark corner and watched. Previously, however, he had carefully explored the street from one end to the other, for it is a very short street, and had ascertained that it was utterly deserted. This necessarily put an end to all idea of a mystification, and so he determined he would wait till midnight, and if by that time no one had come he would recognize his wife's innocence, and retire.

Three windows on the second floor were faintly lighted; and these were precisely those of his wife's sleeping room. Norbert looked at them and reflected. "She is not the kind of woman," he said to himself, "who would receive a lover! No, no! it is impossible." And by degrees he began to think of the manner in which he behaved to his wife. Had he nothing to reproach himself with? Two days after their marriage he had virtually abandoned her; and if during the last few months he had condescended to show her any affection, she owed it, poor thing, to the caprice of another woman—who bestowed it upon her like alms to the starving. Even if a man were with her, what right had he to interfere? The law, of course, gave him every right, but his conscience accorded him none.

He stood against the wall, motionless as the stone itself. He was chilled, and it seemed to him that life and thought were both fading away. How long had he been there—one hour or six? He had no idea. He pulled out his watch, but it was so dark that he could not see the hands. However, just at that moment the clock of the Invalides struck a half hour—What half hour was it? He had already decided to depart, when suddenly he heard a light footfall at the end of the street. It was a man's step plainly enough, but not the decided tread of some dweller in the street returning home. It was timid, undecided, furtive so to say. Could this really be the tread of his wife's lover? Soon he distinguished a shadow gliding along the garden wall over the way. Then came a pause. The shadow halted, moved on again, Norbert heard a sound he could not understand, and finally all became quiet once more. The shadow had disappeared.

It seemed evident to Norbert that the man had entered the garden, and yet he would gladly have doubted still. "It may be a burglar," he thought; "but a burglar would naturally have accomplices. This man might have come to see some servant; but then all the servants were away."

Meanwhile, he had not taken his eyes from the windows of his wife's room. All at once the light became brighter; the shade of the lamp had been taken off, or a candle had been lighted. Yes, it was a candle, for he saw it carried across the windows of the landing and then across those of the grand staircase; ay, he must accept the truth. A lover had certainly entered the house, had given some preconcerted signal, and the duchess was going forward to meet him. Norbert's blood boiled in his veins, the chilly fog now seemed to him like the fumes of a brazier. How could he punish the wretches who thus outraged his honour, what punishment could he devise, adequate for the crime? All at once, he uttered an exclamation. An infernal idea had just crossed his mind, and he accepted it as a divine inspiration. He ran to the door, forced the lock, and rushed into the garden.

XVI.

THE person who penned that anonymous letter was only too well informed. The Duchess de Champdoce was expecting George de Croisenois—it was the first time. Alas! the poor woman had ended by falling into the snare set for her by the woman whom she believed to be her most devoted friend.

The evening before she had been for a short time in Madame de Mussidan's drawing room, alone with George. She had been moved by his passion, and could not resist his ardent words. Finally she lost her head, and promised the rendezvous he begged for on his knees. "Ah well," she said, "so be it, then. Come to-morrow night, at half-past ten, to the little garden gate—it will be merely pushed to, kept closed by a stone—push it open, and when you are inside the garden, warn me by clapping your hands together several times."

These words had been overheard by Diane (as usual listening at the keyhole), and as she esteemed her friend sufficiently to know that swift repentance would follow these mad words, she remained with her the whole evening, dined with her the next day, and did not leave her to herself till the appointed hour was near at hand. It was only when she was at last left alone that the duchess fully realized her imprudence, and the enormity of her fault. She repented of her weakness, and would have given anything to have been able to retract that fatal promise. But, alas! the hour was nigh. Still, after all there was one means of safety left, she might go down and bolt the garden door. Seized with this idea, she started up; but it was too late — at that very moment Croisenois' signal was heard! Poor woman! Those handclaps, which announced her lover, sounded in her ears like a death-knell. She stooped to light a candle at the fire; but her hand shook to such a degree that the heated wax blazed, but the wick did not light. She fancied that Croisenois was still in the garden as she had not replied to his signal. It had not occurred to her that he had dared to open the hall door. Hence she intended going down at once and entreat him to retire without entering the house. But she counted without her host. In such an artless, natural way that her infernal purpose could not be guessed, Diane had allowed Croisenois to know that the Champdoce mansion would be quite deserted that night. He had ascertained, moreover, from other sources, that the duke was at Maisons, and that all the servants were dancing and making merry at a wedding. Accordingly George did not hesitate ; he entered the house and went softly up the stairs, so that when the duchess, with the lighted candle in her hand, reached the landing, she found herself face to face with her lover, whose footfall she had not even heard. She started back with a cry of despair. "Fly !" she stammered ; "fly, or we are lost !"

But he did not seem to hear ; and the duchess drew still further back— back, indeed, into her room, whilst he still followed her, after pushing to the door behind him.

But the brief moment this required had sufficed to bring Marie to her senses. "If I allow him to speak," she thought, "if he once suspects my miserable weakness, I am lost !"

"You must depart at once," she said. "I was mad yesterday. You are too noble and too generous not to realise that I am speaking the truth when I tell you that my reason has returned to me. Listen to me—my frankness will convince you that I love you."

De Croisenois uttered an exclamation of joy.

"Yes," continued Marie, "to become your wife I would gladly abandon everything. But it cannot be. I love you, George, but the voice of duty speaks more loudly than that of love. Maybe I shall die of grief ; but, at all events, I shall die without remorse, without a stain on my honour. Adieu !"

The marquis could not consent to being dismissed like this.

"Go !" repeated the duchess, as severely as she could ; "go at once !" And as he did not move she continued :

"If you love me, my honour should be as as dear to you as your own. Withdraw, and never try to see me again. Our present peril shows me clearly that we never ought to see each other. I am the Duchess de Champdoce, and must keep the name I bear intact and pure. I will neither deceive nor betray."

"Why did you speak of deception ?" he asked. "No doubt I despise the woman who smiles at the husband she betrays ; but I also say that she is noble and courageous who boldly abandons everything to follow the fortunes of the man she loves. Leave your name here, Marie, your title, your fortune, and your luxury, and fly with me."

"I love you too much, George," she answered softly, "to ruin your future. The day would come when you would regret your abnegation. A dishonoured woman must be a heavy burden."

George de Croisenois misunderstood her. "Ah ! you doubt me !" he exclaimed, "I see. You think I might abandon you ! Ah ! Marie, never. I swear it, never ! But stay—you need, perhaps, some tie that shall bind us together irrevocably for all time to come. You will be dishonoured, you say. Very well, I will dishonour myself. To-night, at the club, I will cheat at cards, let myself be detected, and go out with lowered head. Folks will call me a thief. Ah ! I would accept dishonour gladly, if to-morrow you would but fly with me to any distant land you choose !"

"I must not listen to you," she cried. "It is too late now—impossible —impossible!"

"Impossible! and why?"

"Ah, George!" she sobbed; "because—if you knew!"

He dared to clasp her round the waist, and was about to press his lips on her brow, when all at once he felt Marie totter, whilst she extended one arm towards the door.

The door was open, and there, motionless on the threshold, stood Norbert de Champdoce. The marquis realised at once what a terrible, irreparable situation he had created by his own impetuosity. "Come no nearer!" he cried in a threatening voice. "No nearer!"

What! at the dead of night, unarmed, he was in another man's house, with his arm round the waist of that other man's wife, and yet he dared to threaten! A sardonic laugh from Norbert recalled him to the truth, and made him realise the folly of his words.

He carried Madame de Champdoce to a sofa and laid her on it. She was almost unconscious, but for one instant she opened her eyes, and, dim as they were, George read therein love and forgiveness for the man who had blasted her happiness forever. This look restored his *sang froid*, and he turned to Norbert.

"Whatever appearances may be," he began, "you have here but one person to punish—not even the shadow of a suspicion should rest on your wife. It was without her knowledge—without any encouragement from her—that I dared to enter your house, knowing all the servants to be away."

Norbert did not speak. He also needed to collect himself. He knew when he ascended the stairs that he was about to surprise the duchess with a lover; but he could not foresee that this lover was precisely the man whom he hated most in the world. When he saw Croisenois, it was with difficulty that he resisted the temptation of springing at his throat

This man, whom he had suspected of stealing Diane's heart, had now robbed him of his wife. He was silent, simply because his mind was in such confusion that he did not dare to speak. If he seemed as cold and rigid as marble, when all the flames of hell rioted in his heart, it was because he could not move—a physical impossibility prevented him. With all this appearance of impassibility, Norbert was mad—absolutely mad.

Meanwhile Croisenois continued, with his arms folded across his breast, "I had just come here, sir," he said, "when you arrived. Would to God you had only heard our conversation from the beginning—you would then realise all the nobility and grandeur of this lady's character. My offence is very great, I admit; but I hold myself at your orders, and am ready to give you all the satisfaction you desire."

As these last words fell from the marquis's lips, Norbert seemed to awake from a dream. With a heavy, uncertain step he entered the room, shut all the doors, and put the keys in his pocket. Then taking up his stand near the mantelshelf, with Croisenois in front of him, he exclaimed, "If I understand you aright, you propose a duel. That is to say, having dishonoured me to-night, you propose to kill me to-morrow; you are too kind."

"Sir!"

"Allow me! I am perhaps a child, as you were once good enough to say to Madame de Mussidan; but at least I've sufficient experience to know that it is foolish to abandon advantages. In the game you have been playing, sir, a man risks his life—and you have lost, I think."

Croisenois bowed mechanically. The mention of Madame de Mussidan's name came to him as a revelation of Norbert's true feelings. "I am a dead man!" he thought, as he looked at the duchess, "and not on your account, poor Marie! but for a very different woman."

In the meanwhile Norbert went on, becoming more excited by the sound of his own voice: "What do I care for a duel? I come to my own house in the middle of the night, I am armed, and I blow out your brains—the law sustains me—" As he spoke, he produced his revolver and deliberately took aim at George.

This was a terrible moment, but Croisenois did not flinch. However, as Norbert did not pull the trigger, the suspense became well nigh intolerable to him. "Fire!" he cried. "Fire!"

"No!" said Norbert coldly. "On reflection, I've decided that your body would be a great inconvenience to me!"

"My patience has its limits, sir; what do you mean to do?"

"I mean to kill you!" answered the duke, in such a tone of concentrated rage and hatred that George shuddered; "but not with a bullet. It is said that blood washes mud away. It's false. If all yours were shed, the spot on my escutcheon would still be there. One of us must disappear from the face of the globe in such a way that not a trace is left."

"Very well, sir; point out the means."

"I know a way," said Norbert, "if I were sure that no human being suspects your presence here to-night."

"No one can know it, sir. I swear it."

"In that case," resumed the duke, "instead of taking advantage of my rights, which justified me in killing you, I consent to risk my life against yours."

Croisenois, with difficulty, repressed a sigh of relief. "I am at your orders, as I told you before," he said.

"I hear and understand; but it will be no ordinary combat, in broad daylight, with seconds—"

"We will meet wherever you choose, sir."

"Very well. That being the case, we will fight with swords, this very moment, in the garden."

The marquis glanced towards the windows.

"You probably think that the night is too dark for us to see to fight," observed Norbert.

"That's true."

"You need not be troubled, however; there will be light enough to die —for one of us must die—you understand me?"

"I understand. Let us go down at once."

Norbert shook his head. "You are in too much hurry," said he; "you have not allowed me to fix my conditions."

"Speak, sir."

"At the end of the garden there is a vacant place, which is so damp that nothing is grown there, and no one ever goes there. Nevertheless, there I shall take you. We shall each of us take a pickaxe and a spade, and in very little time we can dig a hole deep enough to bury the one who is killed. When this is done, we will lay down our spades and take our swords, and fight till one or the other drops. The one who is left standing must finish the other, if he is not quite dead, and then roll him into the pit and cover him over with earth."

"Never!" exclaimed Croisenois; "never will I accept such conditions."

"Take care, then!" said Norbert; "I shall use my rights. In four minutes that clock strikes eleven—if at the first stroke you don't consent, I fire."

The muzzle of the revolver was but twelve inches from Croisenois' breast, the finger of a mortal enemy was on the trigger, and yet he was quite insensible to this danger, though it came after so many emotions. He merely understood that he had four minutes to reflect and deliberate. The events of the last half hour had succeeded each other with such rapidity that they seemed almost incredible, so incoherent and absurd, that he wondered if he were not suffering from some odious nightmare.

"You have only two minutes left," said Norbert suddenly.

Croisenois started. His mind had been a thousand leagues from his present position. He glanced at Norbert, and then at Marie, who was still extended on the couch. She might have been regarded as dead, but for the hysterical sobs which shook her from head to foot at long, irregular intervals. To leave her in this state, without aid of any kind, seemed absolutely barbarous; but Croisenois clearly realised that any indication of compassion on his part would merely be looked upon as a new insult.

"God have pity on us," he said to himself; "we are at the mercy of a madman!" And he asked himself with a shudder what would become of this woman he loved so deeply, were he now to die. "For her sake," he thought, "I must kill this man, or her life will be one slow agony—and I *will* kill him, too."

"I accept!" he cried, in a loud voice.

It was time enough, for the light vibration which precedes the striking of a clock was just heard, and then came the first stroke.

"Thank you, sir," said Norbert coldly.

But Croisenois had now determined to sell his life dearly, if not for his own sake, at least for Marie's. "Yes, I accept," he said; "but I, too, have conditions to make."

"It was decided—"

"Allow me to explain. We are about to fight in your garden, without witnesses and in the dark. We two are to dig a grave, I believe, and the one who survives is to bury the other; am I right? But how can you be sure that this will be the end—that the earth will retain our secret?"

Norbert shrugged his shoulders.

"You don't know, and you don't care," resumed Croisenois, violently. "But I know, and I care—and if it came to pass that some day our secret were discovered—"

"Ah!"

"The survivor—be that survivor you or me—would be accused of murder. He would be arrested, imprisoned, dragged, into a court of justice, condemned, and sent to the galleys or the guillotine."

"Unquestionably."

"You say 'unquestionably,' and yet you think that I would consent to run such a risk as that?"

"Such are the risks, certainly," answered Norbert. "but these very risks are the best possible guarantee that should you kill me, you would conceal my death as I wish to have it concealed."

"You must rely on my word, sir."

"Ah! take care, or you will force me to think you afraid."

"And I am afraid of being accused of murder."

"But it is a danger I am exposed to as well as yourself."

Croisenois was fully determined not to yield. "You say our chances are equal," he rejoined. "Is that so? If I disappear, who on earth would dream of looking for my body here? You are in your own home, you can take every imaginable precaution. But if I kill you, what then? Can I ask the Duchess de Champdoce to assist me? Will she not be herself under suspicion? Shall she say to her gardeners—when all Paris is on the *qui vive* in reference to your disappearance, 'Take care not to disturb the ground at the end of the garden?'"

Norbert now suddenly remembered the anonymous letter he had received, and realized that whoever wrote it possessed his secret, and might noise it about. "What have you to propose then?" he asked.

"Simply, that each of us, without referring in any way to the causes of our duel, shall write down the conditions, with an acceptance of them signed in full."

"Very well; but hasten."

Thereupon the two adversaries drew up the *procès-verbaux* agreed upon, and moreover, again at Croisenois' suggestion, they each penned two short notes dated from abroad, so that the survivor might have them posted with the view of misleading any inquiry, or search that might follow the disappearance of either of them.

When this was done, Norbert rose. "One word more," said he. "A soldier is just now leading my horse up and down the Esplanade des Invalides—the horse on which I came here. If you kill me, go and fetch this horse, and give the man twenty francs—I promised them to him."

"Very well."

"Now let us go down."

They left the room, but as Norbert stepped back to allow Croisenois to pass before him, he felt himself pulled by his coat-tails. He turned and found that the duchess, too weak to stand, had dragged herself to him on her knees. Poor woman! she had heard everything, and with clasped hands, and in an almost inaudible voice, she pleaded in agonized entreaty: "Mercy! Norbert—I am innocent. I swear to you that I am innocent! You never loved me! Why do you fight? Mercy! To-morrow I swear to you I will enter a convent—you shall never see my face again. Mercy!"

"Pray God, madame, that your lover may kill me—that is your only hope. Then you will be free—"

As he disengaged himself with brutal violence, the poor woman fell back on the floor, and fainted away.

XVII.

TWENTY times during that last quarter of an hour had Norbert de Champdoce been on the point of bursting into a furious passion, but twenty times he had been restrained by his excessive vanity. Now, however, he could contain himself no longer; when he left his wife's room, he evinced savage earnestness and impatient ferocity. As he lighted Croisenois down the grand staircase, he over and over again exclaimed, "Make haste, make haste." It needed very little to disconcert his plans—merely a servant returning earlier than the others.

When they reached the ground floor Norbert took Croisenois into a large room which looked as if it belonged to an arsenal, so crowded was it with weapons of every epoch, and every kind. "I think we shall find what we need here," he said in a tone of sardonic raillery, and jumping on to the divan which ran round the room, he took down several pairs of swords and threw them on the table. "Choose for yourself," he said.

George de Croisenois was as desirous as Norbert of putting an end to all the suspense—anything was preferable to this mental agony. That last look from the duchess had entered his heart like a dagger; and when he had seen Norbert thrust aside his kneeling wife, he had only with difficulty restrained himself from felling him to the ground. He did not condescend to look at the swords which were offered to him for inspection, but snatching up one of them, he exclaimed, "This will do, as well as another!"

They then went out into the garden, but the fog was so thick one could not even distinguish one's own hand at arm's length. "It is impossible,' said Norbert, "to do anything in darkness like this. However, I've an idea. Follow me down this narrow passage, if you please, so that we may not awaken the suspicion of the concierge."

They reached a stable where Norbert found a large lantern and lighted it. "With this," said he in a tone of intense satisfaction, "we shall be able to see all night."

"Yes, but the neighbours can see as well. This light, at this hour, would certainly attract attention."

"Don't be concerned, no one can see into my grounds."

They then returned into the garden, which they crossed diagonally, finally reaching the spot which Norbert had spoken of. He hung his lantern on to a tree. It gave rather more light than an ordinary street gas burner.

"We will dig the grave over there in that corner," said the duke to Croisenois, "and then we can cover the ground with some of that straw near by." He took off his overcoat, as he spoke, and handing a spade to Croisenois, he took another, exclaiming grimly: "To work! to work!"

It would have taken Croisenois the whole night to complete this task; but the duke had not forgotten the days when he dug in the fields at Champdoce. He exerted all his strength and displayed marvellous skill, working on with a kind of mad rage, till the sweat gathered in large drops on his brow. Thus, thanks to his superhuman exertions, in forty minutes the grave was dug.

"Enough!" said Norbert; and throwing down his spade, he took up his sword, adding, "On guard, sir!"

But Croisenois did not move—impressionable and nervous by nature, he felt a cold chill at his heart. The night—the vacillating light—all these hideous preparations affected his imagination. He could not take his eyes from that yawning grave—it fascinated and attracted him.

"Well," said Norbert, impatiently.

Croisenois started. "I will speak," he said at last, in a solemn tone. "In a minute, sir, one of us will be lying there dead; a man does not lie in the face of death. Hear me. I swear to you on my honour, and on all my hopes of salvation, that the Duchess de Champdoce is innocent."

"You have said that before, why repeat it?"

"Because it is my duty, sir—because I think with horror that my mad passion has ruined the noblest and purest of women. Believe me, sir, I entreat of you, you have nothing to forgive her. See here, I am not ashamed to entreat you—yes, to entreat you humbly—to allow my death, if you kill me, to serve as full expiation. Be humane towards your wife—treat her kindly—do not make her life one long torture."

"Enough! or I shall look upon you as a coward."

"Alas!" cried Croiseuois, "on guard, then, and may God decide between us!"

Their swords crossed, and the combat began—quick and violent. The space which the lantern lighted was but small, and whenever one of the adversaries was driven into the shadow as frequently happened, the other remained in the light, exposed to thrusts he could not parry, as he did not see them come. This proved fatal to Croisenois; for on one occasion, as he advanced, Norbert lunged forward and pierced him in the breast. The poor fellow threw up his arms, and dropped his sword—his knees bent under him, and he fell back without a cry or sound of any kind. Three times he tried to rise, but thrice his strength failed him. He wished to speak, but could only pronounce a few unintelligible words, for the blood already choked him. A convulsion—one long-drawn breath—and he was dead.

George de Croisenois was dead. Yes, he was dead, and Norbert de Champdoce stood beside him, with eyes dilated in terror, with his hair rising on end, quivering horribly from head to foot. He realized then, for the first time, what it is to see a man die by one's own hand.

And yet Norbert was not so much disturbed by the thought that he had killed Croisenois, for he believed his cause just, and considered he had acted rightly. But sweat gathered on his brow, and he felt mortal anguish at the thought that he must lift that body in his arms, and throw it, yet warm and palpitating, into yonder grave. He hesitated and struggled with himself for at least ten minutes—he recapitulated all the reasons which made it necessary he should do this at once. The risk of discovery—the honour of his house. At last he stooped, put out his arms, but recoiled before his hands touched the body. His heart failed him, and he straightened himself up again. It was only after another long struggle with himself that he once more stooped down. This time he seized hold of the body, and with extraordinary strength threw it into the grave where it fell with a dull thud, which sounded to Norbert like the noise of an earthquake. Then snatching up the spade which poor George had used so clumsily only a little while before, he swiftly filled up the grave and battered down the earth, finally covering it all over with straw and dried leaves. "And so," he said aloud, "this is the end of a man who wronged a Champdoce—this is what it cost him."

He stopped short, for a few paces off in the shade, under the trees, barely a foot or two from the ground, he fancied he could detect a human face with a pair of shining eyes fixed upon him. The shock was so great that he staggered; but in a moment he recovered himself, and snatching up his bloody sword, he rushed to the spot where he had perceived this frightful apparition. At his first gesture, however, a human form—a woman's form—had started up and fled like the wind towards the house. But Norbert caught her on the steps.

"Mercy!" she cried, falling on her knees, "mercy! Do not kill me."

Without replying, he dragged her by her clothes to the end of the garden, under the lantern. She was a girl of eighteen or nineteen—ugly, dirty, and poorly clad. Norbert examined her, and could not recognize her, though he fancied he had seen her before. "Who are you?" he asked at last.

Her answer was a torrent of tears, and he realised he should never be able to get her to speak if he did not begin by reassuring her. "Come, now," he said, more gently, "don't weep in this foolish way, I'm not going to hurt you. Who are you?"

"I'm Caroline Schimmel."

"Caroline?" he repeated.

"Yes, Monsieur le Duc; I have been a scullion here for three months."

"How does it happen you are not at the wedding with the others?"

"Alas! it wasn't my fault; I was invited, and wanted to go, but I hadn't a decent dress to wear: I've only fifteen francs wages a month. I'm very unfortunate, for not one of the women in the house would lend me one."

"How did you happen to be in the garden?" interrupted Norbert.

"Oh! Monsieur le Duc, I felt so very unhappy, and I was sitting at my attic window crying, when all at once I saw a light in the garden. I thought it might be robbers, and I went down the servants' stairs on tip-toe."

"And what did you see?"

"I saw everything."

"What do you mean by everything?"

"Well, when I got here you and the other man were digging. I made certain you were searching for hidden treasure. But, bless me! how mistaken I was! The other began to talk to you, but I couldn't hear a word, you, either of you said; and then you began to fight. I was horribly frightened, but I couldn't turn my eyes away. Then I saw the man fall back—"

"And then?"

"Then," she repeated, with evident hesitation, "I saw you—bury him—then—"

"Did you have a good look at this man?"

"Yes, Monsieur le Duc."

"Had you ever seen him before? Do you know his name?"

"No, Monsieur le Duc."

Norbert reflected for a moment. "Listen, my girl," he said. "If you know how to hold your tongue—if you know how to forget—it will be a great piece of luck for you that you came into the garden to-night."

"I will never say a word, Monsieur le Duc, to any human being. I swear to you I never will."

"Very well. If you keep this oath your fortune's as good as made. To-morrow I'll give you a handsome sum, and you can return to your province, and marry any good fellow you may happen to fancy."

"Can that really be, Monsieur le Duc?"

"It will be. Now go up to your room again and go to bed. To-morrow my valet Jean will tell you just what you are to do, and you must obey him as you would obey me."

"Oh! Monsieur le Duc!—oh! Monsieur le Duc," and in her transports of joy, the ugly scullion wept and laughed together.

To know that his name, honour, and life were in the hands of a girl like this, meant the loss of all repose and sense of security for Norbert. And yet, he was at her mercy! For it resolved itself into that. He realised that in future this girl's merest wishes would be orders he must obey. No matter what absurd notions and fancies she might take into her head, he must comply with them all. What means could he employ to liberate himself from this odious slavery? He only knew of one—murder; but surely there had been enough blood spilt on that one night.

Four persons now possessed, or were on the point of possessing Norbert's secret. First, the unknown person who had written the anonymous letter, then the duchess, and Caroline, and finally, Jean, whom he would be compelled to confide in. But this was not the moment to reflect. Danger was perhaps at hand. The servants might at any moment return. Accordingly, Norbert obliterated the last traces of the duel, and then went to his wife's room.

He expected to find her unconscious, lying where she had fallen when he pushed her back. But the duchess was seated in an arm-chair beside the fire. She was very pale, and her eyes shone with fever. She rose when he entered the room, fixing such a strange look upon him that he involuntarily bowed his head.

But ashamed of his own moral cowardice, he swiftly raised it again. "My honour is avenged," he said, with a bitter sneer. "The Marquis de Croisenois is dead. I have killed your lover, madame."

She was apparently prepared for this blow, for she did not start; only her expression became more haughty, and the lurid light in her dark eyes grew more intense. "You are mistaken," she said, in a wonderfully calm voice. "You are mistaken, Monsieur de Croisenois—George—was not my lover."

"Oh! spare yourself the trouble of lying; I ask no questions."

Norbert was inexpressibly irritated by his wife's calm impassibility, and would have given anything to have been able to dispel this mood, which to him was utterly inexplicable. But in vain did he use the most mortifying words, and speak in the most sarcastic tone; she had reached heights he could not attain.

"I am not lying," she answered, coldly. "Why should I deceive or feign? What have I to fear or dread any more in this world? You wish the truth? Very well, you shall have it. Learn, first, that it was with my knowledge and my permission that George came here this evening. He came because I expected him, I left the small gate open for him."

"Madame!"

"When you came, he had not been five minutes in my room, where he had never been before. I might have left you, fled from you, perhaps; but living under your roof and bearing your name I could never have betrayed you. When you entered the room, he was begging me to fly with him. At that moment his life and his honour were mine. Ah! why did I hesitate? Had I said, yes, he would have been living, and in some country far away; we two might have learned that this life was not all sorrow."

She became more and more animated as she spoke; all her usual timidity seemed to have vanished. "Yes, I will tell you all," she continued—"all, since you desire it. Ah! I loved him before I even knew that there was such a person as yourself in existence. It was my broken love I wept for on the day when I was weak enough to obey my father, cowardly enough to give my hand to such as man as you! And it is my own folly I now deplore—my own miserable weakness. Why did I ever consent to be your wife? You have killed George, you say? No; not so. His memory will live for ever in my heart, radiant and imperishable."

"Take care!" cried Norbert; "take care! If—"

"Ah! you will kill me, too? Do so! I will make no struggle for life; it is worth nothing without him. He is no more. I have lived, and life can have no charms for me henceforth, death would be welcome. To kill me would be the only boon you could now bestow on me! Strike! You would unite us in death, and my lips would murmur, till they grew cold and rigid : 'Thanks! thanks!'"

Norbert listened, confounded, astonished that he had still any power of feeling left him, after the terrible scenes he had passed through. Was this she—Marie, his wife—who expressed herself with this unheard-of violence—who braved him thus, and defied his anger? How could he have so misunderstood her? He had often compared her to polar ice, and now she burst forth into volcanic passion. He forgot all his resentment in his admiration. She seemed to him absolutely transfigured, her beauty was something unearthly, her eyes glistened like stars, and her superb hair fell around her shoulders in heavy masses. Yes, this was passion—real passion—not the mocking shadow he had so long pursued. Marie was capable of loving, really loving ; whilst for Diane, the fair-haired beauty with the steel-blue eyes, love was only a battle or a jest! This was a revelation, indeed. Ah! what would he not have given to have been able to efface the past? An absurd, preposterous idea entered his mind. He really fancied that his wife might possibly forgive him, and so went towards her with extended arms. "Marie!" he said, "Marie!"

"I forbid you," she answered—"I forbid you to call me Marie."

He did not reply, but approached still nearer—when, all at once, she threw herself back with a fearful shriek. "Blood!" she cried—"blood on your hands!"

Norbert looked at his hands. It was true. The palm of his left hand was crimson red, and on his right shirt-cuff there was a large spot of blood. The sight well nigh overwhelmed him, and yet he once more made a pleading gesture.

But the duchess pointed to the door. "Go!" she cried, with extraordinary vehemence—"go! I will not betray you—I will keep the secret of your crime. But never forget that there lies a corpse between us, and that I hate you!"

Rage and jealousy tore Norbert's heart. Croisenois, although dead, would harm him still. "And you," he answered, in a hoarse voice—"you seem to forget that I am your husband—that you are mine—that I can make your life one long agony. Let me remind you of that. To-morrow, at ten o'clock, I shall be here."

He left the house just as the clocks were striking two, and hurried to the Esplanade des Invalides. Steady at his post, the soldier was still leading the horse about. "Upon my word!" he exclaimed, however, when Norbert appeared, "you make long visits! I only had leave to go to the theatre, and I shall get into trouble."

"Pshaw! I told you I would give you twenty francs. Take a couple," and Norbert handed him two louis.

"Ah!" exclaimed the soldier, in delighted astonishment, and saluting the duke as deferentially as if he had been a marshal of France, he hurried off.

An hour later, Norbert rapped at the window of the wine shop, where Jean was waiting. "Take care not to be seen when you take the horse in," he said, "and then come to me ; I need your advice and experience."

XVIII.

GRIEF, anger, and horror had imparted wonderful strength and energy to the Duchess de Champdoce, whilst she was in her husband's presence; but as soon as she found herself alone, all her excitement subsided, and exhausted by the stupendous effort she had made, she sank on to a sofa, half fainting and sobbing. Her despair was all the greater, as she reproached herself for Croisenois' death. "If I had not granted him that fatal rendezvous," she said to herself, "he would be living now; it is my love that killed him!"

Her distress was truly terrible. At one moment the idea of going to her father occurred to her; but she rejected it, for what good would it do? The Count de Puymandour would hardly listen to her, or at the most merely say: "You are a duchess, you have five hundred thousand francs a year; you must be happy, or at least you ought to be!"

The night was passed in untold anguish, and when her maids entered her room, about ten o'clock the next morning, they found her stretched on the floor, dressed as they had last seen her at dinner. Her limbs were stiff and cold, her head was burning, and her eyes glistening. This discovery caused quite a panic in the house. No one knew what to do, and four messengers had been despatched, one after the other, for a doctor, when Norbert arrived from Maisons. He went at once to his wife's room. She did not recognise him. Finding her in this condition, he became very uneasy as to what had taken place in his absence. Accordingly he began to question the maids as skilfully as he could, and while thus occupied not one physician, but two arrived. They declared that the duchess was in an alarming state, expressed doubt whether she would even live through this strange attack, and advised a consultation for the afternoon. Then, after urging the strictest adherence to their prescriptions, and the most careful watchfulness, they retired.

These injunctions were superfluous. Norbert took his place at his wife's bedside, determined not to leave her until she was either better or dead. She was now in a terrible fever, and the language delirium brought to her lips made Norbert shudder. This was the second time he had been compelled to guard a secret in the same way. Formerly, at Champdoce, it was his father he watched—the father who could disclose the terrible crime he had attempted. And now he had to guard his wife, and prevent the story of Croisenois' fate escaping her lips. Forced to sit at Marie's side—forced to the contemplation of the past—he was horror-stricken to think that, at twenty-five, he had to look back upon such appalling crimes, and forward to a life filled with such remorse and gloom. What a future was in store for him after such a past! And his wife's delirium was not his only care. Every ten minutes he rang to ascertain if Jean, his faithful valet, had not yet arrived.

At last, after repeated inquiries, Jean came, and Norbert at once led him to the embrasure of a window. "Well?" he asked.

"It is all arranged, sir—be easy."

"This Caroline—"

"Is gone, sir. I put her into the train myself, after giving her twenty thousand francs. She has left Paris, and proposes going to America to find a cousin, who will marry her in all probability—at all events she hopes so."

Norbert breathed more freely—the thought of this Caroline Schimmel had been a fearful weight. "And the other matter?" he asked.

The old servant shook his head sadly. "Ah! It's very perilous," he said.

"What have you done?"

"I have discovered a young commercial traveller, an honest fellow I'm told, who thinks I wish to send him to Egypt to buy cotton. He'll start to-day, and post the two letters written by M. de Croisenois—one at Marseilles, and the second at Cairo."

"And you don't see that these letters will make me perfectly secure?"

"I see that the least carelessness on the part of our agent, or the merest accident, may betray us."

"And yet it must be done."

Jean made no rejoinder. He did not know how to resist his master's orders, so the traveller started, and the letters were posted in due course.

During the two next days Norbert had not a minute to himself. After their consultation the physicians had given a ray of hope, but it was a very faint one. It was suggested that the duchess's reason might always be impaired. And during these hours, which seemed an eternity, Norbert dared not even close his eyes, and it was with a sick dread that he allowed the maids even to enter their mistress's room—for her delirium persisted, and Croisenois' name was constantly mentioned in her ravings. However, on the fourth day the fever turned, Marie slept, and Norbert had leisure to reflect.

How was it that Madame de Mussidan, who usually came every day, had given no signs of life? This circumstance seemed to him so extraordinary that he ventured to write her a brief note informing her of his wife's illness. An hour later he received this laconic reply: "Do you believe there is any reason for Monsieur de Mussidan's sudden announcement that we are to spend the winter in Italy? We leave to-night. Farewell!
"D."

So she abandoned him them—abandoned him, and thus his last hope vanished. And yet he was still so blind that he fancied this separation was really as great a blow to her as to himself.

A few days later, when Madame de Champdoce was out of danger, although he himself was still bowed down by this last misfortune, the doctor took him aside in a mysterious manner; he had to announce a startling though delightful piece of news: the Duchess de Champdoce was *enceinte*.

Such indeed was the case, and this was the secret that Marie had been on the point of revealing to George de Croisenois when her husband's arrival interrupted their interview. It was the thought of her condition that had prevented her from leaving her husband's roof, and had given her courage to resist her lover's entreaties to elope with him. Unfortunately, she had not disclosed the fact to Norbert, and now that the news came to him, after that terrible scene, after the duel and the death of Croisenois, it was bound to rekindle all his rage. Persuaded of his wife's guilt, despite all her protestations, he could only imagine that the child she had conceived was none of his. As the physician spoke to him he turned pale, and his eyes flashed fire. "Thanks, doctor," he stammered—"thanks for this good news. It makes me very happy, of course. Excuse me—I must go to the duchess at once."

However, instead of going to his wife, he repaired to his library and locked himself in. He needed solitude to look this new situation full in the face, and regain his self-possession. The more Norbert reflected, the more he persuaded himself that he had been miserably duped. Must he welcome the child of George de Croisenois and rear it as his own? Must he accept this living testimony of his degradation? This child would grow up in his house, bear his name, and inherit the enormous fortune of the Champdoce family. "No! never," he cried, "never? I would strangle it sooner with my own hands!"

The more he thought of the disgust he would be compelled to hide—of the caresses and affection he must feign, to avoid the suspicions of the world—the more impossible it seemed to him that he could play such a monstrous farce. And yet although he longed for vengeance, he deter-mined to dissimulate. The fact is, he feared his wife's revelations. The mysterious disappearance of De Croisenois had created a great sensation, and although the letters posted by Jean's emissary thickened the mystery of the affair, they did not satisfy either the police or the public. However, the world grows tired of everything in turn, other strange events occurred, Croisenois was forgotten, and Norbert at last began to believe that he could hope with impunity. He led a miserable life. He felt utterly worn out and exhausted. He was not yet twenty-five, and yet there did not seem to be a ray of hope in the future. For three months Diane had given him no sign of life, a river of blood separated him from his wife; among all his associates he had not a single true friend, and dissipation utterly palled on his taste.

Thus in the seclusion of his own house he pondered on what had now become his one fixed idea: how could he get rid of that child which was coming into the world, how could he free himself from bringing it up as his own? It seemed to him that there was only one plan possible. He must procure another child no matter where or how, and substitute it for the infant the duchess was about to give birth to. Yes, that was the only feasible scheme he could think of, and accordingly he explained it to Jean, whom devotion had made his accomplice. For the first time, since Norbert had been his master, Jean resisted. This substitution seemed to him abominable, and he did not hesitate to express his conviction that it would certainly entail misfortune for all who took part in it. Still, Norbert was so pressing and imperative, that, at last, the old valet reluctantly consented to assist him, being all the more influenced as his master had talked of applying to some one else, who might prove less scrupulous and skilful in carrying out this infernal scheme.

The enterprise was a perilous one, difficult to conduct with due secrecy; special coincidences were needed to insure success, and even when every possible precaution was taken, something must still be left to chance. No matter. A month later Jean informed his master that it would be advisable for the duchess to establish herself at once at the Château de L——, a place owned by the Champdoce family near Montoire. Once there, the old valet would answer for the rest. Accordingly, the very next day Norbert took his wife to L——. Poor woman! she was the mere shadow of herself. Of recent times she and Norbert had lived like strangers under the same roof —weeks sometimes elapsing without their seeing each other, for when they had anything to communicate they usually wrote it down.

The Château de L—— was marvellously adapted to Norbert's plan—for once there the duchess was entirely at her husband's mercy and discretion. She could look nowhere for assistance; she had not even the faint hope of her father's help, for a month previously he had died suddenly, from disappointment and vexation, at having been beaten at an election. What exactly occurred at L—— when the duchess was confined? It is difficult to say, so well was the secret kept. The note in which the poor mother wrote: "Have mercy, give me back our child," alone reveals something of the terrible struggle which undoubtedly took place. However, this much is certain—the child which the duchess gave birth to was left by Jean at the Foundling Hospital of Vendôme; and it is moreover beyond question that the infant, baptised under the name of Anne-René-Gontran de Donpair, Marquis de Champdoce, was really the son of a poor girl of the environs of Montoire, who was called the "Witch."

* * * * * * * * *

XIX.

AT this point B. Mascarot's manuscript abruptly ended. Paul Violaine laid the leaves on the table, saying with some surprise, "And that's all?" It was, however, quite time he finished, for his voice was well-nigh broken by this perusal of six hours' duration, with but one or two pauses of a few minutes. The narrative had certainly been listened to with due attention. Neither Catenac nor Hortebize had interrupted, either with remark or gesture. As for B. Mascarot, he had apparently listened with the satisfaction of an author who is proud of his work, but in reality, as he sat leaning back in his arm-chair, twirling his thumbs, he was keenly watching his companions. The effect of the narrative had been just what he had anticipated. The perusal was over, and Paul, Catenae and Hortebize, still looked at each other, with an air of mingled terror and stupefaction. The lawyer was the first to break the silence. "Ah! ha! I always said that our friend Baptistin was born for literature. As soon as he takes up a pen the business man disappears, and instead of notes and memoranda, we have a romance!"

"Do you really look on this as a romance!" asked Hortebize.

"A romance in form, certainly—you will admit that."

"Catenac," said Mascarot, in a sarcastic tone, "ought, better than any one else, to be able to judge of the veracity of this tale, he being the adviser of the noble Duke de Champdoce, this very Norbert whose youth I have described."

"I don't deny the foundation," said Catenac, quickly.

"Then what do you deny?"

"Nothing, in fact; I was merely jesting. I merely object to the somewhat romantic form in which you have stated your case."

"Catenac," resumed Mascarot, "has heard several important statements from his noble client, but he has taken good care never to communicate them to us. Knowing as much as he did, he had every reason to believe we were going straight on to the rocks, and should be wrecked. Indeed, he positively hoped such would prove the case, and that he would thus get rid of us for good!" The advocate tried to protest and deny, but Mascarot silenced him with a threatening look and an imperious wave of the hand. "As for this narrative being a romance," he resumed, "my work has merely been so much editing—so much classification and curtailment. The romantic element, if such it be, is entirely the work of Norbert and Madame de Mussidan. Certain things may have seemed to you far fetched, but don't blame me. I have merely been a copyist."

"It seems to me—"

"It seems to me," interrupted Mascarot, "that you have forgotten Madame de Mussidan's correspondence. She is a very careful woman, and had preserved not only her own letters, which Norbert returned to her, but also his answers."

"And we have them ?"

"Most certainly we have, and my narrative is mainly a *resumé* of their contents, supplemented by information from the instigator of the original intrigue—'judge' Dauman."

"The 'judge' indeed ! What, is he still living ?"

"Certainly he is, and you know him too. He's one of our people. He is no longer in his *première jeunesse*, no doubt ; in fact, he's rather broken as regards his limbs, but his brain is still intact."

Catenac had become very serious. "You tell me so much—" he began.

"I can tell you even more," interrupted Mascarot. "I can tell you that all the particulars of the duel and death of poor George de Croisenois were written under the dictation of Caroline Schimmel. When this woman left Paris with the 20,000 francs Jean had given her, she meant to go to America, but as it happened she travelled no farther than Le Hâvre. The good looks and persuasive language of a gallant sailor she met there, changed her plans. This sailor was certainly a most amiable man as long as her money lasted, but somehow or other he disappeared just at the same time as her last thousand franc note. Caroline was as poor as ever again, but, however, she contrived to return to Paris, and applied to the Duke de Champdoce. He realised he was caught, and succoured her. Four or five times he tried to assure Caroline a comfortable little position, but her misconduct made all attempts in that direction useless. At last the duke resignedly allowed her to black-mail him whenever she chose, accepting this shame, perhaps, as a kind of penance. She leads a queer life. Now and then she'll seek a situation and work for a week or two, but her dissolute habits soon gain the upper hand, and then she goes off to the Duke de Champdoce and asks him for money. However, the oath of secrecy she swore was until very recently faithfully kept by her. If it hadn't been for her partiality to the bottle, Tantaine would probably have failed to extort a word from her. It may happen, that having recovered, she will remember she has divulged the duke's secret, and go and warn him of the fact."

"Good heavens !" exclaimed Catenac, in alarm, " in that case—"

"Do you think," asked Mascarot, "that I should be as much at ease as I am, if I feared any peril? What would Caroline say. Who would she accuse of having stolen her secret? An old man named Tantaine. Do you suppose the noble duke, your client, would be able to trace any connection between a poor devil like Tantaine, and a highly respected advocate like yourself ?"

"It would be difficult, indeed ! "

"And besides," urged Dr. Hortebize, "at the first sign of danger we should suppress old Tantaine. No trace of him would ever more be found."

B. Mascarot nodded approvingly, and then resumed, "What have we really to fear from the Duke de Champdoce? Nothing at all in my opinion.

We hold him as surely as we hold the Countess de Mussidan. We have his letters, and we know that Croisenois' skeleton could be found in his garden. The identity of the marquis's remains could easily be established, for we know that when he disappeared he had about his person a thousand francs or so in Spanish *onzas*. That fact is distinctly stated in the report of the inquiry which took place concerning his disappearance."

It was amusing to watch Catenac's face, and see how his feelings and views changed as he gradually became convinced that little or no risk was incurred by these proceedings. "Come," said he, "enough speaking. I'm at your discretion. Am I not? And, besides, you've convinced me. I'll act loyally, I give you my word. Explain your plan, and then I'll tell you all I have learned from the duke."

Mascarot smiled with an air of satisfaction. He had really won the day, and no longer doubted the advocate's sincerity. "Before anything else," said he, "I must give you the end of the story which Paul has just read. The Duke and Duchess de Champdoce renounced all hopes of happiness, but they both determined to save appearances, and did not allow the world to suspect the terrible life they led. The duchess, who had become a great invalid, devoted all the time her ailments allowed her to works of charity ; and the duke, after applying himself to remedy the deficiences of his early education, became one of the most remarkable men in Europe."

"And Madame de Mussidan?" asked Catenac.

"Her husband's father was dead. She had now become a countess with great wealth at her disposal. However, with the strange perversity of her character, she did not consider herself completely avenged on Norbert, until he learned that he owed the crowning misfortune of his life to her ; and, in fact, on her return from Italy she sent for Norbert and told him everything. Yes, she dared to tell him that it was she who had, so to say, impelled his wife into Croisenois' arms—she told him that it was she who, having heard of the rendezvous, had written him that fatal anonymous letter."

"And he didn't kill her?" cried Hortebize.

"Hadn't she all his letters? And she threatened him with them, moreover. Oh! we need not flatter ourselves that we have the monopoly of blackmailing! This noble countess made the duke shell out just as if she had been a mere adventuress. Only ten days ago she borrowed—she called it borrowing, you observe—a large sum from him, to appease Van Klopen. However, on that point *sufficit*, let us turn to the child who was substituted for the duchess's real son. You knew him, doctor, I believe."

"I often saw him. He was a handsome fellow—"

"Yes, but a miserable scamp after all. He was educated and brought up in the most princely manner ; but he had the tastes and manners of a lacquey, and if he had lived he would certainly have dishonoured the name he bore. He had caused the duke and duchess any amount of despair, when some ten months ago he was carried off by a brain fever. He died, imploring the forgiveness of those whom he believed to be his parents, and they forgot their animosity towards each other at the bedside of this dying youth who had caused them so much sorrow—a sorrow. which Norbert, at least, may have looked upon as divine punishment. Well, this lad being dead, it seemed as if the name of Champdoce was doomed to extinction. However, urged by his wife, Norbert decided to try and find the child, left at the Foundling Hospital of Vendôme. He could not undo what had been done, but still, in accordance with the law, he might adopt this child and bequeath fortune, name, and title to him. He no longer doubted that the boy was really his own ; and so, all hope and expectation, he started for Vendôme provided with all needful information for identification. A terrible disappointment awaited him. It was admitted at the hospital that a child had been received there on the day Norbert named, and clothed as he described. The register proved all this, and the medal the poor little foundling had worn round his neck was even produced. But on the other hand, the child had long since left the hospital, and no one knew what had become of him. When twelve years old, he had run away, and all efforts to find him again had proved unavailing."

It was with a keen pang that Catenac listened to these precise particulars, which showed how well informed his associates were. He had hoped to be able to reveal many of these points himself as an atonement for his past treachery.

However, Mascarot continued, " This new misfortune overwhelmed the Duke de Champdoce. After the crimes and follies of his youth, which he considered he had bitterly expiated by long years of misery and anguish, he had hoped at least to end his days in peace, and to find his home not quite desolate after all ; but even this solace now seemed denied him. He returned home, looking fully twenty years older, and had to tell his poor wife the sad truth. Their son had disappeared—there was no hope of finding him. For some days the duke remained in a state of absolute prostration, but at last it seemed to him that it would be culpable cowardice not to make an effort to try and find the child. The world is wide, no doubt, and a nameless, penniless boy flying from a foundling hospital is a mere speck on its surface ; but then with money miracles can be accomplished, so why shouldn't the duke make an effort? With his great wealth he might obtain the assistance of the most expert detectives. And besides, his life would have an object, and in the search he might utilise all his own energies now running to waste. Seized with this idea, he swore that he would never rest—that he would never despair of finding his son until he held in his hands the indisputable proofs of the lad's death. However, he did not confide his project to the duchess. He feared, for he had learned to have some consideration for her, that alternatives of despair and hope would be more than she could bear. Her health was so shattered, that such excitement might kill her. Having fully reflected, he began by applying to that lesser Providence which watches over society from the Rue de Jerusalem. However the police hardly paid any attention to him. They merely said, ' All right. We'll see what can be done ; call again in a month's time. Good-morning.' The fact is, the duke's peculiar position imposed especial reserve upon him. As he could not tell the truth, he naturally presented the subject weakly, and in fact, awakened no interest. This was very unfortunate for him, for he had been received by a rather clever chap—a fellow who has a big reputation at the Préfecture, who is our friend Martin Rigal's neighbour by the way, and whose name is Lecoq."

To Paul's great surprise, this name produced an appalling effect on Dr. Hortebize, who at once started to his feet, caught hold of the locket dangling from his watch-chain, and looked round the room with haggard eyes. " Stop ! " said he, in a choked voice, " if that Lecoq's mixed up in this, I withdraw, for nothing will go well. Yes, really, I withdraw."

His panic was so singular, that Catenac deigned to smile. " Ah ! ah ! " said the lawyer, " I understand your excitement. But don't be troubled ; Lecoq has nothing to do with us."

This assurance was not enough for Hortebize, who turned and looked at Mascarot. "No, Lecoq has nothing to do with us," repeated the agent. "The simpleton replied that his position prevented him from occupying himself with any private investigation—which is true, by the way. The duke offered him a large sum if he would give up his position, but he refused, saying that he did not work for money, but for art."

"Which is also true," interposed Catenac.

"To make a long story short, it was when Lecoq refused his assistance that the duke applied to Catenac, who introduced him to Perpignan. I believe that is everything—"

"Yes, that's everything," said the advocate, "I will merely add that the duke requested me to superintend the searches."

"Have you a plan?"

"Not yet. The duke's instructions are these: 'Succeed, even if you have to question everybody on earth.' However, operations have not yet commenced, and to say the truth, I am very much of Perpignan's opinion, the enterprise is a senseless one."

"Lecoq thought that success was possible."

"He said so, no doubt; but I fancy that if he had really *thought* so, he would have undertaken the task himself."

"Well," said Mascarot, calmly, "I have felt certain of success ever since the outset."

"Indeed!"

"Yes, and I have been at work—"

"What! You have been to Vendôme!"

"Never mind: I have been somewhere, at all events, and at this very moment I can lay my hand on the Duke de Champdoce's heir."

"You are jesting!"

"I was never more serious in my life—I have found him. Only, as it is quite impossible for me to appear in the matter, I reserve the pleasure of restoring this child to his father to yourself and Perpignan."

Catenac looked at Marscarot, Hortebize, and Paul in turn, as if desirous of assuring himself that he was not being laughed at. "You don't wish to appear?" he said at last to his associate, in a suspicious tone. "And why? Do you fear failure then? Do you want to ensnare me?"

Mascarot shrugged his shoulders. "First of all," he said, "I am no traitor, as you very well know. Then it is our mutual interest that no misfortune should befall you. One of us can't be compromised without harming the others. And besides, as to laying a trap for you, the part you'll have to play is so simple that treachery or bad faith is quite out of the question. You will have nothing to do but to point out the beginning of the scent. Others will follow it up at their own risk and peril, and you will only have to look on."

"But—"

Mascarot's patience was gone; and he frowned severely. "Enough!" he harshly answered. "No further discussion is required; I am the master, and you must obey."

When the agent spoke in this style, it was pure waste of time to try and resist, and so Catenac, albeit humiliated and puzzled, discreetly relapsed into silence. "Now," resumed Mascarot, "sit down at my table and take careful notes of what I am about to say. Success, as I have told you, is certain, but I must be ably seconded. Everything now depends on your exactitude and the precision of your movements—one false step may spoil our game."

XX.

WITHOUT another word, hiding his resentment and jealousy under an equivocal smile, Catenac sat down at the agent's table, opened a large note-book, and provided himself with a well sharpened pencil. In the meanwhile, Mascarot, on his side, took up a dozen of those cardboard squares which he spent his life in studying.

"Now, Paul," said he, "pray listen, and you, Catenac, don't lose a word of what I am going to say. To-day's Thursday; can it be arranged that the Duke de Champdoce, Perpignan, and yourself, shall start for Vendôme on Saturday?"

"Possibly so," answered the advocate.

"Answer me with a yes or no. Are you sure that you can take these people there?"

"Well, then—yes."

"Very well; on Saturday you will start, and on reaching Vendôme you must go to the Hôtel de la Poste."

"Hôtel de la Poste!" grumbled Catenac, with the air of a secretary who repeats the last words of a phrase dictated to him.

"On the day of your arrival at Vendôme," resumed Mascarot, "you will naturally do nothing—you will rest and feel your way. It will be Sunday, as you know. Nevertheless, go to the hospital together, and repeat the in-quiries which the duke previously made alone. The superior, who is a woman of the higher class, and a good woman too, will take the greatest pleasure in answering your questions. Through her you will again obtain the description of the boy, and the precise date of his disappearance. She will tell you that it was on the 9th of September 1856, that his flight was discovered. She will tell you that he was at that time a tall, vigorous lad, with an intelligent countenance, and keen bright eyes, healthy and hand-some, about twelve years and a half old, but looking fully fifteen. She will say that he wore a grey linen blouse, trousers of cotton stuff striped blue and white, a little cap without a peak, and a black silk neckcloth with white spots. She will add that the young fellow also carried away with him a white blouse, a pair of grey trousers, and a pair of new shoes, tied up in a coloured handkerchief."

The lawyer watched the agent with stealthy curiosity. "Upon my word!" he muttered, "you are well informed."

"Passably so, I think," answered Mascarot carelessly; and then in a quick decided tone, he continued: "After this you will return to your hotel, and not until then—you understand—you will hold a consultation as to your first steps. Perpignan's plan is a good one—"

"You know it then?"

"I think so. He will suggest dividing the environs of Vendôme into a certain number of zones, and visiting every dwelling in these zones in succession."

"The project seems reasonable to me."

"It is so. Let him initiate it, but quietly influence its execution. Draw his attention to the fact that a natural division of the surrounding localities in some measure already exists, and that the simplest course is to begin by exploring, first of all, the *communes* depending from Vendôme itself, and then all the *cantons* of the *arrondissement*. In support of your idea ask for Bescherelle's Geographical Dictionary, and determine the others to work in the order the dictionary indicates. That is to say, you will, first of all, visit the *commune* of Areines, then Azé, then Marcilly, but that's already more than enough."

"Areines," repeated Catenac, like an echo; "Azé, Marcilly."

Mascarot leaned over the advocate and touched his shoulder lightly. "Note the order," he said; "the order I indicate. Everything depends on that."

"Never fear—it's written! Look."

The agent nodded his approbation. "When you set out," he continued, "you will naturally require a guide."

"Of course, we shall require such a person."

"Well, here, Catenac, I am obliged to leave something to chance; I can't do otherwise. But there are ninety-nine chances to one that the hotel-keeper will designate a man named Frégot, whom he employs as a commissioner. Still, it may be that his choice will fall on another. In that case you must, in some way or other—skilfully, mind—obtain the services of this particular man."

"But what am I to say to him?"

"Nothing at all. He knows what he has to do. His duties have been even more carefully traced out than your own; he understands everything fully. However, these preliminaries settled, you will, on Monday morning, begin your investigations in the Commune of Areines, under the guidance of Frégot. Leave all the responsibility to Perpignan; but be sure the duke is with you. You will begin by questioning the local authorities, who will not be able to give you any information, and then you must go through the village from door to door. Ask the inhabitants a series of questions which you will previously prepare. Something in this style: 'My friends, we are looking for a child. There are ten thousand francs reward for the person who puts us on the right track. At the beginning of September, 1856, this lad must have been in your neighbourhood after running away from the Foundling Hospital at Vendôme. Do any of you recollect such a child? Did any of you shelter or assist him? The ten thousand francs will be paid at once. He was thirteen years old, &c., &c.'"

The lawyer stopped Mascarot. "Wait a moment," he said; "I can find nothing better than your own words; so I'll just jot them down." And he proceeded to do so.

"On Monday," resumed the agent, "you will receive discouraging answers. Matters will be the same on Tuesday and on the next three days; but on Saturday be prepared for a great surprise. On that day Frégot will take you to a secluded farm, which is tilled by a man named Lorgelin, his wife and two sons. These good people will be at table; they will ask you to take some refreshment, and you will accept. But at the first words you utter about the child, you will see their faces change. The farmer's wife will turn pale and at once exclaim, 'Holy Virgin! these gentlemen are surely speaking of our poor Sans-Père.'"

Since he began to disclose his plan, Mascarot appeared to have grown taller, and his features, usually so composed, seemed animated by the spirit of perversity. His mode of explanation was wonderfully clear, and his gestures were full of authority. He spoke of problematic events as certain to happen, and described them with such strange lucidity, and with such merciless and logical reasoning, that they seemed to be absolutely real.

"What! The farmer's wife will say that?" exclaimed Catenac in surprise.

"Just that, and nothing else. Then the husband will explain that he gave the name of Sans-Père to a poor little fellow whom they found shivering in a ditch by the roadside early in September, 1856. The little fellow was taken home and charitably sheltered by them. You will begin to read your description of the youngster, but the farmer will close your mouth by giving his, which you will find to correspond precisely with your own. Then Lorgelin will sing the praises of this child; how the farm seemed like another place while he was there, so that they never had the courage to take him back to the hospital at Vendôme, as no doubt they ought to have done. The whole family will sing the youngster's praises. Sans-Père was so merry and clever. At thirteen he could write like a notary; and they will even show you some of his writing in an old account book. Finally, mother Lorgelin, with tears in her eyes, will tell you this petted child became an ingrate; for, a year later, in September, 1857, he left the family that had adopted him. Yes, he abandoned them to follow some mountebanks who had been performing in the neighbouring village. You will be touched by the regret these worthy folks will express. Lorgelin will tell you he went to Château Renault and to Blois, in hopes of finding the lad and bringing him back; but all in vain. He couldn't find him."

Catenac had held his breath for the denouement, and was much disappointed. "I confess I am puzzled to see what we shall have gained when we have heard the Lorgelin's story," said he.

"Let me finish," rejoined Mascarot. "In such a case you wouldn't know what to do; but Perpignan won't hesitate for a moment, I'll be bound. He will tell you that he has the end of the thread and can follow up the clew."

"I think you esteem Perpignan too highly."

"Not so. Each man has his trade. Besides, if he wanders off the scent, you must bring him back to it—delicately, cautiously, you understand. His first step will be to take you to the mayor's office in the village of Azé, near this farm. There you will ask to see the register of provisional licenses and permits, and on consulting it you will find that in September, 1857, there arrived at Azé, from Versailles, and bound for Tours, a party of mountebanks, comprising nine persons, with two vehicles and five horses, under the direction of a man called Vigoureux, nicknamed the 'Grasshopper.'"

Catenac had begun writing again, and his pencil flew over the paper. "Softly! softly!" he said; "I can't follow you."

After a pause of a few minutes, the agent continued: "An attentive examination of the register will show you that no other troupe of mountebanks passed through Azé that month. Therefore little Sans-Père must have followed the Grasshopper; and you will then read the description of this same Grasshopper's person, still in the same register: 'VIGOUREUX.—Born at La Bourgonce (Vosges); age, forty-seven; height, six feet two; eyes, small, grey, and near-sighted; complexion, dark. Third finger of the left hand cut off above the first joint.' If with these particulars you mistake any other mountebank for him, you must certainly be very stupid, all of you."

"I should never find him, though," muttered Catenac.

"But you have Perpignan, whose business it is to do so. You will see him bristling with importance, and overjoyed at what he has learned at the mayor's office. He will tell you, loftily, that the investigations in the provinces are completed, and that it is advisable to return to Paris at once. Make no objections. Allow your noble client to reward Frégot and Lorgelin, but take care not to leave him behind you. I presume he will be in a hurry to reach Paris. When you arrive here again, Perpignan will take you at once to the Rue de Jerusalem, where Vigoureux must certainly have his papers like all other travelling artists. The police are very avaricious, and keep a firm hold on all the documents they possess ; but the magic name of the Duke de Champdoce will open all the boxes. Finally, you will be informed that Vigoureux was sentenced to imprisonment for disorderly conduct in 1864, and that now he is still under surveillance, and keeps a wineshop at the corner of the Rue Dupleix—"

"Stop a moment !" exclaimed Catenac ; "let me take down his address."

"When you go to the Rue Dupleix, you will recognise Vigoureux by his missing finger. He will admit that the little rascal followed him, and was with his troupe for ten months. He will say he was a fairly decent lad, but as proud as a peacock and as lazy as a lizard. All he cared for was music, and he became most intimate with an old Alsatian named Fritz, who was the band-master of the troupe. In fact, this old fellow and the lad were so happy in each other's society, that one fine day they went off together. Thereupon you will ask what has become of this Fritz, and Vigoureux will overwhelm you with insults ; but in your capacity as a lawyer threaten him with punishment for carrying off a minor, and then he'll become as mild as a dove, and promise to try and find the old Alsatian. Before a week's over, he'll tell you he has found Fritz, whom you can see at the Hospice St. Magloire, where he has obtained comfortable shelter for his old age."

Catenac, Hortebize, and even Paul Violaine had long since lost their illusions, and the two former, at least, were not easily surprised, and yet they marvelled greatly as they listened to Mascarot still unwinding the thread of this strange search, proceeding from investigation to investigation in the most minute manner, and giving the most precise particulars concerning each successive prediction. "Now," resumed the agent, "this fellow Fritz is a cunning old scamp—tottering and blear-eyed, no doubt—but a great deal more cute than he looks. Tell the Duke de Champdoce not to trust him too much. However, the old rogue will tell you, with many tears, all the sacrifices he made for his dear boy. He will tell you that he went without his tobacco and without his schnapps to pay for the music lessons which he insisted on Sans-Père taking. He will say he had determined that the lad should go to the *Conservatoire* ; for he had recognised his surprising ability, and cherished the hope of seeing him become a great musician some day, like Weber or Mozart. I'm persuaded that Fritz's crocodile tears will touch your noble client. He will see his son rising above the trammels of poverty all unaided. He will recognise this energy as indicating the characteristics of the Champdoce family, and would be ready to accept the lad as his son on the strength of that alone."

It was always a hard task, not to say an impossible one, to divine Mascarot's thoughts, and Catenac had, for three quarters of an hour, been trying to guess what was passing in this spectacled sphinx's mind. What was he aiming at ? Was all this serious, or merely so much joking ? What was true and what was false in all he said and prophesied ? The advocate was utterly at a loss to tell. Still, he was growing impatient, and so exclaimed, "Never mind, never mind about all that. I shall find out if your surmises are correct, later on, from the facts themselves."

"If your penetration requires no further explanations from me," rejoined Mascarot testily, "you will allow me, I trust, to continue for the benefit of our young friend, Paul Violaine, who has a far more difficult part to play than you. So, to resume, the old Alsatian will try and excite your compassion by declaring that as soon as the lad felt himself strong enough to fly alone, he abandoned Fritz, installed himself in a magnificent hotel in the Rue d'Arras, gave music lessons, and played of an evening in a band at a ball. However, you will listen impatiently to old Fritz's grumbling, for you will detect in his complaints the rancour of a disappointed speculator. He will confess to you, moreover, that his very bread comes from that 'ungrateful fellow.' The duke will, of course, leave him some testimonial of his joy, and then you will betake yourselves as fast as possible to the hotel in the Rue d'Arras. The landlord there will state that four years ago he got rid of this artist, the only one who ever dared to install himself in the house ; but with a little skill, and a twenty-franc piece, you will obtain the name and address of one of the young musician's former pupils—Madame Grandorge—a widow in the Rue Saint Louis. This woman, who is still handsome, will tell you, with a blush, that she is ignorant of her former teacher's present address, but that he formerly resided at No. 57 Rue de la Harpe. From the Rue de la Harpe you will be sent to the Rue Jacob, and thence to the Rue Montmartre, at the corner of the Rue Joquelet."

The worthy agent here paused to draw breath, and indulge in one of those quiet chuckles which presage the success of some capital joke. "Be comforted, friend Catenac," he said ; "you have nearly reached the end of your pilgrimage. The concierge in the Rue Montmartre, mother Bregot, who is the most obliging and most talkative woman in the world, will take much pleasure in explaining to you that the artist still has his bachelor apartment under her roof, but that he lives there no longer. 'For he has been lucky,' she will add, 'and I'm glad of it. Last month he married the daughter of a rich banker in our street. This young lady, Mademoiselle Martin Rigal, fell head over heels in love with him !'"

Catenac ought to have foreseen what was coming, and yet he uttered an exclamation of surprise. "Upon my word !"

"Yes, that's precisely what she'll say," rejoined Mascarot, with modest triumph. "The Duke de Champdoce will drag you off to the residence of our excellent friend, Martin Rigal, and there you'll find our young *protégé*, Paul—Flavia's happy husband."

Having thus spoken, Mascarot drew himself erect, re-arranged his spectacles, and then turning once more to Catenac, exclaimed, "Now let's have no spite. Show your common sense, and do obeisance to Paul Gontran, Marquis de Champdoce."

Hortebize had of course foreseen this finish, having long been in Mascarot's confidence and having prepared part of the drama himself. Still he applauded as warmly as a simple spectator, and clapping his hands, called out, "Bravo, Baptistin ! bravo !"

Paul, warned and prepared as he had been, had fallen back on his chair with his head swimming and his breath gone.

"Well, yes," exclaimed Mascarot, in a ringing voice, "I accept your praise without false modesty. We have no reason to fear even that grain of sand which sometimes interferes with the working of the best machinery. Success is certain. I have explained my combinations. If you find the slightest defect in any of them, tell me of it ; it shall be remedied at once. Who is our most valuable tool? Perpignan, of course. And the vain fool will serve us without knowing it. Can the duke have a suspicion after these minute investigations? It is impossible! But to remove the faintest shadow of doubt, I have an additional plan. I will make him go back over the whole ground. He himself shall take Paul to all these various places, and will obtain additional confirmation of everything that has been stated. Paul—Rigal's son-in-law, Flavia's husband—will be recognised in the Rue Montmartre, in the Rue Jacob, and the Rue de la Harpe. He will be recognised in the Rue d'Arras. Fritz will throw himself into the arms of 'the ungrateful fellow.' Vigoureux will remind him of his marvellous aptitude for trapeze exercises. The Lorgelins will press their dear Sans-Père to their hearts! And this will happen, Catenac, because the scent you will follow has been created by myself—because all these people, from mother Bregot back to the Lorgelins, are my slaves who dare not have any other will than mine. So triumph is certain. The twelve millions of the house of Champdoce will belong to us, You cannot say the contrary."

Catenac rose slowly and solemnly. "I admire your patience and your ingenuity Baptistin, only I am going, with one word, to overthrow the edifice of your hopes. I'm sorry for it, but it must be done."

Catenac might be a coward, he might be also a traitor, but he was none the less a clear-sighted counsellor. In former days, when they were all working cordially together, even Mascarot had at times relied on his perspicuity. Thus Hortebize shivered as he heard these words, though the agent's smile was still as victorious as ever. "Speak on," he said to the advocate.

"Very well, then, Baptistin—old comrade—you will not overreach and deceive the duke."

Mascarot smiled pityingly. "Are you sure," he said, "that I wish to deceive him? You have not been frank with me, why should I be honest with you? Am I in the habit of confiding in those I can't trust. Does Perpignan suspect the role he is to play? Why may it not have suited me to keep from you the fact that Paul is really the child the duke seeks after?"

Mascarot spoke so seriously, and what he said was so singular, that Catenac stood with mouth and eyes wide open. His conscience was by no means clear, and he felt ill at ease. He himself had thought of treason, and might not his associates in their turn intend to betray him? He hastily weighed all the probabilities; but no, in all these combinations he could not detect any possible danger for himself. "I sincerely hope," he answered, in some degree regaining his self-possession, "that Paul is what you imply. But mark my words, the duke has an infallible means of preventing or rather of detecting any imposition. What can you expect? It is always so. The most trivial circumstance is sufficient to upset the most sagacious plans—to render the finest inspirations of genius useless."

The agent interrupted his associate. "Paul *is* the son of the Duc de Champdoce," said he gravely.

What did this mean? Catenac felt that he was being trifled with, and he was offended. "As you please," he answered; "but you will allow me, I trust, to convince myself of the truth?" So saying, the advocate approached Paul, and eagerly added, "Have the goodness, sir, to take off your coat."

Paul did as he was bid. "Now," resumed Catenac, "roll up the right sleeve of your shirt—higher still—to the shoulder." Hardly had the young man obeyed, and hardly had the lawyer glanced at his arm, than he turned to his associates, and said: "No it is not he!"

To his infinite astonishment, Mascarot and worthy Dr. Hortebize burst out laughing.

"No," he persisted, "no, this young man is not the abandoned child of the Duke de Champdocc, and the duke will recognise this truth even better than I. You laugh; because you don't know—"

"Enough!" interrupted the agent; and turning to the doctor, he added, "Explain to our loyal friend that we know a good many things."

Worthy M. Hortebize at once came forward, and with the bland semi-jocular air which he usually assumed when expatiating on the merits of homœopathy began, "You declare, Catenac, that our young friend here is not the man we say he is, simply because you don't find certain marks on his arm. However they'll be there, on the day that Paul is presented to the duke, and apparent enough to satisfy even incredulous Saint Thomas."

"What the deuce do you mean?"

"Let me explain in my own fashion, if you please. If Paul had received on his shoulder a burn from boiling water in his childhood, a burn which removed the skin and occasioned a running sore, he would to-day have a large scar, the nature and peculiar form of which would denote its origin."

Catenac nodded. "Quite so," said he.

"Now, then, listen. I am going to take Paul home with me. I shall take him into my private office, where he will lie down. I shall give him ether, poor boy, for I don't wish him to suffer. Baptistin will help me. When Paul is asleep, I shall uncover his body and apply to his skin a bit of flannel, previously dipped in a liquid prepared according to a secret formula of my own. I'm not a fool, as perhaps you know. Well, this bit of flannel, which is already in my drawer, is artistically cut so as to simulate the capricious course of a scalding burn inflicted by hot water falling from above, and straggling hither and thither. A few little scattered bits of flannel will in addition simulate the marks left by the splashes. Remember the currier whom the duke's son was apprenticed to has been found out. He recollects what kind of a burn this was; and the scars I shall inflict will, as nearly as possible, tally with those that must have really resulted. Very well, then, I apply this flannel I spoke of—this blistering bandage—and when in eight or ten minutes it has done its work, I take it off and dress the sore according to my own method. Then I wake Paul up and we go to dinner."

B. Mascarot rubbed his hands.

"But," argued Catenac addressing the doctor, "you have not taken into consideration the fact that time is needed to give a scar a certain appearance—"

"Let me speak," interrupted the doctor. "If it were only time we needed—three months, six months, a year even—we should naturally enough postpone our denouement until then. But I can absolutely promise to show you in less than two months—thanks to a discovery of my own—a scar that will be entirely satisfactory, not possibly to an expert fellow practitioner, but quite so for a man like the duke. Ah! you see Catenac homœopathy has its merits after all."

The advocate reflected. Yes, his associates seemed to possess every element of success, and he began to regret his past hesitation. The Champdocc millions seemed to blaze before him and his eyes sparkled with unwonted fire. "May the devil fly away with all prejudices and scruples!" he suddenly exclaimed. "If we lose, we shall at least have played for high stakes. My friends, count on old Catenac—he's yours, body and soul. You are wise and I'm a fool!"

This time the doctor and Mascarot exchanged a look of triumph.

"Of course, however, we shall go shares," continued the lawyer. "I come in towards the end, it's true, but my work is delicate and important—in fact, you can do nothing without me."

"You will have your due share," answered the agent, evasively.

"One word more," said the advocate. "Are you sure that the duke has no other means of recognition?"

"Remember the duke has never even seen the infant, that it was carried away before the duchess even asked for it."

"But Jean saw it. Jean is still living, mind. He is eighty-seven and very infirm no doubt, but as soon as anything arises of interest to the Champdoce family—to which he has devoted his whole life—his intelligence revives."

"Well! And what then?"

"Why Jean, you know, opposed the substitution of another infant with all his strength. Isn't it possible that he may have foreseen just some emergency like the present one, and have prepared for it?"

The agent had become very grave. "I have thought of that," he said; "but what can be done?"

"I will ascertain," exclaimed Catenac. "Jean has entire confidence in me, and I will question him." The advocate seemed altogether changed. So lukewarm and hesitating before, he was now all zeal and eagerness. "Well that point's settled, then, for the present," he continued. "But who can be certain that no one will recognise Paul as the person he really is?"

"I can be sure of that," answered B. Mascarot, "for I know how entirely his poverty isolated him from every one except a girl named Rose, who's now lodged at Saint-Lazare. She's the very girl you induced Gandelu the builder to file a complaint against. At one time I was a little anxious as I discovered that Paul had had a protector whom I did not know. But this protector turns out to be the Count de Mussidan, his father's murderer; for Paul is really the son of Montlouis."

"The conclusion is clear, then—there is nothing to fear in that direction," interposed the doctor.

"No, nothing. And now, while you attend to your duties, Catenac, I shall hasten Paul's marriage with Flavia Rigal. But this will not prevent my attending to another operation, and before a month, Henri de Croisenois will have organised his company and have become the husband of Sabine de Mussidan.

"It would be as well to go to dinner, I think," now said the doctor, who was beginning to feel very peckish, and turning to the *protégé* of the association, he added, "Come on, Paul."

But Paul did not move, and then only did the three men perceive that the young fellow had fainted. They were obliged to bathe his head with cold water some time before he recovered his consciousness.

"Dear me!" said the doctor, "can it be that the idea of a little operation, which you will not even feel, has put you into this state?"

Paul shook his head sadly. "It isn't that," he answered.

"What then?"

"Simply," he answered, with a shiver, "that there exists some one—I know him—I know where he lives—"

"Who? What?" asked the partners, half thinking that the young fellow had gone mad.

"I know him, I tell you—the Duke de Champdoce's son."

Had a thunderbolt fallen at that moment into the office, it would not have caused more stupefaction. "Let's see," said Mascarot, who was the first to come to his senses. "What do you mean? Explain yourself."

"Gentlemen, what you have just told me has enlightened me, and it is for that I felt so ill. I know a young man, of twenty-three, who was left at the Foundling Hospital of Vendôme, who ran away at the age of twelve and a half, and who has just such a scar as you described on his arm and shoulder. It came from a burn while he was apprenticed to a currier."

"And where is this young man?" asked the agent, quickly. "What does he do? What is his name?"

"He is a sculptor. His name is André, and he lives—"

Mascarot swore a horrible oath. "This is the third time," he exclaimed in a fury, "that this miserable fellow has crossed our path; but it shall be the last, I swear!"

Catenac and Hortebize were deadly pale. "What do you mean to do?" they stammered.

"I shall do nothing," answered the agent, who with a great effort had regained at least a semblance of *sang froid*. "Only this fellow, André, is an ornamental sculptor, and often works at dizzy heights. Haven't you ever heard that the lives of people who work like that in mid-air, hang as it were on a mere thread?"

XXI.

WHEN Mascarot spoke of suppressing the man who hindered his projects, as simply as if it had been a question of snuffing out a candle, he was not aware that circumstances made his task no easy one. In point of fact, André was forewarned, and had been so ever since receiving from Sabine that despairing letter, in which she told him she was about to marry another man—that she was compelled to choose between him and the honour of her family. The young artist's apprehensions were strengthened, moreover, by the long conference he had with De Breulh-Faverlay, and the Viscountess de Bois d'Ardon, when they had all come to the conclusion that the Count and Countess de Mussidan were the victims of an abominable conspiracy, planned by Henri de Croisenois. André did not know whence he might best expect the peril, but he vaguely realised that it hung over his head. Thus he prepared to defend himself. It was not only his life that was in danger, but his love and happiness as well.

M. de Breulh-Faverlay had strengthened the young fellow's distrust by remarking, "I would wage my fortune we have to contend against some gang of blackmailers. The misfortune is, we can't apply for the assistance of the police. In the first place, we have no positive proof to offer, and the police don't move a finger on mere surmises. In the next place, we should render a sorry service to those we wish to save, if we merely attracted the attention of the legal authorities. The secret of M. and Madame de Mussidan may be a terrible one—an indictable offence, indeed it is quite possible the police might intervene rather against them than in their favour. So let us be prudent. And you, André, have a care. Mistrust street corners at night time. Who knows but what some villain might spring out of a dark doorway and stab you?"

The result of this conversation was, that André and De Breulh decided for the present to cease seeing each other openly. They felt convinced that they were watched, and rightly opined that their intimacy would excite the suspicion of De Croisenois, whom it was desirable they should lull into a sense of security. Accordingly, they determined to attach themselves, each in his own sphere, to the marquis's person, and arranged to meet of an evening, and exchange notes at a little café in the Champs Elysées, near the house where André worked.

The young painter's resolution was in no way daunted, but his first reck-lessness had passed away. He was a born diplomatist, and fully realised that he could only succeed in his task by dint of cunning. What should he do? There was his contract with M. Gandelu to attend to, and yet how could he superintend the men he had engaged, and watch De Croisenois at the same time? He must have money as well, and he was altogether un-willing to borrow from De Breulh. On the other hand, if he suddenly gave up his work, questions would naturally arise, and suspicion follow. Re-membering M. Gandelu's kindness, André at last decided that the best thing he could do was to confide in the contractor, and so early the next morning he repaired to the Chaussée d'Antin.

To his great surprise, in the courtyard of the house, he met young M. Gaston, looking sadly woe-begone. The self-created "marquis" was by no means so carefully dressed as usual, and the disconsolate manner in which he was chewing a cigar stump, showed that he was altogether out of sorts. "Hallo," exclaimed the brilliant young "masher," "Here's my artist. Bet you ten louis that you have come to see my father on business."

"You are right. Is he at home?"

"Oh yes; he's at home, but he's sulking—he has locked himself in his room, and refuses to see me."

"You are is jest, of course?"

"I, in jest! not in the least. He's playing the tyrant, and, upon my word, it's altogether supremely ridiculous!"

As the grooms, busy in the adjoining stable, could hear, the young man had sense enough to draw André aside. "Do you know," he resumed, "the governor has put me on short allowance. He swears he will insert an advertisement in the papers, to the effect that he declines to be re-sponsible for my debts. But I can't think he will do it after all, for it would ruin me entirely—." At this thought poor Gaston heaved a bitter sigh. "You don't happen to have ten thousand francs to lend me, eh?" he suddenly asked the young artist. "If you have, I'll give you twenty thousand in return, when I come of age."

"I must admit, sir—" began André in surprise.

"Pshaw!" exclaimed Gaston. "What a fool I am! Say nothing—I understand. You are an artist, of course, and if you had ten thousand francs you wouldn't be here. And yet I must have that amount; I gave certain notes to Verminet, and they're bothering me dreadfully. Do you know Verminet?"

"Not in the least."

"Where on earth do you come from then? Why, he's the manager of the Mutual Loan Society, my dear fellow. The only thing that troubles me is, that, at his suggestion, to facilitate matters I signed another person's name as endorsement."

"But that's forgery, man!" cried André, in alarm.

"Not at all—because I intend to pay; besides, I positively required the money for Van Klopen. You know Van Klopen, I suppose. No? Well, he's the man to dress a woman, and no mistake! I ordered three costumes of him for Zora. But after all, the governor's to blame for everything—

why did he drive me to despair? Yes, he drove me to it. He did not content himself with abusing me, but he revenged himself on a poor innocent, defenceless woman, who never did him any harm—it was a cowardly, contemptible thing to do. Now, Zora—"

"Zora," repeated André, to whom this name recalled nothing.

"Yes, Zora. You remember her—you came to take pot luck with us one day."

"Ah, yes—you mean Rose?"

"Precisely; but you know I don't like any one to call her by that name. Well, then, the governor went perfectly wild about her. Bet you twenty louis you don't know what he did? He filed a complaint against her for leading a minor astray. Truth! As if I were a fellow to be led by any one! But all the same, they arrested her and she's now in prison at Saint-Lazare." This heart-breaking idea brought tears to Gaston's eyes. "Poor Zora!" he resumed, with a moan. "I never cared much about women, but she really pleased me. What style she had! Her hairdresser told me he had never seen such hair as her's before. And yet she's at Saint-Lazare! When the men came to arrest her she thought of me at once, and cried out: 'The poor fellow will kill himself, I'm sure of it.' The cook told me so, and added that the poor dear girl was in such a state of agony, she actually spat blood! Think of that! And she's at Saint-Lazare now! I went to see if I could speak to her, but it was no use." At this point the young fellow was so afflicted that he actually began to sob.

"Courage, M. Gaston, courage!" said André kindly.

"Yes—to be sure. Oh! I'll have courage; and as soon as I'm of age I intend to marry her. You'll see. In the meantime, I don't consider my father altogether to blame, for he had been advised by his lawyer, a man named Catenac. Do you know him? No? Well, to-morrow I intend to call him out—I must select my seconds. By the way, will you be one? I can easily find a second one."

"I really know nothing of such matters."

"Then you wouldn't do, of course. Besides, I must have seconds whose looks and manner will frighten him a little."

"In that case—"

"I know what you mean. You think I had best find some military men. But, after all, the affair's simple enough: I'm the insulted party, and I choose pistols at ten paces. If he's afraid, then he will make the governor give up all his nonsense."

At any other moment André would no doubt have been amused by young Gaston's folly; but now he merely asked himself how he could best get rid of him. However, just at this moment a servant came out of the house and approached him, saying: "Monsieur, my master has seen you from his window, and begs you to go up to him."

"At once," answered André eagerly; and with a few words of encouragement and consolation he hurriedly took leave of the young "marquis."

XXII.

THE young artist found M. Gandelu looking greatly changed. The contractor had evidently been weeping, for his eyes were red and swollen. However, at sight of André, his face brightened, and he half rose from his chair. "Ah! it's you!" he said, in a melancholy voice. "It does me good to see you. I'm thankful for the good wind that blew you in this direction."

"It wasn't a good wind, sir," answered André, as he shook his head.

"What's the matter, then, André?" asked the contractor, now noticing how sad and solemn the young man looked.

"I am threatened with a great misfortune, sir."

"You! what are you saying?"

"Only the truth, sir. And the consequences of this misfortune may be despair and death!"

"Holy Virgin!" exclaimed Gandelu, "is that really so? Ah! what a terrible thing life is. The wicked prosper, and honourable fellows are always in trouble. It's enough to doubt the existence of Providence. However, I'm your friend my lad, and if I can help you in any way it will be with pleasure."

"I came, sir, full of confidence, to ask you to do me a favour."

"Ah! you thought of me, then. Thanks for doing so; you make me feel quite happy. Give me your hand, André. I like to have a loyal manly hand in mine; it warms my poor lonely heart. Come tell me your trouble."

The young artist collected his thoughts. "It is the secret of my life, sir, that I am about to confide to you," he said, with some solemnity.

M. Gandelu did not speak, but with his clinched fist struck himself on the chest—the gesture guaranteeing his discretion better than any oath would have done. Accordingly, André no longer hesitated, but merely suppressing the names, he told the simple story of his love, his ambition and hopes, concluding with a clear statement of the present situation.

"Well, what can I do for you?" asked M. Gandelu.

"Why, sir," said André, "allow me to turn the work you intrusted to me over to one of my friends. In appearance, I should still retain the responsibility and management, but in reality I should only be one of the workmen. This arrangement would give me my liberty to a certain extent, and, at the same time, allow me to earn something during a few hours every morning."

"And is that what you call a service?"

"Yes, sir; a service and a great favour."

"Why, my dear fellow, do what you like with the house. Pull it down if it pleases you. Who do you take me for? When Gandelu likes any one, half measures won't do. Dispose of me and my fortune too." Then rising, and opening a large iron safe in one corner of the room, he took out a packet of bank notes and laid it on the table before André. "You'll need the sinews of war," said he. "Take this, it will be of help to you."

The kindness of this worthy man, who forgot his own troubles in his desire to relieve another, touched André to the heart. "But I don't need money, sir," he began.

Gandelu imposed silence with a gesture.

"Take these twenty thousand francs," he said; "'twill encourage me to tell you why I asked you to come upstairs to me."

It would have been most ungracious to refuse, so André accepted and waited to hear what the contractor had to say to him.

The old man had regained his seat and remained for some moments reflecting. "My dear André," he began at last. "You learned something of my sorrows, the other day. My son is a most unfortunate fellow, and, in fact, I've lost all esteem for him."

The young artist had already divined that his patron intended speaking of Gaston. "Your son is certainly very much in error, sir," he said ; "but then remember how young he is."

Gandelu smiled sadly. "My son is old, " he answered, "at least, old in v ce. I have reflected and judged him. Yesterday he threatened to commit suicide. What preposterous nonsense ! He hasn't enough courage to destroy himself. No, I'm rather afraid that he will end by dishonouring my name."

André shuddered ; he remembered the forgeries which Gaston had just confessed to him.

"Up till now," resumed the contractor, "I have been foolishly weak—it is too late now to be severe. The boy is madly in love with a wretched woman named Rose, whom I have had shut up in jail. However, I have resolved to let her out, and at the same time I'll pay his debts. It's weak and cowardly on my part no doubt ; but what can I do ? After all I'm his father, and if I don't esteem, at least, I love him still. He has broken my heart no doubt, but its fragments belong to him."

André did not speak—he was appalled by the horrible sufferings which this resignation implied.

"I don't deceive myself," continued M. Gandelu, after a pause. "My son is lost. I can only try to attenuate his ruin in some degree. If this girl Rose is not altogether an unworthy creature, one might, perhaps, utilise her influence for good. But then, who will undertake the negotiations, and who can obtain from my son a sincere confession of his debts ? I confess André, that I thought of you."

"And you did rightly, sir," rejoined the young painter. "I will speak to your son this very day, and to Rose as soon as she is at liberty."

It was absolute heroism on André's part to undertake to try and save young Gaston, for at this very moment he needed all his intelligence and energy for his own affairs. It seemed to him almost a crime to forget Sabine, who was threatened with the most terrible misfortune that can overtake a young girl ; and yet, at the same time, he recognised that it was his duty to do what he could to aid this generous man, who had just placed in his hands the one element of success which he previously lacked.

Accordingly, he drew a chair to M. Gandelu's side, and they began to discuss what course they should pursue. Prudence and dissimulation were indispensable. The last events had so demoralized Gaston that anything could be obtained from him, providing he was not made acquainted with his father's real ideas and plans. Still it was necessary to make haste and profit of the young fellow's disposition. Finally, it was decided that André should have *carte blanche*, and that the old contractor should, to all appearance, stand firm in his original course, and only be led to gentler measures by slow degrees, through André's intercession.

Gaston, it may be mentioned, was even more morally crushed than André had imagined, and had been pacing up and down the courtyard in a state of despair, while his father had been talking with the young painter. As soon as the latter appeared on the steps, Gaston hurried to meet him.

"Well," he asked, breathlessly.

"Your father," answered André, "is naturally very irritated against you ; nevertheless, I hope to induce him to grant some concessions."

"Will he set Zora at liberty ?"

"Perhaps so."

Gaston gave vent to a joyful exclamation. "What luck !" he cried, and after a wild kind of dance, he added, "I'll buy her a brougham, as soon as she comes out!"

André had foreseen some answer of the kind.   "Softly, softly," said he.   "If your father heard you, Madame Zora would probably remain where she is for a long time to come."

"You don't mean it!"

"Yes I do.   Your father will only set her free and pay your debts, providing you promise to alter your mode of life and be more reasonable in future."

"Oh, I'm ready to promise anything you like."

"No doubt you are; but then your father asks for something more than promises.   He must have guarantees."

These words considerably moderated Gaston's joy.   "Guarantees?" he answered sulkily.   "Isn't my word enough?   What guarantees can my father ask for?"

"Ah! I can't tell you, you must suggest them yourself.   I will propose them to him, and coming from me I'm quite sure he'll accept them."

Gaston looked at his companion in astonishment.

"Do you mean to say that you can make my father do anything you choose?" he asked.

"Not precisely; but you must see for yourself that I have a great deal of influence over him.   Do you need a proof of it?   Well, I've just obtained from him the money to pay those notes of your's."

"Verminet's, do you mean?"

"I suppose so.   I speak of those which you were mad enough to endorse with another man's name."

For a moment Gaston averted his glance.   Foolish as he was, his imprudence nevertheless made him feel very anxious.   He vaguely realised that it might have terrible consequences, which even all his father's influence and wealth might be powerless to save him from.   Still he strove to regain his assurance, and clapping his hands, exclaimed, "What! my father's parted with the coin!   That's capital!   Just give it me."

But André shook his head with a knowing smile.   "Excuse me," said he, "the money won't leave my hands until I receive the notes.   My orders on this point are precise; but the sooner we settle the affair and take up the notes the better."

M. Gaston did not reply at once.   A grimace of disappointment followed his triumphant smile.   "Come, that's really too bad," he said, at last.   "My father's a cunning old fox, as Augustin said in the play the other night; but I suppose he must have his own way, so come on.   I'll just put on an overcoat and go with you."

With these words he hurried into the house, whence he returned in less than a quarter of an hour, arrayed in all his usual splendour.

"It's in the Rue Sainte-Anne," he said, taking André's arm.   "We'll walk if you don't mind."

It was, indeed, in that street that M. Isidore Verminet had installed the office of the "Mutual Loan Society," of which he was the sole director.   The house he had selected and adorned with his name in gilt letters on a marble slab was far from attractive in appearance, and passers-by noticing its dirty front, its tumble down shutters and filthy windows, might well inquiringly exclaim, "What kind of business can be carried on in there?"

It is, indeed, scarcely easy to define M. Isidore Verminet's business.   According to the prospectuses of the Mutual Loan Society, it was founded with the sole object of procuring credit and money for those who never had any.

At first sight this would seem a very philanthropic but scarcely a practicable scheme ; and yet Verminet's "financial system," to use one of his favourite expressions, was simplicity itself. Suppose some unfortunate tradesman on the eve of failure applied to him ? Verminet began to console him, made him sign promissory notes for the sum he needed, and in exchange presented him with other notes, signed by some other tradesman equally on the verge of ruin.

To each of these unfortunate dealers he would say, "You can't discount your signature ? All right. Well, here's another man's signature which is as good as gold, and which you can discount as easily as you might change a bank note."

This little bit of trickery performed, he pocketed his commission of two per cent. in ready cash on both transactions. To those whom a single signature did not satisfy he gave two, three, and four signatures. What did it matter to him, so long as his commission was forthcoming ?

It may be asked how he obtained customers ? But then it should be remembered that a luckless merchant, pursued by the phantom of failure, is ready to do anything ; he seems to lose his head, and clutches at a signature like a drowning man at a blade of grass. At times this exchange of signatures succeeded for a few days. Some men whose real situation was known found credit on the strength of the signature of some other man whose position, although equally shaky, was less notorious. One thing is certain, application to Verminet robbed the luckless trader of his last chance of salvation.

However, the Mutual Loan Society transacted other business as well—business of even a less legitimate character than the foregoing. It dealt largely in purely "circulation notes," which were the terror and despair of bankers ; and receivers in bankruptcy had a hard time of it with the fancy "shares" fabricated in the Rue Sainte-Anne.

But, at all events, whether the transactions of the society were moral or not, it at least seemed certain that Verminet made money.

XXIII.

GIFTED with that quick perception which artists of talent usually possess, André divined the character of the Mutual Loan Society by a mere look at the house.

"H'm," said he, "I hardly like this."

"To be sure," rejoined M. Gaston, looking as wise as he could. "To be sure the house isn't a handsome one, but it has its merits, I assure you. Ah ! Verminet's a fellow who knows a thing or two ! "

"So I should fancy," rejoined André ; and indeed there could be but one opinion in regard to a person who was capable of taking advantage of the folly and ignorance of a simpleton like Gaston, to induce him to utter forged notes.

However, the young artist said nothing more, but quietly followed young Gandelu, who was evidently familiar with the place. They turned down a long, narrow, dark, and ill-smelling passage, crossed a damp courtyard, and with the assistance of a sticky hand-rail, climbed a slippery, disjointed flight of stairs.

On reaching the second floor, Gaston paused in front of a door covered with various placards, announcing at what hours the office was open and the particular time to call for payment of accounts. "Here we are," said young Gandelu.

They entered a large, lofty room, the wall paper of which was soiled and torn. A light railing divided this apartment in two; on one side there being sundry benches for the accommodation of customers, whilst beyond, five or six clerks were feeding at their desks, for it was now the luncheon hour. The smell and heat of the stove, the perfume of the food, and the scent of the pomatum with which the clerks' heads were well greased, were well calculated to affect the olfactory senses of new comers, and André was at first almost overcome with nausea.

"Where is Monsieur Verminet?" asked Gaston with an air of authority.

"Busy," carelessly answered one of the clerks with his mouth full.

This reception angered young Gandelu beyond expression. "Eh!" said he; "what do you mean? None of that behaviour, come." And producing one of his address cards, bearing the coronet which so exasperated his worthy father, he added, "Whether Verminet's busy or not, just go and tell him that I want to see him—I, Gaston de Gandelu."

The clerk was so impressed by the young fellow's conceited air, that, without another word of objection, he took up the card and disappeared through a door in the rear. This was quite a victory for Gaston, and he glanced at André with a proud smile.

In a moment the clerk reappeared. "Monsieur Verminet is at this moment much occupied with a client; he begs you to excuse him, and wait a few minutes—he will receive you presently." And anxious, probably, to win the favour of such a distinguished mortal as young M. Gaston, he added deferentially, "My master is with the Marquis de Croisenois."

"Think of that, now!" cried Gaston, turning to André. "Why, Croisenois is a particular friend of mine. Bet you ten louis he would be only too delighted to shake hands with me!"

André had started, and his face had flushed when he heard this name of Croisenois. Croisenois! 'Twas the very man whom he loathed and hated above all others; the wretch who, armed with some stolen secret, was constraining Sabine de Mussidan to marry him. It was the scoundrel whom M. de Breulh-Faverlay, Madame de Bois d'Ardon, and himself had sworn to unmask. So far, André had never seen the marquis. He had intended that very day to begin his supervision, watch and follow him, note his present life and inquire into his past; but as yet he was physically unacquainted with him. The young artist trembled with eagerness at the thought that a mere door separated him from his mortal foe, that he was about to meet him, see him pass along, and maybe hear his voice. André could barely conceal the emotion he felt; but fortunately his companion did not notice it.

Gaston had, in fact, sat down, and crossing his legs and adjusting his thumbs in the armholes of his waistcoat, he was offering himself to the admiration of the ill-fed, slovenly-looking clerks behind the railing.

"You know this dear marquis, I presume?" he asked André in a voice loud enough to be heard by the clerks.

André's reply was fairly unintelligible; but Gaston accepted it as a negative. "But you must have heard of him?" he urged. "Where in the world do you live, then? Henri de Croisenois is one of my best friends. Why, he still owes me the bagatelle of fifty louis that I won from him one night at Ernestine's.

André was not listening. He was blessing chance, or rather Providence, which in its mysterious ways so greatly helped him in his task. He was on the track at last. He felt sure that he had judged Verminet rightly, and, in that case, Croisenois' connection with this shady personage was highly significant. The matter must be investigated. Hitherto, André had been in darkness, but now he beheld a gleam of light. He had been on the point of rushing hither and thither, in hap-hazard fashion, and now it seemed as if he held the end of a string which would guide him through the labyrinth of Croisenois' iniquities.

Moreover, it so chanced that young Gaston was personally acquainted with the marquis. Might he not therefore obtain some information from him? "So you are intimate with M. de Croisenois?" he asked.

"Intimate! I should rather say I was!" answered young Gandelu. "Just ask Adolphe at Brébant's about us! By you shall see for yourself by-and-bye. I'm on the best possible terms with a lady who costs him a pretty penny, though I've never given her a sou myself. However, it's a mystery—"

He stopped short, for at that moment the door of the manager's office opened, and Verminet and the marquis appeared on the threshold.

Henri de Croisenois wore a fashionable, elegant morning costume. As usual, he had a cigar in his mouth, and he twirled in his well-gloved hand a light cane with a gold knob. At one glance, but a glance in which André concentrated all his intelligence, he saw enough of Croisenois never to forget him, no matter how long he might live. He considered that the marquis had a false, traitor-like look, and divining that his carelessness and scepticism were merely affected, realised that he must be a man of determination, coldly cruel and expert in villainy. The marquis's eyes particularly struck the young painter. They were restless, ever on the *qui vive*, like the eyes of a man who, having committed a crime, knows he must remain on his guard; for danger may spring up on all sides at any moment. Seen a short distance off, the marquis, with his coquettish silky moustache, seemed yet a young man; but André's artist eyes were not to be deceived. This fellow was plainly a rake, and cold cream and rice powder alone attenuated the stigmas of vice. Gambling and debauchery, and the anxieties of a precarious existence, had wrinkled his temples, tampered with his hair, creased his eyelids, and divested his lips of their youthful ruddiness. All this was evident, albeit, that the marquis plainly had recourse to the most approved artifices of the toilette table.

For the nonce, Croisenois seemed to be in the best possible humour, and it was right gaily that he finished his conversation with Verminet. "Then it's understood," said he; "I haven't to bother myself about the matters which only concern ourselves."

"Quite so; I'll see to them."

"Pray don't forget. The least delay or forgetfulness might have serious consequences."

This caution seemed to suggest an idea to Verminet, for he said something in a low voice to his client, whereupon they both laughed.

Gaston felt considerably disconcerted at not having been immediately recognised, and soon, unable to control himself, he advanced towards M. de Croisenois, at the risk of interrupting the latter's conversation. "Eh, eh!" said the brilliant youth with a conceited smile. "The dear marquis indeed! 'Pon my word, 'tis a long time since I've seen you. And Sarah, how is she? Does she still give some of those nice little card parties?"

If the marquis was pleased at meeting Gandelu, he certainly did not show it. He seemed surprised—he frowned, in fact, and just extended his gloved hand with a careless, "Glad to see you."

This was all, and then, with small ceremony, he turned his back on Gaston and continued his conversation with Verminet. "As regards the other matter, all the difficulties are conquered," he said, "and so there is not a moment to lose. You must see the banker, Martin Rigal, and Mascarot to-day."

André started. Were these people accomplices of Croisenois? He saw accomplices everywhere now, to be sure! At all events, these names remained engraven in his memory.

"Tantaine was here this morning," answered Verminet, "and gave me an appointment to see his master at four this afternoon—Van Klopen will be there, too. Shall I speak to him for your fair friend?"

The marquis shrugged his shoulders with a laugh. "Upon my word!" he said, "I had nearly forgotten her! After all, it's carnival time; she will be wanting silks and laces. Speak to Van Klopen by all means, but no extravagance, mind. Remember that I don't care a sou for Sarah's whims, now."

"I understand," rejoined Verminet; "but be cautious. Don't have any quarrel—keep things as smooth as possible with her; an amicable separation would be best."

"Certainly—to be sure," answered Croisenois, and after shaking hands with the manager of the Mutual Loan Society, he walked swiftly across the office, just touching his hat to Gaston, and altogether ignoring André's presence. However, the young artist was by no means offended, quite the reverse; for he was doing his best to escape attention.

"At your orders, gentlemen!" now exclaimed Verminet. "Walk in, please. Excuse me, but greatly hurried. One o'clock already—not been to Bourse yet—customers anxious."

When André and Gaston had entered the private room, the financier sat down in his leather-covered arm-chair. He was better than his office. In the first place, he was clean; in the next, his clothes did credit to his tailor. Was he young or old? Who could say? His age was no more apparent than that of a five-franc piece. He was plump and fresh, pink and white; wore English whiskers, and had a pair of vitreous eyes, as expressionless as a cellar window. His great preoccupation was to seem a serious, very serious man, well acquainted with the value of all things; and it was because he was so convinced of the axiom that "time is money," that he usually spoke in a curt, telegraphic style.

Young Gandelu was also in a hurry. "One word, if you please—as Geoffroy said in the play the other night—one word. You lent me some money last week—"

"Precisely. Do you want some more?"

"No. I wish, on the contrary, to take up my notes."

A cloud came over Verminet's face. "The first payment isn't due until the fifteenth," he said.

"That's no matter; I have the money now, and so, you understand, I should like to take them up."

"Impossible."

"Eh! Impossible! Why, pray?"

"Negotiated!"

Gaston started with surprise. "Come, you don't mean it?" he stammered. "You've negotiated them! It can't be. That's too much of a joke; for of course, Verminet, you're joking?"

"Joking! Oh! no, indeed; I never joke."

The young fellow could not believe his ears, could not imagine that this statement was serious, and his surprise and alarm could be read in his eyes. "Come now," said he, "don't play the fool. You know very well that when I signed those notes, it was agreed they should never leave your hands—it was so understood by both of us. You promised—"

"I don't say the contrary. But to make a promise and keep it are very different things. I was compelled—needed money—some one ready and so disposed of the notes— "

André was not surprised by this answer, for to tell the truth he had anticipated something of the kind, and seeing that Gaston had now utterly lost his head, he thought it advisable to intervene.

"Excuse me, sir," he said, to the laconic director, "but it seems to me that certain circumstances—peculiar circumstances—should have made you respect your agreement."

Verminet made a stiff bow, and, instead of replying directly, asked, "Honour of speaking to whom?"

André, who was becoming more and more suspicious, thought it prudent not to give his name.

"I am a friend of M. Gandelu's," he said evasively.

"In his confidence?"

"Quite so; you lent him I think, ten thousand francs— "

"Excuse me, five thousand— "

André turned in astonishment to his companion, who grew crimson.

"What does this mean?" asked the artist.

"Can't you see? I said ten thousand, because I needed the difference for Zora."

"Ah, indeed!" answered André, lifting his eyebrows slightly. "Then M. Verminet, it was five thousand francs you lent M. Gandelu. That was natural enough. But it was not so natural, in my opinion, that you should have induced him to forge a signature."

Verminet started off his chair, "I!" he answered, "I didn't know it was a forgery!"

This impudent denial aroused poor Gaston from the stupor into which he had fallen. "That's too strong," he cried, "altogether too strong! Did you not yourself tell me, Verminet, that for your own personal safety you must insist on another name in addition to mine? Did you not yourself hand me a letter, and say to me, 'Imitate the signature—it's that of Martin Rigal, the banker, in the Rue Montmartre?' I didn't want to do it, but you declared it was a mere formality so as to make sure I should pay you punctually. And besides, you declared the notes should never leave your drawer. Now, however, you deny it. Come, that's hardly delicate, and I'm quite surprised at you."

The honourable director of the Mutual Loan Society listened with a frigid air. "False accusation—absence of proofs," he said at last. "Society incapable of any act punishable by law."

"And yet, sir," insisted André, "you had no hesitation in putting these notes into circulation. Have you calculated the frightful consequences of this breach of faith? What would happen if this forged signature was presented to M. Martin Rigal?"

" Unlikely—notes signed Gandelu ; endorsed, Rigal. Notes, when due, are always presented to person signing them."

Gaston indulged in violent recriminations, but André realised that further discussion was useless. Plainly enough a trap had been set for young Gandelu, though with what object the artist could not divine. " Enough words," said he at last, " we have but one thing to do, we must follow these notes and take them up."

" Right ! "

" But to do this, you must first tell us to whom you disposed of them."

Verminet waved his hands like a person whose memory is at fault. " Don't know, I'm sure," said he ; " forgotten ! "

André had promised himself he would be patient and remain calm. But human forbearance has its limits, and the cool cheek of this scoundrel, Verminet, proved too much for his good resolution. " Come," said he, in a tone of concentrated fury, " in that case, it would be greatly to your interest if you made an energetic appeal to your memory— "

" Threats ! "

" And if this appeal be unsuccessful," resumed André, " the consequences may prove very serious indeed for you."

It was easy to see that the young painter was in earnest, and Verminet rose exclaiming, " I'll look through the books in the next room."

He evidently meant to slink off, but André was too quick for him, and stationed himself in front of the door. " Oh ! you can find the information here, without leaving the room," said he ; " and, by Jove ! I advise you to make haste."

For a couple of minutes these two men stood motionless, looking at each other, Verminet green with fear and André pale with anger.

" If this villain lifts a finger," thought André, quite beside himself, " I will pitch him out of the window."

" This big fellow's a positive Hercules," thought Verminet ; " and he looks as if he were capable of anything."

The idea of summoning his clerks to his assistance occurred to him, but he dismissed it for reasons André could not suspect. Finding himself caught, he resolved to yield, and, suddenly striking his forehead, exclaimed. " How forgetful of me ! I have memoranda there." He hastened to his desk, drew a large diary from a drawer, and began turning over the leaves. André who was hard by saw that the volume was upside down. Still, with marvellous affectation, Verminet pretended to have found what he was seeking.

" Ah," said he, " here it is ! Notes for five thousand francs, Gandelu and Rigal—transferred to Van Klopen, the ladies' tailor."

André was silent. A remark of Croisenois' had informed him that Verminet had dealings both with Van Klopen and Martin Rigal. Now, why had the bill discounter proposed Rigal's signature to Gaston, as the one he should imitate? and why had he passed these same notes over to Van Klopen? Was it mere accident that had prompted the selection of these names ? No ! some secret tie must exist between these three men and the Marquis de Croisenois. Of that, André felt as good as certain.

" Is this all ? " asked the director of the Mutual Loan Society. " Are you satisfied."

" Has Van Klopen still got the notes ? " inquired Gaston.

" Don't know, I'm sure."

" Never mind ! " said André, " he will tell us where they are."

They immediately withdrew, and as soon as they reached the street, the young artist caught his companion by the arm and hurried him along in the direction of the Rue de Grammont.

"I don't wish this Verminet to have time to warn Van Klopen of our intentions," said he. "I mean to fall upon him like a bullet."

XXIV

HAD André been better informed, he would have known that no one ever fell like a bullet on Van Klopen.

Entrenched in the innermost sanctuary of his inspirations, this fashionable tyrant was well nigh as inaccessible as an Asiatic despot in the depths of his harem. The women, his customers, at times managed to escape the probation of the waiting-room, but masculine visitors never. And this was but natural, for the latter were usually indignant husbands whom the illustrious ladies' tailor had good reason to fear.

Accordingly when Gaston and André, out of breath, reached the ante-room, they were confronted by two stalwart footmen, whose gold-laced liveries were eloquent indications of their master's prosperity.

"Monsieur Van Klopen is engaged," they said.

"But our business is most important," urged André.

"Our master is working."

Prayers, threats, and even the offer of a hundred francs, proved all in vain. André saw that he was about to be check-mated, and was tempted to take the footmen by their collars and dash them aside; but he had already repented of his anger at Verminet's. Reluctantly enough he decided to submit and wait, and followed by Gaston he entered the famous salon which Van Klopen called his "purgatory."

"While we are dawdling here," thought the young artist, "Verminet will have time to warn this dressmaker, and we sha'n't learn anything."

However, the footmen had told the truth, Van Klopen was really working, and in the salon several women of the highest fashion were awaiting the good pleasure of this glass of fashion and mould of form. They all turned with surprise as the two young men entered the room—all but one, who sitting beside a window was looking idly into the street, and drumming lightly on the glass with her pretty fingers. However, it was precisely this lady who attracted André's attention, for to his infinite surprise he recognised Madame de Bois d'Ardon.

"Is it possible?" he said to himself. "Can the viscountess have come here again, after the infamous manner in which Van Klopen treated her. So De Breulh was mistaken when he said she would prove a devoted ally."

In the meantime young Gandelu, realising that five pair of eyes were watching him, selected the most graceful posture he could, and complacently allowed himself to be admired.

André from amazement soon passed to disgust and indignation. "I will learn the truth at any cost," he said to himself, and rising from his chair, careless of the presence of so many strangers, and without reflecting that he might grievously compromise the viscountess, he crossed the salon and approached her with a low bow. But she was absorbed in something that was going on in the street and did not turn.

"Madame la Vicomtesse," said André.

At the sound of his voice she started—and when she looked round and recognised him, she could not restrain an exclamation of surprise"
"Heavens! Is it you!"

"Yes, it is I—here."

The look which accompanied his words was so expressive, that Madame de Bois d'Ardon, divining his thoughts, flushed scarlet. "My presence here astonishes you," she said, "and you think I have little memory, and less pride."

André did not answer, his silence was a sufficiently significant reply.

"Let me tell you, then," continued the viscountess with a reproachful look, "you do me great injustice. If I'm here, it's because De Breulh this very morning told me that in the interest of your projects, I ought to forgive Van Klopen and come here as I did before. You see, Monsieur André, it is never safe to judge by appearances—a woman above all things."

"Will you ever forgive me, madame?" replied the young artist in an earnest tone.

With a rapid gesture which he alone could see she cut his apologies and protestations short. Clearly enough this gesture implied : "Take care, we are being looked at."

At the same time she turned her face to the window and André did the same. By this means their features at least escaped observation. Their conversation had been carried on in too low a tone for anyone to overhear it, and the other ladies looked intensely scandalised at what they considered a preconcerted rendezvous. As for young M. Gaston he was overcome with jealousy. "Why that artist pretended to be virtuous," he muttered. "But, dear me, this looks rather the reverse."

In the meanwhile, the viscountess had resumed speaking. "De Breulh," said she, "has found out several things about M. de Croisenois, and nothing to his credit. However, in the present case, this information would not suffice, for it is clear that De Mussidan has a knife at' his throat. We must rake out of the past some really infamous act of this man's, the revelation of which will force him to withdraw of himself."

"I shall find one," muttered André between his teeth.

"But, my dear sir, there is no time to lose. According to our agreement, I am altogether charming to him; he thinks I am entirely devoted to his interests, and to-morrow I have agreed to present him to the Mussidans. The count and countess have promised to receive him."

André started, and was barely able to restrain a gesture of rage.

"As soon as I saw the Mussidans," resumed Madame de Bois d'Ardon, "I realised that you were quite right in your opinion : in the first place, Mussidan and his wife, who always lived on the most wretched terms, are now most friendly, almost affectionate towards each other, as if they felt that they could best resist danger by remaining united. Then, their faces are careworn and anxious—they watch their daughter with the saddest, dreariest eyes. I think they regard her as their salvation, and deplore the necessity of the sacrifice !"

"And she ?" asked André eagerly.

"She is sublime—yes, sublime ! She accepts the sacrifice, which she has decided on, fully and entirely, without a word, without a murmur. Her devotion is admirable, and so great is her heroism, that she hides from her parents the real extent and the horror of her sacrifice. Noble girl ! She is calm and grave as she always was, but not more than usual. Perhaps she is a little thinner and a trifle paler. When I kissed her, her forehead was so hot that it fairly burned my lips. But except that, nothing betrayed her sufferings. Modeste told me, however, that her poor young mistress was merely playing a part, affecting calmness she did not feel. At night time, said Modeste, Sabine is utterly exhausted; and the poor girl wept as she told me that her poor mistress was killing herself!"

Big tears pearled forth from André's eyes. "What can I do," he said, "to deserve such a woman?"

But at this moment a door opened, and the young artist and the viscountess turned round abruptly. It was Van Klopen coming from his sanctum, after dismissing the customer with whom he had just been engaged. "Well! whose turn is it next?" asked the illustrious ladies' tailor, in his usual brutal style.

But when he saw Gaston his face changed, and it was with the most amiable smile that he went towards him, waving away the patient lady whose turn it should have been, and who protested against the injustice.

"Ah!" said Van Klopen, in a gay, good-natured tone, "you have come, I presume, M. Gandelu, to order some surprise for that exquisite creature, Zora de Chantemille?"

This may have been unintentional irony, but it was none the less extremely bitter for poor Gaston, who heaved a terrible sigh. "Not just now," he answered. "Zora is not quite well."

But André, who had arranged the little story he intended to lay before the mighty Van Klopen, was in too great a hurry to waste time in useless chatter. "We have come," he said, hastily, as soon as they had reached the privacy of the modern Mantilini's sanctum, "on a matter of importance. My friend, M. Gandelu, is about to leave Paris for some months, and, before leaving, he is desirous of withdrawing all his notes of hand from circulation, for his father would be very displeased if he knew he had been discounting his signature."

"I can understand that."

"Well, sir, you can be very useful to him."

Intelligent M. Gaston already considered himself saved. "Come, Van Klopen," said he, "pray let us have the notes of mine you received from Verminet."

The illustrious ladies' tailor looked perplexed. "Yes, I remember those notes," he said slowly. "I had them once—five notes of a thousand francs each, signed Gandelu, and endorsed by Martin Rigal. I received them from the Mutual Loan Society, as you say, but I have them no longer."

"Is that really so?" murmured Gaston, faintly.

"Yes; I sent them in part payment to my ribbon merchants at Saint Etienne—Rollon, Vrac, & Co."

Van Klopen was certainly a clever rogue, but, born at Rotterdam, he was, like most other Dutchmen, deficient in a certain *finesse* of detail; and, besides, apart from his extraordinary professional impudence, he was easily disconcerted. In proof of this, André's fixed stare so worried him that he added, "If you don't believe me I can show you these gentlemen's acknowledgment."

"It is not necessary, sir," answered André; "your word is sufficient."

"And I certainly give it to you, sir. Nevertheless, I should like to show you the letter." And he began turning over a pile of papers on his desk.

"Oh! don't take so much trouble, pray," said André, quietly, as if he were really duped by this comedy, which was far from being the case. "It can't be helped. The notes are at Saint Etienne; I am sorry for it.

However, we will wait until they come due. M. Gandelu won't disinherit his son for that. I have the honour of wishing you a very good morning."

In reality, the young artist's blood was boiling in his veins, and he feared he should not long be able to control himself. So, although Gaston was anxious to consult Van Klopen about sundry dresses for Zora when she left Saint-Lazare, André hastily dragged him away from the tailor's sanctum. He paused when they were in the street, and more as a mere formality than anything else, just jotted down the name of Van Klopen's ribbon people. Then turning to Gandelu he asked, "What do you think of your man-dressmaker?"

Gaston now felt quite comfortable. "I think," he said, "that Van Klopen's no fool. He knows me. As Philippe says in the play, I'm a good fellow, but I don't care for practical jokes."

"Then where do you think your notes are?"

"At Saint Etienne, of course."

Young Gandelu's obstinate confidence elicited from André a gesture of impatient commiseration. He could not understand such idiotic simplicity on the part of a young fellow who moved in one of the most corrupt circles of Parisian life. "Come," said he, looking at his watch when they had reached the corner of the Rue de Richelieu, "it's three o'clock, and I've still another quarter of an hour to give you. Now listen to me, and try, if you can, to realise the frightful position you stand in."

"I'm listening, my dear fellow; go on."

"It was because Van Klopen refused to give you longer credit—in fact, it was in order to pay him that you applied to Verminet?"

"Precisely."

"Then how do you explain the fact that this same man, who, on Monday, did not think your credit good enough to open an account with you, should, on Wednesday, accept your notes from Verminet, with the intention of sending them to his manufacturers?"

The objection was so forcible, and it so clearly defined the situation, that even obtuse M. Gaston was struck by it. It was like a sun ray piercing suddenly through the fog that obscured his mind.

"The deuce!" he muttered, anxiously. "I never thought of that; it's queer. Does he mean to do me a bad turn — he, Van Klopen, or Verminet?"

"It is clear to me that the two together have a charming little project of blackmailing you."

This expression seemed peculiarly offensive to Gaston, who indignantly exclaimed, "Blackmail me! Indeed they won't. I know a trick worth two of that, and they won't make much out of me."

André shrugged his shoulders. "Then," he said, "have the goodness to tell me what you propose to say to Verminet when, the day your notes are due, he comes to you and says, 'Give me a hundred thousand francs for these five bits of paper, or I shall take them to your father?'"

"I should say—well, upon my word, I don't know what I should say."

"You could say nothing at all. You would realise that you have been imposed on in the most shameful manner, and you would implore Verminet to wait, as he would no doubt consent to do, providing you agreed to give him a hundred thousand francs the day you came of age."

"A hundred thousand fiddle strings! that's all Verminet will get from me! That's my way, you see. If people treat me badly, I am apt to kick and upset their plans. Pay this fellow! No, not I. I know very well there would be a tremendous row with the governor; but rather than knuckle down to Verminet I'd bolt."

The young fellow was no doubt very indignant, and yet such was the force of habit that he could only express his feelings in this slangy style.

"I think," resumed André, " that your father would forgive you this—imprudence, though it would no doubt be even harder for him to do so than it was when he forgave you for engaging a physician to count how many hours he still had to live. But, after all, he *would* forgive you, I've no doubt; for he's your father—and he loves you."

"Of course. Let Verminet go to the deuce!"

"By no means," insisted André. "If Verminet discovered you were not afraid of your father, he would threaten you with someone else—in fact, with the public prosecutor—"

Gaston stopped short, and looked aghast. "Come, now," said he, "you're joking."

"By no means. This isn't a joke—this is forgery, and a forgery, when it's detected, means, first of all, the assize court, and afterwards the galleys."

Gaston had become ghastly pale, and shook like a leaf from head to foot. "The galleys!" he stammered. "No, I won't stand that. Anatole says a man may get along pretty comfortably there, providing he's protected; but no, I'd rather not try." He reflected for a moment, then, with sudden violence, resumed: "They've got me in a corner have they? Well, all the same, they sha'n't blackmail me! I'll do like Cartex did—invite all my friends to a grand dinner, and then, just after the coffee, blow my brains out. 'Twould be a splendid advertisement for the restaurant. All the women would be begging the waiters to let them dine in the same private room. Yes, that's what I'll do; to be sure I will. And besides, I'll prepare a witty letter for the newspapers. It shall be found on my body when I'm dead!"

Gaston seemingly forgot he was on the Boulevards, for he raised his shrill, falsetto voice well-nigh to its full pitch, and gesticulated furiously. Several passers-by turned, and looked at him in astonishment; but André, fearful of a scene, managed to drag him on.

"Ah, me!" said Gaston, resuming his soliloquy in a lower voice, "after all, I pity the governor; it might kill him, you know. I might have made him so happy, and yet I've proved such a torment. Ah! if I could begin life again—but of course it can't be. What a fix! And at my age too. Rich and fashionable, loved by a woman like Zora, and compelled to turn off the gas all the same. It isn't a nice look out. But then the assizes—no, I can't stand that! I much prefer a bullet! After all, I'm the son of an honest man."

In his turn André paused, examining his companion much as a professor of vivisection might examine some animal he was experimenting on. "Do you really mean what you say?" he asked.

"To be sure I do. I can be serious sometimes." And, really, resolution seemed to sparkle in young Gandelu's eyes.

"Well, don't despair yet a while," said André. "I think that we may be able to arrange this unfortunate affair, only you cannot be too prudent. Keep quiet, and by all means remember that I may have imperative need of you at almost any moment."

"Agreed! But look here, I can't make up my mind to abandon Zora."

"Do not be troubled, I will see her to-morrow. And now, good-bye for to-day ; I've not another minute to lose." So speaking, and leaving Gaston still in a state of confusion, André rushed away.

The reason for his excessive haste was that he had heard Verminet say to Croisenois, "I shall see Mascarot at four o'clock," and he had taken it into his head that he would wait until he saw the director of the Mutual Loan Society leave his office, and then follow him. In this way he hoped to get at Mascarot, whom he had already decided must be an accomplice of some kind. He sped down the Rue de Grammont like an arrow, and half-past three was striking at the Imperial Library in the Rue Richelieu when he reached the Rue Sainte Anne. He breathed again, and recollecting that he had not lunched, looked round him for some place where he might break a crust. Just in front of the office of the Mutual Loan Society there happened to be a wine shop. André entered, and asked for two sous' worth of bread, a slice of ham, and a pint of wine. He paid his score in advance, so that nothing might delay him in starting after Verminet as soon as the latter appeared ; and then taking up his stand near the window, he began to eat, at the same time keeping his eyes fixed on the opposite side of the way. He was somewhat anxious, for Verminet had also said that he intended going to the Bourse. Would he return home after he had been there, and before he went to see Mascarot ? All depended on this. If he did, André would be able to carry out his plans ; if not, his hour of waiting was lost. It was not lost, however, for just as he had finished his bread and ham, he caught sight of Verminet leaving his office. At one gulp André swallowed his wine and rushed out after him.

XXV.

As seen in the street, Verminet appeared to be a highly successful man, a capitalist, the fortunate manager of a thriving and lucrative business. He walked along in a jaunty style, with head erect and smiling face, glancing at the shops with the air of a millionaire able to purchase the whole of their contents, and ogling all the good-looking women he met, in the most impertinent style. André had no difficulty in following him, although he was entirely new to the profession of a *fileur*, which is a more difficult matter than is generally supposed, although, like most other things, it has its recognised rules, which simplify it wonderfully.

Profiting of the fine weather, the director of the Mutual Loan Society chose the longest route, like a man with a quiet conscience, who, after a day's hard work, allows himself the recreation of a stroll. Thus, instead of taking the Rue Neuve des Petits Champs he gained the Boulevards, and walked on enjoying his cigar, and constantly bowing to the right or left, or exchanging shakes of the hand. André, who was not more than fifteen paces behind, kept his man well in sight, and wondered at the many persons who knew this surprising financier. Somewhat disconcerted, he asked himself, "Am I mistaken ? A man scarcely sees aright when he looks through the prism of passion. This fellow may not be what I suppose. Have I taken the chimeras of my imagination for positive evidence ?" In point of fact, André had no knowledge of that large fraction of Parisian society which forgives every sin, providing the sinner be well off—the society that always bows to a man with a plethoric purse, no matter how he may have filled it.

Meanwhile, Verminet, having reached the Boulevard Poissonnière, threw away his cigar, and changed his air and walk. He walked rapidly along the Rue du Petit Carreau, and having almost reached the end of the Rue Montorgueil, near the Halles, he suddenly stopped short and disappeared under a vast *porte-cochère*. André had only to glance at the boards on either side of the door to ascertain where the financier had gone. He had gone into the office of B. Mascarot, and this Mascarot simply kept an employment agency. André had expected a more brilliant, certainly a more significant, discovery, and he felt somewhat disconcerted. Still he determined to wait for Verminet, and to give himself an air of doing something, he crossed the street, without losing sight of Mascarot's door, and pretended to be absorbed in watching three men who were fitting sliding shutters to the shop-windows of a new house. However, André was not obliged to wait long. In less than a quarter of an hour he saw Verminet come out with two men—one of them tall and thin, wearing coloured glasses ; the other, stout, smiling, and ruddy, with the air and bearing of a man of the world. They all three advanced from under the *porte-cochère*, and, standing on the kerbstone, remained talking with no little animation.

André would have given half of the twenty thousand francs in his pocket to have heard their conversation, or at least some portion of it, and he was executing an adroit manœuvre destined to bring him closer to the group, when, suddenly, two sharp shrill whistles resounded above the hum of the street traffic. These whistles were so oddly modulated that they struck André, and he was not the only one to notice them, for the tall, thin, spectacled personage who was talking to Verminet started, and looked hastily around. Hidden behind several passers-by, however, André still advanced, when suddenly the three men he was watching separated. The man with the spectacles went into the house again, while Verminet and the stout fashionable-looking man walked away together.

André hesitated. . . Should he try and find out who these men were ? There was a young chestnut vendor under the *porte cochère*. Could he not first find out something from him ?

"No," he thought, "that fellow will always be there, while I shall never, perhaps, get hold of Verminet again, so I had best begin by following him."

So saying, he started in pursuit of the director of the Mutual Loan Society, who, with his jovial-looking companion, walked down the dark passage of the Reine de Hongrie, and turning to the right in the Rue Montmartre entered a handsome-looking house. Whom had they gone to visit ? A man with any experience in detective business would not have been embarrassed, but the young painter was extremely so, until as he got nearer he espied at the end of the vestibule a marble slab bearing the words : "Office on the first floor." This was a ray of light. "Ah !" he thought, "the banker Martin Rigal must live here."

He entered and questioned the concierge, and ascertained that his surmise was a correct one. "Upon my word," he thought, "I'm in luck to-day. And now if that young chestnut vendor can only tell me the names of Verminet's companions I shall have done well. It is to be hoped he hasn't gone."

Not only was he still there, but he had a companion with whom he was so eagerly disputing, that André's presence remained for a moment unnoticed. "Come now," said the young chestnut dealer, to his "pal," "that's enough beating about the bush. I told your guv'nor just what I'd do. You want my place, and furnace, eh? Well, you can have 'em for two hundred and fifty francs."

"But the old boy will only give two hundred."

"Then he may go to blazes. Two hundred francs for a place like mine! Why, some days I've made ten francs, and over—I give you my word for it, the word of Toto-Chupin."

Toto-Chupin! Yes, the chestnut vendor was our familiar young friend. This name tickled André's fancy, and without more ado he spoke to the young scamp. "I say, my good fellow," he exclaimed, "you were here just now. Did you happen to notice three gentlemen who came out of this house, and stood talking together for a few minutes?"

Toto turned, and with an insolent air surveyed the person who had presumed to interrupt him; then in a brutal tone, he replied: "What can it matter to you? Mind your own business, and go your own way."

André was acquainted with more than one specimen of the engaging class to which Toto-Chupin belonged. He knew the language and the ways of the *gamins de Paris*, and so he resumed. "Well, you might as well answer, it wouldn't burn your tongue."

"Well, yes, I saw them. What then?"

"What then? Why, I should like to know their names, if you happen to know them yourself."

Toto-Chupin lifted his cap and scratched his head, as if to stimulate his intellect, but while he set his yellow tow-like hair on end, he examined André inquisitively. "And if I did know these men, and could tell their names," he said at last, "what would you give me?"

"Ten sous."

The young scamp puffed out his checks, and gave them a resounding slap, as a superlative expression of contempt and irony. "Look out for your suspenders!" he exclaimed, with an air of supreme pity. "Ten sous! Upon my word! Shall I lend 'em to you?"

André smiled blandly. "Did you think I meant to offer you twenty thousand francs?" he asked.

To his infinite surprise Toto burst out laughing. "I've won!" he cried. "I bet with myself that you weren't a fool, and I've won, as I said. I owe myself a new hat."

"And why do you think I'm not a fool?"

"Because a fool would have offered me five francs to begin with, and when I asked for more, he'd have advanced to ten—as many francs, as you did sous."

The painter smiled.

"But you were not to be caught," continued Toto. He paused and frowned, for he was in great perplexity. He knew these names, of course, but should he give them? He instinctively scented an enemy. Well intentioned persons do not usually address themselves to chestnut vendors with such questions. To speak was, in all probability, to do some harm either to Mascarot or Beaumarchef, or perhaps, to that sweet and gentle Tantaine.

This last thought settled the point. "Keep your ten sous," said Toto; "I'll tell you what you want to know for nothing. I've taken a fancy to you! The tall fellow was Mascarot, and the other, the stout one, his friend Dr. Hortebize; as to the third—wait a minute till I think—"

"Oh, I know *him*, *his* name's Verminet."

"Yes, that's it!"

André was so delighted with Chupin that he drew a five-franc piece from his pocket and tossed it on to the cover of the furnace. "Here! take this for your pains," he said.

With an apish grimace Toto caught up the coin. "Thanks, my prince!" he said, and he was no doubt about to indulge in one of his usual witticisms, when he happened to glance down the street, and at once his expression changed. He became very serious, almost anxious, and fixed his eyes on the young painter with a most singular expression.

"What's the matter?" asked André, much surprised.

"Nothing," answered Toto—"oh, nothing at all! Only as you seem to be a nice sort of fellow, and not a bit proud, I should advise you to look out."

"Look out? And for what?"

"I mean—be careful—I don't know just what I do mean. It's only an idea that's come into my head—an idea that some one wants to blackmail you. But that's enough—I don't mean to say another word."

André only concealed his astonishment with infinite difficulty. He realised that the young scamp knew a great many things, the knowledge of which would be wonderfully useful to himself; but he also perceived that Toto did not mean to tell them, at least at present, and that it would be folly to try and elicit another word from him. Besides, the hour fixed for meeting M. de Breulh was now approaching. Accordingly, as an empty cab passed by André hailed it, and bade the Jehu drive him to the Rond-point of the Champs Elysées.

If he did not give the name of the café where he was to meet his friend, it was because, in obedience to Toto's counsel, he had resolved to be careful —yes, extremely careful. He remembered the two odd whistles he had heard, which had made Mascarot start, and had apparently broken off the conference which the agent, Verminet, and Hortebize were having together. He recollected also, that it was after a glance down the street that Toto-Chupin had suddenly become serious, and had given him that strange, mysterious warning.

"Zounds!" he cried, suddenly enlightened by the recollection of a story he had been told not long before, "I'm being followed! That's it evidently." André was too perturbed for the time being to draw any conclusions from this discovery. Besides, the more essential point was to put the person who was following him off the scent.

He lowered the glass in front of the cab, and pulled the driver by the sleeve to attract his attention. Then, when the man turned and leaned his head towards him, he exclaimed: "Listen to me attentively, and don't change your pace. First, I wish to pay you your five francs in advance."

"But—"

"Listen. Drive as quickly as possible to the Rue de Matignon; when you get there turn round, and, as you turn, check your horses for one half minute. Then go on like the wind. When you are once in the Champs Elysées, you can go where you choose, for I sha'n't be inside."

The driver gave a little chuckle. "Ah, ah!" he said, "I understand; you are followed, and you want to give somebody the slip?"

"Something like that, I confess."

"Then listen to me. Look out when you jump, for I shall turn short, and don't take the side next the foot-walk—the roadway's less dangerous."

The driver was not only intelligent, but skilful as well, for on reaching the Rue de Matignon, he so managed matters that André was able to spring out without hurting himself, and had time to turn into a dark alley before anyone else entered the street. "Like this," thought he, "I shall be able to ascertain who it is that follows me."

But all in vain did he listen and watch, entrenched behind a door for fully five minutes, which seemed endless; neither foot-spy nor vehicle appeared—there was nothing to justify his precautions in the smallest degree. "Have I been frightening myself for nothing?" he thought. "No, such coincidences cannot be accidental."

However, when a quarter of an hour had elapsed, André decided to abandon his post and join M. de Breulh. "For I am sure he must be waiting!" said he.

And he was right; for as he approached the little café in the Champs Elysées chosen as their meeting place, he perceived M. de Breulh's brougham waiting close by, and the baron himself walking up and down smoking a cigar. On catching sight of André, M. de Breulh advanced to meet him, and exclaimed: "I have been waiting for you for fully twenty minutes."

André began to excuse himself, but his friend stopped him. "Never mind," he said; "I know, of course, that you must have had an excellent reason for your delay. Only to tell you the honest truth I had become a little anxious."

"Anxious? And why?"

"Don't you remember what I said the other evening? How I recommended you to be careful. Henri de Croisenois is a villain of the deepest dye."

André did not speak, and his friend put his arm familiarly through his. "Let us walk," he said, "it will be better than shutting ourselves up in the café. Yes, I believe Croisenois to be capable of anything and everything. Ah! you guessed him aright the first time. He constantly talks of the large fortune left by his brother George, which he will one day come into possession of; but it's really only a bait for his creditors. He has long since devoured this fortune by anticipation. A man driven to extremities is not to be trifled with you know."

"Oh, I'm not afraid of him—"

"But I am, for your sake, friend André! I am somewhat relieved, however, by the idea that he doesn't know you."

The young painter shook his head. "Not only does he know me," he answered, "but I am inclined to believe that he suspects my designs."

"Impossible!" exclaimed M. de Breulh.

"Nevertheless, this very day, I've been followed about. I have no actual proof of this, but still I'm certain of it." Thereupon, without waiting for a reply, André briefly recounted everything that had befallen him.

"Yes, you are right," said M. de Breulh in a serious voice. "You are on the track of the scoundrels who mean to blackmail the Count and Countess de Mussidan; but they evidently know it and have taken their precautions. Yes, you have been followed, no doubt of it, and, in future, at each step you take, you will be watched by spies. Why, at this very moment, no doubt, we are being observed."

He looked round as he spoke, but it was already dusk, and he could see nothing suspicious. "Ah well," he added with a laugh, "we'll give your spies the slip for to-night, and if we dine together, they'll hardly know where." Thereupon, approaching his brougham, he gave the coachman some orders in an undertone.

"Come," said he to André, and they both took their seats in the carriage. The horses at once started off at a tremendous pace in the direction of the Avenue de l'Imperatrice. "What do you think of this expedient?" asked Monsieur de Breulh, gaily. "We shall keep up this pace for an hour, and return to town by way of the Avenue de St. Ouen and the Rue de Clichy. At the corner of the Chaussée d'Antin we'll stop, jump out, and then be free. Those who are minded to follow us to-night must have good legs."

The programme was carried out, only just as De Breulh alighted, he saw a shadowy form slip from behind the carriage and disappear among the crowd on the Boulevard. "By jove!" he cried, "I thought I was leading the spy off the trail, and I was only giving him a drive!"

And then to make certain, he went behind the carriage, and felt the springs and axles. "There can be no doubt of it," he said to André. "Feel for yourself, the iron is still warm. The scoundrel had passed his legs here, and held on there."

The young painter now realised why he had seen no one, when alighting from his cab at the corner of the Rue de Matignon. Whilst he darted into the dark alley, the spy perched behind the vehicle had gone on with it as far as the Champs Elysées. This adventure saddened the dinner, and a little after ten André excused himself and retired.

XXVI.

The Viscountess de Bois d'Ardon had accurately described the situation at the Hôtel de Mussidan, when she said to André in Van Klopen's salon, "Misfortune and sorrow have brought the count and countess near together, and Sabine has decided that it is her duty to save the honour of the family. Sabine is sublime in her self-abnegation."

It was indeed a fact, that M. and Madame de Mussidan had realised that their hate ought to subside in presence of the common peril, and that their united efforts would be none too many to resist the scoundrels who threatened them. Unfortunately, this change had not taken place as early as it should have done. After Dr. Hortebize's threatening communication, and when she had ascertained that all her letters had really been stolen, Diane's first impulse had not been to confess everything to her husband, but rather to implore the help of Norbert, who was in reality as much compromised by this correspondence as herself. However, her first letter to the Duke de Champdoce elicited no reply. She wrote a second, and, finally, a third one in which she said enough to acquaint Norbert with the persecution she was a victim of, and the peril which threatened Sabine.

This third letter was brought back to her by one of the Champdoce footmen. The duke had certainly read it, for across it he had written: "The weapons you intended to use against me are turned against yourself. God is just."

She almost lost her reason on reading these words, and, for the first time, her heart of marble knew remorse. The duke's reply seemed to her a prophecy—a voice from Heaven, telling of evil days to come—saying that the hour of chastisement was near at hand, and that she must now expiate her crimes. Poor fool! She implored God to efface the past, as if the divinity had that power! At last, she realised that all was lost, and that she must speak to her husband, if she did not wish copies of the letters stolen from her to be sent to him.

It was one evening, in a small salon adjoining Sabine's room, that the

Countess de Mussidan told her husband the peril which menaced her, and what she had been asked to do. Alas! she was compelled to speak of those fatal letters and their contents; she did so with that marvellous dexterity of women who avoid lying, and yet do not speak the truth. However, she could hardly gloss over the share she had had in the death of the old Duke de Champdoce, and the mysterious disappearance of George de Croisenois.

The count was stupefied. However skilfully she presented the facts, they were still so odious, that he could hardly believe his senses. He looked at his wife, who was still handsome, and asked himself how it was possible that such a face could hide so much perversity. He recalled his youthful days, and remembered Diane as he had first seen her at Sauvebourg, where he had learned to love her. How pure and candid she had seemed, and yet she had instigated a parricide! But yet another circumstance struck M. de Mussidan. He had hitherto believed that Diane's relations with Norbert de Champdoce had been more than questionable, and that they had continued even after her marriage. And yet the countess denied it, denied it absolutely, with all her energy. And the moment was a solemn one. She was reduced to reveal the secret of her life. After the terrible confession she had made, there seemed no reason why she should not admit her guilt on this point also, if guilt there was. But on the contrary, she warmly asserted her innocence, and given all the circumstances, she was certainly worthy of belief.

The count believed her; but he remembered with a pang that he had often doubted whether Sabine was his child, and now felt himself condemned to self-reproach for the indifference he had shown her. He did not speak, but when the countess had finished he rose and left the room, staggering like a drunken man.

Whilst talking, the count and countess had believed their daughter to be asleep, but they were mistaken. Fearing what she might say in her delirium, they had sent the faithful Modeste to rest, while they sat in the small salon, with the door of Sabine's room half open, so that they could hear the slightest movement she made, and, if need be, instantly hurry to her side. Yes, they had been guilty of this imprudence; and Sabine had heard the significant words—ruin, dishonour, infamy, despair.

At first she did not understand. Were not these words part of her delirious fancies? She made an effort to shake off this nightmare. But soon she realised that the whispers were grim realities, and she lay in bed, shuddering with terror. Many of the words exchanged by her father and mother escaped her, but the conclusion was too clear. Her mother's crimes would be divulged and punished if she, Sabine, did not consent to marry this man, who was unknown to her—the Marquis de Croisenois.

With a shudder she resigned herself. Duty was there; she must obey its dictates. At least, her agony could not be of long duration. To tear her love for André from her heart, was equivalent to killing her. Still she must have courage enough to live until her sacrifice was consummated and her parents safe; and then, she thought, she would have a right to accept the repose and forgetfulness of the grave. But her flesh was weaker than her spirit. Her fever returned during the night, and a relapse imperiled her life again. Fortunately, her youth and good constitution gained the victory, and, when she recovered, her resolution was in no degree weakened. Her first act was to write that letter to André, which had sent the poor fellow nearly wild. Then, as she feared her father might take some desperate step in his despair, she went to him and confessed that she knew everything. "However, I never loved Monsieur de Breulh," she said, with a wan smile, "and so, it will not be so great a sacrifice on my part."

Was the Count de Mussidan duped by this generous falsehood? Certainly not. Alone, he would have braved the consequences of the murder of Montlouis; but could he suffer the divulging of his wife's sins, of the trap set for poor George de Croisenois and the midnight duel he had fought with the Duke de Champdoce?

Time was going on, however, and the scoundrels who had threatened the Mussidans gave no signs of life. Dr. Hortebize didn't show himself. What did this silence mean? Sometimes the countess ventured to hope. "Have they forgotten us?" she asked herself.

No, they were not forgotten. Honourable B. Mascarot never for one moment lost sight of any of the pieces on the vast chessboard he had selected for his last game, and it was with admirable precision, and always at the right moment, that he made a move. Everything had been arranged for the success of the Champdoce matter. All precautions were taken to avoid detection in the substitution of Paul for the duke's real son, and Mascarot had now time to turn his attention to the marriage of M. de Croisenois and Sabine. First of all, the count and countess's consent must be wrung from them, and then the marquis must be compelled to start that famous company, intended to mask the blackmailing practices of B. Mascarot and his associates.

Our old friend, Father Tantaine, was commissioned to interview the Count de Mussidan, and obtain a decisive promise from him concerning Sabine's marriage. Any one else but the old clerk would, no doubt, have considered it indispensable to make some little improvement in his dress —to clean his boots, possibly, and brush the accumulated dust from his coat. But Tantaine disdained cleanliness, which he indeed called nonsense, declaring that the coat did not make the man. He had once been heard to say that he never quitted an article of clothing; he waited till the garment dropped from him in shreds, and, judging from his appearance, this was perhaps true. He clung to his rags as to his personality, saying that if he changed them he should not be the same man, and should fail to recognise himself in new clothes. So this is why the servants at the Hôtel de Mussidan, on seeing this dirty, shabby old man enter the vestibule, and ask to see the count or countess, replied with a jocular sneer that their master and mistress had gone out several hours ago.

However, the jest in no way disconcerted old Tantaine. Drawing one of Mascarot's address cards from his pocket, he implored these "good gentlemen," to take it up-stairs, saying that as soon as their master saw it, he would send for him to come up. The name of the honourable employment agent had magic influence among menials, and yet the footmen still hesitated, when Florestan entered the hall and consented to take the card to the count.

The Mussidans were at lunch, and when the count read Mascarot's name, he turned deadly pale, and barely had strength to stammer, "Show the gentleman into the library, and tell him I will join him soon."

Florestan left the room, and the count passed the card to his wife, saying, "You see!"

Madame de Mussidan did not look at it. "I can guess," she answered.

"Ah, yes!" said the count, "settling day has arrived. This name on this strip of card is the signification of our sentence." He rose to his feet with such a violent movement of rage that half the things on the table were overturned. "And to think I can do nothing against the scoundrels," he exclaimed, "nothing! It is enough to drive one mad!" His emotion was too much for him, and sinking on to a chair again, he covered his face with his hands and burst into tears.

At sight of his despair the countess rose, and kneeling beside him, took hold of one of his hands and kissed it tenderly. "Pardon, Octave," she murmured, "forgive me. I am a wretched woman. God is unjust. I alone committed these crimes, and alone ought to be punished."

M. de Mussidan repelled her gently. He suffered so much, that the idea never occurred to him of reproaching this woman, his wife, who had made of his life one long agony, and who alone had caused this supreme catastrophe. "And Sabine," he resumed, "must she, a Mussidan, marry one of these ignoble scoundrels! That cannot be. It would be abominable cowardice, a more odious crime than all the others to sacrifice our daughter in order to save ourselves from infamy!"

Sabine was the only one of the three who retained a semblance of calmness, and yet her sufferings were even more terrible than her parents', and besides, she was innocent; but then she possessed that heroism which is the outgrowth of duty, and her countenance was firm and composed.

"Ah! dear father!" she said, with a gaiety that was heart-breaking under the circumstances, "why despair? Who can say that M. de Croisnois won't prove a good husband?"

The count turned to Sabine and gave her a look of the tenderest affection and gratitude. "Dear child!" he murmured—"dear Sabine!"

Her example, in some measure, restored his self-possession, and he rose again. "Let us resign ourselves in appearance, at all events," he said. "Time alone can bring us succour. Let us wait. Rescue may come before we reach the church door." Then going to the table he poured himself out a large glass of water, swallowed it at one draught, and left the room, muttering, "Come, I must be brave!"

XXVII.

GENIAL Father Tantaine had guessed that some such scene would take place between Mascarot's luckless victims, and was by no means surprised at being asked to wait. Florestan had conducted him to the superb library where B. Mascarot had been received, and to kill time he took as it were an inventory of its contents. He inspected the fine old carved furniture, felt the heavy hangings, examined the costly bindings of the books, and admired the magnificent bronzes on the consoles.

"Ha! ha!" he muttered, as he tried the springs of the arm-chairs, "it is very comfortable here, and when everything is arranged, I'm not sure I shouldn't like such a nest for myself. I'm quite sure that Flavia—"

He stopped short, hearing a foot-fall on the stairs; the next moment the door opened, and the count appeared, calm and dignified, but very pale.

Tantaine bowed to the very ground, pressing his shabby hat against his breast. "Your most humble servant—" he began.

But the count had paused abruptly on the threshold. "Excuse me," he said, "was it you who sent me a card soliciting an interview?"

"I had that honour," answered Tantaine humbly.

"But you are not the person whose name I read on this card?"

"True, I am not M. Mascarot; but I used that respectable name, Monsieur le Comte, because I knew that my own would convey no information to you. My name is Tantaine, Adrien Tantaine, a lawyer's clerk by profession."

It was with the greatest surprise that M. de Mussidan looked at the shabby individual before him. He realised well enough that Tantaine's simple expression and amiable smile were only affected, and that it would be folly to trust to them.

"However," continued Tantaine, "I have come on the same business, sir. It must be finished as soon as possible."

The count shut the door and locked it. This filthy looking old man compelled him to feel the ignominy of his position even still more sensibly.

"I understand," he said, "perfectly; but why have you come, and not the other—I mean the one whom I saw before?"

"He meant to come, but at the last minute he declared he wouldn't."

"Ah!"

"Yes—he was afraid. Mascarot, you see, has a great deal to lose; while I—" He stopped, and holding out the tails of his coat, turned round, so as to fully display his tattered sordid garments. "What I have on my back is all I have to lose," he added, with mock joviality.

"Then, I can treat with you?" asked the count.

"Certainly—and in fact all the more easily as I'm not an intermediary. I am the owner of the documents."

"What, is it you who—"

Tantaine bowed with an air of modest virtue. "Yes, it is I, Monsieur le Comte, who hold the leaves torn from M. de Clinchan's journal; and—why not confess it?—the correspondence of Madame de Mussidan as well. If, originally, I divided the operation, it was because I didn't think it prudent to put all my eggs in one basket. But now that you, sir, and madame are on good terms, we can, I think—"

"Enough!" answered the count, unable to conceal his disgust. "Sit down!"

Father Tantaine does not care a straw whether folks despise him or not, but he never forgives them for showing their feelings in his presence. Thus the result of the count's curt, imperious, disdainful manner, was that all the old fellow's seeming humility vanished at once. "I will be brief," he said, sharply. "Have you any intention of filing any complaint, or making any charge against us?"

"I have already said I should do nothing of the kind."

"We can transact our business, then?"

"Yes—if—"

The old man shrugged his shoulders. "There are no 'ifs in the matter!" he answered. "We dictate the conditions, which you can accept or reject as you choose."

He spoke so impudently that the count's face flushed, and he felt tempted to pitch the scoundrel out of the window. However, he had determined to keep his temper, and accordingly replied, "At all events, state your conditions."

Tantaine produced a greasy portfolio, and drew a paper from it. "These are our terms," he said, slowly. "The Count de Mussidan promises the hand of Mademoiselle Sabine, his daughter, to the Marquis de Croisenois; he gives six hundred thousand francs dowry, and agrees that the marriage shall be solemnised as early as possible. To-morrow the Marquis de Croisenois will be officially presented at the Hôtel de Mussidan, and will be well received. Four days later he will be invited to dinner. In a fortnight hence M. de Mussidan will give a grand fête for the signing of the marriage contract. The leaves of M. de Clinchan's diary, and the correspondence of Madame de Mussidan, will be handed to M. de Mussidan, immediately after the marriage has been solemnised."

The count sat with compressed lips and clinched hands, listening to these atrocious conditions. "Very well," he said, coldly; "but who can tell me that you will keep your engagements, and that the papers will be restored to me after all?"

Tantaine gave him a glance of commiseration. "Your own good sense!" he answered. "What more could we hope from you when we have your daughter and your fortune?"

This was logical enough. Assuredly he would be left quiet when nothing more could be extorted from him. However, the count did not speak at first. For some minutes he walked up and down the library, glancing askance at the old clerk, and employing all his penetration in trying to discover some flaw, some weak point in the armour of his impudent, cynical adversary. "Well," he said at last, in a deliberate tone, like a man who has made up his mind : "I renounce struggling. You hold me; I must admit myself conquered. Exorbitant as your conditions are, I accept them."

"That's the way to talk !" said Tantaine, cheerfully.

"Only let us have a frank explanation without reticence. It seems to me that all artifice of language is unnecessary."

"Quite so."

"Then," rejoined the count, in whose eyes there sparkled a gleam of hope, "why do you talk to me of giving my daughter to M. de Croisenois? It is perfectly unnecessary. What you want is simply the six hundred thousand francs, is it not? Well, take them, and leave Sabine to me. I offer you her entire dowry—"

He checked himself, and waited for the result. He believed he had won the battle, but he was mistaken.

"It wouldn't be the same thing," answered Tantaine. "We should not attain our object in this way."

"I can do more even. Grant me another month, and in that time I shall be able to increase the sum to a million."

But Tantaine was not moved by the magnitude of this offer. "You have forgotten what I told you, Monsieur le Comte," said he. "Our conditions are final, irrevocable." He rose to his feet, and added, "I think, it would be best to end this interview, which might become irritating. You have agreed to accept the conditions ; M. de Croisenois will be welcomed to-morrow—"

The count replied with a gesture of assent, but he dared not trust himself to speak.

"Then," continued Tantaine, "I can now retire. As you, sir, keep your engagements, so will we keep ours."

His hand was on the door, when the count stopped him. "One word more," said M. de Mussidan. "I can answer for myself and my wife, but as to my daughter—"

Tantaine's face changed. "I don't understand," he interrupted, speaking in a tone that showed he understood only too well. "I don't know—"

"It may be that my daughter will reject M. de Croisenois."

"Why should she ? The marquis is good-looking, witty, and amiable."

"Nevertheless, she may reject him all the same."

"But surely Mademoiselle de Mussidan is too well born and bred to question her parents' decisions."

The count knew he was surrounded by spies, but he had no notion that his persecutors were acquainted with Sabine's admirable devotion. Hence he rejoined, "However, it is as well to foresee all contingencies. My daughter has always had a firm will. She was expecting to marry M. de Breulh-Faverlay, and perhaps—"

"If mademoiselle resists," interrupted the old clerk, peremptorily, "you will, if you please, let me see her for a few minutes. After that I am inclined to believe you will have no further difficulty."

"What would you presume to say to my daughter?"

"I should tell her—well—I should tell her that if she loves any one it is certainly not this M. de Breulh!" As he finished speaking, worthy Tantaine tried to bolt, fearful of the consequences his words might have, but the count, with a kick, closed the door which the old fellow had already partially opened.

"You will not leave this room," said the count, sternly, "without explaining that insulting remark. What do you mean?"

Tantaine seemed to be reflecting. His impatience had carried him farther than he meant to have gone, and he was rather at a loss for an answer. "Good heavens!" he replied at last, as he adjusted his spectacles, "I had no intention of offending you. I merely—" He hesitated, and finally, in a tone of the most delicate sarcasm, which was strange in a man of his apparent condition, he resumed : "I am aware that a noble heiress may do many a thing without being in the slightest degree compromised—many a thing which would hopelessly ruin the reputation of a girl of a different social grade. So no doubt M. de Breulh-Faverlay knew that the young lady he expected to marry was in the habit of passing her afternoons in the room of a young man—"

"Scoundrel!" roared the count. "Wretch, you lie!"

M. de Mussidan's gesture was at the same time so threatening, that Tantaine started back and pulled out the revolver which never left him, and which he had already produced on the occasion of his memorable visit to Perpignan. "Gently, count, if you please," said he. "Insults and blows never pay. I am simply better informed than yourself, that's all. I, myself, have often had the honour of seeing your daughter enter No—, Rue de la Tour d'Auvergne, ask the concierge for M. André, the painter, and then dart up the staircase like a hare."

The count was fairly choking. "Proofs!" he gasped. "Proofs!"

As they talked, the old clerk had manœuvered so successfully that the great library table now separated him from M. de Mussidan. Entrenched behind this improvised rampart he felt comparatively secure. "Proofs!" he answered; "do you think I carry them in my pocket? I couldn't furnish you with any of the correspondence of these young people under a week, and that's too long to wait. However, you can satisfy yourself very easily. To-morrow, before eight o'clock, go to the address I have just given, and climb the stairs to M. André's studio. There, behind a green baize curtain you will find Mademoiselle Sabine's portrait—and a good portrait it is, too. I presume you will admit that this could not have been painted without a sitter."

"Leave this room at once!" cried the count, who felt as if he were going mad.

Tantaine did not wait for the injunction to be repeated. He hurried to

the door, and when he was quite outside, popped his head in and cheerfully added, "Don't forget the address, Monsieur le Comte—André. artist,
Rue de la Tour d'Auvergne, No.—, and go early, before eight o'clock."

At this supreme insult, the count bounded forward, but he was too late.
Tantaine pulled the door to, and darted down the staircase. "It was
better than I expected," he muttered ; "but, after all, I have yet to see
the man who is not subdued by a fortnight's agony of suspense !" When
he reached the vestibule his face had regained its usual expression, and it
was with the greatest respect that he bowed to the footmen, and left the
house.

"Eh ! eh !" he said to himself, as he walked down the Rue de Matignon,
"it seems to me I didn't arrange that so badly. The count will certainly
verify my information about André. They will be brought together, and
what will be the result ? Was I not rather too prompt ?—But no, on the
contrary, it was a happy inspiration of mine. André knows himself
watched, and of course I shall discover nothing more through him ; whilst
on the other side, M. de Mussidan, now certain that his daughter has had a
lover, and what a lover too ! a low born ornamental sculptor, will almost
thankfully accept the Marquis de Croisenois as his son-in-law."

In saying this, worthy Tantaine felt convinced that Sabine had been
André's mistress. He was quite unable to imagine the possibility of such
a noble honest love as that which bound the young artist and Mademoiselle
de Mussidan together. "What will be the result of the count's visit to
the studio?" he asked himself. "The old nobleman's frightfully hot-
tempered. Suppose they quarrelled, we might have a duel then, and who
knows?—that cursed André might be killed. Well in that case, good
riddance to bad rubbish, that's all I say."

XXVIII.

THE old clerk had by this time reached the Champs Elysées, and he looked
anxiously around him, and then made the tour of the summer circus
building. He was seeking for Toto-Chupin with whom he had made an
appointment, and as usual on these occasions, the young scamp was not to be
found. Tantaine not only felt uneasy but out of temper also, but at last near
one of those stalls where imitation lotteries for worthless gewgaws and pieces of
crockery are organized, he saw Toto conversing earnestly with its owner.
Chupin was no longer radiantly attired as at the "Grand Turk" but wore
a dirty patched blouse, and a greasy cap—"Eh, Toto !" called worthy Tantaine—"Toto-Chupin !"

The lad heard him, plainly enough, for he looked round, but did not
move. The conversation he was engaged in was evidently of great interest. However, Tantaine shouted again, and more imperiously than before,
and Toto reluctantly left his companion and went towards the old clerk.
"What an idea !" he grumbled. "As soon as you come, I must leave
everything else. Do you feel ill, that you set up such a squeal? If you
do, I'll go and get a physician."

"I'm in a great hurry, Toto."

"I daresay. So's the postman when he's late. I'm busy too."

"With that person you just left ? "

"Yes, to be sure : 'that person,' as you call him, is wiser than I am.
How much do you make each day, Father Tantaine ? Well, that fellow

there with that little stall pockets thirty or forty francs every night, and he has literally nothing to do for it either. It must be nice to see people make such fools of themselves. I should like that business, and I think I shall start on it soon. Patience!"

Patience! Father Tantaine realised that he had never so much needed it as at this precise moment. "I thought," he said, quietly, "that you were going into business with the two young men you were drinking beer with at the 'Grand Turk.'"

At this suggestion Toto howled with rage. "Business with them!" he cried. "I won't have anything more to do with the rascals!"

"Have they done you any harm, my poor Toto?"

"Yes, utterly ruined me at cards—won all my coin, and even my new clothes, that's why I'm in this old blouse. They were in force, the beggars, and made me strip. If you like to lend me a hundred sous, I shall just have five francs in my pocket. Fortunately, I saw Mascarot yesterday, and he gave me leave to sell the furnace. He's a good fellow, is Mascarot."

Tantaine pouted disdainfully. "Good fellow!" he answered. "He's good and friendly enough, no doubt, as long as no one asks a favour of him."

It was so strange to hear the old clerk say a word against Mascarot that Toto was astounded. "That isn't the way you used to talk," said he.

"Ah, I didn't know Mascarot then. But since he lets me half starve while he rolls in gold, I say to myself, 'That'll do; I've had quite enough of you.' And, in fact, Toto, as you are a bright boy, I don't mind telling you that I'm only waiting for an opportunity to leave Mascarot and set up in business on my own account."

"Work for oneself, indeed," said Toto in a tone which betrayed bitter deception. "That is easier said than done; I know that right enough."

"You've tried, then?"

"To do something alone? Yes, I have, but I came to grief. Besides you know all about it as well as I do myself. Don't tell me you didn't listen that evening when you were looking for Caroline at the 'Turk.' Well, never mind, I can tell you all the same. One day then, I saw a lady looking frightened to death get out of a cab. I followed her at once. My plan was already made, and I knew just what I meant to do. I was well-dressed at the time, so I rang at the door, and I felt so certain I was going to make something out of her, that I wouldn't have taken eighty francs down for the hundred I expected to have. Well, then, I rang. A servant opened the door, and in I went. What luck I had! Why a great big fellow pummelled away at me, and finally kicked me down stairs." So saying, Toto lifted his cap and showed a couple of scars, which reddened his manly brow, "That's the bloke's mark," he added, grimly.

Whilst talking, Tantaine and Toto had walked slowly up the Champs Elysées, and they had now just reached the house which was being built by M. Gandelu—the house where André worked.

Tantaine took a seat on a bench just across the road. "Let's sit down a moment," he said; "I'm horribly tired."

And when Toto had installed himself at his side, he added: "Your story, my boy, only proves that you are lacking in experience. Now I've plenty of that. With Mascarot, it was really I who was at the head of most things. If I were to start on my own account, I should have a carriage this time next year; only one thing deters me, and that's my age, for unfortunately I'm growing old. At this very moment I have a superb affair on hand with half the coin paid in advance.   Only I must give it up, for to bring it to a successful issue I need some one who's young and quick."

Chupin looked up with eager eyes.   "Wouldn't I do?" he asked.   The old clerk shook his head.   "You are too young," he said—"just as I'm too old.   The heart, at your age, speaks too loudly.   You would recoil just at the critical moment.   And then you have your conscience."

"So I have!" cried Toto, "but it's a conscience much like yours, Papa Tantaine; it has a deal of elasticity about it, and can be rolled up and tucked away when one takes the omnibus."

"Well! well! perhaps we can come to terms."

The old clerk produced a checked rag, which did duty as a handkerchief, and wiped his spectacles without removing them.   "Listen to me, Chupin," he resumed; "listen to a mere supposition.   You hate your two quondam friends—the fellows who were stronger than you, and who fleeced you of your money and clothes.   Well, suppose you knew they ran about like squirrels all day long in the scaffolding of that big house opposite, what should you do?"

Toto scratched his head.   "If your supposition were truth," he answered at last, "those chaps might as well say their prayers; for I'd slip into the house at night-time and just saw the planks nearly apart, so when one of my brigands the next morning stepped forward—whew!   You under-stand, Father Tantaine?"

"Not bad!" said the old man paternally, "not at all bad, upon my word, for a lad of eighteen."

Toto-Chupin swelled with pride.   "And I'd manage it all so well," he added, "that no one would ever suspect me.   I know all about the build-ing trade.   Why I worked for a mason myself once on a time."

"The more I listen to you, Toto," said the old clerk seriously, "the more I'm convinced you are precisely the partner I need.   I'm sure we could make heaps of money together."

"Oh, I'm sure of that."

"The more so, as you know all about the building trade.   Well, just let me tell you that among my acquaintances there's a very wealthy old gentleman who has a mortal enemy—a young man who ran off with a woman he adored."

"The old fellow must have been awfully wild."

"He wasn't pleased, certainly.   Now it happens, Toto, that this young man spends ten hours out of the twenty-four on those very scaffolds op-posite.   The old gentleman, who's a clever fellow, had much the same idea as you, but he's too stout and too old to try the game himself, and to cut a long story short, he'd give four thousand francs to the persons who put his idea into execution.   If we went into partnership, that would be halves for each of us.   Two thousand francs for a little sawing!—what do you think of that, Toto?"

Despite the elasticity of Chupin's conscience, this significant suggestion made him turn pale, and he shuddered.   Trying, however, to master his feelings, he exclaimed, "The thing might p'r'aps be done."

His agitation was too evident to escape Tantaine, but the latter pre-tended not to notice it.

"First of all, Chupin," he said, "I must explain to you how the old gentleman's plan differed from yours.   If any plank were sawed as you suggest, why we should run the risk of some other fellow breaking his neck, and our man escaping scot free."

"'That's true," said Toto, who scratched his head and added, "however, anyone who hit on a better way would be a smart fellow,"

"I've hit on one, Toto."

"Pshaw! I'm not curious, but I should like to know it."

Tantaine smiled genially. "Listen to me," he said using his forefinger as an indicator. "You see that little wooden shanty up there among the scaffolding?"

"That's where the ornamental sculptors perch."

"Open your eyes and shut your mouth," said Tantaine severely. "That little shanty a hundred feet up in the air has a window, as you see. Now, the supports of that window ought to be sawn through, down to the floor of the shanty."

"That's easy enough; but what then?"

Tantaine shook his head compassionately. "Ah!" he said, in a tone of reproach, "I thought you more intelligent than that; I really did. Suppose my old gentleman's enemy—whose name is Pierre—was in that little box at work! All of a sudden, he hears in the avenue the voice of a woman shrieking, 'Help! Pierre, help! It's I—your Adèle!' What would Pierre do, do you think? He would rush to that window and lean out, and as the supports have been sawed through, why, he'd come a cropper on the pavement."

"It's awfully well planned," said Toto admiringly.

"Not badly, certainly; but the point is, would you undertake the job?"

Driven to the wall, Chupin hesitated. "I don't say no," he muttered; "but will the old gentleman pay promptly? We might do the work, and then, p'r'aps, he'd leave us in the lurch."

"He will pay; and, besides, didn't I tell you that he had paid half in advance?"

Toto's eyes sparkled. The old clerk unbuttoned his coat, and mysteriously produced two bank-notes of a thousand francs each. "There!" said he.

"By jove!" exclaimed Toto covetously. "If I undertake the work, are one of these for me?"

"Of course; and you'll have a second one afterwards," said Tantaine.

"All right, then, count on me." And when the old clerk had handed him the note, the young scamp, carried away by delight, positively kissed it, and then, careless what passers-by might think, executed a frantic *pas de danse*.

After these preliminaries, the rest was easily settled. It was agreed that Toto should, that very night, enter the building and set to work. Beyond sawing the supports, he would only have to stroll about in the neighbourhood and watch for the result. This last point was particularly specified by Father Tantaine, who, on his side, undertook to select the right moment, which might only occur in a few days' time, for some one to call out in such a manner as to bring the young sculptor to the window. The old man thought of everything, and even explained to Toto the kind of hand-saw he had best choose, giving him the address of a maker who was unrivalled for the quality of his tools. "Above all," he added, "take care not to leave any marks that might cause suspicion. Remember that the merest atom of sawdust on the floor might disclose the whole secret. It would be wise, moreover, to furnish yourself with a dark lantern. Grease your saw well, and when you have finished, conceal the marks it will leave. I should suggest doing so with a little putty, over which you might sprinkle some plaster. There'll be lots lying about."

Toto listened to the old man with astonishment ; he had never supposed him so practical. He promised that he would attend to all these details, and presuming that his instructions were over, he rose to go.

But Tantaine had not finished. "By the way," he said, "just tell me the truth about Caroline Schimmel. You told Beaumarchef that she ac-cused me of making her drunk, and that she was looking everywhere for me to avenge herself. Is that true ? "

"Oh ! you weren't my partner then," answered the lad with a laugh ; "and I only said it to frighten you. The truth is, you made the poor woman drink so much that she's very ill, and is in an hospital now."

Tantaine looked pleased. He rose, and before turning away, asked, "Where do you lodge at present ? "

"I don't know. Yesterday I slept at the Carrières d'Amerique ; but now, as I've some coin, I shall be furnishing a place for myself."

"In the meantime, will you have my room for a few days ? " asked Tan-taine. "I've moved, but the attic belongs to me for another fortnight."

'All right. Where is it ? "

"You know ; in the Rue de la Huchette, at the Hôtel du Pérou. I'll write a word to the landlady, Madame Loupias." As he spoke, he tore a leaf from his notebook, and wrote with a pencil a request "that a young relative of his, M. Toto-Chupin," might have his room.

Toto carefully secured this letter with the bank-note in the folds of his neckcloth, which seemed to be both his strong-box and his archives. "And now," said he, "I'll just have a look at the building, so as to plan how I'll do the job."

The old clerk watched him cross the avenue and stand on the opposite pavement, looking up at the men at work. At this very moment, M. Gandelu, the builder, came out with his son, and stopped to give some directions. For two or three minutes, Toto and Gaston stood side by side, close to each other. A strange smile flitted over Tantaine's lips as he noticed this. "Two children of Paris," he mused, "charming examples of its vaunted civilisation—both gifted with similar instincts, but one of them stultified by vice, and the other sharpened by necessity. However, the dandy struts about on the pavement, while the gamin plays in the gutter. Why is it that Toto doesn't buy cigars at a franc a-piece, and let Gaston pick up the stumps ? "

But he had no time to spend in philosophising, as the omnibus he needed was within sight. He hailed it, took his seat, and, half an hour later, entered the house in the Rue Montmartre, where he had installed Paul Violaine.

Madame Bregot, the excellent concierge, who was ready to swear that Paul had resided in her house for years, happened to be in the courtyard watching one of the tenants, who was bottling wine, when she caught sight of Tantaine. She rolled up to him with a most ingratiating smile ; but still absorbed in thought, the old clerk neglected to touch his shabby hat, and merely asked, with an absent air, "How is our young man getting on ? "

"Better, sir ; much better. I made him some good soup yesterday, and he enjoyed it immensely. He looks like a king this morning, and the doctor has just sent a dozen of wine, which will set him all right again."

Tantaine listened as carelessly as he had spoken, and he was already half way towards the stairs when mother Bregot stopped him and mysteri-ously added, "A person was here last night making inquiries about M. Paul."

This information roused Tantaine from his reflections, and he eagerly, anxiously asked, "Who was it?"

"A gentleman. He asked me if I were well acquainted with M. Paul, what he did, if he had several friends, and where he lived before he came here?"

"Well, what did you answer him?"

"Oh! just what you told me to say—neither more nor less."

"What sort of a person was this gentleman?" asked Tantaine, after a brief pause.

"Well, he was a man much like other men—neither tall nor short, neither thin nor fat, well-dressed but stingy, for after questioning me for a quarter of an hour, he went off without giving me a farthing."

This description of the visitor was hardly calculated to enlighten Tantaine, and he looked disappointed. "Then you remarked nothing about him in particular?" he asked.

"Yes—his spectacles, with gold bows as fine as hair; and his watch-chain, which was as thick as my thumb."

"And is that all?"

"Yes," she said, "that's all. Oh! one thing; this gentleman must know you come here."

"Indeed! What makes you think so?"

"Because, while he was talking to me he was in an awful fidget—he never took his eyes off the door. He was as restless as Minette, my cat, when she has stolen a piece of meat while my back's been turned."

"Thank you, mother Bregot. Be prudent and watchful," said Tantaine, as he continued his way upstairs far more slowly than was his habit. He stopped every two or three steps to think. "Who can this person be?" he asked himself.

With wonderful promptitude he surveyed the whole field of probability and possibility, and still he was at a loss to answer his own query. "That man must know me," he pondered. "If he was nervous and fidgety, it must have been that he feared being surprised by me. He must be working against us. He can't have come with any good intentions." As the old clerk reflected, his anxiety developed into fright. "Thunder!" he muttered. "Are the police at my heels?" He tried to reassure himself; but only succeeded partially, for his nerves were strangely shaken. "At all events," he said, "I must make haste. After succeeding, I can certainly annihilate all proofs. I must finish the work as speedily as possible."

He had now reached the third floor, and stood at the door of Paul's apartment. He rang, and the door was instantly opened: but at the sight of the person who had answered his ring, he started back and uttered a cry of angry astonishment. It was a woman who stood before him—a young girl, the daughter of Martin-Rigal, the banker. At one glance, Tantaine, a keen observer, realised that Mademoiselle Flavia had not been with Paul merely for a few minutes; for she was without her hat and cloak, and held a piece of embroidery in her hand. "What do you wish, sir?" she asked.

The old clerk tried to speak, but, strange to say, he could not utter a word. An iron hand seemed to be clutching at his throat, and he looked like a man who was about to have an apoplectic fit. Flavia gazed at him with some curiosity and considerable disgust. This shabby, sordid-looking old man repelled her. She fancied she had seen him somewhere before. In fact, there was an inexplicable air about him which puzzled her.

"I should like to speak to Monsieur Paul," said the old clerk at last, in a voice so low and husky that it was almost unintelligible ; "he expects me."

"In that case, sir, come in ; but I ought to warn you that his doctor is with him just now."

As she spoke, Flavia retreated close to the wall, so that Tantaine might enter without touching her dress. He passed her with a low bow, and crossed the little salon with the air of a person who knew where he was going. He did not even knock, but opened the door of the bedroom and went in.

A singular spectacle met his eyes. Paul, who looked very pale, was sitting up in bed with his shoulders bare, and Hortebize was hovering round him with an air of eager interest. On Paul's arm, from shoulder to elbow, there extended an enormous wound or burn, which must have been intensely painful. The doctor was applying to this appalling wound strips of gold-beater's skin, which had previously been moistened with a solution contained in a phial standing on a side table.

When Tantaine entered, Hortebize turned, and so readily did these two men understand each other, that a gesture and a glance sufficed for them to exchange their thoughts. "Flavia here !" was what Tantaine's gesture signified. "Is she mad ?" "I daresay, but I can't help it," was the answer to be read in the doctor's eyes.

However, Paul also had turned, and it was with an exclamation of delight that he greeted the old clerk, who of all the people round about him pleased him the most. In fact, he thought him less evil-minded than the other associates. "Come here," he said gaily, "and see what a pitiable state the doctor and M. Mascarot have reduced me to."

It was with the attention and curiosity of a connoisseur that Tantaine examined Paul's wound. "Are you sure," he asked Hortebize, "that the scar will deceive, not only the duke, who will believe just what we choose, but also his wife and friends, and even his physicians?"

"We will deceive them, one and all !" answered the doctor decidedly.

"The next point," continued Tantaine, "is, how long we shall have to wait for the scar to become white and acquire an appearance of age."

"Before a month has elapsed, we can present Paul to the Duke de Champdoce."

"Is that really so ?"

"Understand me : the scar will not be altogether natural, but there are several other things I intend to do to it."

The dressing was now completed, and Paul's shirt was pulled up over his shoulders, and he was allowed to lie down again, and instructed to move and turn about as little as possible. "Oh ! I'll keep still," he said, "as long as I have the nurse who's waiting in the next room. By the way, I'm sure she's waiting with great impatience for your departure."

Hortebize frowned, and gave his patient a furious look, as much as to say, "Hold your tongue !" but the young fellow was blind.

"How long has this nurse been with you?" asked Tantaine, in a constrained voice.

"Ever since I've been in bed," answered Paul, with the most conceited air. "I wrote to say, I could not go and see her, as I was ill—and so she came here. She received my note at nine o'clock, and at ten minutes past she made her appearance."

The judicious doctor contrived to get behind Tantaine, and made a despairing gesture to Paul to induce him to say no more ; but all in vain.

"It seems," continued the conceited simpleton, "that M. Martin-Rigal spends his life in his private office. As soon as ne is up in the morning, he shuts himself up in his private room, and is never seen again all day. So Flavia is free as air. As soon as she knows that the worthy banker is busy with his papers, she throws a shawl over her shoulders and flies to me. Upon my word, no one could be more obliging or prettier." Then with an impudent little chuckle he added, "Why, I could send M. Mascarot about his business."

"Believe me, it would be most unwise to do so," rejoined the doctor severely.

Paul perceived the gesture with which M. Hortebize underlined these words, but he mistook their meaning. "Oh I don't intend to do so," he said. "Only it would hardly do for M. Martin-Rigal to think of refusing me his daughter's hand. Flavia wouldn't hesitate between her father and me—"

Tantaine, who for some minutes had been pulling frantically at his spectacles, now stammered, "You are no doubt flattering yourself."

"And why? Flavia loves me, you know that, of course—and this is the point. Poor girl! I ought to marry her, and I will; but still, if I chose— "

"Miserable scoundrel!" cried the gentle Tantaine. "Only a fool and coward would dare speak like that of a poor girl whose only misfortune is that she loves a conceited whipper-snapper unworthy of her. Do you think I'll allow— "

His gesture was so furious, and his voice so threatening, that Paul was frightened, and drew back to the wall; but Tantaine went no further, for Hortebize had seized him by the arm and now fairly dragged him from the room.

<h2 style="text-align:center">XXIX.</h2>

PAUL was utterly at a loss to imagine why Tantaine had burst into such a rage. No doubt he had spoken improperly of Flavia, who was really entitled to his respect and tender deference. But conceited as his language had been, did it really justify such an outburst? And, besides, why was it that each time he affected that scorn of all morality which his associates gloried in, they should turn round on him, and treat him with contempt? After all, he would have understood and accepted a remonstrance from the doctor, who was Martin-Rigal's intimate friend. But what earthly connection was there between that cynical old beggar Tantaine and the rich banker?

Forgetful of the suffering which the slightest movement caused him, Paul sat up in bed and listened eagerly, with extended neck, hoping to hear something of what was going on in the next room. But there was a thick wall between the salon and bedroom, and he could hear nothing. "What are they doing?" he asked himself. "What are they plotting?"

Father Tantaine and Hortebize had rapidly crossed the salon, only pausing on the landing where the doctor tried to console his companion, who seemed utterly desperate. "Courage!" he said, in a low voice—"courage! What on earth is the good of getting into a state like this? How can you mend matters? No—it's too late. Besides, even if you could, you wouldn't, as you know very well yourself."

The old clerk had drawn out his handkerchief to dry—not his glasses, but his eyes. "Ah!" he said, "now I understand only too well what Monsieur de Mussidan must have felt when I proved to him that his daughter had a lover. I have been cruel, hard, and pitiless, and I am punished—yes, bitterly punished."

"You mustn't attach too much importance, old friend, to this nonsense. Paul is a mere lad."

"Paul is a miserable, cowardly hound," replied Tantaine in a fierce whisper. "He does not love Flavia, but she adores him. Oh, what he says is true, too true—I feel it. Between her father and himself she would not hesitate a moment. Poor girl, what a future lies before her!" He checked himself abruptly, and appealing to all his energy, succeeded in regaining some semblance of his usual composure. "However," said he, "she must not remain here, and as I cannot speak to her myself, try, doctor, and make her listen to reason."

Hortebize shrugged his shoulders. "I fear my eloquence will be of no avail," he answered. "And in that case, no doubt, you will be unable to restrain yourself. However, remember that one word might reveal to her the secret of our lives."

"Go at once. I swear to you that whatever happens, I will remain calm."

The doctor returned to the room as he spoke, while Tantaine sat down on the stairs outside with his head in his hands.

Mademoiselle Flavia was just returning to Paul when the doctor appeared. "Back again!" she said, pettishly; "I thought you far away."

"I wanted to say a few words to you," answered Hortebize, "and serious ones, too. You need not draw down those pretty eyebrows—I see you understand me. Yes, you are right. I came to tell you that this is not the place for Mademoiselle Martin-Rigal."

"I know that," she answered, with such cool calmness that the smiling doctor was evidently disconcerted.

"It seems to me— " he began again.

"What? that I ought not to be here? However, I place duty above propriety. Paul is very ill—he has no one with him; so who ought to take care of him, except the woman he is soon to marry? Has not my father given his consent?"

Hortebize was reflecting for some good argument. "Come," he said at last, "listen to the voice of my experience. Men are so constituted that they never forgive a woman for compromising herself, even for themselves. Do you know what would be said of you twenty-four hours after your marriage, if it were known you had been here? Why, people would say that Paul had been your lover, had, in fact, seriously compromised you, and that your father had only for that very reason consented to your marriage. Believe me, don't lend yourself to slander which might trouble all your married life."

Flavia was as red as a poppy. The doctor's words had hit home, and she hesitated. "But can Paul be left all alone?" she objected. "What will he think?"

"Paul's nearly cured, and, come, if you are reasonable, I promise he shall go and see you to-morrow."

This last argument put an end to Flavia's resistance. "Very well then," she said, "I obey you—and don't ever tell me again that I'm obstinate. Just let me say one word to Paul, and then I'll go!"

The doctor retired, well pleased with his victory, and not in the least suspecting that he owed it to a suspicion awakened in Flavia's mind.

"We've won," he said to Tantaine on the stairs. "Now let's make haste. She'll follow us at once."

When Tantaine was in the street again he semed to have recovered his wonted self-possession. "Ay, we've won," he said, "for to-day; but how about to-morrow? This marriage must be hastened. It can take place now without danger to any one. In forty-eight hours the only obstacle separating this youth from the Champdoce millions will have disappeared."

Worthy Dr. Hortebize turned pale at this information, although it was not unexpected. "What!" he stammered; "André—"

"André's very ill, doctor! I have arranged the scheme I spoke to you about, and the most difficult part of the undertaking will be accomplished this very night by our young friend, Toto-Chupin."

"By that boy? Why, only the other day you declared you suspected him, and thought of getting rid of him for good."

"That's still my intention, but I mean to kill two birds with one stone. When it's discovered after André's fall, as will certainly be the case, that the window supports had been sawed apart, the perpetrator of the deed will be searched for. My precautions are taken. Master Toto will be found at the Hôtel du Pérou; it will be proved that he purchased a saw, and changed a thousand-franc note at the time."

Dr. Hortebize looked greatly alarmed, "Are you mad?" he cried. "Why, Toto will denounce you."

"I daresay he will, but by that time poor Tantaine will be dead and buried. Then will come the interment of B. Mascarot. Beaumarchef, the only one who has faithfully served us, will be in America. The play will have finished, and we shall be able to snap our fingers at the police!" He talked like this, the genial Tantaine, so as to stimulate the doctor's confidence, and yet at that very moment, mindful of mother Bregot's visitor, he was asking himself whether he hadn't a detective at his heels.

"Decidedly," said Hortebize, "you were made for success. But for heaven's sake make haste! All this incessant suspense and these fluctuations of hope and despair will make me seriously ill."

The two honourable associates talked thus at the corner of the Rue Joquelet, partially concealed from observation by a van. They were waiting, anxious to ascertain if Flavia's promise had been sincere. Yes, she had been truthful, for in less than ten minutes they saw her pass.

"Now," said the old clerk, "I can go in peace. Good-bye, doctor, till to-morrow." And without waiting for a reply, he walked rapidly away in the direction of the Rue Montorgueil. "Ah," he muttered to himself, "how can I find out about that chap with the gold spectacles. I dare not confide anything to Hortebize! However, when a man's three persons at the same time he surely ought to be able to save one individuality!"

He was interrupted by Beaumarchef who breathlessly barred his passage, just as he turned under the *porte cochère* leading to B. Mascarot's agency. "I was looking for you," cried the ex-sub-officer. "M. de Croisenois is in the office, abusing me like a pick-pocket, because M. Mascarot isn't there."

"Go up stairs," replied Tantaine, "and occupy this penniless marquis. Make him be patient. The master will be there before long." Then as soon as Beaumarchef had disappeared, he darted down the Passage de la Reine de Hongrie, turned into the Rue Montmartre, and entered Martin-

Rigal's house. "Dash it," he grumbled, "Beaumarchef may think what he likes. In another fortnight he'll be far away."

He was wrong to suspect Beaumarchef, who having been told to go upstairs, had at once obeyed. He had been told moreover to occupy the marquis, and he was doing his best, though his best did not have much effect on M. de Croisenois. "Great business people, to be sure," the latter grumbled, "to have forgotten the engagments they made themselves."

He suddenly stopped, for the door of the inner sanctuary had opened and B. Mascarot appeared in person. "I'am not late, M. le Marquis," he said. "Punctuality does not consist in arriving before the time, but in keeping an engagement exactly at the appointed hour. Pray consult your watch and walk in."

The marquis, so impertinent with Beaumarchef, became the veriest schoolboy when he was seated opposite Mascarot, and it was with a most anxious eye that he followed the movements of the agent, who seemed to be looking for something among the papers on his desk. Having found what he wanted, he turned to M. de Croisenois. "I desired to see you, sir," he said, "in reference to the company you are to start, according to our agreement."

"Yes, I know; we must discuss it, fully understand it, and feel our way."

The agent whistled disdainfully. "Do you think," he asked, "that I am the sort of person to stand and cool my heels while waiting for you to feel your way? If you do, you had better undeceive yourself as quickly as possible. When I undertake anything it is promptly done. You have been amusing yourself while Catenac and I have been working for you; and everything is ready."

"Ready! What do you mean?"

"I mean that the offices are taken in the Rue Vivienne, that the company's statutes are deposited with a notary, and that the members of your board of directors are chosen. The printer came here yesterday with the prospectuses and circulars. You will find that you can begin to morrow."

"But—"

"Read for yourself," answered Mascarot, extending a sheet of paper. "Read, and perhaps you will be convinced."

Croisenois took the paper in a bewildered sort of way, and began to read it aloud :—

THE COPPER MINES OF TIFILA
(ALGERIA).
MARQUIS DE CROISENOIS & Co.
Capital—Four Millions of Francs.

This company does not appeal to rash speculators who are willing to run great risks for the sake of high dividends. Our shareholders must not expect more than six, or at the most, seven per cent. profit on their investments, &c., &c.

"Well," asked Mascarot, "what do you think of that as a beginning?"

The marquis did not at first reply, he was finishing his perusal to himself. "It all seems very real and very true," he muttered, trying to conceal his agitation, which was intense, for although driven to the wall he was still anxious to shirk the task imposed upon him. But what objection could he raise? "The prospectus," he said at last, "is so tempting that I fear we shall have other subscribers than those we contemplate. What should we do in that case?"

"We should refuse to take them, that's all. Ah! Catenac would settle them soon enough. Read your bye-laws. Article 20 says expressly that the Board of Directors reserve to themselves the right of accepting or refusing the subscriptions they please."

"Very good," said M. de Croisenois, "but what should we do if one of the persons whom you mean to compel to take a certain number of shares happened to dispose of them to someone else? Might not this other party interfere with us?"

"Article 21 has provided for that trick. Listen to it : 'A transfer is only valid when it has been certified to and authorized by the Board of Directors, and inscribed on the register of transfers.'"

"And how will this comedy end?"

"Naturally enough. You will announce, one fine morning, that two-thirds of the capital being absorbed, you are compelled to go into liquidation, according to Article 17. Six months later you will let it be understood that the net results of the liquidation are—nothing! You wash your hands of the whole affair, and it's all over!"

Croisenois felt that he was beaten on all points, but he tried one more argument. "It seems to me," said he, "that it's rather hazardous to undertake this enterprise just now. May it not interfere with my marriage? May not the Count de Mussidan be unwilling to give me his daughter, under the circumstances, and risk her dowry? Now, on the contrary, when once I'm married—"

The agent gave a little sniff of disdain. "You mean, I suppose," he interrupted, "that when you are once married and have received Mademoiselle Sabine's dowry, you will say good-bye to us! Not so, young man. If that's your idea, put it out of your head, for it's sheer nonsense. I shall keep my hand on, then as now."

It was clear that further resistance was quite useless, so Croisenois murmured. "Well, begin your advertising then."

"That's what I call speaking!" exclaimed Mascarot. "The first announcements shall appear in the morning papers, and to-morrow afternoon you will he officially introduced to the Mussidans. Put on a bold front and try and please Mademoiselle Sabine."

* * * * * * * *

When M. Martin-Rigal emerged from his private office that evening, his daughter showed herself far more affectionate than usual. "How I love you, dear father!" she said, as she kissed him. "How good you are!" Unfortunately, he was too pre-occupied to ask Flavia the reason of this sudden display of tenderness.

XXX.

THE danger which threatened André was immense. However, he knew that he was being watched, and considered, not unnaturally, that it was with the object of putting him out of the way at the first favourable moment. Now, were he to perish Sabine would be lost, and for this reason, he resigned himself to a prudence that was very far from his character. He knew that he could claim assistance from the police, but in doing so, he might risk the honour of Sabine's family.

He felt certain that with time and patience he would be able to confound the scoundrels who persecuted not merely the Mussidans, but himself as well; but on the other hand, great as was his patience, time was wanting. Only a few days now separated Sabine from the terrible, irreparable sacrifice she was called upon to make, and would they suffice for the mighty task he had undertaken?

Having risen at daybreak, André was seated in his studio before his work table, and with his head in his hands he pondered—recapitulated the various events that had occurred, and tried to connect them together, like a child tries to fit the pieces of a puzzle-map one into the other. He was searching for the connecting link, which to his idea must exist between all these people he had come across—Verminet, Van Klopen, Mascarot, Hortebize and Martin-Rigal. Whilst analysing the various incidents of the last few days, he came at last to thinking of young Gaston Gandelu.

"Is it not strange," he said to himself, "that this unfortunate fellow should be victimised by the same scoundrels who are persecuting us—by Verminet and Van Klopen? It is really very strange."

He stopped with a short start. A new idea had occurred to him. On superficial examination, it was no doubt monstrous, improbable, fantastic, and yet after all might it not be founded on fact? A presentiment seemed to tell him that young Gandelu's ruin was connected with his own, that they were both the victims of the same intrigue, and that this affair of the forged promissory notes was but part and parcel of some general scheme. André would have sworn that such was the case, and yet he had of course no means of explaining to himself how it happened that he and Gaston were thus mixed up together. But stay, who had denounced young Gandelu to his father? Catenac. Who had advised the incarceration of Zora-Rose? Catenac again. Now this Catenac, who was Gandelu's lawyer, was also Verminet's and de Croisenois' man of business. Had he not obeyed their instructions? All this was certainly vague and entangled. How could all these strange presumptions be linked together? It seemed almost impossible to accomplish such a task, and yet André determined to pursue his investigations on this basis.

He had just taken a pencil with the view of jotting down the main features of some general scheme of investigation, when suddenly he heard a knock at the door. He glanced at his clock: it was not yet nine. Who could this matutinal visitor be, André wondered; nevertheless, he rose to his feet and called out, "Come in."

The door was thrown open, and the young artist staggered back, for who should stand before him but Sabine's father. He had only caught a glimpse of the Count de Mussidan on two previous occasions, but he would have recognised him under any circumstances.

The count also was ill at ease. He had passed a sleepless night, and it was only after a severe mental struggle that he had decided upon taking this step. However, he had had time to prepare himself, whereas André was taken unawares.

"You will excuse me, sir," began M. de Mussidan, "for intruding upon you at so unseasonable an hour, but I thought I should be more likely to meet you."

André bowed. A thousand suppositions, each more unlikely than the other, flashed through his mind. Why had the count come there? Was it as a friend or as an enemy? Who had given him his address?

"I am an amateur," continued Sabine's father, "and one of my friends, who has an excellent judgment has spoken to me, most warmly, of your talent. This will explain to you the liberty I take, curiosity has induced me, I have felt desirous of seeing—" He did not finish his phrase; but stopped short, and then added, "I am the Marquis de Bivron."

Thus M. de Mussidan gave a false name; he did not imagine André knew him; he wished to retain his *incognito*. This circumstance in some measure enlightened the young painter as to what course he had better pursue.

"I am extremely flattered by your visit," answered André. "Unfortunately, I have nothing completed just now. I have only a few studies and sketches, but if you like to see them—"

The count at once assented. He felt greatly embarrassed, and could hardly help flushing when his eyes met the young artist's frank, honest gaze. He was, moreover, still further disturbed by seeing in a corner of the studio the veiled picture which Tantaine had spoken to him about. In response to André's suggestion, he began to inspect the studies hanging on the walls, at the same time making heroic efforts to keep calm, and hide the awful agony he suffered. Ay, the cynical old tatterdemalion who had called upon him had spoken the truth. That green baize curtain hid his daughter's portrait. This man, then, was Sabine's lover. She came here—she spent hours here. Alas! whose fault was it? Had her mother ever showed her any affection? Had he, her father, ever treated her with aught but callous frigidity? Could she be blamed? She had listened to her heart. She had accepted from a lover the affection her parents had never bestowed on her.

The count was forced to admit that Sabine's choice was not an unworthy one. At first sight he had been struck with the young artist's manliness, and the energetic, intelligent expression of his face.

"Ah! You come to me under a borrowed name," André was thinking. "Very good, I will respect your *incognito*, but I will take advantage of it in one way, for I will tell you the truth, which, perhaps, I should never have dared to reveal under different circumstances."

Great as was his preoccupation, he noticed his visitor's eyes turned again and again towards the veiled picture. "Some one must have spoken to the count about that portrait," he thought. "He has come here on account of it. Who can have mentioned it to him? Our enemies? In that case Sabine must have been slandered."

Meanwhile, M. de Mussidan had gone round the room, and had time to gather his energy together. He now approached André again. "Accept my congratulations, sir," he said. "My friend's praise was not misplaced. I regret, however, that you have no finished work to show me—for you have nothing, I believe?"

"Nothing, sir."

"Not even that picture, the frame of which extends beyond that green curtain?"

Although he had expected this question, André flushed scarlet. "Excuse me, sir," he answered, "that picture is certainly completed, but I never show it to any one."

The count could now no longer doubt the correctness of Tantaine's information. "I understand," said he, "it is no doubt a woman's portrait."

"You are right, sir; it *is* a woman's portrait."

The situation was so strange; they were both of them equally perturbed, and averted their faces in embarrassment. But the count had sworn he would go on the bitter end.

"I see," he said, with a forced laugh, "you are in love. After all, all great painters have immortalised the beauty of their mistresses."

André's eyes flashed. "Stop, sir—you misunderstand me. This is the portrait of the purest and most innocent of girls. I love her, and it would be as impossible for me to cease loving her, as to stop by an effort of will the circulation of the blood in my veins. But I respect her as much as I love her. She, my mistress! Why, I should loathe myself forever if I had ever breathed to her one word that her own mother could not have heard!"

Never in his life had Monsieur de Mussidan experienced so delicious a sensation of relief. "You will excuse me," he said; "but a portrait in a studio suggests that there must have been a model."

"And there was one, sir. She came here, unknown to her family, risking her honour, her reputation, and her life, and thus giving me the strongest possible proof of her affection." He shook his head sadly and resumed: "I was wrong, very wrong, to accept this devotion; and yet, not only did I accept it, but I went on my knees to beg for it. How else was I ever to hear her voice or see her? We love each other, but, alas! such a great social difference, so many prejudices keep us apart! She is an heiress, belonging, unfortunately for our love, to a very great and noble, a very proud and wealthy family; whilst I—" He paused, as if hoping for some remark, a word of encouragement or blame. None came, however, and somewhat emphatically André resumed: "Do you know what I am? A poor foundling, dropped in the basket at an hospital door by some poor girl who had been betrayed. One morning, when I was twelve years old, I ran away from the hospital at Vendôme with twenty francs in my pocket, and found my way to Paris. Since then, I have earned my bread by daily toil. You see only the brilliant side of my life. Here, I am an artist; elsewhere, I am a common workman. Look at my hands; they tell the truth. Still, I hope to succeed; one day, perhaps, I shall. But I have had to study and at the same time earn my livelihood."

If M. de Mussidan still kept silent, it was because he could not help really admiring André, and he wished to conceal his true sentiments.

"She knows all that," resumed the young artist; "she knows it, and yet she loves me. She has confidence in me. When I despaired, she bade me persevere. Here, in this very room, she swore she would never be another man's wife. I have faith in her promise. Not a month ago, one of the most brilliant men in Paris solicited her hand. She went to him and told him our story, and he generously withdrew, and to-day he is my best friend." He paused, for he was stifling. He was pleading for his own happiness in life, and his anxiety was overwhelming. At last, however, he managed to speak again. "And now, sir," he asked, "do you wish to see the picture of this young girl?"

"Yes," answered the count; "I should be grateful to you for that mark of confidence."

André went to the picture; but as he touched the curtain his hand dropped, and he hastily turned round again. "No!" he exclaimed, "no! I cannot continue this comedy. It is unworthy of me!"

Monsieur de Mussidan turned pale. These words might have a terrible signification. "What do you mean?" he stammered.

"I mean that I knew you, sir—that I knew I was speaking to the Count de Mussidan, and not to the Marquis de Bivron. I will not uncover this picture without warning you, without telling you—"

With a kindly gesture the count interrupted him. "I know," he said, "that I am about to see Sabine's portrait. Uncover it, sir, if you please."

The young painter obeyed, and for a moment M. de Mussidan stood in silent ecstacy before this really remarkable painting. "Yes, it is she," he said; "her very smile, the light in her eyes! It is beautiful!" He spoke a few more words, but in so low a tone that they were lost for André, and then slowly turning to the young painter's arm-chair, he sat down and seemed lost in reflection.

Misfortune is a true master. A few weeks before, M. de Mussidan would have smiled and shrugged his shoulders at the idea of giving his daughter in marriage to this insignificant painter. He was then thinking exclusively of M. de Breulh-Faverlay. But now, he would have received as a boon from heaven the liberty to choose André for Sabine. Must she really marry that hateful Marquis de Croisenois? At this thought the count started.

André had shown so much assurance that he could hardly be acquainted with the real situation. But on questioning the young artist, M. de Mussidan was undeceived. Conscious of having won the day, André told the count exactly what he knew, spoke of M. de Breulh's generous assistance and the part that Madame de Bois d'Ardon had consented to play, revealed his plans and investigations, his conjectures and his hopes. Such was his vehemence and energy, so brightly did his eyes sparkle with conviction of success, that the count's spirits began to revive. At last they studied the situation together at great length, and agreed that prudence and dissimulation were requisite above ought else; that it would be better not to confide their hopes even to Sabine, and that the Marquis de Croisenois must be received with apparent good grace. Moreover, they must abstain from seeing each other; they must hide their understanding from everyone.

Eleven o'clock was striking when M. de Mussidan rose with the view of retiring. After again contemplating his daughter's portrait for some minutes, he turned to the young painter, and grasping his hand, exclaimed, "Monsieur André, you have my word for it, if we ever free ourselves from these scoundrels, Sabine shall be your wife."

XXXI.

When M. de Mussidan had gone, André sunk on to the divan. His head and heart were burning. Yes! Sabine was promised to him, but on conditions he won her; and to win her he must unmask and confound Croisenois and his associates. However, with the promise of such a prize, the young painter felt strong enough to dare them all. "To work!" he cried, springing to his feet again, "to work!"

He stopped short, for on the stairs outside he could hear some woman laughing noisily, whilst a man seemed to be scolding in a sharp, high-pitched key. André had no time to ask what this meant, for his door was well-nigh burst open, and a whirlwind of velvet, silk, and lace burst into his studio. To his astonishment, he recognised that this whirlwind was the beautiful Zora-Rose de Chantemille. In her wake came young Gaston de Gandelu, who was the first to speak. "Ay, here we are, in the flesh," he shouted. "Did you expect us?"

"Not at all."

"Ah, indeed! Well, it was a surprise of the governor's. Upon my word, I intend to make his declining years happy, as Leontine said in the play. This morning he came into my room, and he said to me : 'I took all the necessary steps yesterday to release a person you are very fond of. Go and find her.' Now what do you think of that? So I rushed off, found Zora, and here we are ! "

André gave him only imperfect attention, for he was watching Zora, who was looking about the studio. She was on the point of pouncing on Sabine's portrait, when the young painter hastily intervened. "Excuse me," said he, "I have to place a picture to dry." And then, as the portrait stood on a movable easel, he rolled it into his bedroom.

"Now," resumed Gaston, "I want to celebrate Zora's deliverance. Will you come and lunch with us ? "

"Thank you ; no. Indeed I can't, for I have to work."

"I daresay—and work is a very good thing ; but just now you must go and dress—"

"Indeed, it's quite impossible ; I can't go out."

Gaston reflected for a moment, and then exclaimed, "I have it; you won't come to lunch. Well, then, lunch shall come to you. An excellent idea. It's the reverse of Mahomet and the mountain. Well, I'll just go down and order the needful." So saying he bounded out of the room.

André rushed after him ; but it was in vain that he shouted down the stairs. Gaston hurried on, and the young artist returned to his studio considerably out of temper. Rose noticed how annoyed he looked. "That's the way Gandelu goes on," said she, shrugging her shoulders ; "and he thinks himself very witty. Pshaw ! "

Her tone indicated such utter contempt for her lover that the painter looked at her in astonishment.

"Why are you so amazed?" she asked. "It's easy to see that you don't know him. And all his friends are just like him. If you listen to them for an hour you are absolutely sickened. Merely to think of the evenings I've spent in their society makes me yawn." And she did yawn, as if inexpressibly wearied. "If he only loved me ! " she sighed.

"Loved you ! Why, he adores you ! "

Rose made a little gesture that would have excited Toto-Chupin's envy and admiration. "Do you really think so ? " she asked. "Come, do you know what he loves in me ? When people look at me as they pass and say, 'Heavens ! what *chic !* ' my idiot is proud and happy. But if I wore a cotton wrapper, he wouldn't as much as look at me ; and yet, after all, I'm not so very ugly."

The fact is, that Rose had improved, despite her incarceration. Her impudent beauty had never been so brilliant. She was glowing with youth, and life, and passion. "My name didn't please him," she continued. "His dainty lips couldn't condescend to utter the name of Rose, and so he called me Zora—a dog's name, by the way—and I have to bear it. He has money, no doubt; but I don't care much for money after all. My little Paul had no money, and yet I loved him well enough. I have forgotten how to laugh, I think, and yet I was merry once."

"But why did you leave Paul ? "

"Why ? Well, just tell me why there's velvet at forty-five francs the yard ? I thought I should like to know how women feel when they put on an India shawl, and so, one fine day, I took to flight ; but, after all—who knows?—perhaps Paul would have left me. There was a fellow doing his best to separate us—a neighbour of ours at the Hôtel du Pérou—an old monkey named Tantaine, a *huissier's* clerk."

At this name André fairly gasped. An old fellow—Tantaine—a *huissier's* clerk ! It must be the same. However, he tried to master his emotion. "Nonsense !" he said, with affected carelessness ; "what interest could he take in separating you ?"

"I don't know," answered Rose, becoming all at once very serious ; "but I am sure he had one. Men don't give bank-notes to people for nothing, and I saw him give Paul one for five hundred francs. More than that, too, he promised him he should make a great fortune with the help of a friend of his named Mascarot."

This time André did not start. He was prepared for some such revelation. However, he felt alarmed at the development the intrigue was taking. All these manœuvres which he discovered one by one must have a common object. He recalled the visit that Paul had paid him on the pretext of returning the twenty francs he owed, and he remembered that Paul had boasted he could make a thousand francs a month, though he had not said how.

"Paul has forgotten me, I fancy," continued Rose. "I met him once at Van Klopen's, and he did not say a word to me. It is true he was with that Mascarot. However, I'll find him out, and no doubt he'll forgive me."

Rose's statements all pointed to one conclusion. Paul was protected by the members of this mysterious association ; hence he must be useful to them. Rose, on the contrary, was persecuted by them, so she was in their way. "And indeed," thought André, "if Catenac had Rose shut up, it looks as if he were afraid of her. It seems as if her mere presence deranged their combinations."

But he had not time to finish his deductions, for Gaston's falsetto voice was now again heard on the stairs. Presently he appeared. "Room for the feast !" he cried. "Let the fête begin."

In his rear came a couple of waiters laden with baskets of provisions. At any other time André would have been enraged at this intrusion, and have dreaded the prospect of a lunch likely to last two hours at the least, and put his studio in a state of confusion. Now, however, hoping to learn something that would facilitate his investigations, he was inclined to bless Gaston for the inspiration, and it was with the best grace in the world that, assisted by Rose, he cleared a large table, on which the cloth was laid.

In the meanwhile, Gaston perorated. "Ah !" said he, "I must tell you a story—a good joke. Henri de Croisenois, one of my intimate friends, has just organised a company."

André nearly dropped a decanter he held. "Who told you so ?" he asked.

"Who told me so ? A great yellow poster told me so !—'Tifila Mines—capital, four million of francs.' I call that the joke of the season. Poor dear marquis, and he has hardly a penny to buy a loaf of bread with."

The young painter looked so utterly bewildered that Gaston laughed aloud. "You look just as I did," he said, "when I stood with open mouth in front of that poster. Croisenois chairman of a company ! If I had read in a paper that you were elected pope, I really shouldn't have been more astonished. Tifila Mines, indeed ! shares 500 francs each ! 'Pon my word, that's coming it rather strong."

Meanwhile, the lunch had been laid on the table, the waiters had retired, and Gaston bade his guests sit down. But, alas ! gaily as the banquet began, it was fated to end tempestuously. Young Gandelu, whose head was none of the steadiest, drank most inordinately, and before long the fumes of the wine mingled with the fumes of vanity in his shallow brain. The small amount of good sense he possessed disappeared entirely, and he began to overwhelm Zora with bitter reproaches—not being able to understand, as he told her, how a serious man like himself, destined to play a great rôle in society, could have been led away by such a person as she was. Gaston possessed a goodly store of invectives, but Rose was even stronger than himself in this respect.   Being attacked, she defended herself so effectually that finally the young fellow lost his temper, or what remained of it, and went off declaring that never, no never, would he see Zora again. She might keep all he had ever given her—furniture and jewels—said he, and he should consider himself well rid of her at the price.

His departure delighted André, who, now that he was alone with Zora, hoped to obtain some further information from her, and notably an exact account of Paul, whom he now numbered among his adversaries.   The hope was vain, for the young woman herself was so exasperated that she would not listen to a word.   She hastily put on her hat and mantle and darted off, declaring she meant that very moment to go in search of Paul, who in her conviction would speedily punish Gaston for his insults.   All this transpired so rapidly that the young painter felt as if he had been visited by a tornado.

As quiet and calm fell on his studio again, he began to realise that Providence had manifestly interposed in his favour, by sending this interesting pair to furnish him with new facts, which were of the greatest importance. Indeed what Rose had said, incomplete as it was, threw light on a portion of the intrigue which had hitherto been enveloped in darkness.   Paul's intimacy with Tantaine explained the pains Catenac had taken to have Rose shut up, as well as the forged signatures wrung from the weak-minded Gaston.

But, on the other hand, what was the meaning of this business enterprise started by the Marquis de Croisenois, at the very time when he was applying for Sabine's hand ?   André decided to turn his attention first to this detail ; and, at once, ran down stairs and hastened to the corner of the street, where Gaston had told him he had seen the poster.   There it was, dazzling and conspicuous, and sufficiently fascinating to attract even the most timid capitalists.   Nothing was lacking, not even a charming view of Tifila (Algeria), showing a number of workmen loading barrows with copper ore ; whilst, just above, the name of De Croisenois stood out in letters six inches high.

André had surveyed this masterpiece for five minutes, or more, when all at once he had a gleam of common sense and prudence.   " Idiot ! " he said to himself, " what am I doing here ?   Who can tell how many knaves may be reading my countenance, and deciphering all my plans in my eyes."   As this thought crossed his mind, he turned swiftly round, but no one suspicious was in sight.   " Never mind," muttered André " those fellows must lose my scent.   I must disappear."   Success depended on this point, and when he returned to his room he sat for an hour revolving every possible plan in his mind.   At last, he fancied he had discovered a feasible one. Under his windows there extended a large garden, or rather play-ground belonging to a school, which was entered by the Rue de Laval.   A wall, not more than seven feet in height, separated the courtyard of André's house from this garden.   Why couldn't he escape unperceived in this direction.   " I might," he thought, " disguise myself in such a way as not to be recognised, and to-morrow in the small hours of the morning, climb the wall and get out by way of the Rue de Laval, while the spies are watching my door in the Rue de la Tour d'Auvergne. It isn't necessary for me to sleep here. No! I can ask Vignol to accommodate me, and besides he'll assist me in every possible way."

This Vignol was the friend who, in André's absence, was superintending the work going on at the Gandelu mansion. "In this way," continued the young artist, "I can escape completely from Croisenois and his banditti. I can watch their game without their suspecting me. Of course, I must cease to see all those who are now assisting me: De Breulh, Gandelu and M. de Mussidan. But that can't be helped. Besides, I have the post-office and the telegraph in cases of emergency. Indeed, I will write and tell them my intentions."

It was dark before he had finished his letters. He then went and dined at the nearest restaurant; and, having posted his letters, returned to his rooms to arrange his disguise.

His costume was ready, for he found it among his old clothes, an old blue blouse, a rusty pair of trousers, shabby shoes, and an equally shabby cap, were all he required. However, it was important he should change his face. He began by clipping off his beard, and then cut his hair in such a way as to leave on either side two long locks which he affixed with cosmetic to his temples. This done, he looked for some water colours, and set to work with a camel's hair brush, seeking to modify the complexion and expression of his countenance. The task was more difficult than he had supposed, and it was only after long and patient toil that he was satisfied with the result. He then dressed himself, wrapped an old handkerchief round his throat, and stuck his cap on one side, with the visor pulled down over the right eye. Thus equipped, he gave himself a glance in the looking-glass, and thought himself absolutely hideous. However, like a conscientious artist, he was about to correct certain faults he detected in his make-up, when he suddenly heard a knock at his door.

It was nine o'clock. He was expecting no one. The waiters from the restaurant had taken their baskets and crockery away; and the person outside could only be his concierge, whom he did not choose should see him in his disguise, for he had but limited confidence in the discretion of worthy Madame Poileveu. "Who's there?" he asked.

"It is I," answered a plaintive voice—"Gaston!"

Was there any reason to distrust this young fellow? André decided not, and accordingly he opened his door.

"Has Monsieur André gone out?" asked young Gandelu faintly; "I thought it was he who spoke."

Then he was deceived by the disguise! This was a triumph for André, but showed him at the same time that his voice must be changed as well as his face. "What!" said he, "don't you recognise me?"

Gaston started with surprise, and made some confused remark. It was plain that some terrible catastrophe had befallen him. His morning excesses alone could not have reduced him to that state.

"Tell me," said André kindly, "what has gone wrong with you?"

"Why, I've come to say good-bye to you. I'm going to blow out my brains at once—"

"Are you mad?"

Gaston struck his forehead in a dreary way. "Not in the least," he said, "it is simply this—those notes have turned up. To-night just as I was leaving the dining-room—having dined with the governor—the butler whispered to me that an old man was waiting for me outside. I went out and found a dirty old beggar, with his coat collar turned up about his ears."

"Old Tantaine!" cried André.

"Ah! Is that his name? I didn't know it myself. However, he said to me in the sweetest voice that the holder of my notes had decided to lay them before the authorities at twelve o'clock to-morrow, but that a means of escape was open for me."

"And that was to go to Italy with Rose."

Gaston's surprise was so great that he started to his feet. "Who told you so?" he cried.

"Nobody; I guessed it. It was part of their plan, when you were first induced to forge M. Martin-Rigal's signature. And what did you say?"

"That the proposition was utterly absurd, and that I wouldn't move a foot. Besides, I see their plan. As soon as I'm out of the way, they'll go to my father and blackmail him. But it shan't be. Why it'll kill him to learn that his son is a forger. However, I've bought a revolver, and in an hour from now, it'll all be over."

André was not listening. What should be done? he asked himself. To advise Gaston to depart and take Rose with him was to deprive himself of a considerable chance of success. But on the other hand, to let the young fellow kill himself was not to be thought of; ordinary humanity forbade that, and besides André was under great obligations to his father.

"Listen to me," he said finally. "I have an idea, Gaston, which I will disclose to you when we are out of the house. Only for certain reasons, which would take too long to tell you now, it's necessary I should get into the street without leaving this house by the door. I can manage it, if you will only help me. Go away now, and at midnight—precisely—ring at the door of No. 29 Rue de Laval. The concierge will pull the string, go in, and ask some question of her. In the meanwhile leave the street door ajar. I shall be in the garden of the house, and while you are with the concierge, I will get out into the street and wait for you."

Gaston complied with these instructions, the plan succeeded, and at ten minutes past midnight he and André were walking along the outer Boulevard. The young painter was full of hope. He was convinced he had put the spies who were watching him off the scent, and besides he had conceived the idea of executing a powerful diversion, thanks to Gaston, whilst personally he continued tracking Croisenois and the rest of the band.

XXXII.

MONSIEUR LE MARQUIS DE CROISENOIS resided in a superb new house on the Boulevard Malesherbes, near the church of Saint Augustin. In a modest suite of rooms, rented for four thousand francs a year, he had assembled sufficient vestiges of his former opulence to impress superficial observers. To guard against the annoyances of creditors, his apartment was taken in the name of his valet. His brougham and horse belonged, in the same way, to his coachman. For, low in funds as he was, the marquis still drove about in his own natty "pill-box." He had no other servants besides his coachman and valet—the former doing most of the rough work indoors, whilst the latter knew enough of cooking to prepare a bachelor's breakfast.

Mascarot had only seen the marquis's valet on one occasion, and the man had so singularly impressed him that, in his distrust, he tried to find out who he was and where he came from. Croisenois had told the agent that he had only engaged the fellow on the recommendation of an English friend, Sir Richard Wakefield. Morel, as the valet called himself, certainly seemed to have lived in England, for he spoke English passably well. He was, moreover, expert in all his duties, and so dignified in manners and appearance, that ignorant folks fairly believed his master to be a perfect grandee.

André knew but little of all this; he had merely obtained some trifling information from M. de Breulh, when he asked the latter for Croisenois' address. However, on the morning of his escape from his studio, he came, still in his disguise, to a wine-shop close to the marquis's residence. Providing Croisenois' servants patronised this establishment, as seemed probable, there being none other in the immediate vicinity, he would no doubt be able to overhear their talk and pick up some useful information. The young artist's confidence had increased since the previous evening; for not only had he saved Gaston, but the young fellow's escapade seemed likely to yield an advantageous result.

This is what had occurred. After infinite trouble, he had induced Gaston to return to his father's house; and on reaching the Chaussée d'Antin, at two o'clock in the morning, he had made bold enough to have old Gandelu woke up. Then, after explaining the reason of his own disguise, he told the contractor how his son had been victimised and induced to commit a forgery, and how, but for his own intervention, the young fellow would have committed suicide. He naturally insisted on Gaston's repentance, the good sentiments he expressed, his separation from Rose, and his promises to become serious.

The old man was much moved and shed tears. This would no doubt prove a decisive lesson for his son, and really modify his conduct for the better. "Go and fetch him," said the poor contractor; "tell him to come to me, and say that we two will save him."

André had not far to go, for Gaston was waiting in the next room in an agony of suspense. He was weeping, weeping with repentant sorrow, bewailing his own foolishness and the misery he must have caused his good, indulgent father. "Come in, Gaston," said André.

But with unusual energy, the young fellow exclaimed, "Never call me by that name again. It is as false as the coronet on my cards. Call me Pierre Gandelu. My father is only too kind to allow me to bear his name."

Thus begun, the reconciliation was bound to prove complete. The worthy contractor had not felt so happy for many years. The next thing was to decide what course to take to rescue the lad from the consequences of his folly. "I do not believe," said old Gandelu, "that these wretches will dare to carry their threat into execution, and apply to the legal authorities. At all events, my son cannot remain exposed to this intimidation. I myself will lay a charge against the whole band. I will call on the public prosecutor before noon, and we will see what happens to this Mutual Loan Society, which lends money to minors and extorts forged signatures in return! It will be best, however, for my son to go to Belgium in the morning; but he won't stop there long, as you'll see."

André remained in the old gentleman's house throughout the night, and it was in Gaston's room that he made himself up again in the morning. The future looked rosy indeed, as he walked lightly up the Boulevard Malesherbes. Thanks to the contractor's intervention, the police would now deal with Verminet's malpractices. The inquiry would, moreover, probably result in the detection of the other members of the band, and this enormous result would be gained without any mention being made of M. de Mussidan, the countess, or Sabine. For his own part, André was determined to cling to Croisenois like a shadow. The establishment where he installed himself was wonderfully adapted for his purpose. From the table where he sat he could see all the windows of De Croisenois' apartment, as well as the door of the house, which no one could leave or enter unperceived by him. Moreover, as there was no other wine-shop in the vicinity, André felt certain that the marquis's servants would come there, in which case he could talk with them, offer them something to drink, creep into their confidence, and obtain important information. He sat down at a table near the window and ordered breakfast, keeping his eyes and ears on the alert. The shop was full of customers, nearly all of them servants, and André wondered whether any of these were in the employ of M. de Croisenois. He was racking his brain for some excuse for questioning the landlord, when the door opened and two more servants entered, one of them attired in a coachman's livery, and the other wearing the discreet black of a *valet de chambre*. "Ah, ha!" exclaimed an old man with a placid countenance, who was struggling with a tough beefsteak at the table next to André's. "Ah, ha! here come Messrs. Croisenois."

Servants, as is well known, often call each other by their masters' names; and thus André obtained the information he desired without having to make any suspicious inquiries. "If these men," he thought, "only had the happy thought of sitting near this old fellow, who knows them, I could hear every word they say."

This they did, at the same time begging the landlord to serve them as speedily as possible, as they had not a moment to spare.

"What are you in such a hurry about?" asked the old man near whom they seated themselves.

"Why," answered the younger of the new-comers—M. de Croisenois' coachman, "I have to drive my master to his office; for he has an office now. He's the chairman of a mining company—copper mines—a splendid thing it is, too. Why, 'Geese plucked here' ought to be written up over the door! If you have any savings, Monsieur Benoît, as you ought to have, this is a good chance to invest them."

Benoît shook his head gravely. "Who can tell?" said he. "All that looks good isn't good, and what seems bad isn't bad." Benoît was evidently a prudent man, who had seen much of life, and was not disposed to commit himself lightly. "But come," he continued, "if your marquis is going out, Monsieur Morel will be free, and we can have a game of piquet together."

"No, sir," answered the valet.

"Are you engaged as well, then?"

"Yes, sir; I'm just going to put on some white gloves and carry a heap of flowers to the marquis's future wife; for he's going to be married. It's official. A splendid dowry, so I hear; as for the young lady, she's a bit haughty; but I wouldn't mind taking her myself for three months, just on trial."

This fellow in the preposterously high, stiff collar was actually speaking of Sabine in this disgraceful style, and André had to appeal to all his powers of self-restraint not to spring at his throat and strangle him.

"Ah, well!" said the coachman, with his mouth full, "ah, well! I don't mind betting that the marquis won't invest his wife's dowry in his new business."

This remark elicited no rejoinder, and the two ceased talking of M. de Croisenois to speak of their own affairs, which naturally had no interest for André. He waited in vain. They settled their score and went away without so much as mentioning the marquis's name again; and the young artist was reduced to reflect over the difficulties a spy encounters. The other customers were looking at him most suspiciously, and the fact is, he scarcely had a pleasing aspect. Moreover, he had not yet acquired the art of observing things without appearing to do so. It was easy to see that he was there for some other reason than lunch; that he was waiting for some one or something, and was growing impatient. He had enough penetration to realise the impression he had created, and his embarrassment became all the greater.

Having finished his meal, he took some coffee, sipping it as slowly as possible, and now he called for a glass of brandy. There were only some five or six customers left, sitting at a table near the door, and playing a game of cards which seemed to amuse them immensely—that is, judging from their constant shouts of laughter. André half thought of retiring, and hurrying to the marquis's offices to wait for his arrival there; but on consideration, he decided to make quite sure that M. de Croisenois was going out, and wait till he saw him drive off in his brougham. So he still lingered in the wine-shop and called for another glass of brandy.

It had just been served him, when as evil a looking individual as himself entered the establishment. The new comer was a tall, ungainly, impudent-looking fellow, with a tuft of red hair on his chin. He wore a dirty black jacket and a dilapidated cap, and was, to all appearance, as fine a specimen of a *barrière* bully as could anywhere be found. In a husky, drawling voice he ordered a plate of beef and a pint of common wine, and while passing in front of André to reach a vacant table, he upset the young artist's glass of brandy. This might be a mere accident, hence André made no remark; but as the new comer sat down, far from apologising, he gave the artist a most contemptuous look. He was smoking, this big fellow, and setting his cigar on a corner of the table, he relieved himself by spitting—not on the floor, but on André's trousers.

This time the insult was so flagrant, that André reflected as to its meaning. Had he not eluded his spies as he fancied he had done? Was it not possible that this individual had been purposely sent to pick a quarrel with him and give him a blow that would settle him? Prudence bade him depart at once; but he felt he could not do so until he had satisfied himself positively of the truth of his surmises. However, there seemed little doubt of their exactitude; for as the fellow cut up his beef, he tossed every bit of skin or muscle he found over on to his neighbour. Finally, he drank a draught of wine, and leaving a little at the bottom of his glass, deliberately threw it—not on to André's legs, but on to his shoulders.

This was more than the young artist could put up with. "Just observe," said he, "that some one is sitting here."

"I know that very well. Aren't you pleased?"

"No, I'm not."

"Ah, well, with me you must be pleased, or else—" And so saying the bully shook his fist but an inch or two from André's nose.

The young artist had powerful reasons for remaining calm, but nature mastered will, and rising to his feet, he lunged out, the result being that the bully rolled under the table. The noise made the card-players turn round. They had been so absorbed in their game that they were not acquainted with the origin of the fray, and could not tell who was in the right or who in the wrong. They only saw André standing erect, with flashing eyes and lips trembling with rage, while the other fellow lay on the floor among the chairs.

"No fighting here, do you understand?" said one of the players. "Just settle your quarrel in the street."

André's adversary, however, had just struggled to his feet, and now made a rush at the young artist, who, with an adroit application of his left foot, succeeded in stopping him midway. It was altogether so skilfully done that the card-players applauded. They now found the fight as exciting as their game had been. Three times did André's adversary charge, and each time the young artist cleverly repulsed him. Finally there was a great scrimmage, a table was overturned as well as a stove, and several glasses were smashed, as well as a couple of window panes. The landlord, who had momentarily absented himself, hurried to the scene on hearing this last crash. With the assistance of a waiter he parted André and his adversary, and then, noticing that the damage done represented some twenty francs, he bade the antagonists settle for it between them and then clear out. André would gladly have paid the whole of what was owing, in view of effecting a speedy escape ; but his opponent flew into such a rage, and began shouting to such an extent, that at last the landlord despatched the waiter for a couple of policeman, who, strange to say, entered the shop the very next moment, as if they had indeed been purposely waiting outside. At all events, before André had time to breathe, he found himself with his adversary in the street, between a couple of *sergents de ville*, who bade them both walk straight and keep civil tongues in their heads.

It would have been sheer folly to resist, and the young painter resigned himself to the inevitable. But on the way he could not help pondering over this strange scene. The whole affair had been so sudden and so swift, that as yet he could not see it clearly. Still it was certain that this brutal aggression had some secret motive, which he could not fathom. Meanwhile, the police agents had reached a narrow alley. They ordered their prisoners on in front, and André now realised that they were not being taken to the lock-up, but to the office of the district commissary of police. A moment later they entered a bureau where the commissary's secretary and a couple of clerks were at work.

"Well, the job's done," said the *sergents-de-ville*, with a hearty chuckle ; and thereupon they withdrew, leaving André and his opponent in the office.

André opened his eyes. This was really a most extraordinary arrest. However, there was more to come, for his assailant tossed his cap aside, smoothed his hair, and shook hands most cordially with the commissary's secretary. What did it all mean?

"Allow me to congratulate you, sir, now," said the young painter's recent opponent. "You've a good stout fist, and no mistake. Fortunately I backed down under the table just in time when you lunged out, on the first occasion—otherwise you might have killed me. However, I wasn't able to escape your foot when I charged ; that was really a masterly defence on your part."

The young painter listened in amazement. But at this moment a door was thrown open, and a voice could be heard calling out, "Send him in." André was thereupon pushed by his recent adversary through the doorway into a narrow corridor, and presently found himself in a room which seemed to be the commissary's private office. On the right hand side, before a desk in front of a window, sat a man who looked between forty or fifty years old, and who wore a white choker and a pair of gold-rimmed spectacles. "Please to sit down, Monsieur André," said this personage with the most exquisite politeness.

The young artist took a chair in a semi-stupefied condition and waited. Was he dreaming? Was he awake? He was uncertain. He doubted himself, his own intelligence, even the testimony of his senses.

"Before proceeding further," said the spectacled gentleman, "I must apologise for what must seem to you the very singular manner in which you have been treated. However, I really had no choice. I particularly wished to speak with you. You are closely watched, and it was essential that the folks who watch you should not imagine there was any connivance between you and me."

"I am watched!" stammered André.

"Yes, by a certain La Candèle; a bright fellow—in fact, I may say the brightest fellow for that sort of work in Paris. Does this astonish you?"

"Yes, for I thought—"

The spectacled gentleman smiled benevolently. "You thought," he interrupted, "that you had succeeded in eluding your spies. So I supposed this morning, when I saw you in your present disguise. Unfortunately you were bound to lose your time. The people who watch you know very well that you yourself are watching the Marquis de Croisenois. So by stationing himself near the marquis's house, La Candèle made sure of meeting you again."

"Ah! Of course, I had not thought of that," stammered André, with considerable confusion.

"On the other hand," resumed the spectacled gentleman with increased urbanity of manner, "you must allow me, my dear Monsieur André, to tell you that your disguise leaves much to be desired. The first attempt of a man in a new trade is, I admit, always to be viewed with indulgence. But La Candèle would not be taken in. Even at this distance, I can detect your entire 'make up,' and what I see, others, of course, can see as well." So speaking, he rose and approached André. "Why on earth," he said, "have you decked your face with all these colours, which make you look like a North-American Indian in his war-paint? In order to change a man's countenance, only two strokes of a crayon are necessary, red or black—here at the eyebrows, there at the nostrils, and here again at the corners of the mouth. See for yourself—"

He joined a practical demonstration to his theory; for producing a pencil case as he spoke he corrected the young artist's imperfect work. When he had finished, André glanced at himself in the looking glass over the mantelpiece, and was fairly astonished. No one would ever have recognised him. With his eyebrows which almost met, his deformed nose, and his enlarged mouth, he had a sinister, impudent look, such as he himself would never have known how to acquire.

"Now," continued the unknown gentleman, "do you realise the futility of your attempts? La Candèle knew you at once. However, I wished to speak to you so I sent for Palot, one of my agents, and bade him pick a quarrel with you. Two policemen then arrested you, and so here you are. No one knows that we are together. Pray, efface my touches, for they would be remarked when you go out, and would necessarily awaken suspicion."

André obeyed, and while he rubbed his face with the corner of his handkerchief, his bewildered mind sought for some elucidation of this mystery. He was evidently in presence of some important functionary of the Préfecture of Police ; but what was wanted of him? How had the police found him out? What had they discovered?

Meanwhile the spectacled personage had resumed his seat in his arm-chair, and was handling his snuff-box in a style which the most finished actor at the Comédie Française might have envied. "Now," he said, "let us have a little talk together, if you please. As you see I know you— Jean Lantier, your old master who engaged you eleven years ago when you arrived in Paris, after running away from Vendôme, tells me he'd answer for you under any circumstances, and Lantier's son-in-law, Dr. Lorilleux, asserts that he knows no character higher than yours—he declares your probity to be without a stain, your courage undoubted—"

"Really, sir— " stammered the young painter, flushing scarlet.

"Let me proceed. Monsieur Gandelu tells me he would be willing to confide his whole fortune to you ; your comrades, one and all—Vignol at the head of them—have the highest respect for you. So much for the present. As to the future, two painters of the greatest renown assert that you will one day stand at the head of the French school. At this moment, your work brings you in about fifteen francs per day. Am I correct in my in-formation?"

"Quite so," stammered the bewildered André.

The spectacled gentleman smiled. "Unfortunately," he continued, "my information ends here. The means of investigation in the hands of the police are necessarily very limited, they can only act on facts, and not on intentions. So long as volition is not accompanied by action, the police are helpless ; and it must always be so until a detective finds some way of taking the top of a man's head off like the cover of a box, and looking down into it to see what's going on there. However, I heard of you only forty-eight hours ago for the first time, and I already have your biography in my pocket. I know that the day before yesterday you were walking about with young Gandelu, and driving with Monsieur de Breulh-Faverlay, and that La Candèle was behind the vehicle. These are all facts, but— " He paused, and after giving André a piercing look, slowly resumed, "But no one has been able to tell me why you followed Verminet, or why you watched Mascarot's house, or why you have disguised yourself to follow the honourable Marquis de Croisenois about. It is the motive we can't get at—the facts are clear."

André moved restlessly on his chair, disturbed by his questioner's mag-netic gaze, which seemed to draw the truth from him, despite the resist-ance of volition. "I cannot tell you, sir," he said, at last—"I really can-not. It is a secret which does not belong to me."

The spectacled gentleman smiled : "You don't choose to trust me? Very well, then, I will speak. Remember that I have told you all I knew positively ; but I have also drawn my inferences and deductions, from the facts laid before me. You are watching Croisenois. Why? On account of his Mining Company? No. Then it must be because he is going to marry a rich heiress—Mademoiselle de Mussidan. Come don't blush. We haven't got to the end of it yet. Well, we'll conclude then that you wish to prevent this marriage—and why? Do you happen to love Mademoiselle de Mussidan, and does she love you in return? That is of course a reason; but it doesn't explain your disguise. So there is something more no doubt. I have heard that Mademoiselle de Mussidan was at one time to marry

Monsieur de Breulh-Faverlay. Do the Count and Countess de Mussidan
prefer a ruined marquis to one of the most remarkable men of the day?
That isn't possible ! It is clear to me that they give their daughter to
Croisenois under compulsion of some kind. What kind of compulsion?
That's the point. Doesn't the marquis happen to hold some terrible secret
over their heads ? "

" Your theory is at fault, sir ! " cried André. " You are wrong—en·
tirely wrong."

" All right," rejoined the spectacled gentleman, shrugging his shoulders.
" If you cry out with such superfluous energy that I'm wrong, it's simply
because you know me to be right. I need no proofs. Yesterday Monsieur
de Mussidan paid you a visit, and my agent said that his face was much
brighter when he came out of the house you live in than when he went in ;
consequently, I infer that you promised to rid him of Croisenois, and he, in
turn, agreed to give you his daughter. And this explains your present disguise. Now just tell me if I'm mistaken ? "

The young painter could not lie, and therefore did not dare to speak.

" And the secret," continued the spectacled gentleman—"didn't the
count tell you the secret ? I don't know it myself, and yet I think I could
find it out if I tried. People fancy the police forgets things. 'Tis a great
mistake. The police has a terrible memory. I'm acquainted with some
apparently forgotten crimes which three generations of detectives have
worked at. For instance, did you ever hear that your Croisenois had a
brother named George, a brother older than himself ? This George disappeared one fine evening twenty-three years ago, in a most mysterious
way. What became of him ? No one has ever been able to tell. However this very George was a great friend of Madame de Mussidan's. Might
not that disappearance of years ago account for this marriage of now-a-
days ? "

André rose, quivering, to his feet. " Who are you ? " he cried, " I want
to know who's speaking to me."

The spectacled gentleman smiled and answered, " I am Monsieur Lecoq."

At the name of this celebrated detective, André recoiled in absolute
amazement. " Monsieur Lecoq ! " he stammered.

The detective's vanity was agreeably tickled by the impression his name
had produced on the young artist. " And now that you know me, dear
Monsieur André," he said, " may I venture to hope that you will be more
reasonable."

M. de Mussidan had not confided his secret to the young painter, but he
had said enough for him to realize that the detective's surmises were not
far from the truth.

" If we could only understand each other, fully," continued M. Lecoq ;
" and indeed, upon my word, it seems to me that my frankness ought to
elicit yours. I need you, and on my side I can be useful to you. Let us
assist each other. Pure chance has made me acquainted with you. I discovered that you were being watched by certain people, whom I myself was
watching, and I said to myself, this young man must be an important personage of the intrigue. I had you followed, and for a couple of days you
have had at your heels not merely the other folks' spies but mine as well.
To-day, everything considered, I have come to the conclusion that my surmises are correct. Yes, you and you alone will furnish the finish, the
dénoûment, I am seeking for— "

" I, sir ? "

"Yes you, the artist and ornamental sculptor, called André for the time being."

For the time being!—The expression seemed strange to the young painter, but he did not venture to question the detective.

"For several years," resumed M. Lecoq, "I have felt certain that an organised association for blackmailing existed in this city. Family differences, sorrows and shame, imprudences, and the like, prove absolute gold-mines to a party of scoundrels who make at least a hundred thousand francs per annum."

"Ah!" muttered André, "I suspected something of this kind."

"Of course, when I was quite sure of it, I said to myself: 'I must nab these fellows.' But it was easier said than done. Blackmailing, you see, has one peculiarity: those who practise it feel well-nigh certain of impunity. Suppose you are asked for a thousand francs, and are threatened in default thereof with the revelation of some secret calculated to overwhelm you with shame or ridicule; naturally you would pay the money and keep quiet. Why, a score of times I have found out some pigeon or other who had just been plucked, but never would one of them furnish me with weapons against the scoundrels who had victimised them. It was all very well for me to say, confide in me, the police is discreet, your secret will be respected, I can promise it, swear it. No one would ever believe me. The fools doubted my word! Such being the case, I soon realised that it was impossible to reach the scoundrels through their victims. Accordingly, I decided to try and reach their victims through them. Ah! I have needed patience. For three years I have been waiting for an opportunity. During the last eighteen months one of my agents has been acting as the Marquis de Croisenois' valet. The scamps! I'm sure that at the present moment they've cost the house at least ten thousand francs!"

As André realised, "the house," was no other than the Préfecture of Police.

"Yes, ten thousand francs," repeated M. Lecoq, "to say nothing of the worry. Why, I owe a dozen white hairs to Mascarot alone! For I believed that Tantaine really existed, and Martin Rigal as well, whereas Tantaine and Rigal and Mascarot are simply one and the same person! It was a long time before I thought of a door of communication between the banker's house in the Rue Montmartre and the Employment Agency in the Rue Montorgueil. Ah! the scamp's a cunning fellow!"

Cunning indeed, but he was to find his master: such was evidently the meaning of the detective's smile. "This time," said he with increased animation, "this time they have gone too far, and I have them. The idea of establishing a company so as to net the coin of all their victims was really a very pretty one; but then I'm there and the scamps are lost. Ah! I know them all now, from their chieftain Mascarot, *alias* Rigal and *alias* Tantaine, down to Toto-Chupin, their lowest agent, and to Paul their docile instrument. We will trap the whole band. Hortebize and Verminet, Croisenois and Beaumarchef. We may, perhaps, also collar Van Klopen. As for Catenac he can't escape. Just now, he's travelling in the country near Vendôme, with the Duke de Champdoce and a fellow named Perpignan. But two of my guardian angels are at the party's heels, and send me news of their progress almost hourly. My trap is well set, well baited, and we'll catch them all as you shall see. And now, Monsieur André, do you still hesitate to confide to me what you know? I swear to you, on my honour, to respect your confidence, no matter what may happen."

The young painter felt half bewildered, but still, thanks to the detective's statements, he divined that he had to contend against truly terrible adversaries—adversaries so powerful and expert, that alone, unaided, he had little prospect of success. Moreover, like everyone else who approached Lecoq, he was fascinated by him ; and besides, what was the use of hiding anything ?—what he concealed from the detective to-day would surely be known to-morrow. Thus the wiser plan was rather to try and win his good graces. With the utmost frankness, therefore, André told everything he knew.

When he had finished, Lecoq rose to his feet. "Now," cried he, "I see clearly before me. Ah ! They wish to compel Gandelu to go off with Rose, do they ? Well, we'll see about that."

His eyes flashed behind his gold spectacles ; he had just decided on his plan of battle. "From this moment," said he, "you may sleep in peace, Monsieur André. In another month Mademoiselle de Mussidan will be your wife. I promise it you. And when Lecoq promises, he means what he says. I answer for everything." He stopped, reflected for a moment, and then resumed more slowly. "I answer for everything except for your life. Such great interests are centred in your person that every means will be tried to get rid of you. Don't forget that for one moment. Never eat twice in succession at the same restaurant ; throw away any food that has a peculiar flavour ; keep away from all street crowds, hold all kinds of vehicles in suspicion ; never lean out of a window unless you know that the supports are solid. In a word, fear everything and suspect everything."

André warmly thanked the detective, and was on the point of retiring, when Lecoq exclaimed, "One moment. Do you happen to have such a thing as a scar or a sign on your arm or shoulder."

"Yes, indeed, I have the scar of a severe burn."

M. Lecoq did not take the trouble to hide his satisfaction. "Ah ! ha !" said he, "I thought as much. Everything's going on capitally." And as he gently pushed the young artist out of the room he saluted him with the the same words that Mascarot had so often used to Paul : "Till we meet again, my Lord Duke of Champdoce !"

XXXIII.

ANDRÉ turned hastily round, but the door had been closed behind him, and he could hear the key grating in the lock. He was now again in the outer office, where the commissary's secretary, the two clerks, and his whilom opponent in the wine shop looked at him and smiled. André was, however, too preoccupied to notice them ; he mumbled a word or two, which may have been " good morning" or not, and then hurried out into the street. He was greatly perplexed by M. Lecoq's parting words. Were they a joke ? But in that case what was their point ? Now André was a clear-headed, practical man, he had proved it ; but on the other hand he was a foundling, he had never known either father or mother, and the field of conjecture was immense. Who could tell ? Perhaps he belonged to a noble family—a family that had been compelled to abandon him, but would seek for him once more. Such strange things happen at times, who can be certain of his destiny ? " What a child I am," he muttered at last ; "is joy troubling my brain ?"

At all events, he now possessed a formidable ally, a protector, who took, indeed, even greater interest in him than he imagined. Immediately after his departure, M. Lecoq had opened his door, and summoned his agent Palot. "My lad," said he, "you saw that young man who just went out?"

"Yes, sir."

"Well, he's a worthy fellow, with heart and energy, as honest as daylight, and as true as steel. I esteem him thoroughly, and he's my friend."

Palot's look and manner signified that he should henceforth consider André a sacred being.

"Now you must follow him," resumed M. Lecoq, "and closely too, for this isn't merely a case of watching him, but of defending him, if needs be. I'm sure that the Mascarot gang want to murder him, and it must be prevented, mind. You are my best, most faithful agent, and I trust him to you. He's warned, but he lacks experience. You will see danger where he would never dream of any. If there's any trouble, throw yourself into the breach, have every one marched to the lock up, but try not to let any one discover who and what you are. If at any emergency it is imperative you should speak to him, do so; but only as a last extremity. Whisper in his ear my servant's name 'Janouille,' and he'll understand that you come from me. Now, remember, you are to answer for him. But Mascarot's men mustn't recognise in you the fellow of this morning's quarrel. They would guess everything then. How are you dressed under that blouse?"

"Like a commissioner."

"Good. Now arrange yourself, and be very particular about your head."

Palot at once approached the looking glass, pulled a carroty beard and wig from his pocket, and adjusted them with all the dexterity that habit imparts. Twenty minutes later, he approached his superior, who was waiting, and asked, "Shall I do?"

M. Lecoq scrutinised him most carefully, and finally replied: "Not bad!" The fact is, the fellow was the ideal type of a Paris commissioner, and any Auvergnat would have saluted him instantly as from his own province.

"Where shall I find this young artist now, sir?" he asked.

"Somewhere near Mascarot's den, for I advised him not to relinquish his rôle of spy without my orders. Come, make haste after him!"

Palot darted off, and overtook his "ward" half-way down the Rue Montmartre. André was sauntering slowly along, ruminating over M. Lecoq's advice always to be careful, and look out for his adversaries, when a handsome young fellow with his arm in a sling walked rapidly past him, proceeding in the same direction as himself. André felt certain that this young fellow was Paul Violaine, and as he did not fear being recognised, he overtook him in his turn and had a good look at him. It was, indeed, Rose's former lover. But why had he his arm in a sling? This was the first question that occurred to André, and by a phenomenon which is not uncommon when the mind is concentrated on one particular point, he had an intuition of the truth. "At least," he thought, "I can discover where he goes."

Accordingly, he followed him, and saw him enter the house where M. Martin-Rigal resided. Two women were talking near the door, and André heard one of them say, "That's the young man who is engaged to Mademoiselle Flavia, the banker's daughter."

So Paul was to marry the daughter of the leader of the band? Was M. Lecoq acquainted with this point? No doubt he was. Still André decided he would write and inform him of it; for the detective had given him his address. He lived in the same Rue Montmartre, but a few yards from Martin-Rigal's house.

But time was flying, and André decided to hasten to the mansion M. Gandelu was building in the Champs Elysées, and, in accordance with his plan, ask his friend Vignol to lodge him for a few days. He walked so fast that it was still broad daylight when he arrived, and all the workmen were still about the building. They did not prove as lynx-eyed as Mascarot's agents, for not one of them knew him when he asked for M. Vignol.

"He's up there," they said, "at work on the frieze; take the staircase on the left."

This frieze was the main decorative element in the new building, and it was in front of the central and more important design that the little wooden shanty previously spoken of had been erected. Vignol was there alone when André entered the cabin, and he uttered an exclamation of astonishment when his friend named himself, for he had not recognised him in his disguise. Naturally enough Vignol was eager for an explanation. "Oh, it's nothing of any consequence," replied the young painter carelessly; "only a little love affair."

"Was it to win a girl's heart that you have made such a guy of yourself?" asked his friend, with a laugh.

"Hush! I will explain everything another time," rejoïned André. "I came to ask if you could lodge me—"

He stopped short, listened for a moment, and then turned frightfully pale; he fancied he had heard his name, a scream, and then the word "Sabine." He was not mistaken. The same voice, a woman's voice, despairing and desolate—repeated the cry? "André! it is I—Sabine—help!"

With one bound the young painter reached the window of the shanty, opened it and leaned out. Alas! Toto-Chupin had earned the money given him by genial Tantaine. The whole window frame and its supports yielded at the same moment, and André was precipitated into space. The little shanty was certainly sixty or sixty-five feet from the ground; the fall was bound to be a terrible one—and indeed it proved all the more appalling as fully two seconds elapsed between the moment when André was launched forward, and that when his bleeding, mutilated body reached the ground. Two seconds—two centuries of frightful agony—an eternity in which he fully realised the trap into which he had fallen. Death, inevitable death, was there on the pavement below. And during these two seconds of suspense, a world of thought traversed his brain. All his past, from the moment that he had left the hospital of Vendôme, rose as it were before him; and in the future—as a supreme, intolerable pang—he saw Sabine in the arms of the Marquis de Croisenois. His last thought was for her. He dead, who would defend her? Mascarot, the doughty plotter, had won the day!

This frightful fall was witnessed by fully three hundred people—promenaders who habitually hie to the Champs Elysées in the afternoon. At Vignol's shriek of despair they all stopped, and spell bound with horror, watched André as he was hurled downward in virtue of the laws of gravitation. Falling head foremost, the young painter had first struck against one of the cross-beams supporting the scaffolding. From below his hands could be seen desperately clutching at the empty air. He tried to catch at something—the corner of a plank, the end of a rope—he would have snatched at a bar of red hot iron. But he caught nothing, and fifteen feet lower he was dashed against a stone window-sill, whence he bounded to the first floor of the scaffolding. The planks bent under his weight, and then with a rebound, threw him right across the footway, not on the asphalte fortunately, but on the sandy walk.

A formidable outcry now arose from the crowd, and a compact circle formed around the poor fellow, who lay an inert, unconscious mass, in a pool-of blood ; but the workmen, headed by Vignol, who had at last made them understand that this stranger was their friend and comrade, André, were soon on the spot, and speedily pushed aside the inquisitive individuals, who just wished to see if a person who had fallen from such a height still breathed. Alas ! poor André gave no sign of life. His face was fright-fully bruised, his eyes were closed, and a stream of blood poured from his mouth, when Vignol, pale as death, raised his head and supported it on his knee. "Oh, he is dead !" said the bystanders ; "he'll never come to !"

But the workmen were not listening—they were deciding among them-selves what had best be done. "He must be taken to the Beaujon Hospital," said Vignol at last, " we are close by."

In the meantime a man had hastened to the nearest police station, and speedily enough some police agents arrived with one of those dreary litters, covered with striped cotton, which are only too often to be met with in the streets of Paris. The sculptors raised their unfortunate com-rade, and laid him in the litter, which was at once borne down the Rue de l'Oratoire towards the hospital. It was urgent that poor André should be examined as soon as possible.

Had the crowd been less preoccupied, it would no doubt have found food for some strange conjectures in an incident which occurred just as André fell. A red-bearded commissioner had suddenly darted after a young woman—one of those wretched creatures who sweep the Champs Elysées with their trailing skirts every afternoon and evening. It was she whose shouts had attracted André's attention. At sight of the commissioner coming down on her like a tornado, the woman tried to escape, but he caught her by the arm, exclaiming, "Keep still, and hold your tongue."

His voice, gesture, and look, filled the woman with abject terror, and she at once obeyed him ; she neither moved nor spoke. "Now, why did you call out like that ?" asked the commissioner.

" I don't know."

" You lie."

"No ; I swear it's the truth. A man came to me a minute or two ago, and said to me. 'If you'll call out twice, within an interval of half a minute : ' André, it's I, Sabine ! Help ! I will give you two louis.' Of course I agreed ; whereupon he handed me forty francs, and then I did what he wished."

" And what sort of a man was this ? "

" He was tall and old, very shabby and dirty, and wore coloured spec-tacles. I'm sure I never saw him before."

The commissioner reflected for a moment. "Do you know, you wretch !" he said at last, " that those words you uttered have, perhaps, caused a man's death—the death of the poor fellow who just fell from that house?"

" Well, what did he go there for ? " asked the woman.

This stupid indifference so exasperated the commissioner that, without another word, he dragged the woman towards the nearest policeman and gave her in charge. "Take her to the lock-up," said he, after explaining that his name was Palot, and that he was M. Lecoq's lieutenant. "Don't let her escape on any account. She'll be wanted as a witness at an important trial."

Palot could not conceal from himself that the woman had no doubt spoken the truth. "Plainly enough," thought he, "she didn't know what she was doing, and it was old Tantaine who gave her those two louis. He shall pay for this. But, unfortunately, even if the whole gang's hanged, it won't restore this poor fellow's life."

However, Palot hadn't time to indulge in meditation now. He must collect all the evidence he could. How had this accident happened? It was easy to ascertain, for the window frame had fallen with André, and had broken into several pieces as it reached the pavement. Palot picked up one of the fragments, and the crime which he had already suspected became manifest. The plank had been sawed through on both sides, and still retained traces of the plaster and putty with which the saw-marks had been concealed. This was too important a bit of circumstantial evidence to be neglected, and accordingly Palot called one of the workmen—an intelligent looking fellow—explained the discovery he had just made, and advised him to put the fragments of the window frame in a place of security, as they would surely be needed at the judicial inquiry which was bound to take place.

This duty fulfilled, Palot could at last join the spectators crowding round the spot where André had fallen, but the young painter had already been carried away.

The detective looked round, asking himself what course he had now best adopt, in view of obtaining further information, when suddenly on a bench, hard by, he perceived a fellow whom he had often followed in the days when M. Lecoq was still uncertain as to the identity of B. Mascarot, Father Tantaine, and Martin-Rigal. This fellow was our young friend, Toto-Chupin. He no longer wore his sordid rags of a day or two previously, but was clothed from head to foot in the newest raiment. Still, well dressed as he was, he scarcely looked at his ease. His face was livid, his eyes were wild, and his jaw worked convulsively as if seeking for saliva to moisten his parched mouth. These circumstances struck Palot forcibly, and he muttered to himself, "That young blackguard must be the guilty party, and he's frightened at his crime."

The surmise was correct enough. Toto-Chupin was struggling against remorse, which with him was quite a new sentiment. In fact he was positively deliberating whether he should not go and give himself up at the nearest police station, not because he thought confession would make his judges more merciful, but because he longed to revenge himself on old Tantaine, who had made him an assassin.

Naturally enough, the idea of arresting Toto crossed Palot's mind, but on reflection he decided to abandon it. "By nabbing this scamp," thought he, "I might warn the whole band. Big as Paris may be, we are certain of finding him again whenever we need him. Perhaps I even made a mistake in arresting that woman." Accordingly, he returned to his inquiries, and on learning that André had been removed to the Beaujon Hospital, he determined to go there. On his way he began to think of the consequences of the catastrophe. "Good heavens!" he thought, "M. Lecoq will declare I'm not fit to be trusted. I'm disgraced for ever. I knew that this poor fellow's life hung on a thread, and yet I allowed him to enter an un-finished house. Why, I might just as well have killed him with my own hand."

Thus Palot was in a great state of apprehension when he reached the hospital, and asked one of the assistant-surgeons what had become of the young man who had been brought there half-an-hour previously. "You mean number seventeen?" said the assistant-surgeon; "he is in a most deplorable state. We fear internal injury—a fracture of the skull—in short, we fear everything."

Sixty-four hours had elapsed, when André at last regained sufficient consciousness to think of his situation. It was in the middle of the night; the large hospital ward was lighted up by a single lamp; still, at a glance, he realised where he was. It seemed to him strange that he was yet alive, and still stranger that he felt no pain. Suffering only returned to him when he tried to turn in his bed, and yet he found he could move his legs and one arm. "How long have I been here?" he asked himself. He tried to think, but his thoughts flickered like those of a man who has been under the influence of chloroform, and he fell asleep.

When he awoke again it was broad daylight, and the ward was full of life and motion. It was the hour when the chief surgeon made his rounds. This chief surgeon, a middle aged man, with a bright, kind face, was going from bed to bed, followed by a score of students—demonstrating and lectur-ing, and scattering among his patients encouraging words. At last came André's turn, and the surgeon told him that he had a shoulder out of joint, an arm broken in two places, and a deep cut on his head, whilst his whole body was but one large bruise; still he was a lucky fellow to have escaped with such little harm. André listened with only a dim conception of the meaning of the words he heard. With revived reason, remembrance of Sabine had returned to him, and he asked himself, with a sinking heart, what would happen while he lay there in bed.

In his bitter anxiety he was shedding tears, when a stout gentleman with large carroty whiskers, a high white neckcloth and a venerable-looking hat —looking for all the world like one of those provincial doctors who, when visiting Paris, make it a point of frequenting the hospitals—suddenly stepped forward from the group of students, and approached his bedside. This stout gentleman leaned over André and whispered, "Janouille." On hearing this name, the password which had been agreed upon by himself and M. Lecoq, the young painter started. "I see that you don't recognise me," said the old gentleman in an undertone.

André could not believe his eyes. The art of disguise became genius when carried to such perfection. "Monsieur Lecoq!" he gasped.

"Hush! who can tell who is watching us? Quick—only two words—I 'came to tranquillize your mind, which will do more for your recovery than all the medicine you can take. Without committing you in any way, I have seen Monsieur de Mussidan, and have furnished him with a pretext for postponing his daughter's marriage to Monsieur de Croisenois, for another month. In the meantime, you will remain here in comparative safety. Still, be careful. Eat nothing coming from outside, unless it is brought you by some one possessing our password. Some spy might be sent here, so don't confide in any one. M. Gandelu will no doubt come to see you. His son is in safety. If anything extraordinary happens to you and you wish to write me, apply to the patient in bed on your right hand. He's one of my men. Poor Palot is so grieved about your accident, that I haven't had courage to scold him. Now good-bye. You will hear from me every day, and you must be prudent and patient."

"I can wait," murmured André, "since I hope!"

"Ah!" murmured Lecoq, as he moved away, "ah! isn't hope the sum total of life?"

XXXIV.

If M. Lecoq advised André to be prudent and patient, and instructed his agents to be exceedingly cautious and discreet, it was because he realised, and willingly admitted, the ability and cunning of the scoundrels he had to deal with. They would scent his supervision from a distance, just as crows scent powder, and he foresaw that at the least sign of danger they would all decamp, each in a different direction. His agents, weary of difficult work which seemed to lead to nothing, had frequently begged him to act, but he had mastered their impatience saying, "It isn't a good plan to chatter or make a noise when a man goes fishing."

Events had proved that he was right in delaying operations. This time the mysterious association of blackmailers had been obliged to unmask itself in prosecuting its final and most complicated scheme. It could already be proved that the leader, who tried to conceal himself under three names, had instigated an assassination. But M. Lecoq preferred not to utilise this circumstance at once. He was desirous of apprehending the whole band. And his investigations had been so secretly conducted, that the association suspected nothing whatever. Yet, B. Mascarot was irremediably lost at the very moment when he considered himself more certain of success than ever.

On the morrow of the accident which had befallen André, he forwarded to the Prefect of Police a most explicit anonymous letter in which he denounced Toto-Chupin's culpability, and furnished sufficient particulars to lead to his apprehension. "Of course," mused he, "Toto will try to turn all the responsibility on Father Tantaine, but the worthy old man no longer exists, and I defy even the police to resuscitate him."

That very morning, indeed, he had lighted a large fire, and burned to the very last thread the rags and tatters he wore whenever he assumed the name of Tantaine for the needs of his dark designs.

He laughed at the success of his ruse as he watched the thick smoke that rose. "Search, my friends," he chuckled. "Toto's accomplice has gone up the chimney!"

The next thing was to get rid of B. Mascarot, which was a more delicate and difficult operation. Tantaine had been an old nomad, and nobody would trouble themselves about him; but Mascarot could not disappear in the same style. He was a man of position, paying considerable rental and large taxes. He was widely known and esteemed in his capacity as a servants' agent. His disappearance would have created a great sensation—the whole neighbourhood would have gossiped about it, and the police would have taken the matter in hand. The simplest thing, therefore, was to make open arrangements for departure, and so the honorable agent began by telling everyone that family affairs and ill health compelled him to dispose of his business, which he would sell for a modest sum. At the same time he searched for a purchaser, found one, and in four-and-twenty hours the whole transaction was completed. Ah! Mascarot had a hard night's work, on the eve of his successor's entry into possession. Assisted by Beaumarchef, he carried all the papers which filled the private office of the agency into the sanctum of M. Martin-Rigal, the banker. This was accomplished by means of an aperture which the ex-sub-officer had certainly never so much as suspected, and which aperture, pierced at the back of a cupboard, placed Mascarot's bedroom in direct communication with the banker's private office.

When the last scrap of paper had been carried through this huge hole, Mascarot showed his faithful Beaumarchef a pile of bricks and a bag of mortar. The aperture must be filled up. The task was a long and fatiguing one, for neither of them were accustomed to such work. Still at last it was accomplished; all traces of bricks and mortar were effaced, and the bedroom floor was carefully swept and waxed.

Then followed a heart-breaking scene. Beaumarchef had already received a sum of twelve thousand francs, on conditions he started at once for America. The time for his departure had now arrived, and the poor fellow wept bitterly at the thought of leaving his master for good. He had served Mascarot with unflinching devotion, blindly obeyed every order; and as he could not boast any great amount of acumen, a great many suspicious circumstances had escaped him. He had unconsciously had a hand in many a piece of iniquity. However, he turned away with a sad face and drooping moustaches, just as the new "agent," M. Robinet, arrived.

Mascarot was eager to finish the business. The floors of this house seemed to burn his feet. He had annihilated Tantaine in order to disembarrass himself of Toto; but by Tantaine, he, the old clerk's soi-disant master, might perhaps be reached, and—who knows?—possibly arrested. Then farewell to his last and best personality, the one he had selected for his old age. However, it was necessary he should explain the machinery of the employment agency to his successor, acquaint him with the rules and usages of the servants' lodging-place attached to the establishment, hand over the books and lists of clients, and generally enable M. Robinet to turn his new investment to account. All this, and some visits to tradespeople in the neighbourhood, occupied the better part of the day, and it was past four o'clock when his trunks were piled upon the roof of a four wheeler which he had sent for. Henceforth, he was to evaporate, pass away out of recollection. On the boards outside, people could already read: "*J. Robinet, successor to B. Mascarot.*"

Knowing as he did how trifles bear on great events, he drove to the Western Railway Station, and took a seat in a train bound for Rouen. He was suspicious, for he might have been watched, and he had determined not to leave behind him a single clue whereby he could be traced. It was only at Rouen that he ventured to get rid of the trunks and clothes he had taken away with him, and before doing so, he obliterated everything that in his mind could possibly serve as proof against him. At Rouen he abandoned the long black coat, the spectacles, and beard he had worn as an employment agent. He annihilated B. Mascarot just as he had already annihilated Tantaine, and when on the morrow he returned to the banking offices in the Rue Montmartre, of the three personalities he had simultaneously assumed for twenty years, there only remained that of Martin-Rigal, the father of the pretty coquette Flavia, the respectable, steady old banker with the bald head and closely-shaven face. *En route*, he had not paid any attention to a young man who made the same journey as himself—a very dark young man, with quick flashing eyes, and a mocking mouth, who looked like a commercial traveller.

On reaching the Rue Montmartre, Mascarot, or rather Martin-Rigal as we shall henceforth call him, tenderly embraced his daughter, and then betook himself to his private room, the key of which never left him.   There was here a space of rough brick wall, occupying the place of the aperture which had formerly existed.   "This won't do," muttered the banker, "it must be finished with plaster, and then re-papered."

In the meanwhile, he carefully gathered up all the bits of mortar on the floor and threw them into the fire-place, where he pulverised them and mixed them with the cinders.   He next swept up the dust, and going down on his hands and knees, rubbed the carpet to efface any spots that remained. Then in front of the space of rough brick wall he placed a cheffonier, which had always stood there in view of concealing the aperture, and which he had been in the habit of moving as he went in and out.

This being accomplished, and having satisfied himself that everything was in order, he sank with a sigh of satisfaction into his arm-chair.   After a long period of anxiety, there now came the conviction of absolute security and impunity, and a delicious sensation of beatitude filled his mind.   He was glorying in the success achieved by his courage and audacity, when the smiling Hortebize entered the room.

"Now then, sceptic," cried the banker, before the door had fairly closed, "do you still doubt?   At last you have fortune within your very grasp.   Baptistin and Tantaine are dead, or, rather, they never existed. Beaumarchef is on board a transatlantic steamer ; La Candèle will be in London in a week.   You can throw away your locket with the poison. The millions belong to us ! "

"God grant it ! " answered the doctor, piously.

" Has He not granted it already ? "

" But you know the saying, ' Never holloa till you are out of the wood.' "

" Pshaw !   We have nothing more to fear ; and you would say the same if you knew all the points of the case as well as myself.   Who was the enemy we had most reason to fear?   André.   Well, he's not dead, to be sure, but he is laid up for a month or more, and that's enough.   Besides that, he has given up the contest.   The day before yesterday I received a report from one of our men, who succeeded in getting into the Beaujon Hospital, and he assures me that the young artist has not received a visit nor written a line during the whole fortnight that has elapsed since he regained consciousness."

" He had friends, though."

" Have you any friends who would trouble themselves about you after a misfortune and a fortnight's absence?   Your simplicity is refreshing ! Who are these friends you speak about?   Monsieur de Breulh-Faverlay ? But the racing season has begun, and he doesn't move from his stables. Madame de Bois d'Ardon?   Why the new spring fashions are enough to fill her empty brain.   Monsieur Gandelu?   His son is enough to keep him occupied.   There is no one else of any consequence."

"And young Monsieur Gandelu ? "

" He has yielded to Tantaine's advice, my friend ; he is reconciled with the charming Rose, and they have both taken flight for Florence."

Favourable as were these tidings they did not altogether dispel the cloud on the doctor's brow.   "The Mussidan family worries me," said he.

"And why, pray ?   Croisenois has been recieved in a very courteous manner, I assure you.   I don't say that Mademoiselle Sabine has fallen into his arms, but every evening she thanks him graciously for the bouquet he sends her every morning. What more can you expect?"

"I should have preferred no postponement of Sabine's marriage with our friend the marquis. Why did M. de Mussidan postpone it? I must confess this point worries me exceedingly."

"It's annoying, certainly. But his reasons were not pretences. I thoroughly investigated everything. We must wait; that's all."

The banker soon succeeded in infusing his own confidence into Dr. Hortebize, and the latter finally expressed himself as satisfied.

"Everything is going on well respecting the Tifila Mines," resumed Martin-Rigal. "The subscribers are not at all reluctant. It's true, I haven't been too hard on them. I have taxed each one according to his means, from a thousand up to twenty thousand francs, and we are already promised at least a million."

"And with us," murmured the doctor, "promising means something."

"Precisely; none of these folks will have their compromising papers back unless they pay up. Why, when it's all settled, doctor, you'll have at least a million francs for your own share."

The doctor rubbed his hands at this magic word. A million! What an infinite prospect of delicious dinners and exquisite joys of all kinds.

"I have seen Catenac," resumed Martin-Rigal, "since he returned from Vendôme, where everything was carried out as I ordered and predicted. The Duke de Champdoce is wild with impatience and hope, and eager to follow the track which he thinks will take him to his son. Ah! doctor, I look on this false trail as my *chef-d'œuvre*. The idea is well worth the price it will bring us in. But then what trouble we had to perfect the scheme. The late Father Tantaine and the defunct Mascarot did not spare themselves in the task."

"And Perpignan? You said he was cunning."

The banker shrugged his shoulders with profound contempt. "Perpignan," said he, "is duped just as much as the duke. He imagines that he himself has discovered this trail leading from the Hospice de Vendôme to Paul. The day before yesterday they interviewed Vigoureux, the ex-mountebank, at his wine shop in the Rue Dupleix. Very shortly he'll give them the address of old Fritz, the musician, and before long, we shall see the whole party arrive here. But by that time Paul will be my daughter's husband and Flavia will become Duchess de Champdoce, with an income of six hundred thousand livres."

He checked himself, for at this very moment there was a gentle tap at the door, and Flavia entered. Flavia was very pretty, but her beauty had never been so great as in these days of hope and joy, when she fancied she had won the heart of the man she loved, and would soon become his wife. She bowed to the doctor in a cordial, friendly way, and then, lightly as a bird perches on a branch, she seated herself on her father's knees, and putting her arms round his neck, kissed him again and again.

Hortebize looked on, and although the sight was no new one to him, he was astonished to see how the banker changed under the influence of these sweet caresses. It was, indeed, almost impossible to recognise him as the same man who, ten minutes before, had spoken with cool indifference of a murder he had planned. As soon as Flavia appeared, a most singular change took place in him; all the keen intelligence of his features vanished, and in lieu thereof came an expression of admiring, beatified simplicity. "Oh, oh!" said he, gaily, "this is a very nice little preface, my dear. The favour is granted, for of course you have one to ask—have you not, my darling?"

Mademoiselle Flavia shook her head, and in the same tone that she would have used towards a naughty child, exclaimed, "Oh! what a bad papa! Am I in the habit, sir, of selling you my kisses? When I want anything, is it necessary for me to say more than that I want it?"

"No, of course not; only—"

"I merely came to tell you that dinner is ready, and that Paul and I are both very hungry—and I only kissed you because I love you. Yes, I love you because you are good—yes, if I had to choose a father from among all the fathers in the world, I should choose you!"

He smiled, half-closing his eyes like a cat does when her head is scratched. "Come," said he, "confess it. During the last six weeks, you have loved me a little bit more than you used to do."

"No," she answered, "not during the last six weeks only since a fortnight or so."

"And yet it is more than a month since our good friend, the doctor, brought a certain young man to dinner for the first time."

Flavia laughed—a pretty, frank, girlish laugh. "I loved you for that," she replied, "yes, very dearly, indeed; but I love you more for something else."

"And what's that?"

"Ah! that's a secret which mustn't be told."

"Oh, come now, let me coax it out of you."

"How anxious you are! And besides it would make you angry."

"No, it wouldn't, I'm sure."

"Well, I'll tell you then. It is only during the last fortnight that I have realised all your love for me. Poor, dear papa! Ah! I cried when I knew all the pains you took to please your naughty daughter, when I realised all the difficulties you had to contend against to bring me my dear artist. To think you put on those wretched clothes, that horrid beard, and those spectacles! Ah, how awfully ugly you looked, poor papa!"

Martin-Rigal at these words started so abruptly to his feet, that Flavia was nearly thrown on to the floor. He was deadly pale. "What on earth do you mean?" he stammered.

"Do you suppose a father can impose on a daughter? Others may not have recognised you, but I—"

"I don't understand you, Flavia."

"Do you mean to say," she asked, fixing her eyes upon him, "that you did not come in disguise one day to Paul's, when I was there myself?"

"You are crazy—listen to me."

"No, papa, I'm nearly as cunning as you are. When you came to Paul's, in spite of your ragged clothes, I had a vague suspicion, a presentiment; and when you went out with the doctor I listened at the door, and heard a few words you said. And that is not all, for when I came home I hid myself in the passage, and I saw you come into this very room."

The banker no longer thought of denying. He seemed overwhelmed. "Ah," murmured he, "this is the result of a single act of imprudence. It was necessary to get in doors—into Mascarot's office. Croisenois was waiting for me and I feared his suspicions." Then suddenly, as a terrible idea crossed his mind, he eagerly asked, "But, Flavia, you have said nothing to any one—"

"No, indeed—certainly not."

He breathed again.

"Of course I don't count Paul," she added; "but he is the same as myself."

"Unfortunate child!" cried Martin-Rigal. "Unfortunate child!"

His gesture was so terrible, his voice so threatening, that for the first time in her life Flavia felt afraid of her father. "But what have I done?" she asked, with tears in her eyes. "I only said to Paul: 'Dear Friend—We should be monsters of ingratitude if we did not worship my father. You do not know what he does for us. He even dressed in rags to go and find you out, and—'"

The doctor, who had hitherto been a mute spectator of the scene, now interrupted Flavia: "And what did Paul say?" he asked.

"Paul? Oh! he stood still, looking quite confused for a moment, and then he shook his head, saying, 'I understand!' At last he began to laugh as if he would kill himself."

The banker, who was walking up and down the room in a state of great agitation, now stopped before his daughter. "And you, poor child," he said, in a bitter tone, "didn't you understand the meaning of that laugh? Paul, at this very moment, thinks you have been my accomplice. You have shown him that it was in obedience to your orders that I went in search of him."

"Well, what then?"

"Alas! a man like Paul would never love a woman who has sought after him. No matter how great her beauty and her love for him, he would always think and say that she threw herself at his head. He will accept all tokens of tenderness and devotion, and make no more return for them than if he were a wooden idol, before which worshippers burn incense. You don't see this? God grant that this bandage may never fall from your eyes! Can you not yet read the character of this poor, foolish boy, who lacks every manly quality! who is inflated by vanity, who has neither energy nor independence, nor will nor heart?"

Flavia had flushed scarlet. "Enough!" she exclaimed, interrupting her father, "enough! I am not such a coward as to allow you to insult my husband. I will defend him against all comers, even against my father."

Martin-Rigal shuddered at the thought that his words might cost him his daughter's affection, and he was asking himself how he could manage to attenuate the effect of his fit of anger, when Hortebize interposed. The doctor put his arm round Flavia's waist, and hurried her from the room. Then, when he was alone with the banker again, he exclaimed, "I really can't understand your anger. At the outset it depended on you yourself to prevent this marriage ever taking place. You lacked the courage to do so. Why? That's no business of mine. However, at the present hour, recrimination is quite out of place."

Martin Rigal was in consternation. "You speak as if it were nothing," said he; "but here I am at the discretion of this miserable Paul."

"Not more, it seems to me, than before your daughter's indiscretion. Isn't Paul our accomplice? Are we any the more compromised because he has penetrated the mystery of your triple personality?"

"Ah! your are not Flavia's father! Paul until now believed that I did not know Mascarot, and that I was a victim of blackmailing. All my strength was in that. As a dupe he respected me—I held him; but as an accomplice he escapes me! I think we must hasten this disastrous marriage as well as the Duke de Champdoce's search. Let's go to dinner. The evil can't be remedied. I'll write to Catenac to-morrow."

The marriage took place at the end of the next week, and Paul left his simple bachelor abode to take possession of the magnificent suite of rooms prepared for him by the banker under his own roof. The transition was abrupt, but Paul was no longer astonished at anything. The simpleton was so imbued with Mascarot's and Hortebize's theories that he imagined that adventures like his own were common in Paris. And he reflected with admiration how easy and how profitable it is to be dishonest. He had not a shadow of remorse. He feared only one thing—that he might make some blunder and fail, when came the decisive scene which was to give him a high social position and a ducal title. He longed for that moment to arrive, and flushed with pleasure when one day Martin-Rigal said to him, "Gather your strength together. It will be for this evening."

"Oh, I'll be brave," replied Paul. And, indeed, when in the course of the evening the Duke de Champdoce appeared, accompanied by Perpignan and Catenac, the young impostor rose to the level of his masters, and played his difficult part with consummate skill. However, he might have been clumsy had he chosen. The duke would have detected nothing. This man, whose life had been one long agony, was as if siezed with vertigo. Had his wishes been complied with, Paul would have at once established himself with his wife at the Champdoce mansion. But here Martin-Rigal interposed with objections.

The banker pretended to be only moderately pleased at finding that his son-in-law was a marquis and ten times a millionaire. He objected that it was very late, and that the Duchess de Champdoce was no doubt hardly prepared for the emotion the recovery of her son would cause her. Finally it was agreed that the duke should come and lunch the next morning at Martin-Rigal's, and that afterwards he should take his son away with him.

The appointment was fixed for eleven o'clock, but it was only ten when the Duke de Champdoce was ushered into the banker's private room, where the master of the house, Catenac, Hortebize and Paul were already assembled in council. Almost immediately behind the duke came Flavia. She had no suspicion of this ignoble comedy, and the thought that her husband was the only heir of a great house filled her with joy. It was not that she was dazzled by a title, but she saw in all this the justification of her choice. "Come now," she had said to her father, whom she kept on thorns by her enthusiastic expressions of delight, "you can laugh no more at me for loving a poor Bohemian. You see that this artist is a Champdoce, and that his father possesses millions!"

She entered her father's room on tiptoe, and stood near the door with a smile on her pretty lips. The Duke de Champdoce was sitting on the sofa by the side of Paul, whose hand he held and whom he fully believed to be his son. He was relating what an anxious night he had passed. He had wished to prepare the duchess, his wife, for this great joy, all the more unexpected by her as he had concealed his investigations from her; and yet a few words of vague, faint hope, had now sufficed almost to imperil her life. "This morning," he added, "she is better, and she hopes—"

He was abruptly interrupted. A succession of loud quick thuds could be heard against one of the walls. "Dear me," said M. de Champdoce, "the neighbours don't seem to be very particular."

Certainly not, indeed. They were evidently attacking this wall with pickaxes, without the least care for what other people might think. The whole house shook, and the stack of drawers standing against the wall visibly oscillated. The three honourable partners had become livid, and looked at each other in consternation. It was clear to them that some one was attacking the brick work raised by B. Mascarot and Beaumarchef. Why was this being done? The lack of all precautions seemed to indicate that the men at work considered they had a perfect right to demolish this brick work, and yet it was difficult to imagine that anyone possessed such a right.

The Duke de Champdoce was amazed. The terror of the three accomplices was perfectly evident; he felt Paul's hand tremble in his own, and he could not understand why these blows on the wall should cause such fright. Flavia was the only one who suspected no evil, and accordingly she said, "We must ascertain the reason of this noise."

"I will send and see," said her father, rising to his feet.

But hardly had he opened the door than he started back with dilated eyes, contracted features, and extended arms, as if to ward off a terrible apparition. In the passage beyond stood a most respectable looking gentleman, wearing gold-rimmed spectacles, and behind him appeared a commissary of police, wearing his scarf of office, with half a dozen agents in the rear. The same name came to the lips of the three associates: "Monsieur Lecoq!" And at the same time this terrible conviction entered their brains: "We are lost!"

The famous detective advanced, curiously watching the strange scene before him. His countenance, despite its gravity, evinced something similar to the intense satisfaction which a dramatist feels when he beholds his master-scene—conceived and combined in the seclusion of his work-room—admirably rendered on the stage. "Eh, eh!" said he, "I knew very well that by making a noise against yonder wall I should bring some one out in this direction."

But already, thanks to a mighty effort of will, the banker had succeeded in regaining at least a semblance of self-possession. "What do you want?" asked he in an arrogant tone. "What is the meaning of this violation of a private residence?"

M. Lecoq shrugged his shoulders. "Here," said he, "is the commissary of police, who will explain that point to you. In the meanwhile, I—I arrest you, yes, you—Martin-Rigal, *alias* Tantaine, *alias* Mascarot, formerly an employment agent in the Rue Montorgueil."

"I don't understand you."

"Indeed! Do you think that Tantaine has so thoroughly washed his hands that not one drop of André's blood clings to the fingers of Martin Rigal?"

"Upon my life, I don't comprehend."

Lecoq smiled blandly, and drawing from his pocket a neatly folded letter, he rejoined, "You are probably familiar with your daughter's handwriting. Well, then, listen to what she wrote, not a month ago, to Monsieur Paul, here present. 'Dear Friend—We should be monsters of ingratitude if we did not worship my father—'"

"Enough!" interrupted the banker in a hoarse voice, "enough!" And no longer having sufficient energy to remain erect, he sank into an arm-chair, stammering, "Lost! Lost by her—by my child—by Flavia!"

Of the three accomplices, individually so different in temperament and character, the calmest now was the one who usually was the most readily alarmed—smiling Dr. Hortebize. On recognising M. Lecoq, the worthy doctor had drawn from the locket dangling on his watch-chain a little pill-like ball of grey paste, which he held in the hollow of his hand. With his eyes fixed on Martin-Rigal, it seemed as if, before despairing, he were waiting for this chieftain, of so many and such tried resources, to declare that all was really lost.

However, leaving the banker, the detective had now turned towards Catenac. "And you, too," said he ; "in the name of the law I arrest you !"

"I? What do you mean ?"

"Your name is Catenac, I believe ? You are an advocate ?"

Perhaps, precisely for that very reason that he was an advocate, Catenac did not deign to answer M. Lecoq. It was to the commissary of police that he replied, "I am the victim of a most deplorable error ; but I enjoy sufficient consideration at the Palais de Justice for you not to hesitate—"

"At all events," interrupted the commissary, "the warrant against you is in regular form. I could show it to you, if you choose."

"That's not worth while. I will merely beg you to conduct me at once before the magistrate who signed it. In less than five minutes I shall have justified myself."

"Do you think so ?" asked M. Lecoq in a bantering tone. "You are ignorant, I see, of the event which caused such a sensation at La Varenne, in the environs of Paris, only two days ago. Some labourers engaged in opening a trench discovered the body of a new-born child wrapped in a silk handkerchief and an old shawl. The police, having been warned, lost no time, and they already have the mother, a girl named Clarisse."

If Lecoq had not restrained him, the advocate would have flown at Martin-Rigal's throat. "Scoundrel !" he yelled. "Traitor ! Coward ! You have sold me—"

"Ah !" stammered the banker, "my papers have been stolen."

He now realised that the blows struck on the other side of the wall were but a ruse. M. Lecoq had wished to frighten the confederates, so as to crush them the more easily.

"The papers !" grumbled an agent. "There was a hole in the wall; we profited by it."

Worthy Dr. Hortebize no longer smiled. The game was lost, ay, irremediably lost. "I have honest relatives who bear my name," he thought. "I will not dishonour them. There is no time to lose." Whereupon he swallowed the contents of his medallion, muttering to himself, "At my age, and with such a digestion, too ! Never was I in better health ! Ah ! it would have been better if I had contented myself with a decent little medical practice."

No one noticed the doctor. M. Lecoq had just had the cheffonier moved aside, and he was showing the commissary of police the rough brick wall through which a hole, sufficiently large for a man to pass, had now been pierced. But a sudden noise cut his explanations short. Dr. Hortebize had fallen on the floor in terrible convulsions. "How stupid !" exclaimed M. Lecoq ; "how stupid of me not to have foreseen that ! He has taken poison ! He escapes us ! Run for a doctor ! Put him on a bed at once !"

While these orders were being hastily obeyed, the banker and Catenac were led downstairs to a cab, which awaited them in the street. Martin-Rigal seemed struck by imbecility. His mind, so powerful for purposes of evil, had apparently given way beneath the weight of mortal anguish. "And my daughter," he stammered, "Flavia ! What will become of her ? She has no fortune, and she is married to a man who cannot even earn his living. My child ! my child ! Will she herself always have bread ?"

The commissary of police leaving to superintend the removal of Dr. Hortebize, M. Lecoq now remained alone with the Duke de Champdoce, Paul, and Flavia. The poor young woman had seen her father led away by the police agents without having force to say a word. She was stretched helplessly in an arm-chair, and the wild light in her eyes told that her mind was wandering. She could not believe in the reality of the horrible scene which had just been enacted.

For a moment the celebrated detective looked at her with an air of compassion which was certainly not feigned. He was reluctant to strike another blow—a more terrible one than all the others—at this poor child, who, being innocent, was necessarily the greatest sufferer. However, time was passing, in the interests of justice the truth could not be deferred, and so he approached the Duke de Champdoce, who seemed to have been struck dumb with surprise. "I must warn you, Monsieur le Duc," said M. Lecoq, "that you have been odiously imposed upon. This young man here is not your son. His name is Paul Violaine, and his mother, originally a poor work-girl at Châtellerault, kept a petty thread and needle shop at Poitiers during the last years of her life."

Hard as was this blow for Paul, he still tried to continue playing his part—he began to bluster and deny ; but at a sign from M. Lecoq, an agent ushered in a young woman most fashionably attired. Paul recognised at once his discarded mistress—Rose, and without even letting her speak, he confessed everything. "It is true," he stammered, bursting into tears. "I was persuaded, threatened, led away. I did not know how to resist ; forgive me ! "

With a disdainful gesture M. Lecoq repelled him. "It is not of me you should ask forgiveness," said he, "but of this poor young woman, your wife, who is dying, I think."

The Duke de Champdoce had entered the banker's house with a joyful heart, and now he was about to leave it in a state of despair, when the celebrated detective suddenly led him aside. "Let me tell you, Monsieur le Duc," said he, "these scoundrels have only half deceived you. The child you seek exists, and they know him. But I know him also, and to-morrow I—Lecoq—will take you to him ! "

XXXV.

OBEDIENT to the instructions of his new protector, André had resigned himself to wait patiently at the Beaujon Hospital for the finish of the great game which M. Lecoq was playing on his behalf. Moreover, he had enough courage to assume that air of utter indifference for the future which had duped B. Mascarot's spies. It is true that he received all the comfort and solace possible under the circumstances. Every day his neighbour on the right hand side—the patient whom M. Lecoq pointed out as one of his agents—stealthily slipped into his hand a note acquainting him with the march of events. André read these notes in secret, and then carefully destroyed them.

But time was rolling on, the days seemed interminable ; and as the decisive moment approached, André was beginning to lose patience, when, one afternoon, his neighbour openly handed him a note which thrilled his heart with joy. "We are winning the fight," wrote Lecoq ; "all danger is over. Ask the surgeon to sign your permission to leave. Make yourself a swell, and to-morrow morning, at nine o'clock, you will find me waiting for you outside the hospital door."

André had not yet fully recovered. He must still carry his arm in a sling for several weeks to come; but no consideration of this kind would have deterred him from complying with the detective's instructions. Rising at an early hour on the morrow, he arrayed himself in his best clothes, which he had sent for, and then, after taking leave of the Sisters of Charity, who had carefully tended him, he went downstairs, crossed the courtyard of the hospital, and passed into the Faubourg St. Honoré beyond. He remained for a moment on the threshold of the great entrance-gateway, inhaling the fresh air with delight. The day before he had still suffered from his wounds; but now he forgot them, as if he had been touched by some magic wand. Never had he felt so young, so strong and lithe; never had his heart palpitated so intensely with hope. However, he was surprised not to see his new protector, and he was deliberating as to what he had better do, when an open vehicle, drawn by a fast trotter, dashed up the Faubourg and stopped just in front of the hospital. André at once recognised the respectable-looking old gentleman with gold spectacles who was seated inside, and so, hastening towards him, he exclaimed, "Thank Heaven you have come, sir. I was beginning to feel very anxious."

"You are right!" said M. Lecoq, consulting his watch. "I am five minutes behind time, but I was detained at the Préfecture." Then as André began to thank him most effusively, he added, "Jump in beside me. I want to talk to you; the weather's delightful; we'll go as far as the Bois."

As he took his seat beside the detective, André was struck by the unusual expression of his features, as a rule so placid and composed; and feeling anxious, he ventured to ask, "Has anything unfavourable occurred, sir."

"Not in the least."

"I was afraid—"

"Ah, I see, you detect a strange expression in my face? It may be so, for I'm tired out. I've spent the night looking over Mascarot's papers. And, besides, I have just witnessed a most painful scene—one of the most painful of my life, and yet I have seen a good many strange and terrible things in my time." He shook his head, as if he hoped to dispel the impression, and then resumed. "Martin-Rigal's reason has not resisted this catastrophe. This villain had one sublime passion, he adored his daughter. Suddenly separated from her, knowing her to be without fortune, and married to a fellow with a worthless character, Rigal has given way to the delirium of despair and become mad. He will go to an asylum instead of to the galleys. He escapes the punishment of man, but not the punishment of God, and this last is the more terrible."

"Martin-Rigal mad!" muttered André.

"Yes; and do you know what form his madness has taken? He imagines that Paul and Flavia are without resources, without shelter, without bread. He fancies that Paul means to speculate on his wife's beauty, and live on the fruits of her shame. He thinks he can hear his daughter constantly crying to him for help. Yes, he hears this voice—a bitter, pleading, agonising voice. Then he calls for the gaolers, and on his knees implores them to let him out only for a day, an hour, swearing he will return as soon as he has rescued his child from infamy and shame. And when his prayer is refused he becomes frenzied, he wounds himself in trying to loosen the window bars and break the locks. This morning he had to be fastened on his bed, where I just saw him making vain efforts to free himself. I saw him with his features frightfully convulsed, with his eyes starting from their orbits, with a foaming mouth, and howling like a wild beast. He recognised me and exclaimed, 'Do you hear Flavia's voice?' And this agony, mind, will perhaps last for years, the doctor told me so. Until his death he will unceasingly hear his daughter's despairing voice. Each minute of the years to come will contain more intolerable torture for him than he ever inflicted on all his victims."

A pause followed. André could not help pitying this scoundrel, although he had tried to have him murdered, and had endeavoured to rob him of Sabine.

"You see," resumed M. Lecoq, "the battle is won. Dr. Hortebize is agonising. The poison which he relied on as instantaneous has betrayed him, and his sufferings have already lasted twenty-four hours. Catenac is trying to hold his own, but he will be convicted of infanticide or complicity therein, and will at the least have ten years' hard labour. Martin-Rigal's papers have furnished me with proofs against Perpignan, Van Klopen, and Verminet, who will all serve out a comfortable sentence. Toto-Chupin's fate is not yet settled. We shall remember that he came and surrendered himself, and shows very great repentance."

But all this did not fully reassure André. "And Croisenois?" he asked timidly.

The detective repressed a smile. "Ah, ha!" said he, "you are not confident in me, I see."

"Oh! I assure you, sir—"

"Well, don't be nervous, I promised you that the Count de Mussidan's name should not be mentioned in the matter, and so I have allowed Croisenois to escape me. Last night he slept at Brussels, at the Hôtel de Saxe, room No. 9. The Tifila Mining Company will be treated as an ordinary swindle. No funds have been paid in so far; the promised subscriptions will be returned to the persons they emanate from, and Croisenois will be sentenced by default to a couple of months' imprisonment. Finally, to-morrow young Gandelu will have his notes of hand returned to him."

The vehicle had been rolling through the Bois de Boulogne; and now M. Lecoq made a sign to the coachman to turn and go back. "The time has come, Monsieur André," said he, "to explain to you why, at our first interview, I saluted you as the Duke de Champdoce. I had guessed your history, but only last night did I learn its details."

And without waiting for a reply he rapidly analysed, for André's benefit, the voluminous manuscript prepared by B. Mascarot, and read aloud by Paul. He did not tell everything, however. He concealed as far as possible the crimes and faults of the Duke de Champdoce and Madame de Mussidan. He wished to spare André the pain of loathing or ceasing to respect his father and Sabine's mother.

The detective had managed his narrative so well, that he had just brought it to a conclusion when the coachman drew up at the corner of the Rue de Matignon. "Now, just alight here," said M. Lecoq; "and take care of your arm." André mechanically obeyed. "Now," resumed the detective, turning towards the carriage again, "listen to me. The Count and Countess de Mussidan are expecting you to lunch. Here is the invitation they requested me to give you. However, don't linger too long near Mademoiselle Sabine. At four o'clock be at your studio, and I will then have the honour of presenting you to your father. Until then not one word."

The young painter wished to speak and express his gratitude; but before he was able to do so M. Lecoq's driver had whipped his horse, and the vehicle rolled rapidly away. So much happiness overwhelmed the young artist. Everything came to him at once—a great name, an immense fortune, and the girl he loved. However, he gathered himself together, and walked with a firm step towards the entrance of the Hôtel de Mussidan. He wondered how he would be received. Would M. de Mussidan remember his promises, or the peril no longer existing? Would he merely frigidly express his thanks? The respectful manner of the servants made him judge that he was expected and recommended. This was of good augury, and yet, in the hall, when the head valet asked him his name, he could hardly articulate it. The door of the grand salon was thrown open, and he staggered as he crossed the threshold, for there on the opposite wall was Sabine's portrait, the portrait which he himself had painted. How came it there? Fortunately, the Count de Mussidan understood the young artist's embarrassment, and came towards him with extended hands. Then leading him towards the countess, he exclaimed, "Diane, this is our daughter's husband."

André bowed low, while words of gratitude rose confusedly to his lips; but the count had already led him to where Sabine stood, and putting his hand in her's, resumed in a feeling voice, "If happiness, here below, is a reward, you will be happy."

It was only after a moment's pause that André recovered sufficient self-possession to look at Mademoiselle de Mussidan. Poor child, she was but the shadow of her former self—she had suffered so intensely during that long month when she had forced herself to receive the homage of the Marquis de Croisenois, and smile to him. "Oh darling!" whispered André in her ear, "how terribly you must have suffered."

"Yes," she said, quietly, "I should certainly have died if it had lasted longer."

Ah! the young artist needed great courage to keep his secret from Sabine during the delightful afternoon he spent near her, during the glowing hours when she told him what had been her anguish and her hopes; and it was only with a superhuman effort that he tore himself away at half-past three o'clock.

He had not been five minutes in his studio when he heard a knock at the door. He opened it, and M. Lecoq entered, followed by an old gentleman of somewhat haughty mien. This was the Duke de Champdoce—Norbert! "Monsieur," said the duke to André, without a preamble, "you know the reasons that bring me here. You know who you are, and who I am—"

André bowed affirmatively.

"This gentleman," resumed the duke, indicating M. Lecoq, "has told you under what deplorable circumstances I abandoned you—my son. I will not try to excuse myself—though I have cruelly expiated this crime. Look at me, I am only forty-eight years of age."

He looked sixty at the least, and André was able to form some idea of what this man, his father, must have suffered.

"My fault follows me still," continued M. de Champdoce. "To-day, although it is my dearest wish, I cannot claim you as my son. The law only allows me to give you my name and fortune by adoption."

The young painter remained silent; and the duke at last resumed, with evident hesitation, "You can of course institute proceedings against me; but in that case I must say—I must confess—"

"Ah! Monsieur," interrupted André, "what can you imagine my feelings to be? What! Before assuming your name, which is mine as well, do you think I should try to dishonour it?"

The duke breathed more freely. André's manner had chilled him. What a difference there was between the young painter's haughty reserve, and the pathetic scene enacted by Paul, the day before!

"However, Monsieur le Duc," resumed André, "before anything else, I must ask you to allow me to address you a few observations?"

"Observations?"

"Yes; 1 did not dare to say conditions—but I think you will understand me. For instance, I have never had a master. My independence has cost me enough for me to cling to it. I am a painter, and for nothing in the world can I ever renounce art."

"You will always be your own master," rejoined the duke.

Just as the latter had hesitated a moment earlier, so André hesitated now. He had become very red. "This is not all," he said: "I love a young lady and am loved by her. Our marriage is arranged, and I think—"

"I think," interrupted the duke, "that you can only love a woman who is worthy of our name."

As André heard this he smiled sadly. "But I was a nobody yesterday," said he, softly. "However, you may be at ease, monsieur, she is worthy of a Champdoce, both by her fortune and by her name. From a social point of view she was far above me. She is—the daughter of the Count de Mussidan!"

At the mention of this name M. de Champdoce turned livid. "Never!" he cried, "never! I would rather see you dead than see you become Mademoiselle de Mussidan's husband."

"And I, sir, would suffer ten thousand deaths rather than renounce her!"

"If I refused my consent—however—if I forbade—"

André sadly shook his head. "Paternal authority," said he, "is acquired only by long years of protection and affection. I owe you nothing. Forget me, as you have hitherto done. Follow your road, and I will follow mine."

The Duke de Champdoce remained silent. A frightful struggle was going on in his mind. He bitterly realised that either he must renounce this son, so miraculously restored to him, or else he must see him married to Diane's daughter. Both alternatives seemed to him equally terrible. "Never!" he muttered at last; "besides, the countess would never consent. She hates me as much as I hate her."

M. Lecoq, who had looked on in silence, now thought it time to interfere. "I will undertake," said he, "to obtain Madame de Mussidan's consent."

On hearing this the duke no longer resisted. He opened his arms to André, and exclaimed, "Come, my son, let it all be as you desire."

But the young painter soon drew himself from the embrace to give free course to the emotion which was stifling him. "My mother!" he cried, pressing the duke's arm. "Lead me to my mother."

*   *   *   *   *   *   *   *

That evening, when embracing the son for whom she had so often wept,

Marie de Puymandour, Duchess de Champdocc, realised that happiness is not a mere word.

The duke had surmised correctly. On learning that André was Norbert's child, Madame de Mussidan formally opposed his marriage with Sabine. But M. Lecoq never promises in vain. Among B. Mascarot's papers he had found the correspondence stolen from the countess. He returned it to her and in exchange she gave her consent. The celebrated detective assures us that this is *not* blackmailing.

André and Sabine now-a-days reside at the Château de Mussidan which has been magnificently restored. Perhaps they will establish themselves there for good, so dear to them are the beautiful woods of Bivron where they first learned to love each other. Above the balcony of the château, André willingly shows his visitors the unfinished garland of volubilis, which he began by way of justifying his prolonged sojourn in old Madame de Chevauché's time. He declares that he means to finish it speedily, but this is very doubtful, for he has really become extremely lazy.

At all events this much seems certain : Before the end of the year there will be a christening at Mussidan.

THE END.